"Chokshi has created an inclusive and authentic cast with obvious chemistry and affection for one another and infuses the tale with witty banter and twists." —*School Library Journal* (starred review)

"An opulent heist adventure that will leave readers voracious for more." —*Kirkus Reviews* (starred review)

"Evocative writing, sumptuous set pieces, and vividly sketched, authentically flawed characters distinguish this immersive tale of found family and star-crossed romance." —*Publishers Weekly* (starred review)

"In this delicious first entry in a new series from a veteran young-adult author, readers will find sumptuous visuals, deep characters, and a maddening eleventh-hour twist." —BookPage (starred review)

"*The Gilded Wolves* sets up a fantastical great heist with a series of clues and problems the well-developed, diverse group of teens must decipher. Chokshi's world is lush and her characters distinct and engaging—this first in a new series is as sharp and lustrous as the title suggests." —Shelf Awareness

"There can be no doubt that Chokshi has grown as a writer with each book, and *The Gilded Wolves* takes us to a new level of intrigue." —NPR.org

"Chokshi's writing is vivid and lovely." —*Entertainment Weekly*

"Thrilling and gorgeous, *The Gilded Wolves* is another captivating book from one of YA's most brilliant voices."

—*Paste*, "10 of the Best Young Adult Novels of January 2019"

"This rag-tag team will face danger, deception, puzzles, and of course delicious secrets that hide in the opulence of Paris. This is a story you will not soon forget."
—The Nerd Daily

"A gorgeously layered story with characters that make you laugh and ache and cheer."
—Renée Ahdieh, *New York Times* bestselling author of *The Wrath and the Dawn*

"A masterpiece of imagination. You will want this book to steal your heart so that you will never have to leave this story."
—Stephanie Garber, *New York Times* bestselling author of *Caraval*

"*The Gilded Wolves* is the smart, dark adventure young-adult readers have been waiting for."
—Adrienne Young, *New York Times* bestselling author of *Sky in the Deep*

Also by Roshani Chokshi

The Star-Touched Queen
A Crown of Wishes
Star-Touched Stories

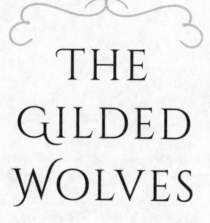

THE
GILDED
WOLVES

Roshani Chokshi

Wednesday Books
New York

First published in the United States by Wednesday Books,
an imprint of St. Martin's Publishing Group

THE GILDED WOLVES. Copyright © 2018 by Roshani Chokshi. All rights reserved.
Printed in the United States of America. For information, address
St. Martin's Publishing Group, 120 Broadway, New York, NY 10271.

www.wednesdaybooks.com
www.stmartins.com

Case Stamp Courtesy of Kelli McAdams.

The Library of Congress Cataloging-in-Publication Data is available upon request.

ISBN 978-1-250-14454-6 (hardcover)
ISBN 978-1-250-22620-4 (international, sold outside the U.S.,
subject to rights availability)
ISBN 978-1-250-14456-0 (ebook)
ISBN 978-1-250-14455-3 (trade paperback)

Our books may be purchased in bulk for promotional, educational, or business use. Please contact your local bookseller or the Macmillan Corporate and Premium Sales Department at 1-800-221-7945, extension 5442, or by email at MacmillanSpecialMarkets@macmillan.com.

First Paperback Edition: 2020

10 9 8 7 6

For Aman, who said:
"Say something cool about me."

Nope.

Fléctere si néqueo súperos Acheronta movebo.
If I cannot move heaven, I will raise hell.

—VIRGIL

Once, there were four Houses of France.

Like all the other Houses within the Order of Babel, the French faction swore to safeguard the location of their Babel Fragment, the source of all Forging power.

Forging was a power of creation rivaled only by the work of God.

But one House fell.

And another House's line died without an heir.

Now all that is left is a secret.

PROLOGUE

The matriarch of House Kore was running late for a dinner. In the normal course of things, she did not care for punctuality. Punctuality, with its unseemly whiff of eagerness, was for peasants. And she was neither a peasant nor eager to endure a meal with the mongrel heir of House Nyx.

"What is taking my carriage so long?" she yelled down the hall.

If she arrived too late, she would invite rumors. Which were a great deal more pesky and unseemly than punctuality.

She flicked at an invisible speck of dust on her new dress. Her silk gown had been designed by the couturiers of Raudnitz & Cie in the 1st arrondissement's Place Vendôme. Taffeta lilies bobbed in the blue silk stream of her hemline. Across the gown's low bustle and long tulle train, miniature fields of buttercups and ivy unfurled in the candlelight. The Forging work had been seamless. As well it should be, given the steep price.

Her driver poked his head through the entryway. "Deepest apologies, Madame. We are very nearly ready."

The matriarch flicked her wrist in dismissal. Her Babel Ring—a twist of dark thorns shot through with blue light—gleamed. The ring had been welded to her index finger the day she became matriarch of House Kore, successfully beating out other members of her family and intra-House scrambles for power. She knew her descendants and even members of her House were counting down the days until she died and passed on the ring, but she wasn't ready yet. And until then, only she and the House Nyx patriarch would know the ring's secrets.

When she touched the wallpaper, a symbol flashed briefly on the gilded patterns: a twist of thorns. She smiled. Like every Forged object in her home, the wallpaper had been House-marked.

She'd never forget the first time she'd left her House mark on an artifact. The ring's power made her feel like a goddess cinched to human shape. Though that was not always the case. Yesterday, she'd stripped the mark of Kore off an object. She hadn't wanted to, but it was for last week's Order auction, and some traditions could not be denied . . .

Including dinners with the head of a House.

The matriarch marched toward the open door and stood on the granite threshold. The cold night air caused the silken blooms on her dress to close their petals.

"Surely the horses are ready?" she called into the night.

Her driver did not answer. She pulled her shawl tighter and took another step outside. She saw the carriage, the waiting horses . . . but no driver.

"Has *everyone* in my employ been struck by a plague of incompetence?" she muttered as she walked toward the horses.

Even her courier—who was merely to show up at the Order auction, donate an object and leave—had failed. To his lists of clear-cut errands, he'd undoubtedly added: Get fabulously drunk at L'Eden, that gaudy sinkhole of a hotel.

Closer to the carriage, she found her driver sprawled facedown in the gravel. The matriarch stumbled backward. Around her, the sounds of the horses stamping their hooves cut off abruptly. Silence fell like a heavy blade through the air.

Who is there? she meant to say, but the words collapsed noiselessly.

She stepped back. Her heels made no sound on the gravel. She might have been underwater. She ran for the door, flinging it open. Chandelier light washed over her and for a moment, she thought she'd escaped. Her heel caught on her dress, tripping her. The ground did not rush up to meet her.

But a knife did.

She never saw the blade, only felt the consequence of it—a sharp pressure digging into her knuckles, the snap of finger bones unclasping, hot wetness sliding down her palm and wrist and staining her expensive bell sleeves. Someone prying her ring from her fingers. The matriarch of House Kore did not have time to gasp.

Her eyes opened wide. In front of her, Forged moth lights with emerald panes for wings glided across the ceiling. A handful of them roosted there, like dozing stars.

And then, from the corner of her vision, a heavy rod swung toward her head.

PART I

From the archival records of the Order of Babel
The Origins of Empire
Master Emanuele Orsatti, House Orcus of the Order's Italy Faction
1878, reign of King Umberto I

The art of Forging is as old as civilization itself. According to our translations, ancient empires credited the source of their Forging power to a variety of mythical artifacts. India believed their source of power came from the Bowl of Brahma, a creation deity. Persians credited the mythical Cup of Jamshid, et cetera.

Their beliefs—while vivid and imaginative—are wrong.

Forging comes from the presence of Babel Fragments. Though none can ascertain the exact number of Fragments in existence, it is the belief of this author that God saw fit to disperse at least five Fragments following the destruction of the Tower of Babel (Genesis 11:4-9). Where these Babel Fragments scattered, civilizations sprouted: Egyptians and Africans near the Nile River, Hindus near the Indus River, Orientals from the Yellow River, Mesopotamians from the Tigris-Euphrates River, Mayans and Aztecs in Mesoamerica, *and the Incas in the Central Andes. Naturally, wherever a Babel Fragment existed, the art of Forging flourished.*

The West's first documentation of its Babel Fragment was in the year 1112. Our ancestral brethren, the Knights Templar, brought back a Babel Fragment from the Holy Lands and laid it to rest in our soil. Since then, the art of Forging has achieved levels of unparalleled mastery throughout the continent. To those blessed with a Forging affinity, it is an inheritance of divinity, like any art. For just as we are made in His image, so, too, does the Forging artistry reflect the beauty of His creation. To Forge is not only to enhance a creation, but to reshape it.

It is the duty of the Order to safeguard this ability.

It is our task, sacred and ordained, to guard the location of the West's Babel Fragment.

To take such power from us would be, I daresay, the end of civilization.

I

SÉVERIN

One week earlier . . .

Séverin glanced at the clock: two minutes left.

Around him, the masked members of the Order of Babel whipped out white fans, murmuring to themselves as they eagerly awaited the final auction bidding.

Séverin tipped back his head. On the frescoed ceiling, dead gods fixed the crowd with flat stares. He fought not to look at the walls, but failed. The symbols of the remaining two Houses of the French faction hemmed him on all sides. Crescent moons for House Nyx. Thorns for House Kore.

The other two symbols had been carefully lifted out of the design.

"Ladies and gentlemen of the Order, our spring auction is at its close," announced the auctioneer. "Thank you for bearing witness to this extraordinary exchange. As you know, the objects of this evening's auction have been rescued from far-flung locales like the deserts of North Africa and dazzling palaces of Indo-Chine. Once more, we give thanks and honor to the two Houses of France who agreed to host this spring's auction. House Nyx, we honor you. House Kore, we honor you."

Séverin raised his hands, but refused to clap. The long scar down his palm silvered beneath the chandelier light, a reminder of the inheritance he had been denied.

Séverin, last of the Montagnet-Alarie line and heir to House Vanth, whispered its name anyway. *House Vanth, I honor you.*

Ten years ago, the Order had declared the line of House Vanth dead.

The Order had lied.

While the auctioneer launched into a long-winded speech about the hallowed and burdensome duties of the Order, Séverin touched his stolen mask. It was a tangle of metal thorns and roses gilded with frost, Forged so the ice never melted and the roses never wilted. The mask belonged to the House Kore courier who, if Séverin's dosage had been correct, was currently drooling in a lavish suite at his hotel, L'Eden.

According to his intelligence, the object he had come here for would be on the auction block any moment now. He knew what would happen next. Light bidding would take place, but everyone suspected House Nyx had fixed the round to win the object. And though House Nyx would win, that artifact was going home with Séverin.

The corner of his lips tipped into a smile as he raised his fingers. At once, a glass from the champagne chandelier floating above him broke off and sailed into his hand. He lifted the flute to his lips, not sipping, but once more noting the ballroom's layout and exits just over the glass rim. Tiers of pearly macarons in the shape of a giant swan marked the east exit. There, the young heir of House Nyx, Hypnos, drained a champagne flute and motioned for another. Séverin had not spoken to Hypnos since they were young.

As children, they had been something of playmates and rivals, both raised almost identically, both groomed to take their fathers' rings.

But that was a lifetime ago.

Séverin forced his gaze from Hypnos and looked instead to the lapis-blue columns guarding the south exit. At the west, four Sphinx authorities stood motionless in their suits and crocodile masks.

They were the reason no one could steal from the Order. The mask of a Sphinx could sniff out and follow any trace of an object that had been House-marked by a matriarch's or patriarch's ring.

But Séverin knew that all the artifacts came to the auction clean, and were only House-marked at the auction's conclusion when they were claimed. Which left a few precious moments between time of sale and time of claiming in which an object could be stolen. And no one, not even a Sphinx, would be able to trace where it had gone.

A vulnerable unmarked object was not, however, without its protections.

Séverin glanced at the north end, diagonally from him, toward the holding room—the place where all unmarked objects awaited their new owners. At the entrance crouched a gigantic quartz lion. Its crystalline tail whipped lazily against the marble floor.

A gong rang. Séverin looked to the podium where a light-skinned man had stepped onto the stage.

"Our final object is one we are most delighted to showcase. Salvaged from the Summer Palace of China in 1860, this compass was Forged sometime during the Han Dynasty. Its abilities include navigating the stars and detecting lies from truth," said the auctioneer. "It measures twelve by twelve centimeters, and weighs 1.2 kilograms."

Above the auctioneer's head, a hologram of the compass shimmered. It looked like a rectangular piece of metal, with a spherical indentation at its center. Chinese characters crimped the metal on all sides.

The list of the compass's abilities was impressive, but it was not the compass that intrigued him. It was the treasure map hidden inside. Out the corner of his eye, Séverin watched Hypnos clap his hands together eagerly.

"Bidding starts at five hundred thousand francs."

A man from the Italian faction raised his fan.

"Five hundred thousand to Monsieur Monserro. Do I see—"

Hypnos raised his hand.

"Six hundred thousand," said the auctioneer. "Six hundred thousand going once, twice—"

The members began to talk amongst themselves. There was no point trying in a fixed round.

"Sold!" said the auctioneer with forced cheer. "To House Nyx for six hundred thousand. Patriarch Hypnos, at the conclusion of the auction, please have your House courier and designated servant sent to the holding room for the customary eight-minute appraisal. The object will be waiting in the designated vessel where you may mark it with your ring."

Séverin waited a moment before excusing himself. He walked briskly along the edges of the atrium until he made it to the quartz lion. Behind the lion stretched a darkened hall lined with marble pillars. The quartz lion's eyes slid indifferently to him, and Séverin fought the urge to touch his stolen mask. Disguised as the House Kore courier, he was allowed to enter the holding room and touch a single object for exactly eight minutes. He hoped the stolen mask would be enough to get him past the lion, but if the lion asked to see his catalogue coin for verification—a Forged coin that held the location of every object in House Kore's possession—he'd be dead. He hadn't been able to find the dratted thing anywhere on the courier.

Séverin bowed before the quartz lion, then held still. The lion did nothing. Its unblinking gaze burned his face as moments ticked past. His breath started to feel sticky in his lungs. He hated how much he wanted this artifact. There were so many *wants* inside him that he doubted there was room for blood in his body.

Séverin didn't look up from the floor until he heard it—the scrape of stones rearranging. He let out his breath. His temples pulsed as the door to the holding room appeared. Without the lion's permission, the Forged door would have remained unseen.

All along the walls of the holding room, marble statues of gods and creatures from myth leaned out of recessed niches. Séverin walked straight to a marble figure of the snarling, bull-headed minotaur. Séverin raised his pocket knife to the statue's flared nostrils. Warm breath fogged the Forged blade. In one smooth line, Séverin dragged the blade's tip down the statue's face and body. It split open; the marble hissed and steamed as his historian stumbled out of it and fell against him. Enrique gasped, shaking himself.

"You hid me in a *minotaur*? Why couldn't Tristan make a hiding dimension in a handsome Greek god?"

"His affinity is for liquid matter. Stone is difficult for him," said Séverin, pocketing the knife. "So it was either the minotaur or an Etruscan vase decorated with bull testicles."

Enrique shuddered. "Honestly. Who looks at a vase covered in bull testicles and says, 'You. I must have you.'?"

"The bored, the rich, and the enigmatic."

Enrique sighed. "All my life aspirations."

The two of them turned to the circle of treasure, many of them Forged ancient relics looted from temples and palaces. Statues and strands of jewels, measuring devices and telescopes.

At the back of the room, an onyx bear representing House Nyx glowered at them, its jaws cracked wide. Beside it, an emerald eagle representing House Kore shook its wings. Animals representing the other Order factions all around the world stood at attention, including a brown bear carved of fire opal for Russia, a wolf sculpted of beryl for Italy, even an obsidian eagle for the German Empire.

Enrique dug inside his costume of an Order servant and pulled out a rectangular piece of metal identical to the compass House Nyx had won.

Séverin took the fake artifact.

"Still waiting on my thanks, you know," huffed Enrique. "It took me *ages* to research and assemble that."

"It would have taken less time if you didn't antagonize Zofia."

"It's inevitable. If I breathe, your engineer is prepared to launch warships."

"Then hold your breath."

"That should be easy enough," said Enrique, rolling his eyes. "I do it every time we acquire a new piece."

Séverin laughed. Acquiring was what he called his *particular hobby*. It sounded . . . aristocratic. Wholesome, even. He had the Order to thank for his acquisition habit. After denying his claim as heir of House Vanth, they'd blackballed him from every auction house, so he could not legally purchase Forged antiquities. If they hadn't done that, perhaps he wouldn't have gotten so curious about what objects they were keeping him from in the first place. Some of those objects were, as it turned out, his family's possessions. After the Montagnet-Alarie line was declared dead, all the possessions of House Vanth had been sold. In the months after Séverin turned sixteen and liquidated his legal trust, he had reclaimed each and every one. After that, he'd offered his acquisition services to international museums and colonial guilds, any organization that wished to take back what the Order had first stolen.

If the rumors about the compass were right, it might allow him to blackmail the Order, and then he could acquire the only thing he still wanted: his House.

"You're doing it again," said Enrique.

"What?"

"That whole nefarious-whilst-looking-into-the-distance thing. What are you hiding, Séverin?"

"Nothing."

"You and your secrets."

"Secrets keep my hair lustrous," said Séverin, running his hand through his curls. "Shall we?"

Enrique nodded. "Room check."

He tossed a Forged sphere into the air where it hung, suspended. Light burst from the object, sliding down the walls and over the objects to scan them.

"No recording devices."

At Séverin's nod, they positioned themselves before the onyx bear of House Nyx. It stood on a raised dais, its jaws parted enough so the red velvet box holding the Chinese compass shone bright as an apple. The moment Séverin touched the box, he had less than eight minutes to return it. Or—his gaze went to the beast's shining teeth— the creature would take it back forcefully.

He removed the red box. At the same time, Enrique drew out a pair of scales. First, they weighed the box with the original compass, then marked the number before preparing to switch it with the decoy.

Enrique cursed. "Off by a hair. But it should work. The difference is hardly discernible by the scales."

Séverin's jaw clenched. It didn't matter if it was hardly discernible by the scales. It mattered if the difference was discernible to the onyx bear. But he'd come too far to back away now.

Séverin placed the box in the bear's mouth, pushing it in until his wrist disappeared. Onyx teeth scraped against his arm. The statue's throat was cool and dry, and entirely too still. His hand shook.

"Are you breathing?" whispered Enrique. "I'm definitely not."

"Not helping," growled Séverin.

Now he was up to his elbow. The bear was rigid. It didn't even blink.

Why hasn't it accepted the box?

A creaking sound lit up the silence. Séverin jerked his hand back. Too late. The bear's teeth lengthened in a blink, forming narrow little bars. Enrique took one look at Séverin's trapped hand, turned pale, and bit out a single word: "Shit."

2

LAILA

Laila slipped into the hotel room of the House Kore courier.

Her dress, a discarded housekeeper uniform fished out of the dregs of storage, snagged on the doorframe. She grumbled, yanking it, only for a seam to unravel.

"Perfect," she muttered.

She turned to face the room. Like all the L'Eden guest rooms, the courier's suite was lavishly appointed and designed. The only piece that looked out of place was the unconscious courier, lying face-down in a pool of his saliva. Laila frowned.

"They could've at least left you in your bed, poor thing," she said, toeing him so he turned over onto his back.

For the next ten minutes, Laila redecorated. From the pockets of her housekeeper's dress, she threw women's earrings on the floor, draped torn stockings over lamp fixtures, mussed the bed, and poured champagne over the sheets. When she was done, she knelt beside the courier.

"A parting gift," she said. "Or apology. However you see fit."

She took out her official cabaret calling card. Then she lifted the man's thumb and pressed it to the paper. It shimmered iridescent, words blooming to life. The Palais des Rêves' calling cards were Forged to recognize a patron's thumbprint. Only the courier could read what it said, and only when he touched it. She slid the card into the breast pocket of his jacket, scanning the lettering before it melted into the cream paper:

Palais des Rêves
90 boulevard de Clichy
Tell them L'Énigme sent you . . .

A party invitation sounded like a poor consolation prize for getting knocked unconscious, but this was different. The Palais des Rêves was Paris's most exclusive cabaret, and next week they were throwing a party in honor of the hundredth anniversary of the French Revolution. Invitations currently sold on the black market for the price of diamonds. But it wasn't just the cabaret that had people excited. In a few weeks' time, the city would host the 1889 Exposition Universelle, a gigantic world fair celebrating the powers of Europe and the inventions that would pave the way for the new century, which meant that L'Eden Hôtel was running at full capacity.

"I doubt you'll remember this, but do try and order the chocolate-covered strawberries at the Palais," she said to the courier. "They're utterly divine."

Laila checked the grandfather clock: half past eight. Séverin and Enrique weren't due back for at least an hour, but she couldn't stop checking the time. Hope flared painfully behind her ribs. She'd spent two years looking for a breakthrough in her search for the ancient book, and this treasure map could be the answer to every prayer. *They'll be fine*, she told herself. Acquisitions were hardly new to any of them. When Laila had first started working with Séverin, he was trying to earn back his family's possessions. In return, he helped in her search for an ancient book. The book had no title she knew of . . . her only lead was that it belonged to the Order of Babel.

Going after a treasure map hidden inside a compass sounded rather tame in comparison to former trips. Laila still hadn't forgotten the time she ended up dangling over Nisyros Island's active volcano in pursuit of an ancient diadem. But this acquisition was different. If Enrique's research and Séverin's intelligence reports were correct, that one tiny compass could change the direction of their lives. Or, in Laila's case, let her keep this life.

Distracted, Laila smoothed her hands across her dress.

A mistake.

She should never touch anything when her thoughts were too frenzied. That single unguarded moment had allowed the dress's memories to knife into her thoughts: *chrysanthemum petals clinging to the wet hem, brocade stretched over the carriage footstool, hands folded in prayer, and then—*

Blood.

Blood everywhere, the carriage overturned, bone snapping through the fabric—

Laila winced, snatching back her hand. But it was too late. The dress's memories caught her and held tight. Laila squeezed her eyes shut, pinching her skin as hard as she could. The sharp pain felt like a red flame in her thoughts, and her consciousness wrapped around that pain as if it would lead her out of the dark. When the memories faded, she opened her eyes. Laila pulled down her sleeve, her hands shaking.

For a moment, Laila crouched on the floor, her arms around her knees. Séverin had called her ability "invaluable" before she told him *why* she could read the objects around her. After that, he was too startled, or perhaps too horrified, to say anything. Out of the whole group, only Séverin knew her touch could draw out an object's secret history. Invaluable or not, this ability was not . . . normal.

She was not normal.

Laila gathered herself off the floor, her hands still shaking as she left the room.

In the servants' stairway, Laila shucked off the housekeeper uniform and changed into her worn kitchen uniform. The hotel's second kitchen was dedicated strictly to baking, and during the evening hours, it belonged to her. She wasn't due on the Palais des Rêves stage until next week, which left her with nothing but free time for her second job.

In the narrow hallway, L'Eden's waitstaff bustled past her. They carried chilled oysters on the half shell, quail eggs floating in bone marrow soup, steaming coq au vin that left the hall smelling like burgundy wine and buttery garlic. Without her trademark mask and headdress, not one of them recognized her as the cabaret star L'Énigme. Here, she was simply another person, another worker.

Alone in the baking kitchen, Laila surveyed the marble counter strewn with culinary scales, paintbrushes, edible pearls in a glass dish, and—as of this afternoon—a croquembouche tower nearly two meters high. She had been up at dawn baking choux pastry balls, filling them with sweetened cream, and making sure that every sphere was the perfect coin-gold of dawn before rolling them in caramel and stacking them into a pyramid. All that was left was the decoration.

L'Eden had already won all manner of accolades for its fine dining—Séverin would accept nothing less—but it was the desserts that lit up the guests' dreams. Laila's desserts, though absent of Forging, were like edible magic. Her cakes took the shape of ballerinas with outstretched arms—their hair spun sugar and edible gold, their skin pale as cream and strewn with sweet pearl dust.

Guests called her creations "divine." When she stepped into the kitchen, she felt like a deity surveying the slivers of a universe not yet made. She breathed easier in the kitchen. Sugar and flour and salt had no memory. Here, her touch was just that. A touch. A distance closed, an action brought to an end.

An hour later, she was putting the finishing touches on a cake when the door slammed open. Laila sighed, but she didn't look up. She knew who it was.

Six months after Laila had started working for Séverin, she and Enrique had been playing cards in the stargazing room when Séverin walked in carrying a dirty, underfed Polish girl with eyes bluer than a candle's heart. Séverin set her down on the couch, introduced her as his engineer, and that was that. Only later did Laila discover more about her. Arrested for arson and expelled from university, Zofia possessed a rare Forging affinity for all metals and a sharp mind for numbers.

When she first came to L'Eden, Zofia spoke only to Séverin and seemed utterly uncommunicative when anyone else approached her. One day, Laila noticed that when she brought desserts for meetings, Zofia only ate the pale sugar cookies, leaving all the colorfully decorated desserts untouched. So, the next day, Laila left a plate of them outside Zofia's door. She did that for three weeks before she got busy one day in the kitchens and forgot. When she opened the door to air the room, she found Zofia holding out an empty plate and staring at her expectantly. That had been a year ago.

Now, without saying a word, Zofia grabbed a clean mixing bowl, filled it with water, and guzzled it on the spot. She dragged her arm across her mouth. Then she reached for a bowl of icing. Laila smacked her hand, lightly, with a rolling pin. Zofia glowered, then dipped an ink-stained finger into the icing anyway. A moment later, she began absentmindedly stacking the measuring cups according to size. Laila waited patiently. With Zofia, conversations were not initiated so much as caught at random and followed through until the other girl grew bored.

"I set some fires in the House Kore courier's room."

Laila dropped the paintbrush. "*What*? You were supposed to wake him up without being in the room!"

"I did? I set them off when I stepped outside. They're tiny." When met with Laila's wide-eyed stare, Zofia abruptly changed the subject. Though, to her, it probably did not seem abrupt at all. "I don't like crocodile musculature. Séverin wants a decoy of those Sphinx masks—"

"Can we go back to the fire—"

"—the mask won't meld to human facial expressions. I need to make it work. Oh, I also need a new drawing board."

"What happened to the last one?"

Zofia inspected the icing bowl and shrugged.

"You broke it," said Laila.

"My elbow fell into it."

Laila shook her head and threw Zofia a clean rag. She stared at it, befuddled.

"Why do I need a rag?"

"Because there's gunpowder on your face."

"And?"

". . . and that is mildly alarming, my dear. Clean up."

Zofia dragged the rag down her face. It seemed Zofia was always emerging from ashes or flames, which earned her the nickname "phoenix" among L'Eden. Not that Zofia minded, even though the bird didn't exist. As she cleaned her face, the ends of the cloth caught on her unusual necklace, which looked like strung-together knife-points.

"When will they be back?" asked Zofia.

Laila felt a sharp pang. "Enrique and Séverin should be here by nine."

"I need to grab my letters."

Laila frowned. "This late? It's already dark out, Zofia."

Zofia touched her necklace. "I know."

Zofia tossed her the rag. Laila caught it and threw it in the sink. When she turned around, Zofia had grabbed the spoon for the icing.

"Excuse me, phoenix, I need that!"

Zofia stuck the spoon in her mouth.

"Zofia!"

The engineer grinned. Then she swung open the door and ran off, the spoon still sticking out of her mouth.

ONCE SHE FINISHED the dessert, Laila cleaned up and left the kitchen. She was not the official pastry chef, nor did she wish to be, and half the allure of this hobby job was that it was only for pleasure. If she did not wish to make something, she didn't.

The farther she walked down the main serving hall, the more the sounds of L'Eden came alive—laughter ribboning between the glassy murmur of the amber chandeliers and champagne flutes, the hum of Forged moths and their stained-glass wings as they shed colored light in their flight. Laila stopped in front of the Mercury Cabinet, the hotel's messaging service. Small metal boxes marked with the names of the hotel staff sat inside. Laila opened her box with her staff key, not expecting to find anything, when her fingers brushed against something that felt like cold silk. It was a single black petal pinned to a one-word note:

Envy.

Even without the flower, Laila would have recognized that cramped and slanted handwriting anywhere: Tristan. She had to force herself not to smile. After all, she was still mad at him.

But that would not stop her from accepting a present.

Especially one he had Forged.

Forged. It was a word that still sat strangely on her tongue even though she'd lived in Paris for two years. The empires and kingdoms of the West called Tristan and Zofia's abilities "Forging," but the artistry had other names in other languages. In India, they called it *chhota saans*, the "small breath," for while only gods breathed life into creation, this art was a small sip of such power. Yet, no matter its name, the rules guiding the affinity were the same.

There were two kinds of Forging affinities: mind and matter. Someone with a matter affinity could influence one of three material states: liquids, solids, or gasses. Both Tristan and Zofia had matter affinities; Zofia's Forging affinity was for solid matter—mostly metals and crystals—and Tristan had an affinity for liquid matter. Specifically, the liquid present in plants.

All Forging was bound by three conditions: the strength of the artisan's will, the clarity of the artistic goal, and the boundaries of their chosen mediums' elemental properties. Which meant that someone with a Forging affinity for solid matter with a specificity in stone would go nowhere without understanding the attendant chemical formulas and properties of the stone they wished to manipulate.

As a rule, the affinity manifested in children no later than thirteen years of age. If the child wished to hone the affinity, he or she could pursue study. In Europe, most Forging artisans studied for years at renowned institutions or held lengthy apprenticeships. Zofia and Tristan, however, had followed neither of those paths. Zofia, because she had been kicked out of school before she had the chance. And Tristan, because, well, Tristan had no need of it. His landscape artistry looked like the fever dream of a nature spirit. It was unsettling and beautiful, and Paris couldn't get enough of him. At the age of sixteen, the waiting list to commission him stretched into the hundreds.

Laila used to wonder why Tristan stayed at L'Eden. Perhaps it was loyalty to Séverin. Or because L'Eden allowed Tristan to keep his bizarre arachnid displays. But when Laila stepped into the gardens, she *felt* the reason. The perfume of the flowers thick in her lungs. The garden turning jagged and wild in the falling dark. And she understood. Tristan's other clients had so many rules, like House Kore, which had commissioned extravagant topiaries for its upcoming celebration. L'Eden was different. Tristan loved Séverin like a brother, but he stayed here because only in L'Eden could he lift marvels from his mind, free of any demands.

Once she stepped into the gardens of L'Eden, she was inside Tristan's imagination. Despite its name, the gardens were no paradise, but a labyrinth of sins. Seven, to be exact.

The first garden was Lust. Here, red flowers spilled from the hollow mouths of statues. In one corner, Cleopatra coughed up garnet amaryllis and pink-frilled anemone. In another, Helen of Troy whispered zinnia and poppies. Laila moved quickly through the labyrinth. Past Gluttony, where a sky of glossy blooms that smelled of ambrosia closed tight the moment one reached for them. Then Greed, where a gold veneer encased each slender plant. Next came Sloth, with its slow-moving shrubs; Wrath with its fiery florals; then Pride with its gargantuan, moving topiaries of green stags with flowering antlers and regal lions with manes of jasmine, until finally she was in Envy. Here, a suffusion of greenery, the very shade of sin.

Laila stopped before the Tezcat door propped up near the entrance. To anyone who didn't know its secrets, the Tezcat looked like an ordinary mirror, albeit with a lovely frame that resembled gilded ivy leaves. Tezcat doors were impossible to distinguish from ordinary mirrors without, according to Zofia, a complicated test involving fire and phosphorous. Luckily, she didn't have to go through that. To get to the other side, she simply unlocked it by pinching the fourth gilded ivy leaf on the left side of the frame. A hidden doorknob. Her reflection rippled as the silver of the Tezcat door's mirror thinned to transparency.

Inside was Tristan's workplace. Laila breathed in the scent of earth and roots. All along the walls were small terrariums, landscapes squeezed into miniature form. Tristan made them almost obsessively. When she asked him once, he told her it was because he wished the world were easier. Small enough and manageable enough to fit in the hollow of one's palm.

"Laila!"

Tristan walked toward her with a wide smile on his round face. There was dirt smudged on his clothes and—she breathed a sigh of relief—no sign of his gigantic pet spider.

But she did not return his smile. Instead, she lifted an eyebrow. Tristan wiped his hands down his smock.

"Oh . . . you're still mad?" he asked.

"Yes."

"Would giving you a present make you less mad?"

Laila lifted her chin. "Depends on the present. But first, say it."

Tristan shifted on his feet. "I am sorry."

"For?"

"For putting Goliath on your dressing table."

"Where does Goliath belong? And for that matter, where do *all* your pet insects and whatnot belong?"

Tristan looked wide-eyed. "Not in your room?"

"Close enough."

He turned to the worktable beside him where a large, frosted glass terrarium took up half the space. He lifted the cover, revealing a single, deep-purple flower. The slender petals looked like snippets of evening sky, a rich velvetine purple hungry for the light of stars. Laila traced their edges softly. The petals were almost exactly the same shade of Séverin's eyes. The thought made her draw back her hand.

"Voilà! Behold your present, Forged with a little bit of silk taken from one of your costumes—"

When he caught her frantic gaze, he added, "One of the ones you were going to throw away, promise!"

Laila relaxed a bit.

"So . . . am I forgiven?"

He already knew he was. But she still decided to draw out the moment a little longer than necessary. She tapped her foot, biding her time and watching Tristan squirm. Then, *"Fine."*

Tristan let out a whoop of happiness, and Laila couldn't help but smile. Tristan could get away with anything with those wide, gray eyes.

"Oh! I came up with a new device. I wanted to show Séverin. Where is he?"

When he caught sight of her face, Tristan's grin fell. "They're not back yet?"

"Yet," emphasized Laila. "Don't worry. You know these things take time. Why don't you come inside? I'll make you something to eat."

Tristan shook his head. "Maybe later. I have to check on Goliath. I don't think he's feeling well."

Laila did not ask how Tristan would know the emotional states of a tarantula. Instead, she took her gift and headed back inside the hotel. As she walked, unease shaded her thoughts. At the top of the stairs, the grandfather clock struck the tenth hour. Laila felt the lost hour like an ache in her bones. They should have been back by now.

Something was wrong.

3

ENRIQUE

Enrique scowled as he held apart the bear's jaws. "Remember when you said, 'This will be fun'?"

"Can this wait?" Séverin grunted through clenched teeth.

"I suppose."

Enrique's tone was light, but every part of Séverin's body felt leaden. The onyx bear held Séverin's wrist between its teeth. Every passing second, the pressure heightened. Blood began to run down his arm. Soon, the pressure of the creature's jaws wouldn't just trap his wrist.

It would snap it in half.

At least the emerald House Kore eagle hadn't got involved. That particular stone creature could detect "suspicious" activity and come to life even when its own object was not in question. Enrique nearly muttered a prayer of thanks until he heard a soft caw. Air gusted over his face from the unmistakable flap of wings.

Well, then.

"Was that the eagle?" Séverin said, wincing.

He couldn't twist his body to turn.

"No, not at all," said Enrique.

In front of him, the eagle tilted its head to one side. Enrique pulled more strongly on Séverin's trapped wrist. Séverin groaned.

"Forget it," he wheezed. "I'm stuck. We need to put it to sleep."

Enrique agreed, but now the question was how. Because Forged creatures were too dangerous to go unchecked, all artisans were legally required to add a failsafe known as somno, which put the object to sleep. But even if he found it, the somno might be further encrypted. Worse, if he let go of the jaws, they'd only crush Séverin's wrist faster. And if they didn't get out by the eight-minute limit, the Forged creatures would be the least of their worries.

Séverin grunted. "By all means, take your time. I love a good slow, painful death."

Enrique let go. Steadying himself, he circled the onyx bear, ignoring the ever-closer jumping of the emerald eagle. He ran his hands along the bear's body, the black haunches and shaggy feet. Nothing.

"*Enrique*," breathed Séverin.

Séverin fell to his knees. Rivulets of blood streamed, dripping down the creature's jaws. Enrique swore under his breath. He closed his eyes. Sight wouldn't help him here. With so little light in the room, he would have to feel for any words. He trailed his fingers across the bear's haunches and belly until he caught something near its ankles: chipped-away depressions in the stone; evenly spaced and close together as if it were a line of writing. The letters and words came to life beneath his touch.

Fiduciam in domum

"Trust in the House," translated Enrique. He whispered it again, running scenarios through his head. "I . . . I have an idea."

"Do enlighten me," managed Séverin.

The bear lifted one of its heavy, jet paws, casting a shadow over Séverin's face.

"You have to . . . to trust it!" cried Enrique. "Don't fight it! Push your wrist farther!"

Séverin didn't hesitate. He stood and pushed. But his hand remained stuck. Séverin growled. He threw himself against the creature. His shoulder popped wetly. Every second felt like a blade pressed tight against Enrique's skin. Just then, the eagle took off in the air. It circled the room, then swooped, talons out. Enrique ducked as the jewel claws grazed his neck. He wouldn't be so lucky the next time. Once more, claws rasped at his neck. The eagle's talons tugged him upward, his heels lifted off the ground. Enrique shut his eyes tight.

"Mind the hair—" he started.

Abruptly, he was dropped to the ground. He opened his eyes a crack. A bare ceiling met his gaze. Behind him, he heard the shuffling of talons on a podium. He raised himself up on his elbows.

The eagle had gone statue still.

Séverin heaved and rose to a stand. He clutched his wrist. Then, yanking his arm, he swung it forward. Enrique grimaced at the wet *snick* of joints popping back into place. Séverin wiped the blood on his pants and plucked out the Forged compass from the mouth of the still, onyx bear. He slid it into his jacket and smoothed back his hair.

"Well," he said finally. "At least it wasn't like Nisyros Island."

"Are you *serious*?" croaked Enrique. He trudged after his friend to the door. "It'll be 'like dreaming,' you said. As 'easy as sleep'!"

"Nightmares are part of sleeping."

"Is that a joke?" demanded Enrique. "You do realize your hand is mangled."

"I am aware."

"You almost got eaten by a bear."

"Not a real one."

"The dismemberment would've been real enough."

Séverin only grinned. "See you in a bit," he said, and slipped out the door.

Enrique lingered to give Séverin a head start.

In the dark, he felt the presence of the Order's treasure like the eyes of the dead. Hate shivered through him. He couldn't bring himself to look at the looming, *salvaged* piles. He might help Séverin steal, but the greatest thief of all was the Order of Babel, for they stole more than just objects . . . They stole histories, swallowed cultures whole, smuggled evidence of illustrious antiquity onto large ships and spirited them into indifferent lands.

"Indifferent lands," mused Enrique. "That's a good line for later."

He could use it in the next article he submitted to the Spanish newspaper dedicated to Filipino nationalism. So far he didn't have the connections that made anyone think his thoughts were worth listening to. This acquisition could change that.

But first he had to finish the job.

Enrique counted down the thirty seconds. Then, he straightened the borrowed servant's outfit, adjusted his mask, and stepped into the darkened hall. Between the gaps of the marble pillars, he could make out the flutter of fans stabbing the air.

Right on time for his meeting, the Vietnamese diplomat Vũ Văn Đinh rounded the corner. A falsified letter poked out of his sleeve. Though he had hated doing it, Tristan was exceptionally good at faking people's handwriting. That of the diplomat's mistress was no exception.

Last week, Enrique and the diplomat had shared a drink at L'Eden. While the diplomat was distracted, Laila had fished out the

mistress's letter from Ðinh's jacket, and Tristan had copied her pen-
manship to orchestrate this very meeting.

Enrique eyed Ðinh's clothes. Like so many diplomats from col-
onized countries, he had outwardly allied with the Order. Once,
there had been versions of the Order all over the world, each dedicated to their country's source of Forging power—although not all
of them called the artistry Forging and not all of them credited
its power to the Babel Fragments. But those versions no longer
existed. Now, their treasures had been taken to different lands;
their artistry changed; and their ancient guilds given two choices:
ally or die.

Enrique straightened his false suit and bowed. "May I assist you
with anything, sir?"

He extended his hand. Fresh panic reared inside him. Surely
Ðinh would look. Surely he would *know* it was him. The very tips of
his fingers brushed Ðinh's sleeves.

"Indeed you may not," said Ðinh coldly, drawing away his arm.

Not once did he look him in the eye.

"Very well, sir."

He bowed. With Ðinh still waiting on a meeting that would never
take place, Enrique walked to the back of the ballroom. He dragged
his fingers down his face and neck. A slight prickling sensation rolled
down the skin he'd touched, and a thin film of color floated above
his skin and clothes, swirling to match the appearance and apparel
of Ambassador Vũ Văn Ðinh.

Thanks to the mirror powder dusting his fingertips, he now
looked identical to the ambassador.

Long ago, mirror powder had been banned and confiscated, and
so the Order had not bothered to ward their meetings against it.
They hadn't counted on Séverin being friendly with the officer of
customs and immigrations.

Enrique moved quickly through the crowd. The mirror powder might be effective, but long-lasting it was not.

Enrique jogged down the main staircase. At the base was a Tezcat door that seemed to date back to a time when the Fallen House had not yet been ousted from the French faction of the Order of Babel, for its borders held the symbols of the original four Houses of France. A crescent moon for House Nyx. Thorns for House Kore. A snake biting its own tail for House Vanth. A six-pointed star for the Fallen House. Of them, only Nyx and Kore still existed. Vanth's bloodline had legally been declared dead. And the Fallen House had . . . fallen. Supposedly, its leaders found the West's Babel Fragment and tried to use it to rebuild the biblical Tower of Babel, thinking it might give them more than just a sliver of God's power . . . but the actual power of God. Had they succeeded in removing the West's Babel Fragment, they might have destroyed the known civilization. Séverin always said that was a rubbish rumor and believed the Order had destroyed the Fallen House as a power grab. Enrique wasn't so sure. Of the four Houses, the Fallen House was said to be the most advanced. Even the Tezcat doors Forged by the Fallen House did more than just camouflage an entrance. Rumor went that they were capable of bridging actual distances. Like a portal. But whatever the House had once possessed, no one knew. For years, the Order had tried to discover what had become of the Fallen House's ring and massive treasure, but none had been able to find it.

Today, thought Enrique, that might change.

Through the Tezcat, Enrique could see glittering corridors, a handsomely dressed crowd, and the glint of far-off chandeliers. It always unnerved him that though he could see the people on the other side, all they would see was a slim, polished mirror. He felt strangely like a god in exile, filled with a kind of hollow omniscience. As much as he could see the world, it would not see him.

Enrique stepped through the Tezcat and emerged in one of the opulent halls of the Palais Garnier, the most famous opera house in all of Europe.

One man looked up, stunned. He stared at the mirror, then Enrique, before scrutinizing his champagne flute.

Around Enrique, the crowd milled about obliviously. They had no idea about the Forged ballroom the Order kept secret. Then again, everything about the Order was kept secret. Even their invitations only opened at the drop of an approved guest's blood. Anyone else who accidentally received one would see nothing but blank paper.

To the public, the Order of Babel was nothing more than France's research arm tasked with historical preservation. They knew nothing of the auctions, the treasures buried deep beneath the ground. Half the public didn't even believe the Babel Fragment was a physical object, but rather a dressed-up biblical metaphor.

Enrique strode through the crowd, tugging his lapel as he walked. His servant costume shifted, the threads unraveling and embroidering simultaneously until he was dressed in a fashionable evening jacket. He flicked his watch, and the slim band of Forged leather burst into a silk top hat that he promptly spun onto his head.

Right before he stepped outside, Enrique hesitated before the verit stone bust. The verit bust wasn't a decorative piece, but a detection device used to reveal hidden weapons. One ounce of verit rivaled a kilo of diamonds, and only palaces or banks could afford the stone. Enrique double-checked that he'd left his knife behind, and then stepped over the threshold.

Outside, Paris was a touch humid for April. Night had sweated off its stars, and across the street, a black hansom glinted dully. Enrique got inside, and Séverin flashed him a wry grin.

The second Séverin rapped his knuckles against the hansom's ceiling, the horses lurched into the night. Reaching into his coat pocket, Séverin pulled out his ever-present tin of cloves. Enrique wrinkled his nose. On its own, the clove smell was pleasant. A bit woodsy and spicy. But over the past two years he'd been working for Séverin, cloves had stopped being a scent and become more of a signal. It was the fragrance of Séverin's decision-making, and it could be delightful or dangerous. Or both.

"Voilà," said Séverin, handing him the compass.

Enrique ran his fingers over the cold metal, gently tracing the divots in the silver. Ancient Chinese compasses did not look like Western ones. They were magnetized bowls, with a depression in the center where a spoon-shaped dial would have spun back and forth. A thrill of wonder zipped through his veins. It was thousands of years old and here he was, *holding* it—

"No need to seduce the thing," cut in Séverin.

"I'm appreciating it."

"You're fondling it."

Enrique rolled his eyes. "It's an authentic piece of history and should be savored."

"You might at least buy it dinner first," said Séverin, before pointing at the metal edges. "So? Is it like what we thought it'd be?"

Enrique weighed the half of the compass in his hand, studying the contours. As he felt the ridges, he noticed a slight deformity in the metal. He tapped on the surface and then looked up.

"It's hollow," he said, breathless.

He didn't know why he even felt surprised. He knew the compass would be hollow, and yet the possibilities of the map reared up fast and sharp in his head. Enrique didn't know what, specifically, the map led to . . . only that it was rare enough to send the Order of Babel into a furtive clamoring. His bet, though, was that it was a map to the lost treasures of the Fallen House.

"Break it," said Séverin.

"*What?*" Enrique clutched the object to his chest. "The compass is thousands of years old! There's another way to pry it, *gently*, apart—"

Séverin lunged. Enrique tried to snatch it away, but he wasn't as fast. In one swift motion, Séverin grabbed both sides of the compass. Enrique heard it before he saw it. A brief, merciless—

Snap.

Something dropped from the compass, thudding on the hansom's floor. Séverin got to it first, and the minute he held it up to the light, Enrique felt as if a cold hand had pushed down on his lungs and squeezed the breath out of him. The object hidden within the compass certainly looked like a map. All that was left was one question: Where did it lead?

4

ZOFIA

Zofia liked Paris best in the evening.

During the day, Paris was too much. It was all noise and smell, crammed with stained streets and threaded with hectic crowds. Dusk tamed the city. Made it manageable.

As she walked back to L'Eden, Zofia clutched her sister's newest letter tight to her chest. Hela would find Paris beautiful. She would like the linden trees of rue Bonaparte. There were fourteen of them. She would find the horse chestnuts comely. There were nine. She would not like the smells. There were too many to count.

Right now, Paris did not seem beautiful. Horse shit marred the cobbled roads. People urinated on the street lanterns. And yet, there was something about the city that spoke vibrantly of life. Nothing felt still. Even the stone gargoyles leaned off the edges of buildings as if they were on the verge of flight. And nothing looked lonely. Terraces had the company of wicker chairs, and bright purple bougainvillea hugged stone walls. Not even the Seine River, which cut through Paris like a trail of ink, looked abandoned. By day, boats zipped across it. By night, lamplight danced upon the surface.

Zofia peeked at Hela's newest letter, sneaking lines beneath every shining lantern. She read one sentence, then found that she could not stop. Every word brought back the sound of Hela's voice.

Zosia, please tell me you are going to the Exposition Universelle! If you do not, I will know. Trust me, dear sister, the laboratory can spare you for a day. Learn something outside the classroom for once. Besides, I heard the world fair will have a cursed diamond, and princes from exotic lands! Perhaps you might bring one home, then I will not have to play governess to our stingy stryk. How he can be father's brother is a mystery for only God to ponder. Please go. You are sending back so much money lately that I worry you are not keeping enough for yourself. Are you hale and happy? Write to me soon, little light.

Hela was half-wrong. Zofia was not in school. But she was learning plenty outside of a classroom. In the past year and a half, she had learned how to invent things the École des Beaux-Arts never imagined for her. She had learned how to open a savings account, which might—assuming the map Séverin acquired was all they'd hoped it to be—soon hold enough money to support Hela through medical school when she finally enrolled. But the worst lesson was learning how to lie to her sister. The first time she had lied in a letter, she'd thrown up. Guilt left her sobbing for hours until Laila had found and comforted her. She didn't know how Laila knew what bothered her. She just did. And Zofia, who never quite grasped how to find her way through a conversation, simply felt grateful someone could do the work for her.

Zofia was still thinking about Hela when the marble entrance of the École des Beaux-Arts manifested before her. Zofia staggered back, nearly dropping the letters.

The marble entrance did not move.

Not only was the entrance Forged to appear before any matriculated students two blocks from the school, but it was also an exquisite example of solid matter and mind affinity working in tandem. A feat only those trained at the École could perform.

Once, Zofia would have trained with them too.

"You don't want me," she said softly.

Tears stung her eyes. When she blinked, she saw the path to her expulsion. One year into schooling, her classmates had changed. Once, her skill awed them. Now, it offended them. Then the rumors started. No one seemed to care at first that she was Jewish. But that changed. Rumors sprang up that Jews could steal anything.

Even someone else's Forging affinity.

It was completely false, and so she ignored it. She should have been more careful, but that was the problem with happiness. It blinds.

For a while, Zofia was happy. And then, one afternoon, the other students' whispers got the better of her. That day, she broke down in the laboratory. There were too many sounds. Too much laughing. Too much brightness escaping through the curtain. She'd forgotten her parents' lesson to count backward until she felt calm. Whispers grew from that episode. *Crazy Jew.* A month later, ten students locked themselves in the lab with her. Again came the sounds, smells, laughing. The other students didn't grab her. They knew the barest touch— like a feather trailed down skin—hurt her more. Calm slipped out of reach no matter how many times she counted backward, or begged to be let go, or asked what she had done wrong.

In the end, it was such a small movement.

Someone had kicked her to the ground. Another person's elbow clashed into a vial on a table. The vial splattered into a puddle, which pooled out and touched the tips of her outstretched fingers. She had been holding a piece of flint in her hand when fury flickered in her mind. *Fire.* That little thought—that snippet of will, just as the professors had taught her—traveled from her fingertips to the puddle, igniting the broken vial until it bloomed into a towering inferno.

Seven students were injured in the explosion.

For her crime, she was arrested on grounds of arson and insanity, and taken to prison. She would have died there if not for Séverin. Séverin found her, freed her, and did the unthinkable: He gave her a job. A way to earn back what she'd lost. A way out.

Zofia rubbed her finger across the oath tattoo on her right knuckle. Luckily, it was only temporary or her mother would have been appalled. She could not be buried in a Jewish cemetery with a tattoo. The tattoo was a contract between her and Séverin, the ink Forged so that if one of them broke the agreement, nightmares would plague them. That Séverin had used this tattoo—a sign of equals—instead of some of the cruder contracts was something she would never forget.

Zofia turned on her heel and left rue Bonaparte behind. Perhaps the marble entrance could not recognize when a student had been expelled, for it did not move, but stayed in its place until she disappeared around a corner.

IN L'EDEN, ZOFIA made her way to the stargazing room. Séverin had called for a meeting once he and Enrique got back from their latest acquisition, which she knew was just a fancy word for "theft."

Zofia never took the grand lobby's main staircase. She didn't want to see all the fancy people dressed up and laughing and dancing. Plus, it was too noisy. Instead, she took the servants' entryway, which was how she ran into Séverin. He grinned despite appearing thoroughly disheveled. Zofia noticed how tenderly he held his wrist.

"You're covered in blood."

Séverin glanced down at his clothes. "Surprisingly, it hasn't escaped my attention."

"Are you dying?"

"No more than usual or expected."

Zofia frowned.

"I'm well enough. Don't worry."

She reached for the door handle. "I'm glad you're not dead."

"Thank you, Zofia," said Séverin with a small smile. "I will join you soon. There's something I'd like to show everyone through a mnemo bug."

On Séverin's shoulder, a Forged silver beetle scuttled under his lapel. Mnemo bugs recorded images and sound, allowing projection-like holograms should the wearer choose. Which meant she had to be prepared for an unexpected burst of light. Séverin knew she didn't like those. They jolted her thoughts. Nodding, Zofia left him in the hall and walked into the room.

The stargazing room calmed Zofia. It was wide and spacious, with a glass-domed vault that let in the starlight. All along the walls were orreries and telescopes, cabinets full of polished crystal, and shelves lined with fading books and manuscripts. In the middle of the room was the low coffee table that bore the scuff marks and dents of a hundred schemes that came to life on its wooden surface. A semi-circle of chairs surrounded it. Zofia made her way to her seat. It was a tall metal stool with a ragged pillowcase. Zofia preferred to balance upright because she didn't like things touching her back. In a green, velvet chaise across from her sprawled Laila, who absent-mindedly traced the rim of her teacup with one finger. In a plushy armchair crowded with pillows sat Enrique, who had a large book on his lap and was reading intently. Of the two chairs left, one was Tristan's—which was less of a chair and more of a cushion because he didn't like heights—and one was Séverin's, a black-cherry armchair

Zofia had custom-Forged so that an unfamiliar touch caused it to sprout blades.

Tristan barged into the room, his hands outstretched.

"Look! I thought Goliath was dying, but he's fine. He just molted!"

Enrique screamed. Laila scuttled backward on her chaise. Zofia leaned forward, inspecting the enormous tarantula in Tristan's hands. Mathematicians didn't frighten her, and spiders—and bees— were just that. A spider's web was composed of numerous radii, a logarithmic spiral, and the light-diffusing properties of their webs and silk were fascinating.

"Tristan!" scolded Laila. "What did I just tell you about spiders?"

Tristan lifted his chin. "You said not to bring him into your room. This is not your room."

Faced with Laila's glare, he shrank a bit.

"Please can he stay for the meeting? Goliath is different. He's special."

Enrique pulled his knees up to his chest and shuddered. "What is so special about *that*?"

"Well," said Zofia, "as part of the infraorder of Mygalomorphae, the fangs of a tarantula point *down*, whereas the spiders you're thinking of have fangs which point and join in a pincerlike arrangement. That's rather special."

Enrique gagged.

Tristan beamed at her. "You remembered."

Zofia did not find this particularly noteworthy. She remembered most things people told her. Besides, Tristan had listened just as attentively when she explained the arithmetic spiral properties of a spiderweb.

Enrique made a *shoo* motion with his hands. "Please take it away, Tristan. I beg you."

"Aren't you happy for Goliath? He's been sick for days."

"Can we be happy for Goliath from behind a sheet of glass and a net and a fence? Maybe a ring of fire for good measure?" asked Enrique.

Tristan made a face at Laila. Zofia knew that pattern: widened eyes, pressed-down brows, dimpled chin, and the barest quiver of his bottom lip. Ridiculous, yet effective. Zofia approved. Across from her, Laila clapped her hands over her eyes.

"Not falling for it," said Laila sternly. "Go look like a kicked puppy elsewhere. Goliath can't stay here during a meeting. That's final."

Tristan huffed. "*Fine.*" Then he murmured to Goliath, "I'll make you a cricket cake, dear friend. Don't fret."

Once Tristan had left, Enrique turned to Zofia. "I rather sympathized with Arachne after her duel with Minerva, but I detest her descendants."

Zofia went still. People and conversation were already a cipher without throwing in all the extra words. Enrique was especially confusing. Elegance illuminated every word the historian spoke. And she could never tell when he was angry. His mouth was always bent in a half smile, regardless of his mood. If she answered now, she'd only sound foolish. Instead, Zofia said nothing, but pulled out a matchbox from her pocket and turned it over in her hands. Enrique rolled his eyes and turned back to his book. She knew what he thought of her. She had overheard him once. *She's a snob.*

He could think what he liked.

As the minutes ticked by, Laila handed out tea and desserts, making sure Zofia received exactly three sugar cookies, all pale and perfectly round. She settled back in her chair, glancing around the room. Eventually, Tristan returned and dramatically plopped onto his cushion.

"In case you're wondering, Goliath is deeply offended, and he says—"

But they would never know the tarantula's specific grievances because at that moment a beam of light shot up through the coffee table. The room went dark. Then, slowly, an image of a piece of metal appeared. When she looked up, Séverin was standing behind Tristan. She hadn't heard him enter.

Tristan followed her gaze and nearly jumped when he saw Séverin. "Must you creep up on us like that? I didn't even hear you come into the room!"

"It's part of my aesthetic," said Séverin, dangling a Forged muffling bell.

Enrique laughed. Laila didn't. Her gaze was fixed on his bloodied arm. Her shoulders dropped a bit, as if she was relieved it was only his arm that was bloodied. Zofia knew he was alive and well enough, so she turned her attention to the object. It was a square piece of metal, with curling symbols at the four corners. A large circle had been inscribed upon the middle. Within the circle were small rows of stacked lines shaped like squares:

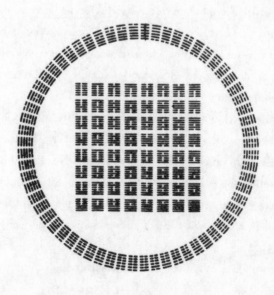

"That's what we planned for weeks to acquire?" asked Tristan. "What is it? A game? I thought we were after a treasure map hidden in a compass?"

"So did I," sighed Enrique.

"My bet was that it was a map to the Fallen House's lost stash," said Tristan.

"My bet was on an ancient book the Order lost years ago," said Laila, looking terribly disappointed. "Zofia? What'd you think it'd be?"

"Not that," she answered, pointing at the diagram.

"Looks like all of us were wrong," said Tristan. "So much for blackmailing the Order."

"At least because all of us were wrong, none of us have to play test subjects to whatever strange poison Tristan makes next," Laila pointed out.

"Touché!" said Enrique, raising a glass.

"I resent that," said Tristan.

"Don't call it a loss yet," said Séverin, pacing. "This diagram could still be useful. There has to be a reason why the patriarch of House Nyx wanted it. Just like there has to be a reason why all of our intelligence was on high alert with this transaction. Enrique, care to enlighten us on what this diagram is? Or are you too preoccupied with praying for my immortal soul?"

Enrique scowled and closed the book on his lap. Zofia glanced at the spine. He was holding the Bible. Instinctively, she leaned away.

"I've given up on your soul," said Enrique. He cleared his throat and pointed at the hologram. "What you see before you might look like a board game, but it's actually an example of Chinese cleromancy. Cleromancy is a type of divination that produces random numbers that are then interpreted as the will of God or some other supernatural force. What you see in this silver diagram are the sixty-four hexagrams found in the I Ching, which is an ancient Chinese divination text that loosely translates to 'Book of Changes.' These hexagrams"—he pointed at the small squares composed of six stacked lines in an eight-by-eight arrangement—"correspond to certain cryptic words, like 'force' or 'diminishing.' Supposedly, these arrangements translate fate."

"What about the spiral things on the edge?" asked Tristan.

The four symbols bore no resemblance to the Chinese characters or sharp lines forming the hexagrams.

"That . . . That, I'm not entirely sure," admitted Enrique. "It doesn't match anything recognizable from Chinese augury. Perhaps it's an added-on signature from whoever possessed the compass after it'd been made? Either way, it doesn't seem like a map to anything. Which, honestly, is disappointing, but that doesn't mean it won't fetch a good price on the market."

Laila drew herself up on her elbows, tilting her head to the side a little more. "Unless it's a map in disguise."

The room fell silent. Séverin shrugged.

"Why not?" he asked softly. "Any ideas?"

Zofia counted the lines. Then she counted them again. A pattern nudged against her thoughts.

"This is nothing we haven't seen before," tried Séverin cheerfully. "Remember that underwater Isis temple?"

"Distinctly," said Enrique. "You said there wouldn't be any sharks."

"There weren't."

"Right. Just mechanical leviathans with dorsal fins," said Enrique. "Forgive me."

"Apology accepted," said Séverin, inclining his head. "Now. When it came to that code, we had to rethink the direction. We had to question our assumption. What if what we're looking at is not just a map, but a hint to what it might lead to?"

Tristan frowned. "A bunch of divination lines do not a treasure make, dear brother."

"Lines," said Zofia distractedly. She tugged at her necklace. "Are they lines?"

"*That*," said Séverin, pointing at her, "is exactly the type of reasoning I'm talking about. Question the very assumptions. Good thinking."

"What if you shine it under a different light?" mused Tristan.

"Or do those symbols at the four corners correspond to something that's a hint?" asked Enrique.

Zofia kept quiet, but it was as if the pattern had peeled off the metal square. She squinted at it.

"Numbers," she said suddenly. "If you change the lines to numbers . . . it becomes something else. We did a similar procedure last year with the coded Greek alphabet riddle. I remember because that was when Séverin took us on that expedition to Nisyros Island."

All five of them collectively shuddered.

Tristan drew his knees to his chest. "I hate volcanoes."

Zofia sat up, excited. A pattern had finally taken shape in her mind.

"Each of those hexagrams is made up only of broken and unbroken lines. If you make every unbroken line a zero, and every broken line a one, then it's a pattern of zeroes and ones. It looks like some kind of binary calculus."

"But that doesn't tell us anything about the treasure," said Tristan.

"I wouldn't be too sure about that. The ancients *were* obsessed with numbers," said Enrique thoughtfully. "It's clear in their art. Which makes me wonder what else might be here. Maybe it's not a strange calculus after all." Enrique tilted his head. "Hmm . . ."

He pointed at the symbols tucked into the four corners.

"Séverin, can you alter the image and break off the four corners?"

Séverin manipulated the mnemo hologram so the four corners broke off. Then, he shrank the I Ching diagram, enlarged the four corners, and placed them beside one another.

"*There*," said Enrique. "I see it now. Séverin, place them in a block and rearrange the order. Turn the first symbol sideways, attach it to symbol two, symbol three should hang down, and the fourth symbol goes on the left."

Séverin did as asked, and when he stepped back, a new symbol took shape:

"The Eye of Horus," breathed Enrique.

Envy flashed through Zofia.

"How . . ." she said. "How did you see that?"

"The same way you saw numbers in lines," said Enrique smugly. "You're impressed. Admit it."

Zofia crossed her arms. "No."

"I dazzle you with my intelligence."

Zofia turned to Laila. "Make him stop."

Enrique bowed and gestured back to the image. "The Eye of Horus is also known as a *wadjet*. It's an ancient Egyptian symbol of royal power and protection. Over time, most Horus Eyes have been lost to history—"

"No," said Séverin. "Not lost. *Destroyed*. During Napoleon's 1798 campaign to Egypt, the Order sent a delegation tasked specifically with finding and confiscating all Horus Eyes. House Kore sent half its members, which is why they have the largest supply of Egyptian Forged treasures in Europe. If there's any Forged Horus Eyes left from that campaign, it's with them."

"But why was it destroyed?" asked Laila.

"That's a secret between the government and the Order," said

Séverin. "My guess is that certain Forged Horus Eyes showed all the somno locations on Napoleon's artillery. If everyone knew how to make his weapons useless, where would he be?"

"What's the other theory?" asked Laila.

"Napoleon thought all the Horus Eyes were looking at him funny and so he had them destroyed," said Tristan.

Enrique laughed.

"But then why have a Horus Eye on an I Ching diagram?" pressed Zofia. "If it's a calculus of zeroes and ones, what would it even see?"

Enrique went still. "*See.*" His eyes widened. "Zero and one . . . and *seeing*. Zofia, you're a genius."

She raised her shoulder. "I know."

Enrique reached for the Bible he'd left on the coffee table and started flipping through the pages.

"I was reading this earlier for a translation I'm working on, but Zofia's mathematical connection is perfect," he said. He stopped flipping. "Ah. Here we are. Genesis 11:4-9, also known as the Tower of Babel passage. We all know it. It's an etiological tale not just meant to explain why people speak different languages, but also to explain the presence of Forging in our world. The basic story is that people tried to build a tower to heaven, God didn't want that, so He made new languages, and the confusion of tongues prevented the building's completion. But He didn't just strike down the building," he said, before reading aloud: "'. . . and they ceased building the city. Therefore its name is called Babel, because there the Lord confused the language of all the earth, but the Lord delighted in His creation's ingenuity and deposited upon the land the bricks of the tower. Each brick bore his touch, and thus left an impression of the power of God to create something from nothing.'"

Something from nothing.

She'd heard that phrase before . . .

"*Ex nihilo*," said Séverin, smiling widely. "Latin for 'out of nothing.' What's the mathematical representation of nothing?"

"Zero," said Zofia.

"Thus, the movement of zero to one is the power of God, because out of nothing, *something* is created. The Babel Fragments are considered slivers of God's powers. They bring things to life, excluding, of course, the power to bring back the dead and create *actual* life," said Enrique.

Across from her, Zofia noticed that Laila's smile fell.

Enrique leaned out of his chair, his eyes uncannily bright.

"If *that's* what the diagram is really about, then what does that mean about the Horus Eye?"

Laila let out a long breath. "You said looking through the Horus Eye revealed something . . . whatever it could see had to be dangerous enough that the instrument couldn't be kept in existence. What would be dangerous enough to threaten an entire empire? Something that has to do with the power of God? Because only one thing comes to my mind."

Séverin sank into his chair. Zofia felt a numb buzzing at the edge of her thoughts. She felt as if she'd leaned over a vast precipice. As if the next words would change her life.

"In other words," said Séverin slowly, "you think this might be telling us that looking through a Horus Eye reveals a Babel Fragment."

5

SÉVERIN

Séverin stared at the luminous dark of the Eye of Horus. In that second, the air smelled metallic. He could almost see it. Gray rippling the sky as if it were hectic with fever. Fanged teeth of light flashing in the clouds—a taunt to snap. This realization felt like watching a storm. He couldn't stop what would come next.

And he didn't want to.

When he first heard about the compass, he imagined it would lead them to the lost treasure of the Fallen House, the only cache of treasure that the Order would do anything to possess. But this . . . this was like reaching for a match only to come out holding a torch. The Order had covered up their hunt for Horus Eyes, and now he knew why. If someone found the West's Fragment, they could disrupt all Forging not just in France, but Europe, for without a Fragment to power the art of Forging, civilizations died. And while the Order might know the Horus Eye's secret, the rest of the world didn't. Including many colonial guilds that had been forced into hiding by the Order. Guilds whose knowledge of the Babel Fragments' inner workings rivaled the Order's. Séverin could only imagine what they'd do to get their hands on this information, and what the Order would do to keep it from them.

"We're not . . ." Enrique couldn't finish his sentence. "Right?"

"You can't be serious," said Laila. She was pinching the tips of her fingers repeatedly, a nervous habit of hers. When she was unhappily distracted, she couldn't touch an object without accidentally reading it and the whole world became dangerously visible to her. When she was blissfully distracted, though, the rest of the world disappeared. Something he couldn't quite forget. "This could *kill* us."

Séverin didn't meet Laila's gaze, but he could feel her dark eyes pinning him. He looked only to Tristan, his brother in everything but blood. In the dark, he seemed younger than his sixteen years. Memory bit into Séverin. The two of them crouched behind a rosebush, thorns ripping at the soft skin of their necks, their hands clutching each other's while the father they called Wrath screamed their names. Séverin opened and closed his hand. A long, silver scar ran down his right palm and caught the light. Tristan had a matching one.

"Are you?" asked Tristan softly. "Serious?"

All this time, they'd been after an artifact that would be a bargaining chip to the Order. An artifact that would force the Order to restore his lost inheritance. Instead, he had information that was either a dream or a death sentence . . . depending on how he played this game. Séverin reached for his tin of cloves.

"I don't know enough to be serious," he said carefully. "But I'd like to know enough to have options."

Tristan swore under his breath. The others looked shocked, even Zofia blankly stared into her lap.

"This information is dangerous," said Tristan. "We'd be better off if you just threw the compass at House Nyx's door."

"Dangerous, yes, but the most rewarding things are," said Séverin.

"I'm not saying we approach the Order tomorrow and tell them we've got hold of one of their secrets. I have no intention to rush anything."

Enrique snorted. "Slow and painful death is far better than getting it over with quickly, sure."

Séverin rose to his feet. For a decision like this, he didn't want to be eye level. He wanted them to look up. They did.

"Think about what this could mean for us. It could bring us everything we wanted."

Enrique dragged his palm down his face. "You know how moths look at a fire and think, *'Oooh! shiny!'* and then die in a burst of flames and regret?"

"Vaguely."

"Right. Just checking to be sure."

"What about Hypnos?" asked Laila.

"What about him?"

"You don't think he'll notice what went missing? He has quite the reputation for . . . zealousness when it comes to his possessions. And what if he *knows* what the compass really contained?"

"I doubt it," said Séverin.

"You don't think he could figure it out?" asked Laila.

"He can't. He doesn't have you." When Laila's eyes widened, he caught himself and gestured to the whole group: *"All* of you."

"Awww . . ." said Enrique. "What a sweet sentiment. I shall take it to my grave. Literally."

"Besides, Zofia and Enrique made a perfect fake artifact. There's no way Hypnos can trace it back to us."

Enrique sighed. "God, I'm brilliant."

Zofia crossed her arms. "I am too."

"Of course you are," soothed Laila. "You're both brilliant."

"Yes, but I'm *more—*" huffed Enrique.

Séverin interrupted them with two sharp claps. "Now that we

have the piece, let's examine it thoroughly. We make no plans beyond that. We make no speculation about what comes next. We don't do *anything* until it's clear what we're working with. Understood?"

The four of them nodded. Just like that, the meeting was concluded. They rose slowly. Enrique was the first to head to the door.

He paused in front of Séverin. "Remember . . ."

And then Enrique hooked his thumbs together and made a strange waving motion with his hands.

"You're a bird?"

"A moth!" said Enrique. "A moth approaching a flame!"

"That's a very alarming moth."

"It's a metaphor."

"It's an alarming metaphor too."

Enrique rolled his eyes. Behind him, Zofia smuggled more cookies on her plate before brushing past him.

"How are the Sphinx masks coming along?"

Zofia did not break her gait or even turn as she said, "Why?"

"Might need them sooner than later," Enrique called after her.

"Mmf."

When Séverin turned back to the room, he went still. Though the room was nearly dark, whatever light clung to its corners now raced to illuminate Laila. It seemed the world couldn't help but want to be near her . . . every beam of light, pair of eyes, atom of air. Maybe that's why sometimes he couldn't breathe around her.

Or maybe it was memory that choked him in those seconds. Memories of one night they'd both sworn to put behind them. Laila had. It was fate that, of course, he couldn't.

Laila practically stormed toward him. Usually, she had a habit of being relentlessly radiant. She hated seeing someone hold an empty plate and always thought everyone was hungry. She knew everyone's secrets even without having to read their objects. At the Palais des

Rêves, she turned that radiance into an allure that earned her star billing and the name, L'Énigme. *The Mystery*. But this evening, she spared him no smile. Her dark eyes looked like chips of stone.

Uh-oh.

"No tea and sympathy for me?" he asked. He lifted his hand. "I am wounded, you know."

"How thoughtful of you to delay the hour of your death so that I might witness it firsthand," she said coldly. But the longer she looked at his wrist, the more her shoulders softened. "You could've been hurt."

"It's the price one pays for chasing wants," he said lightly. "The problem is, I have too many of them."

Laila shook her head. "You only want one thing."

"Is that so?"

He meant it teasingly. But Laila's posture changed almost immediately. More languid, somehow.

She moved closer, sliding her hand down the front of his jacket. "I will tell you what you want."

Séverin held still. This close, he could count her eyelashes, the starlight gilding her face. He remembered the soft flutter of her eyelashes against his cheek when she'd brought him down to her long ago. The heat of her skin seeped through the linen of his shirt. What game was she playing? Laila's fingers slipped into the inner breast pocket of his jacket. She pulled out his silver tin, popped the latch, and withdrew a clove. Eyes still locked on his, she dragged her thumb across his lower lip. The motion felt like the afterburn of sunshine on his retina. Two images lazily superimposed: Laila touching his mouth then, Laila touching his mouth now. It jarred him so much, he didn't remember parting his lips. But he must have because a moment later, a sharp clove hit his tongue. Laila drew back. Cold rushed in to fill the space. All in all, it took no more than a few seconds. The whole time her composure had stayed the same. Detached and sensual, like the performer she was. The performer she had always been. He could see her staging an identical routine at the Palais des Rêves—reaching into a patron's jacket for his cigarette case, placing it on the man's lips, and lighting it before she took it for herself.

"*That's* what you want," she said darkly. "You want an excuse to go hunting. But you have mistaken the predator for prey."

With that, her skirts swirled around her heels as she left. Séverin bit down on the clove and watched her leave. She was right. He was hunting. And so was she. Neither of them could afford to lose sight of their prize, so one night in each other's arms stayed as one mistake, and the memory of it was shoved into the dark. He waited a moment before turning back to Tristan.

He knew what argument he'd have with his brother. He had prepared for it, and yet it still wrenched something from him to see the shine in Tristan's eyes.

"Just tell me," he said wearily.

Tristan looked away from him. "I wish this were enough for you."

Séverin closed his eyes. It wasn't about *enough*. Tristan would never understand. He had never felt the pulse of an entirely different future, only to see it ripped from his grasp and smothered in front of him. He didn't understand that sometimes the only way to take down what had destroyed you was to disguise yourself as part of it.

"It's not about enough," said Séverin. "It's about balancing the scales. Fairness."

Tristan didn't look at him. "You promised you would protect us."

Séverin hadn't forgotten. The day he said that was the day he realized some memories have a taste. That day, his mouth was full of blood, and so his promise tasted like salt and iron.

"Let's say this whole venture doesn't kill us. What if you get what you want? If you get back your House, you'll be a patriarch . . ." His voice pitched higher. "Sometimes I wished you didn't even want to *be* a patriarch. What if you become like—"

"Don't." He hadn't meant for his voice to sound so cold, but it did, and Tristan flinched. "I will *never* be like our fathers."

Tristan and Séverin had seven fathers. An assembly line of foster fathers and guardians, all of whom had been fringe members of the Order of Babel. All of whom had made Séverin who he was, for better or worse.

"Being part of the Order won't make me one of them," said Séverin, his voice icy. "I don't want to be their equal. I don't want them to look us in the eye. I want them to look away, to blink harshly, as if they've stared at the sun itself. I don't want them standing across from us. I want them kneeling."

Tristan said nothing.

"I protect you," said Séverin softly. "Remember that promise? I said I'd protect you. I said I'd make us a paradise of our own."

"L'Eden," said Tristan miserably.

Séverin had named his hotel not just for the Garden of Paradise, but for the promise that had been struck long ago when the two of them were nothing but wary eyes and skinned knees, while the houses and fathers and lessons moved about them as relentless as seasons.

"I protect you," said Séverin again, this time quieter. "Always."

Finally, Tristan's shoulders fell. He leaned against Séverin, the top of his blond head tickling the inside of Séverin's nose until he sneezed.

"Fine," grumbled Tristan.

Séverin tried to think of something else to say. Something that would take Tristan's mind off what the five of them were planning to do next.

"I hear Goliath molted?"

"Don't pretend like you care about Goliath. I know you tried to set a cat on him last month."

"To be fair, Goliath is the stuff of nightmares."

Tristan didn't laugh.

OVER THE NEXT week and a half, Laila spied on the Order members who frequented the Palais des Rêves, keeping an ear out for any rumors of theft following the auction. But all was quiet. Even the notorious Sphinx guards who could follow the trail of any House-marked artifact had not been glimpsed outside the city residences of House Kore and House Nyx.

Everything was fine . . .

It was a hope Séverin was still clinging to when his butler came in with the mail.

"For you."

Séverin glanced at the envelope. An elaborate letter *H* was emblazoned on the front.

Hypnos.

He dismissed the butler, and then stared down at the envelope. Bits of brown flecked the front, like dried blood. Séverin touched the seal. Instantly, something sharp stabbed into the pad of his finger, a Forged thorn concealed in the melted wax. He hissed, drawing back his hand, but a drop of blood hit the paper. It sank into the envelope, and the elaborate letter *H* shivered, unraveling before his eyes until it opened into a short missive.

I know you stole from me.

PART II

Excerpt from *Reports of New Caledonia*
Admiral Théophile du Casse, French faction Order of Babel
1863, Second Republic of France under Napoleon III

The indigenous population, the Canaque, are becoming rather agitated. Through our translators, we have surmised that Forging is considered the provenance of native priests. None of their artisans appear to possess an affinity for mind. Instead, they are mostly gifted in matter affinity of salt water or wood. Each of their homes is adorned with a *fléche faîtière*, a carved finial where their ancestors—whom they worship—supposedly reside. But we have discovered another use of these finials.

As you know, sir, we discovered the presence of nickel along the banks of the Diahot River. While our colonists have taken great pains to extract the mineral, the best instrument for detecting its presence comes from their supposed sacred finial monuments. Regretfully, I must inform you of an event that occurred last week. During the hours of dawn, one of my men had been working hard to tear down the finial from the top of a Canaque hut. Though he was successful in removing the finial, the family refused to tell us how to make the Forged finial respond to nickel. A skirmish arose. The Canaque man took his own life, declaring that "some knowledge is not meant to be known."

We have not found a way to make the Forged finials work.

But I will persevere.

6

ENRIQUE

Enrique had been summoned to the bar of the grand lobby.

In different circumstances, that might be his favorite summons of all time, but Séverin's note had been uncharacteristically brusque. Enrique checked the grand clock of the lobby. Five sharp. His appointment with Séverin wasn't until half past five, which left *just* enough time for one cocktail.

Encircling the lobby was a grand ouroboros, an infinity symbol represented by a snake biting its tail. A huge, Forged brass serpent twined in an endless circle, candlelight rippling off its metal body. Refreshments and bouquets were nestled in the golden scales of its back, and every day at noon and midnight, it finally snapped hold of its tail and shining confetti rained from the ceiling. Around him, heiresses wearing plumed capes and artists with ink-smudged fingers strolled toward the gardens or the dining room. In one corner, politicians schemed together, their heads bent, eyes obscured by the clouds of smoke from their pipes. As usual, Enrique tuned out the sounds. There were too many languages to keep track of, so it was easier to let the sounds wash over him. Here and there, he caught dialects sharpened by the desert sun, languid vowels worn smooth by the waves of coastal regions. All of it unfamiliar music until one phrase caught his ear: *"Magandang gabi po." Good evening.* The language was his native Tagalog. Enrique swiveled toward the speaker and recognized him instantly: Marcelo Ponce. From across the room, Ponce caught his eye and waved a hand in welcome.

Along with Dr. Rizal, Ponce was a member of the Ilustrados, a group Enrique had joined because, like him, all the members were European-educated Filipinos who dreamed of reform to their Spanish-controlled country. But to them, he was only just a member . . . not a visionary. Not someone who charted the course of a new future no matter how much he wanted to be part of their inner circle.

"Kuya Marcelo," said Enrique respectfully.

He still felt a flash of awe that he got to call the great Marcelo "brother," but it was more tradition than intimacy.

"Kuya Enrique," said Marcelo warmly. His gaze dropped to the pen in Enrique's hand. "Working on another article to submit to *La Solidaridad*? Or translating a new language?"

"Um, some of both," said Enrique, flushing. "Actually, if you have time, perhaps I might share my new writing with you? I—"

"That's wonderful news, truly. Keep up the good work," said Marcelo distractedly. He looked over Enrique's shoulder. "I'm actually meeting someone who might help us petition the queen of Spain."

"Oh!" said Enrique. "I-I could help?"

Marcelo smiled. "Ah, but of course! Enrique Mercado-Lopez: journalist, historian, and debonaire spy." Before Enrique could answer, Marcelo patted his cheek. "Of course, it must be easy to spy when you hardly look like one of us. We'll see you at the next meeting. *Ingat ka, kuya.*"

Marcelo squeezed his shoulder as he walked past him. Enrique forced himself to keep walking, even though his face burned and his limbs felt leaden.

Of course, it must be easy to spy when you hardly look like one of us.

Marcelo spoke with no malice. In a way, that was worse. At birth, Enrique had favored his father, a full-blooded Spaniard. In the Philippines, many considered this a good trait. They called him *mestizo*. His aunts and uncles even joked that his dark-skinned mother must not have been in the room when he was conceived. Perhaps this was why the Ilustrados did not let him into their inner circle.

It wasn't his intellect that made him unwanted.

It was his face.

ENRIQUE SAGGED AGAINST the bar counter. One should never drink champagne unhappy, so instead, he tipped his flute back and forth, watching the bubbles slosh down the sides. L'Eden's secret bar was small, designed more like a crypt than a gathering place, and hidden behind a bookcase. Inside, flowering vines crawled down the walls. Their buds put forth no flowers, only dainty teacups or champagne coupes of cut quartz, depending on the time of day. Tristan and Zofia's inventions dominated the room. When building officials deemed a glass chandelier a hazard, Tristan Forged one out of moonflowers and anemone. When the officials declared that lanterns would be a fire risk, Zofia collected phosphorescent stones from the Brittany coast and Forged them into a ceiling net that looked like softly blooming stars.

Looking at the designs, Enrique felt a familiar stab of envy. He had always wanted to Forge. When he was little, he thought it was like magic. Now he knew there was no such thing—neither fairies in the forests nor maidens in the sea. But there was this art, this connection to the ancient world, to the myth of creation itself, and Enrique longed to be part of it. He'd hoped Forging might make him a hero like the kind his grandmother told him about when he was younger. After all, if Forging could reshape objects of the world, why couldn't it reshape the world itself? Why couldn't he be the artist— architect—of change? But his thirteenth birthday came and went, and neither the affinity of mind nor matter called to him. When he realized he didn't have the talent, he chose to study the subjects that felt closest to Forging: history and language. He could still change the world . . . maybe not with something as dramatic or grand as Forging, but in more intimate ways. Writing. Speaking. Human connection.

When he came to Paris, the rallying cry of the French Revolution fitted into the hollows of his dreams: *liberté, egalité, fraternité.*

Liberty, equality, brotherhood.

Those words sang to him as they sang to other students like him. Students who had begun to question the tight grip Spain had kept on the Philippines for nearly three hundred years. In Paris, Enrique had found others like him, but it was Séverin who changed his life, who took a chance on his abilities as a historian when no one else had. Séverin listened to his dreams of changing the world and showed him what needed changing. With one older brother primed to take over the family's lucrative merchant business and the other older brother promised to the church, Enrique had been allowed to pursue whatever he wanted. He knew what he wanted . . . he just had to make the Ilustrados want him too.

Maybe threatening the Order with the Horus Eye's secret was the answer. Enrique let himself daydream what might happen next: Maybe he and Séverin could tell the Order that civilization hung in the balance . . . maybe they could confront them on a stage. Lighting was critical for any dramatic showdown. And there had to be

champagne. Obviously. Then Séverin would become patriarch—
Enrique could make some speech about lineage resurrected, that
would sound nice, perhaps with confetti raining down—House Vanth
would be restored, and, *naturally*, the House would need a historian.
Him. Then, the Ilustrados would clamor for his attention because
they'd finally have an insider who could report on the Order of Babel's workings. It was the only blindspot in their intelligence. After
that, he and Séverin and their whole crew could change the world!
Maybe they could get swords . . . Enrique had no clue what to do
with one, but just holding one sounded rather epic. What if someone
made a statue of him—

"Let's go."

Enrique startled, and his champagne flute fell.

"My drink!" he cried as it smashed on the ground.

"You weren't even drinking. You were daydreaming."

"But I liked holding it—"

"Come on."

Séverin didn't wait for him as he jogged up the short staircase.
Scowling, Enrique muttered something in Tagalog that would have
made his grandmother smack him with her slipper. It wasn't like
Séverin to be that brusque. His shoulders were up to his ears as they
walked past the grand lobby and the entrance to the Seven Sins
Garden.

Near the stables, a carriage discreetly pulled up to the road. Unlike the usual fleet of L'Eden's carriages, this one bore neither name
nor insignia. Enrique clambered in after Séverin. The driver closed
the door, and dark curtains unraveled to block the windows.

Enrique fidgeted with his sleeves. "So . . . *now* do I get to know
what's happening?"

From his pocket, Séverin withdrew an envelope. The bloodred

seal had been split down the middle, but the wax-stamped letter was clear enough. *H.*

Enrique stilled. A beat passed. "Hypnos?"

He knew the moment he spoke the name that it was true. The very air seemed to affirm his suspicions. Wind crept through a tear in the curtain, chilling his skin.

Séverin clenched his jaw. "He knows we stole from him. He's asked for a meeting."

"*What?*"

He thought the plan had been foolproof. No prints. No recording devices. Nothing to give away their presence in the auction's holding room.

As an Order patriarch, Hypnos could have had them arrested. Or worse. That he wanted a meeting spoke of something else . . . a game of give and take and blackmail. Enrique wasn't sure what to make of the fact that Séverin had chosen only him to come along. Was he expendable or invaluable?

Enrique didn't know much about the patriarch of House Nyx, but Tristan had once slipped that Hypnos and Séverin had been playmates, back when both boys were raised as heirs to their Houses. One quick glance at Séverin confirmed they hadn't been in contact since then. Séverin's expression was stony, his eyes drawn. His thumb dragged up and down the silvery scar on his palm.

"What if he . . ." Enrique couldn't bring himself to say the words "kills us."

Séverin seemed to guess his meaning anyway. "Hypnos was always clever," he said slowly. "But if he tries anything, I have dirt on him that could destroy his standing with the Order the moment he lays a hand on us."

"True, but one can't exactly savor vengeance when one is dead."

Séverin pulled down the brim of his hat. "I have no intention of dying."

When the carriage stopped, Séverin leaned forward to unlock the door. As he did so, Enrique caught a glimpse of the letter held in his bandaged hand. He frowned.

It was blank.

HYPNOS HAD NAMED his residence Erebus, after a place in Greek myth where nightmares bloomed next to red poppies. Ridiculous. Enrique found his nickname, Hypnos, just as pretentious. No one would have named an infant after the god of sleep. At least, for the sake of that poor child, Enrique hoped not.

While most of the Houses of the Western world used and collected Forging objects made from both affinities, House Nyx collected treasures of a particular strain: those that showcased an affinity of the mind. House Nyx had objects that spliced memory, soaked dreams, gathered someone's will in a tight fist, and brought forth vivid illusions. Mind was the most regulated form of artistry, used as much in pleasure houses and entertainment venues as it was for prison camps. It was the only affinity that universally required registration, whether or not a person chose to hone that talent. Some mind affinity techniques were even banned. And for good reason. Until about twenty years ago, mind-manipulation objects had been especially popular in the Southern states of the Americas where wealthy landowners kept slaves.

Up ahead loomed the entrance to Erebus. At either side stood two lions carved of diorite, and above the threshold shone a milky jade strip of verit stone. Like the verit entrance at the Palais Garnier, the stone could detect any weapon or harmful Forged object. The only way to neutralize its effect was to carry verit stone on one's person, like two magnets repelling one another. Supposedly, there was nothing in the world like verit, although Enrique had recently come across a treatise on a North African artifact that made him wonder otherwise.

"He's known for his illusions," said Séverin, interrupting his thoughts. "Focus on one thing, and don't lose yourself in his tricks."

The door swung open. Without hesitating, Séverin walked between the two lions. When he passed beneath the verit stone, it glowed bright red and the stone lions growled, their heads whipping toward him. A bulky guard appeared at the entrance.

"Reveal your weapon," he said.

"My apologies," said Séverin mildly. He withdrew a small knife from his pocket. "I always keep one on hand for cutting apples."

Enrique kept his face blank. Séverin was lying.

"You'll have to pass through the verit entrance again—"

"We're already late," said Séverin. "Patriarch Hypnos won't like that, and I can assure you there's nothing else on my person. Here, I'll turn out my pockets in front of you."

Séverin made a show of lifting the bottoms of his trousers and insides of his sleeves. When he got to his pockets, a card fluttered to the floor. The guard picked it up, his eyes widening.

"Ah, and that's a credit for two free nights at the hotel I own. You may have heard of it. It's called L'Eden."

The guard had certainly heard of it.

"Why don't you hold on to it and let me through? Or I could take it for safekeeping as I go through a silly entrance yet again?"

The guard hesitated, then waved Séverin through the doors. Enrique followed after him without incident. He never had reason to carry a weapon.

Erebus, he soon discovered, was aptly named. No sooner had they

crossed into the hall than it shifted. One moment, he glimpsed parquet floors, ebony pillars covered in golden filigree, a sumptuous rug
close to his toes. He should have kept his gaze on the floor, but a
flicker of movement distracted him. He looked up. Instantly, the
room transformed into a wildwood. Silver dusk seeped between
frosted tree branches. The chandelier dissolved into a snowdrift.
What pieces he could see of the carpet looked sugared. Cold touched
his skin. He could smell it. The mineral tang of snow. The inside of
his nose burned from cold. He was in a world of ice and sugar. Blood
spatter on white silk. No, not blood. Poppies. Poppies blooming,
shriveling, budding in glyph-like patterns. Secrets just beneath the
petals and the snow, if he only—

A voice broke the illusion. "Goodness, how rude of me."

The images melted. No more snow or poppies or sugar.

Enrique was on his knees, hands splayed on the scarlet rug as if
he wanted to shred it apart. In front of him, a pair of polished shoes.
He looked up before he realized he should have stood first. The patriarch of House Nyx stared down at him.

Until now, he had only seen Hypnos at a distance. He knew the
other boy's skin, a deep umber like the rain-soaked bark of an oak
tree. He knew the textured hair cropped close to his head. Even
knew his strangely colored eyes, a blue so pale they looked like panes
of frost. Hypnos was beautiful at a distance. Up close, he was just
plain staggering. Enrique stumbled to his feet, hoping the other boy
hadn't noticed. When he looked up, Hypnos's eyes looked darker.
The pupils blown out, as if he was trying to take in all of him too.

"Had I known what pretty company you keep, I might have met
with you sooner, Séverin," said Hypnos, not taking his eyes off
Enrique.

Séverin let out a brittle laugh. "I doubt that. You've been a patriarch for two years, and you still have to run every inhale and

exhale by the Order of Babel. I can't imagine what they must make of your meeting with me. My understanding was that any Order member would be forbidden from speaking to me if they remembered my existence. Do they even know what you're doing right now?"

Hypnos raised one eyebrow. "Do you want them to?"

Séverin didn't answer, and Hypnos didn't push it.

"You requested a meeting," said Séverin. "Why?"

After all this time, Enrique thought.

Hypnos grinned. "I wanted to meet my thieves."

"Well, you found us."

Hypnos made a *tsk* sound. "Now, now. I only did a little bit of the work. *You* did the rest."

Enrique shook off the dregs of the illusion. He took a step closer to Séverin. All his awareness shifted around the inflection of Hypnos's words.

"What do you mean?" he asked.

"Lo! It speaks," exclaimed Hypnos. He clapped his hands. "That fake compass you left me was a pretty decoy, but there was blood on it. And so I performed a little test . . . Whoever had stolen from me had bled all over my poor stone beastie. So, I added a bit of blood Forging to my letter to make sure that none but the thief could read it. I had my men deliver it to every person I could think of. Who, I wondered, would steal from *me*? And *why*? And then, of course, when I ran out of options, I sent it to you. The fancy hotelier with a reputation a *little* too spotless, who's always a *little* too close to every theft of an Order object. So, you see," he said, his expression suddenly quite serious, "I didn't find you. You brought yourself to me."

Enrique squeezed his eyes shut. Too late, he remembered glimpsing Séverin's letter. The curious expanse of blank page. No wonder he couldn't read it.

Séverin betrayed nothing. "Clever."

"One can always rely on a man's hubris. I figured you wouldn't share the letter." Hypnos tilted his head. "How *devastating* for you. To let down your team and admit that you'd failed. Oh, don't look at me like that, Séverin. The Order may not have looked in your direction all this time, but I have."

"I'm flattered you think I'm worth watching."

Hypnos winked. "With a face like that? I must not be the only one."

"What do you want, Hypnos?"

"You know what I can do to you. I can have you arrested, executed, tarred and feathered, et cetera. There's no point, really, in detailing it." Hypnos paused to smile. "But I don't *want* to do any of that. I'm actually quite an exceptional human being, and, I fancy myself rather generous. So instead, I ask only two things. First, that you return the compass. Second, that you turn your acquisition skills to an object I've long desired. In return, I'll give you what you want."

Séverin's face had gone rigid, his mouth flattened to a line, his dark eyes nearly burning.

Slowly, Hypnos raised his hand. His Babel Ring, a thin crescent moon that spread across the middle of his hand, caught the light. From where Enrique stood, it looked like a scythe.

"*Mon cher,* you and I always had so much in common," said Hypnos. "Now, we have even more! Look at us. Two orphaned bastards with colored mothers." He leaned closer to Séverin. "How strange . . . Yours doesn't show up on the skin the way mine does. Mine was the daughter of slaves in a sugarcane plantation my father owned in Martinique. Once I was born, my French aristocrat of a father left her. But I remember *you* had your mother. That always made me rather jealous, I admit. She had the loveliest hair . . . what was she? Egyptian? Algerian? Her name was so beautiful too—"

"Don't," said Séverin, clipped. A muscle in his jaw ticked.

Hypnos shrugged lightly and turned to Enrique, smiling as if he were just another guest and this were just another day.

"Has he told you how the Order's inheritance test works?"

Enrique shook his head.

"It's like this," said Hypnos, walking up to him. "May I, beautiful?"

Enrique managed a nod. Hypnos turned over his hand, sliding his brown thumb down his palm before stopping above his racing pulse.

"In each Babel Ring, there's a core of the matriarch or patriarch's blood. The blood fuels the Ring's ability to House-mark, among other things. When the matriarch or patriarch dies, or if they wish to retire their seat early, a head of House is summoned to administer the inheritance test. First, the Ring that will be passed on is cut into the heir's hand." Hypnos dragged one edge of the crescent moon across Enrique's hand. Through his skin, he felt a hum of power, like lightning traveling through his veins. "Then, the Ring of the witness is held over the bloodied Ring. If the heir is of the same blood as the matriarch or patriarch, both Rings turn blue. If the heir is not . . ."

"You are left with a handsome scar," finished Séverin coldly.

Hypnos dropped Enrique's hand.

"The Order is not above falsifying the inheritance test," he said, facing Séverin. "It's been performed in the past by families wishing to pass over one heir for a different family member."

"On what grounds would they deny an heir his inheritance?" asked Enrique.

Hypnos ticked off the reasons on his fingers. "They might not like how the child's mind works, or who they love, or—"

"Or the Order might like their bloodlines nice and neat," cut in Séverin, his voice distant. "Two heirs of mixed blood would not do. An easy solution is to choose one over the other."

Hypnos's jaw tightened. Gone was his lax demeanor. Regret

twisted his handsome features. "If memory serves, you tried to tell me that years ago," he said quietly.

"And if memory serves, you didn't listen."

Spots of color appeared on Hypnos's cheeks. "As you so aptly pointed out, my very breath has been monitored by the Order since the day my father died and passed the Ring to me. But if you acquire this artifact for me, I will administer the inheritance test myself. No falsifications like last time. I can return your Ring to you . . . I know where it's kept."

Enrique felt as though all the air had been drained from the room. Séverin refused to look at Hypnos as he spoke. "What do you want?"

"A Horus Eye."

Enrique sucked in his breath.

"Where is it?"

Hypnos hesitated for a moment, then said, "The vaults of House Kore."

"No," said Séverin immediately. "I am not stepping into that woman's house."

And no wonder, thought Enrique. The matriarch of House Kore must have helped falsify the results of the inheritance test that stole Séverin's title.

"Just before the auction, she was viciously attacked," said Hypnos. "Her Ring was stolen."

"Probably an inside job," said Séverin. "We don't get involved with those."

We. Enrique felt a thrill of pride. *That's right!* he wanted to say. But he didn't.

"I'm not asking you to find her Ring," said Hypnos. "There are people already dedicated to that search. What I'd like your help for goes beyond that. As I'm sure you haven't forgotten, the Rings of our Houses guard the location of the West's Babel Fragment."

Séverin laughed. "And do you think this mastermind thief knows the Fragment's location and wishes to perform some nefarious activity there with the stolen Ring? Because as I recall, revealing the Fragment's location requires *two Rings*, not *one*. Your precious knowledge should stay safe."

Enrique knew little about the inner workings of the Order, but Séverin had once told him that knowledge about the location of the West's Fragment circulated among the Houses of different empires every century. France was the most recent possessor of the location's knowledge. If the Ring of House Kore had truly been stolen, that knowledge would be in grave danger. And if Séverin was right and the theft was an inside job, then that made all the more sense why Hypnos would want to steal rather than inquire after the Horus Eye.

If House Kore had been compromised from the inside, then no one in the House was trustworthy. And if, by some chance, the thief *had* taken the Ring to the Fragment's location, then looking through the Horus Eye would immediately reveal its whereabouts.

"With a single Ring, the Fallen House nearly threw the world off balance," said Hypnos. "They paid the price, to be certain, but history always repeats itself."

Enrique remembered the Forged threshold of the Palais Garnier as he was leaving the auction. An image stood out in his mind: a peeling hexagram on a gilt mirror. The symbol of the disgraced Fallen House. Something about that hexagram sat heavily in his thoughts.

"And, if I may be so bold, which I am, so I will . . . you have no choice but to help me, Séverin."

"You can threaten me with imprisonment, but I'll get out. You could set your guards on us, but I've already planted an incendiary sphere, and I could have this place up in flames before you take a single step," said Séverin.

Enrique bit back a grin. Séverin's lie at the entrance. The small knife he'd surrendered without complaint. He'd distracted the guard with a false weapon while hiding the real one.

"When did you—"

Séverin smiled. "I had to do something to pass the time while you were making eyes at my historian."

"Wait. I was *bait*?" demanded Enrique.

"You're flattered."

Maybe a little.

When Hypnos looked around the room, Séverin waved his hand. "Don't bother. You won't find it in time. And I won't go anywhere near that House," said Séverin, turning on his heel. "Perhaps we can work out a different agreement. In the meantime, Enrique and I must be going."

Hypnos loosed a breath. "I hate when I have to do this! Flaring tempers, veiled threats, ugh. It ages me, *mon cher,* and I detest that."

Hypnos stomped his foot. An image rippled across the surface of the scarlet rug. Nausea twisted through Enrique. Before him wavered an image of three kneeling bodies in the distance . . . their heads bent forward, hands bound . . . but the shapes were unmistakable.

Laila.

Zofia.

Tristan.

Séverin immediately paled.

"You see? You can walk out and survive. But I can't say the same for the rest. I want an oath that you'll return the compass, go to House Kore, and get me that Horus Eye," said Hypnos, holding out the Forged quill that tattooed oaths. "Do this, Séverin, and I can give you back your House."

Séverin was rooted to the spot. "Are they alive?"

"Do we have a deal or no?" asked Hypnos in a singsong voice.

"Are they alive?"

"They won't be if you don't swear the oath. We'll be equally bound, Séverin. I assure you, it's for the best. You'll like working with me, I promise! I'm fabulous at parties, have excellent taste in menswear, et cetera, et cetera," said Hypnos, waving his hand. "And if you don't agree to this, then I will break every bone in their bodies, and etch your name onto the splinters. That way, your name will be all over their deaths."

Hypnos's smile was sharp as broken glass. "Still unwilling?"

7

SÉVERIN

W rath was the second of Séverin's seven fathers. Some of his fathers lasted for months. Others for years. Some had wives who did not let him call them mother. Some fathers died before he could learn to hate them. Others died because he hated them.

THE LAST TIME Séverin saw his father's Ring, he was seven years old. The Ring was a pinched oval of tarnished brass depicting a snake biting its tail. The underside of the tail was a blade. After the fire killed his parents, the matriarch of House Kore dragged his father's Ring across his palm, and the snake tail cut through his skin like a hot knife to a slab of butter. For a moment, he saw the flash of promised blue . . . the very glow his father had often talked of that proved he was the true heir of House Vanth . . . but then it disappeared, obscured by the sweeping cloak of the patriarch of House Nyx. Séverin remembered how they talked in hushed whispers, these people who he had once called "Tante" and "Oncle." When they turned to face him, it was as if they had never bounced him on their knee or snuck him an extra plate of dessert. The mere span of a minute had rendered them strangers.

"We cannot let you be one of us," said the matriarch.

He would never forget how she had looked at him . . . how she had dared to show him pity.

"Tante—" he managed, but she cut him off with a sharp brush of her gloved hand.

"You may not call me that anymore."

"A pity," Séverin heard his former oncle say. "But we simply cannot have more than one."

A group of lawyers later informed Séverin that he would be taken care of until he came of age to inherit the trust funds of House Vanth, for though he was not the blood heir, his name appeared on every deed and contract, thus entitling him to the assets.

Séverin did not mourn the death of his father as much as he mourned the death of Kahina. His father had not allowed him to call her "Mother," and in public she referred to him as "Monsieur Séverin." But at night . . . when she snuck into his room to sing his lullabies, she always whispered one thing before she left: "I am your Ummi. And I love you."

His first day in Wrath's home, Séverin wept and said, "I miss Kahina." Wrath ignored him. By the second day, Séverin had not stopped weeping and once more said, "I miss my Kahina."

Wrath had stopped on his way to the commode. He turned around. His eyes were so light that sometimes his pupils looked colorless.

"Say her name again," said the old man.

Séverin hesitated. But he loved her name. Her name sounded like how she smelled . . . like fruits from a fairy-tale garden. He loved how when he said her name, he remembered that she used to hunch over him, all that black hair curtaining over his small head, so he could pretend it was nighttime and therefore story time.

The moment he spoke her name, Wrath backhanded him. He did it over and over, demanding that he say "Kahina" until blood replaced the fairy-tale taste of his mother's name.

"She's dead, boy," Wrath had said when he was finished. "Died in the fire along with your father. I don't want to hear her name again."

WRATH'S BASTARD BOY also lived in the house, though he hardly treated him like his own child. The boy was younger than Séverin and had wide, gray eyes. When Wrath was mad, he did not care which boy he took so long as one was taken.

In his study, Wrath kept a Phobus Helmet, a Forged object of mind affinity that coaxed out the wearer's nightmares and played them on a loop . . .

Wrath only watched when the boys started screaming after the Phobus Helmet was secured to their heads. He never touched them except his occasional blows.

"Your imagination hurts you far worse than anything I could ever do," he once said.

One day, Wrath called for the other boy. By then, Séverin had learned his name was Tristan. That day, he saw Tristan crouched in the shadows. Neither boy moved.

"Have you seen him?" demanded Wrath.

Séverin had a choice. He made it.

"No."

Wrath took him instead.

The next day, Wrath called for both of them. Séverin was outside, wandering the grounds. Wrath's footsteps echoed loudly. Séverin might have been caught if he hadn't felt a small tug on his sleeve. The silent boy was hiding in the rosebushes. His lap was full of flowers. He scooted to the side to make room for Séverin.

"I protect you," Séverin whispered.

+ + +

I PROTECT YOU.

One promise.

One promise, and he couldn't even keep it.

Every time he blinked, he saw their bodies. Zofia's bright hair mussed by dirt. Tristan crouching, swaying . . . and Laila. Laila, who should have sugar in her hair, not shards of glass. Laila, who he . . .

He dug his nails into his palm, screaming at the driver to go faster. Beside him, Enrique was a ghost of himself, whispering and turning over rosary beads in his hand. The second they got to L'Eden, Enrique leapt out of the carriage. "I'll check for them inside."

Séverin nodded, then broke into a run across the Seven Sins Garden.

He didn't stop running until he arrived at Tristan's workshop in Envy. Tristan's back was to him. Hunched over. His neck bent. His worktable strewn with small fronds and snippets of petals . . . all the makings of the miniature worlds he obsessively cobbled together.

Séverin couldn't find his next breath. Had they strangled him? Propped him upright like a cruel joke? If so, then what about Laila and Zofia? Were they dead in the kitchens and the laboratory? Or—

Tristan turned.

"Séverin?"

Séverin stood there, swaying.

"Why do you look nauseous? Is it that sleepwalking guest in Room 7? I caught him sleepwalking *naked* in the servants' quarters last night, and if that's what happened, I honestly don't blame you—"

"The others," rasped Séverin. "Are they . . . are they . . ."

Tristan frowned. "I just saw Laila and Zofia in the kitchens. Why? What's wrong?"

Séverin grabbed him abruptly in a hug.

"I feel like I'm missing something important," wheezed Tristan.

"I thought you were dead."

Tristan laughed. "Why would you think that?" But when he caught the flat look in Séverin's eyes, he paused. "What happened?"

Séverin told him everything from Hypnos's proposition . . . to the reward waiting at the end.

"House *Kore*?" Tristan practically spat. "After what she—"

"I know."

"Are you going to take the offer?"

Séverin held up his hand, showing the harsh slash of the oath tattoo. "I have no choice."

In that moment, Tristan's face was inscrutable.

After what felt like forever, Tristan turned over his own hand. The silvery scar down his palm matched Séverin's. Neither of them knew where Tristan had gotten his scar. But it didn't matter.

Finally, Tristan placed his hand over Séverin's, stacking their scars before saying:

"I protect you."

ONE OF THE greatest secrets of the Fallen House was where they had held their meetings.

It was said the key both to their secret meeting locations and to their lost treasure lay in the bone clocks once given to each member of their House. In the fifty years since they had been exiled and executed by the Order, no one had cracked the clocks' code. These days, it was considered nothing more than a rumor that time had smoothed down to the shape of a myth. But that didn't stop interest in acquiring the bone clocks. Of late, the clocks had become something of a collector's item.

One of the few remaining ones sat on Séverin's bookshelf.

In all the time that Séverin had kept the bone clock, it hadn't revealed any of its secrets. Although sometimes the clock stopped at six minutes past two o'clock, which he considered rather strange considering that there was only one word found on the clock: *nocte*.

Midnight.

Séverin often looked at it when he was thinking.

Fifty years ago, it had seemed impossible for anything to ruin the Fallen House. And now . . . to Séverin, the clock was a reminder. Anything could fall. Towers that scraped the heavens, Houses with pockets deeper than empires', shining seraphs who had once been in the confidence of God. Even families who were supposed to love you. Nothing was invincible but change.

Séverin was still staring at the clock face when the letter from Hypnos arrived. He ripped open the envelope, scanned the first line, and scowled.

To be fair, you would have done the same.

Séverin's knuckled grip paled.

Before you throw this in the fire, I do hope you listen to that seed of rationale deep within your fury. We are to work together, and though I might not extract my promises the best way, I always keep them. As I know you do.

Tell me what you need from me.

Séverin hated that word. *Need.* He hated how Hypnos's promise of a new inheritance test had itched that very word to life.

Sometimes he wished he didn't remember life before the Order. He wished someone with a mind affinity could root through his memories and shred those years. He was haunted. Not even by people, but the phantoms of sensations—firelight limning the outlines of his fingers, a cat with a fluffy tail who napped at the foot of his bed, orange blossom water on Kahina's skin, a spoon dipped in honey and smuggled into his waiting hand, wind on his face as he was tossed into the air and caught in warm arms, words that sank into his soul like growing roots steeped in sunshine: "I am your

Ummi. And I love you." Séverin squeezed his eyes shut. He wished he didn't know what he had lost. Maybe then every day wouldn't feel like this. As if he had once known how to fly, but the skies had shaken him loose and left him with nothing but the memory of wings.

Séverin rolled his shoulders. His fingers left damp impressions on Hypnos's letter. He crumpled it in his fist. He knew what he was going to do. What he needed to do. As he walked out the door of his study, a phantom ache curled between his shoulder blades.

As if they craved the weight of wings.

THROUGH THE FROSTED glass door of the kitchen, he saw their shapes crowded around the high-top counters. He heard the chime of bone china, silver spoons hitting tea saucers. The crisp snap of cookies. He could picture them with perfect clarity. Zofia carefully cutting her cookie in half, then dipping each half into the tea. Enrique demanding to know why she was torturing the cookies. Tristan scoffing that tea was hot, watered-down leaves and "Laila, is there any hot chocolate?" Laila. Laila, who moved like a sylph among them, watching them with those eyes that said she knew their worst secrets and still forgave them. Laila, who always had sugar in her hair.

He could sense all of them, and it terrified him.

He placed his hand on the doorknob. The oath tattoos on his right hand glared back at him. They might owe him their service. But he was the one bound to them.

He was the one who would always be left behind. Soon, Zofia's debt would be paid off and leave her wealthy enough to start a new life. Soon, Enrique would join the inner circle of Filipino visionaries and move out of L'Eden. Soon, Laila would leave too. When she offered her services to him and trusted him with her story—as he had trusted her with his—she told him there was an object she was searching for, and she would go wherever that search took her.

Which left Tristan. The only one who would stay of his own free will.

But what if they acquired the Horus Eye . . .

Hypnos would be bound to perform the test, and this time, no one would cheat him. House Vanth would be resurrected. As patriarch, he could give them more than just the connections of the rich. He could get Zofia's sister into medical school; give Enrique access and intelligence for his Ilustrados; help Laila find the ancient book she searched for; keep his promise to Tristan.

He could give them more than just something to tide them over until the next acquisition. He could give them enough to stay.

The four of them stared when he entered. Judging from the empty teacup, they'd been expecting him for a while. After a long moment, Laila poured him tea. Even with her hair in front of her face, he knew she was smiling. He hated that he knew that. Two years ago, he hadn't thought such things were possible.

Back then, Laila had just started working at the Palais as his spy and in the kitchens as a pastry chef. One day she barged into his study, her hair streaked white with flour, carrying a glossy, jewel-bright fruit tart in her hand. Already she'd charmed half the staff and secured more acquisitions than he'd ever been able to do on his own. That she spent most of her free time wandering the library or the kitchens wouldn't have bothered him if she hadn't kept trying to force her creations on him or spouting her opinions on every little thing when he was trying to work. Worse was that she wanted nothing in return. She would leave cakes on his desk, and if he tried to pay her, she'd smack his hand.

"Try it, try it," she had insisted that day, pushing back his chair and holding out a piece.

He'd been too startled by the unexpected way she kept manifesting—like a dream recurring when it was just forgotten—that he didn't have time to say, "I don't want any damn sweets." Her fingers parted his lips. Flavors turned incandescent on his tongue. He might have moaned. He couldn't remember anymore.

"Taste that?" she had whispered. "There's zested yuzu from the orchards, instead of lemon rind, and vanilla bean, instead of only vanilla extract. The glaze is hibiscus jam I made myself. Not some boring apricot. What do you think? Doesn't it taste like a dream?"

That was the first time he realized he could *feel* her smile. Like light pressing against closed lids. He blinked, opening his eyes, watching how her lips pulled into a grinning crescent. Since then, whenever she smiled, he remembered the flavor of that fruit tart, the tang of hibiscus and soft vanilla. Unexpected and sweet.

Enrique cleared his throat, and Séverin shook himself.

"*Finally*," said Enrique. He popped the last cookie in his mouth. "Consider that a penalty for showing up so late," he said with his mouth full.

Séverin pulled up a chair, feeling their eyes on him. Of course, Laila was the first to speak.

"Séverin . . . what are we going to do? Enrique told us what happened back there."

Enrique blushed a guilty red and took a well-timed gulp of tea.

"You're *bound* to Hypnos," said Laila.

He flexed his fingers, watching his scar stretch.

"What happens next is not up to me," he said. "This won't be like our acquisitions of the past. It'll be even more dangerous. And if you choose a different path, I won't hold it against you. I'll deactivate the oath tattoos and pay you accordingly."

Séverin didn't trust himself to look at them until he heard Enrique's resigned sigh.

"I'm in," said Enrique, after a long moment.

"Me too," said Laila.

Zofia nodded her assent.

Tristan swallowed hard, eyes fixed on the counter. He took the longest to raise his gaze to Séverin and nod.

A hot pain spread through Séverin's chest. No physical ache, but the ripping teeth of something cruel. *Hope.* He refused to show it. Instead, he forced a smile.

"Good. Now. To get the Horus Eye out of the vault, we have to focus on two things. First, finding the Eye's exact location inside Kore's vault. For that, we're going to need the catalogue coin so we'll be paying a visit to our old friend, the House Kore courier. Thanks to Laila, we know exactly where he'll be tomorrow."

"The Palais des Rêves," said Laila, smiling.

Enrique made a high-pitched sound. "Wait, no! I want to go there! It's the party of the year!"

Zofia frowned. "What's so great about a party?"

"It's going to be *lavish*," said Enrique, sighing.

"Who said I can get any of you in?" asked Laila.

"Wait wait wait . . . *How*, exactly, are you planning on getting the House Kore courier to part with his catalogue coin?" asked Enrique. "We couldn't even find it when we needed it for the auction."

"That's where the Sphinx mask comes into play, courtesy of Zofia. I pose as a Sphinx. But I'll need someone dressed as a Sûreté officer."

The Sûreté was the detective branch of the armed forces. The only ones authorized to hold an Order member in for questioning. Séverin turned to Tristan, who groaned.

"Why *me*?"

"You have an excellent face."

"What's wrong with my face?" demanded Enrique. "Can I go?"

"He wants to go!" pointed out Tristan. "Why can't he go?"

"Because I chose you."

Enrique whined, "Séverin doesn't think I'm pretty."

"Séverin, tell him he's pretty," said Laila.

Séverin crossed his arms. "Zofia, tell him he's pretty."

Zofia didn't look up from her tea. "I am personally undecided, but if we're assessing based on objectivity, then according to the principles of the golden ratio, also known as *phi*, which is approximately 1.618, your facial beauty is mathematically pleasing."

"I'm swooning," grumbled Enrique.

"It has to be Tristan," said Séverin. "It has to be an honest face. The kind that demands trust."

Séverin heard a thud as Tristan kicked a table leg. A tiny temper tantrum could only mean he was partially persuaded. Tristan glared at him.

"Will it be during the day?"

"Night."

"What about Goliath?"

Everyone sighed.

"Goliath has a very strict feeding schedule. He likes his crickets exactly at midnight. Not before or after. Who's going to feed him?"

"Isn't Goliath big enough?" asked Laila.

"He's probably the one eating all the birds in the garden," said Enrique. "Have you noticed they're all gone?"

Tristan cleared his throat. "*Who will feed Goliath?*"

Enrique raised his hand limply. "Me."

But Tristan wasn't done. "If I do this, *everyone* has to help me with my next miniature project."

Everyone groaned.

Tristan crossed his arms. "Fine, then I won't do it—"

"*You win,*" said Séverin.

Tristan smugly sipped his cocoa.

"Getting the Eye's location sets us up, but that leaves us with House Kore itself. Their Spring Festival is in two weeks' time. Tristan is the only one of us who has been to House Kore multiple times for landscaping Forging, so he'll handle the external layout."

"What about the invitations?" asked Enrique. "They were delivered months ago."

"Hypnos will take care of it," allowed Séverin. "He has to be good for something."

"Our instruments can't get past verit stone," pointed out Zofia.

"She's right," said Enrique. "We'll get stopped at the front door. The only thing that repels verit stone is *verit stone*. And it's not like anyone has a spare piece of verit lying around that would throw off the sensors."

Séverin popped a clove into his mouth.

"Oh no," said Enrique. "I hate when you do that. Now what?"

"I seem to recall you mentioning some North African artifact that purported similar properties."

Enrique's eyes went wide. "I had *no* idea you listened to me."

"Surprise."

"But, uh, yes . . . there's an artifact I wanted to examine, but it's being kept under lock and key at an exhibition. It's part of some exhibit on superstitions from the colonies, but it's not going to open until the Exposition Universelle."

"Very well."

Enrique blinked. "Wait. Do you want *me* to break into the exhibition?"

"Of course not—"

"Thank God."

"—Zofia is going with you."

"*What?*" said Zofia and Enrique at the same time.

"I work alone," said Zofia.

Enrique rolled his eyes. "Most women kill to be alone with me."

"I have learned that something does not have to be animate in order to use the word 'kill,'" said Zofia. "Like how some people say 'kill time.' Perhaps these women you are referencing are killing their expectations?"

Tristan snorted half his cocoa, then looked at the clock and blanched.

"I have to go," he said. "I've got a commission due."

Enrique sighed. "I need to do more research on the artifact. Zofia, you might as well come with me. You'll need to know this too."

Zofia scowled and slid off her chair, leaving Séverin and Laila in the kitchen. Séverin reached for his tea. He was glad the kitchen was bright and that they sat on opposite sides of a wide table. It wasn't as though the circumstances of that one night had ever repeated themselves, but every time he was alone with her, it was as if his thoughts slipped over a cliff . . . where images best left forgotten reared up like ghostly waves.

"Laila."

"*Majnun,*" she said mildly.

Only Laila called him *Majnun,* or madman. Usually, it was said with something like affection, but her tone was cold.

Séverin looked around the kitchen. Laila preferred warm, bubbling chaos in her workspace. Stained recipes papering the walls. Chipped mixing bowls that she insisted had soaked in happiness and were therefore superior to something new. Wooden spoons engraved with the names of the people she cared about, swinging and clanging from the ceiling. But today, everything looked pristine. Nothing on the surface. Everything tucked away. It was the opposite of happy.

"You never learn," she said, sipping her tea. "Perhaps this could have been avoided had you just let me read your correspondence."

"The letter was Forged, there's no way—"

"The *seal* was Forged. The paper itself was ordinary. I could have told you where it had been, how many homes it had traveled to before finding you. I could have told you it was a trap."

She was right, and he knew it. But sharing it with everyone would have only proven that he'd placed them in danger.

"What would you have me do?"

"I would have you trust me," she said. "As I have trusted you."

That trust was the reason why there was no contract or oath tattoo between them. Two years ago, Laila had saved his life by reading the pocket watch of a hotelier who wished him dead just so he could take over the property. She'd proved her abilities to him by reading an old ouroboros pendant passed down from his father . . . and once she'd drawn out the depths of him, she'd offered her own secrets in return. She could have lorded her findings over him, but instead, she gave him a knife of his own, and that was how it was. The two of them smiling, the damning unknown things held like knives at each other's throats.

Barring Tristan, it was the most secure friendship he'd ever known.

"You're making this a far greater deal than it is," said Séverin.

One look at Laila, and he knew he'd said exactly the wrong thing.

"It's my life, Séverin," she said stonily. "And it means a great deal to me."

He flushed. "I didn't mean it like that—"

"I don't care what you meant. I care about something getting in the way of my search," said Laila fiercely. "Your ego included."

Always, Laila returned to her search for the Forged book with the answers to her existence, though not even Laila knew its contents. Just as she was unstoppable and relentless for the ones she loved, she embodied that with her search too. Nothing could hold her back. Not the family she'd left behind in India and, some day soon, not the family she'd made here.

"All I'm asking is that you trust us the way we trust you," she said. "Do you know what I am?"

"Angry?" he tried, with a weak smile.

Laila was not amused. "I'm an instrument. I know that. You know that."

"Don't call yourself that—" he started.

But Laila spoke over him. "And yet you refuse to use me even when I ask it of you. So, it would seem like you're in need of reminding."

Her hand darted forward, reaching for his wrist.

"Laila—" he warned.

"You spilled your box of cloves on your sleeves this morning. You hid one of Zofia's incendiary devices in Hypnos's hall. You stared at the bone clock in your office for nearly an hour. Want more? Because I can do more," said Laila, her voice nearly breaking. "This suit was made by a woman who sobbed into the cloth upon finding that she was pregnant out of wedlock. This suit—"

"*Stop*," he said, standing so fast that his chair smacked the glass behind him.

He looked down to where her fingers still touched his wrist. Neither of them moved. He could hear her breath, shallow and fast, from across the table. Not once since they had agreed to work together three years ago had she read his objects. At her touch, he felt dangerously exposed. He had to leave. Now.

"You're not an instrument. Not to me," he said, not looking at her. "But if you're so insistent, then put yourself to use. Get me on that guest list to the Palais des Rêves."

✦ ✦ ✦

AS EVENING APPROACHED, Séverin heard commotions outside his office. This was nothing new. He ignored it and focused on the papers before him. For some reason, he thought he could smell sugar and rosewater in the air. The perfume Laila kept in a rose quartz bottle. Morning and night, she'd swipe the crystal stopper across her wrists, down the line of her bronze throat. It was a faint scent . . . one he'd only caught when his lips had skimmed down her neck.

Séverin pinched the bridge of his nose.

Get the hell out of my head.

To one side of his desk lay the blueprints of House Kore's palatial layout. To the other side lay Zofia's mock-up of a Sphinx mask. But then he heard a name called out in the corridor: "L'Énigme!"

Oh no, thought Séverin.

"Leave us," said an imperious voice.

Us?

Séverin pushed back his chair, ready to cross the room and lock the door when Laila—not that anyone recognized her at the moment— entered. Séverin had never seen her as L'Énigme. He never went to the cabaret. But he knew the rumors of her effect on the audience. Looking at her now, the rumors were a shadow to the reality. With her peacock headdress and mask, L'Énigme looked more myth than girl. Jewel-toned plumes swept down her back. Pale silk clung to her legs, Forged to billow as if an unseen wind was her constant companion. Her blouse was little more than a corset of pearls.

Laila took a couple steps forward, pausing long enough to let the growing crowd outside the hall see her hand slide up his arm.

"I wanted to surprise you," she said silkily. Then she turned to face the open door and the growing crowd of curious faces. "Are we to have an audience?"

Someone pulled the door shut.

The moment the door closed, Séverin stepped out of her reach.

He glanced at the closed door. Behind it, gossip had probably infested the halls.

"What?"

He didn't trust himself to speak more than that.

"You asked me to get you on the guest list. Voilà."

Laila draped herself in one of the study chairs, then took off the headdress. At her touch, the Forged peacock plumes shrank into a green, silk choker with a resin pendant. Laila pulled her hair to one side as she fiddled with the clasp of her necklace.

"It keeps coming undone," she said, frowning. "I think Enrique clasped it wrong. Help me?"

Every line of her body seemed relaxed. Their fight had passed. It wasn't their first clash, and it wouldn't be their last, and so neither of them bothered to apologize. Séverin moved behind her.

"Explain how that display gets me on the guest list?" he asked, taking the clasp in hand.

"All courtesans are allowed to invite a lover to stay in their private chambers during a performance," she said. "Tonight, that man is you." His fingers slipped, and Laila tensed.

"I haven't forgotten the promise we made," she said lightly.

A year and a half ago, he'd told her, "We can't do this again."

And she'd replied, "I know."

He had a House to reclaim, a whole future to lift out of the dark. He'd had girls in his bed before, but nothing like that night. Nothing that made him, for a moment, forget who he was. Who he was supposed to be.

No fancy was worth his future.

Since then, neither of them had mentioned the promise they'd struck. Both of them pretended that it never happened, and they'd succeeded. They could work together. They could be friends. They could move on.

"This is just a planted rumor," said Laila quickly. "I'll be sure to appear with someone else the next night and thus free you of any association."

He didn't like how his thoughts snagged on the word "tonight."

As he finished clasping her necklace, his thumb brushed against the nape of her neck. Laila shivered, leaning forward. The top of the long scar next to her spine peeked out over the collar.

"Your hands are frigid," she said, scowling. "What kind of lover has cold hands?"

"One who makes up for temperature with talent."

He meant it jokingly, but his voice came out too rough. Laila turned in her seat. Unthinkingly, his eyes went to her mouth. She'd gotten ready in a hurry. A faint dust of white caught the edge of her red lip. *Sugar dust.* Had she been baking when time got away from her? Or was it on purpose? An invitation for someone else to taste?

A burst of red light on his desk made them jump apart.

Laila startled, then winced. Her hand was stuck to the edge of the desk.

"I must have touched it by accident."

Séverin's desk was Forged to answer only to his handprint. If anyone else touched it while it was activated, they would be stuck. He walked over, pressing his palm to the jade table. The red glow subsided, and Laila snatched back her hand. Séverin didn't know what to say. The air was so full of her there was barely enough to draw into his lungs.

"The words you're looking for, *Majnun*, are 'thank you,'" said Laila, rising out of the chair.

And then she headed to the door. Right before Laila reached for the handle, she touched her choker. Her Forged headdress unraveled, twining sinuously across her face and stealing whatever expression had flickered there. Once more, Séverin sat at his desk.

The words you're looking for, Majnun, *are "thank you."*

Laila was almost always right, a fact that he would not admit to her even on pain of death.

But today she was wrong.

8

LAILA

Laila was beginning to panic.

First, she had less than two hours before her performance at the Palais des Rêves. Second, she hadn't picked up her new gown at the couturier, and there was bound to be a line for her favorite tailor. Third, she could not find her Forged choker anywhere, and she refused to leave without it. The necklace held her peacock headdress, and if she didn't wear it, someone might recognize her.

Laila tossed aside one of the many pillows on her bed, then shook the gauzy drapes of her canopy.

"Where is it?" she said aloud. "Did you take it?"

"Why do *I* always get the blame?" demanded Tristan.

He was sprawled facedown on her bedroom floor. One of her pillows was propped under his chin as he painstakingly arranged her whole perfume collection in a line in front of him. Laila recognized every bottle except one, a glass sphere holding a number of black marbles.

"You *could* make yourself useful and help me," she grumbled. "What're you doing in here anyway? You have your own room."

"I'm researching," he shot back.

"Can you research somewhere else?"

"If I go to Zofia's lab, she'll give me a math lesson. If I go to Enrique's office, he'll give me a history lesson."

"What about Séverin?"

Tristan made a face. Laila knew what that meant—the two boys were fighting. Typical.

"You know he cares about you, don't you?" asked Laila.

Tristan ignored her. He reached forward, unstoppering one of her fragrances and taking a whiff. He grimaced.

"This one smells like a dying whale."

Laila snatched the perfume bottle out of his hand.

"I like that one," she said primly.

She looked at her bedroom floor. There were silks from former costumes that she was thinking about turning into drapes, baskets full of unfinished necklaces, an entire assembly line of shoes, and a couple of sketches from the cabaret artists who had drawn her onstage.

Laila tugged on a strand of her hair, agitated. "I can't leave without my choker. I thought it was right—"

A pale glint of ribbon—just behind Tristan—caught her eye. Laila plucked it off the floor and dangled it in front of Tristan.

"Tristan! It was *right* next to you! You couldn't look?"

He blinked at her, wide-eyed. "Sorry?"

"You are *not* sorry," she huffed.

Laila spun on her heel, but the heel slipped . . . She fell backward. Tristan tried to catch her, but he didn't move fast enough, and her head thudded painfully against the floor. Tristan shoved a pillow under her scalp. "Laila! Are you all right?"

As she tried to push herself into a seated position, her arm knocked the glass sphere holding the small, black marbles.

"My experiment!" cried out Tristan.

The glass sphere shattered. Instead of scattering on the floor, the black marbles bounced into the air. She looked up, her lips parted in shock as she stared at the hovering marbles. In a flash, they crashed down. Laila tried to shield her face, but one of them slipped past her lips. She instantly spat it out, and plumes of ink burst into the air, dousing her in thick shadows.

"*Tristan!*" she hollered.

Laila heard a scuffling sound right in front of her. She couldn't tell from what since she couldn't see anything. But then, in a voice that was unmistakably Tristan's, she heard, "Uh-oh."

ONE HOUR LATER, Laila was sitting in her carriage and wiping at a smudge of ink on her thumb.

The black marbles, it turned out, were Tristan's newest Forged invention, combining cuttlefish ink and the cellulose within plant cells. When held in the mouth and spat out, they created a nighttime effect. Hence their name: Night Bites. They had the ability to drench someone in ink and choke off their vision for nearly twenty minutes. This was a very useful thing when one was fighting enemies. It was not very useful when one was supposed to perform before a crowded audience in a matter of hours. At least Zofia had been there to mix a chemical solution to wipe off the ink. Enrique had also "helped," but he mostly laughed while Tristan ran around in circles shouting, "sorrysorrysorry."

As her carriage jostled along the cobblestone road, Laila leaned out the window. In her headdress and mask, she was instantly recognizable. Even her carriage—which boasted a wrought-iron train shaped like peacock feathers—was meant to announce her presence. She preferred it that way. Being loud in one life allowed her to be quiet in others.

Paris expected drama from L'Énigme. L'Énigme burned jewels from ex-lovers (they were actually cleverly designed paste courtesy of Zofia). L'Énigme had rivals (all of whom were friends who agreed on a predetermined schedule of "spats" for the public). L'Énigme was a princess exiled for falling in love with a British nobleman; a demoness let loose upon the streets of Paris. L'Énigme was a heartless temptress who danced because the snap of some poor man's heart between her teeth was far better than any coin.

L'Énigme was Laila, but Laila was not L'Énigme.

The carriage pulled to a stop before 7, rue de la Paix, the fashionable address of Paris's renowned couturier. Other carriages stopped too. Women in various states of costume, plumed hats, and jewel-studded reticules stepped outside, lingering just long enough so the crowd knew where they were entering.

Even though it was unseasonably cold for spring, Laila made a show of shrugging off her black mink pelt. The fur slid down part of her shoulder, exposing the bejeweled strap of her *La Nuit et Les Étoiles* costume. The Night and the Stars.

Dusk drew a shroud of velvet across the rue de la Paix. Faint music melted into the sound of horse hooves on stone. In the distance, the Place Vendôme column looked like a needle that had punctured the sky and stolen its rain. The slicked streets drank in the lantern light, painting streaks of gold down the cobblestones. Around Laila, the crowd surged, loud questioning taking place over the cheers and shouts of admiration.

"L'Énigme! Did you hear that La Belle Otero burned peacock feathers on her stage last night?"

"L'Énigme!" shouted one man. "Is it true that you and La Belle Otero are no longer speaking?"

Laila laughed, covering her mouth with a gloved hand. Her Forged snake rings slithered down her fingers. "La Belle Otero can do many fabulous things with her mouth. Speaking is not one of them."

The crowd gasped. Some scolded her. Others laughed and repeated it. Laila paid them no mind. It was as she and Carolina wanted. Carolina, known by the public as La Belle Otero, had devised the insult herself. The star of the Folies Bergère was a stunning performer, but an even more brilliant strategist when it came to publicity. They had come up with the plan last month over tea. Laila made a mental note to send Carolina her favorite box of dried pineapples.

Inside the salon, Laila walked briskly over the parquet floors and past the tall mirrors. As she walked, she heard the soft murmur of rumors chasing her shadow: "Did you hear who she took as a lover?"

All her "lovers" were either made up or spoken of as favors for male friends who had no interest in taking women to bed. It was a rule she'd kept since she arrived in France.

Only once had she broken it.

With Séverin.

Just once she'd let an attraction turn to an indulgence. What was one time? That was the thought she held on to when she drew him to her. Lust was one thing, but what she'd felt that night was a pull . . . the kind that keeps stars from falling out of the night sky. It was vast. It was unlike what she'd imagined.

It was a mistake.

In the salon, Forged dresses floated down a crystal runway, the fabrics rippling and stretching as if an invisible human body moved them. Couturiers clambered up ladders, hoisting yards of stiff, jewel-toned crinoline or bolts of Forged silk that mimicked anything from a late autumn sky to a smoky twilight flecked with dimming stars.

Her couturier greeted her at the entrance.

"Is my evening gown ready?" she asked.

"Of course, Mademoiselle! You will love it!" he said. "I worked on it all night long."

"And it will match my costume?"

"Yes, yes," he assured her.

Though her Night and Stars costume wouldn't change, she needed an evening gown for her entrance to the Palais des Rêves revolutionary party. The couturier ushered her to a dressing room. Inside, a Forged chandelier of champagne rotated above her. One flute broke off from its companions and drifted down to her hand. Laila held it, but did not drink.

"Voilà!" said the man.

He clapped his hands, and a gown glided into her dressing room. It was ivory satin, with puffed sleeves, a crescent neckline beaded with small pearls, and a black lattice overlay that looked like iron scrollwork. She touched it lightly. At once, the scrollwork twisted, and the black silk lattice seamlessly melded into a new pattern of inky florals.

"Exquisite," she breathed.

"And perfectly themed for the Exposition Universelle," he added. "I have modeled it after the tiered lattices of la Tour Eiffel. I will leave Mademoiselle to evaluate my handiwork. I do hope if Mademoiselle likes her garment, she might consider walking out of the store while wearing it?"

Laila already knew her answer was yes. But her diva persona ruled her for the evening.

She shrugged. "I shall inspect it for myself and decide."

The couturier hid his grimace behind a well-practiced smile. "Of course."

And with that, he left her and the dress. When she was sure he had gone, Laila set down her champagne flute on the small ivory table and began to undress. She wished there were not so many mirrors.

She hated looking at her body.

In the mirrors, her ruined back was reflected a thousand times over. Gingerly, Laila reached over her shoulder, tracing the scar, pushing herself to *read* her own body. Each time she tried, she came away with nothing. Each time, she breathed a sigh of relief. She could read only objects. Not people. Did that mean she was truly human? Or was her own body mute in the way she could read any object except one that had been Forged?

It was a question she had asked her mother every night in India. Before bed, her mother would rub sweet almond oil onto her back, massaging the scar tissue.

"It will fade," she said.

"And then I'll be real?" Laila would ask.

Her mother's hands always stilled when she asked that question. "You are real, my girl, for you are loved."

Her father's hands had not always been so kind. He did not always know what to make of her. His crafted child.

Perhaps it was because she looked nothing like her parents. She had the dark eyes of a cygnet, an uncanny shade of animal black, and glossy hair like the wet pelt of a jungle cat. That had been what the *jaadugar* used after all. A chick stolen from a swan's nest and an unlucky beast trapped in a ditch.

The rest of her had been lifted from a child's grave.

In India, those with the Forging affinity were called magicians. *Jaadugars*. For a price, they could perform complicated Forging techniques. It was said the *jaadugars* of Pondicherry were especially skilled in obscure arts because they possessed an ancient book in a language no longer spoken. Supposedly, the book held the secrets of Forging the likes of which rivaled the powers of the gods themselves.

The *jaadugar* her parents visited was skilled in crafting a new body from broken ones. He could even tease out the consciousness and transfer it to a new vessel. Which was exactly what her parents had asked for when they had brought her—stillborn at birth—to the *jaadugar's* hut outside the town.

Years later, Laila was told that if she had been brought to the *jaadugar* even an hour later, her soul would have unraveled for good. This was a fact her mother loved to remember and her father longed to forget.

They had asked for the beautiful girl they dreamed their daughter would become, and ended up with her. Red and screaming as any newborn. She became stunning, true, but she always bore that seam along her spine. As if she had been sewn together.

When her mother died, her father changed. He turned direction when he saw her, took his meals in his room, barely spoke to her except when she stood in front of him. Laila watched her father grow scared of her and took to wrapping her hands, so that she would not frighten him with her abilities. Her mother called her ability a gift. Her father called it a consequence of her making, for they'd never heard of someone with her gifts. It wasn't until she was sixteen and all her friends were preparing for weddings or agreeing to betrothals that she confronted her father.

One evening, she showed him the bangles her mother had left behind. "Father, may I wear these after you arrange my wedding?"

Her father sat in the dark, his eyes distant. When he looked at her, he laughed.

"Wedding?" he asked. He pointed at the length of her body. "The *jaadugar* who made you said his work won't hold past your nineteenth birthday, child. What's the point of arranging a marriage? Besides, you're a made girl, not even real. Who would have you?"

Those words chased Laila to the ashram of the *jaadugars*, but the man who had crafted her body was long dead, and the book of secrets they had guarded had been stolen . . . taken to a place called Paris by an organization known as the Order of Babel.

She combed for clues to the book's whereabouts in every object she read, but so far her search had proven fruitless. If she could only have direct access to the Order's knowledge, she was certain she'd find it immediately. She couldn't do that, however, unless she had a patriarch at her side. Acquiring the Horus Eye meant she finally would. It was the twisted humor of fate that the patriarch should be the only one who'd ever made her forget she was a crafted thing with an expiration date hanging over her head. Which was all the more reason to pretend that night had never happened.

No distraction was worth death.

Laila watched her scar shift in the mirror's reflection. Delicately, she pressed her fingers along the puckered edges. Part of her wondered if the day she turned nineteen, she would split down the middle, unraveling into a pile of shining pelts and worn bones, the barest glimmer of an almost-girl vanishing into the air like smoke.

If they acquired the Horus Eye, she'd never have to find out.

Laila zipped up her dress, hiding the seam down her back. She left the store wearing the brilliant ironwork gown, the straps of her Night and Stars costume glimmering just beneath the satin.

ON THE BOULEVARD de clichy, the Palais des Rêves embodied its name. The Palace of Dreams. It was designed like a jewel box. On the roof, beams of lights pirouetted into the sky. The Palais's stone façade was Forged with an illusion of dusk-touched clouds, purple-bellied and dream-swollen as they skimmed across balconies. No matter how many times Laila saw the Palais, she always felt trans-formed. As if right then her lungs drew in not air, but the very night sky. Stars fizzed through her veins. The alchemy of the Palais's music and illusions reshaping her from dancer to dream.

Laila stepped through the Palais's secret stairway entrance. In-side, a guard holding a silver lightstick greeted her.

"L'Énigme," he said respectfully.

Laila held still as the lightstick flashed over her pupils. It was rou-tine protocol for any who entered the Palais. The lightstick revealed whether or not someone was under the influence of a Forging affinity of the mind. Mind affinity was a dangerous talent, and the favorite method of assassins who could pass off the blame on an innocent.

Once cleared, Laila entered the Palais. A sense of calm washed over her. The familiar perfume of the stage filled her. Waxed wood, oranges studded with cloves dangling from the ceiling, talc powder, and rubber. Inside, cleverly designed skylights filtered in the star-light. The ceiling arched like a vault over the stage. Champagne chandeliers ghosted over the crowd, glittering like constellations crushed underfoot by feverish dancers.

On the wide, scalloped stage, the singer, La Fée Verte, sang a glori-ous song of revolution. Her gossamer green gown floated out behind her, wings of thinly cut mother-of-pearl slowly opened and closed from her back. The sharp scent of absinthe lingered in the air, and her most fervent admirers raised smoking goblets of the liquor high in their hands. Behind her, she'd chosen a strange backdrop . . . not of the Bastille, the fortress that was stormed by a crowd of revolutionaries . . . but the catacombs of Paris. The ossuaries which held the bones of millions, the remains of voices both terrible and grand from the Revolution. It was a chilling image on the stage: rows upon rows of grinning skulls, femurs bent into hallways and crosses. But it was a reminder too. That every victory had its costs.

The second terrace was reserved for dressing rooms. Each star of the Palais had their own, customized to their specifications. Laila cast a glance over the terrace, quickly scanning the crowd, spotting the mark. The House Kore courier. He looked unsure of himself, sitting in a velvet upholstered chair. On the table before him was a bowl of chocolate-covered strawberries. Laila grinned. *You took my advice.*

A Sphinx stood motionless in the corner, as she and Séverin had known one would. For large parties, the Palais always kept two on hand in the event someone tried to swindle an Order member or smuggle House-marked treasure out the doors. Today, the second Sphinx would not show up until an hour later, thanks to Zofia and Tristan's clever tampering with the Palais's Forged Sphinx sched-ules. But there would be another "Sphinx" to take the guard's place: Séverin. Tristan would be with him, posing as a police officer. A decoy item would be slipped in the courier's pocket. Something that looked as if it might be House-marked, thus letting a Sphinx approach him. From there, the courier would be accused of theft, taken to a holding cell, freed of all personal effects—including the catalogue coin with the Horus Eye location—"interrogated," and let go.

Simple.

In the background, La Fée Vert had just finished to thunderous applause. Next, it would be her turn.

Laila opened the door to her room. Inside, flames danced on stunted candles. The low light turned the room drowsy and golden. On a side table near her vanity lay a bouquet of white roses.

And on her burgundy chaise lounge . . .

A boy. He was reclining on his side, absentmindedly tearing petals off a rose. He must have heard her open the door because he lifted his head and grinned. His eyes were strikingly pale against the lustrous dark of his skin.

"Ah, hello, *ma chère*," said the boy.

"Who are you?"

The boy stood and bowed. "Hypnos."

Laila lifted her chin. "And *what* are you doing here?"

Hypnos laughed. "I adore you already! So imperious! I bet Séverin likes to be bossed around a little, doesn't he?"

At Séverin's name, Laila snapped upright.

"What did you do to him?"

Hypnos clapped his hands together and sighed.

"Oh, goodness, you *care* for Séverin! And why wouldn't you? That boy looks like every dark corner of a fairy tale. The wolf in bed. The apple in a witch's palm."

He winked.

Heat rose to Laila's cheeks. "I don't—"

"I don't really care one way or the other," said Hypnos, waving his hand. His smile held all the danger of a pried-open secret. "And that's not why I came, lovely. I'm here because if we don't act soon, I'm afraid Tristan and Séverin will be dead within the hour."

9

☙⚬❧

ZOFIA

Zofia chewed on a matchstick, her eyes fixed on the exhibition door. The Exhibition on Colonial Superstitions was a glass and steel enclosure the size of a large greenhouse. Inside it were examples of ancient Forging objects throughout France's overseas empire. Any moment now, the security guard's shift would end. After that, she and Enrique would sneak in, steal an artifact Enrique believed would neutralize the effects of verit stone, and meet up with the others back at L'Eden.

"God, this wait is miserable," said Enrique.

At this time of evening, no one was left in the Champ de Mars but vagrants, beggars, and the occasional tourist trying to catch a glimpse of the Exposition before it opened. Over the past few months, preparations for the Exposition Universelle had transformed the city, pulling the skyline into new shapes every day. Colorful tents sprouted up overnight, and the trill of new languages joined the sonorous buzz of electrical lights.

But nothing captured Zofia's attention more than the imposing Eiffel Tower, the official entrance to the 1889 Exposition Universelle. The papers said that, together, Forging and science would pave a new age of industry. But Zofia did not consider Forging separate from the sciences. To her, Forging was not some divine art bestowed by ancient objects, but a science not yet understood.

Zofia glanced at the forbidding Eiffel Tower. Some called it a Tower of Babel for the new age, for both had been built without Forging, and both marked the start of a new era. But the Tower of Babel had been built to reach God and the heavens. Zofia was not sure what kind of god the world sought to reach now.

"What is taking that security guard so long?" Enrique grumbled. "He was supposed to be out by eight o'clock. It's nearly nine."

"Maybe he doesn't have a clock."

He stared at her. "Are you finally making a joke?"

"I'm pointing out a gap in your observation."

Enrique let out a low whooshing breath. "And to think I could've been *dancing* at the Palais des Rêves tonight."

"They didn't want you, remember? Séverin said your face was all wrong."

"Thank you."

"You are welcome."

Past the Forging exhibition loomed the points of stone temples, tops of palm fronds, and silk tents that marked the sprawling colonial pavilions along the Esplanade des Invalides. It was to be the largest attraction after the Gallery of Machines and the Eiffel Tower. According to the newspapers, it contained "a Negro Village with almost 400 Africans in their natural habitat."

That word struck Zofia as wrong. "Habitat." It sounded like it was meant for animals. People were not animals. It didn't seem right that they were there solely to be seen.

"Ugly," she said, not quite realizing she'd spoken until she heard her voice.

"What?" asked Enrique.

He followed her gaze to the tops of the tents, and his mouth twisted into a grimace. "Part of Europe's 'civilizing mission,'" he said quietly.

Zofia knew the definition of "civilize," but she didn't understand why it was being used. In school, "civilize" meant bringing people to a stage of development deemed advanced. But Zofia had seen the illustrations in the traveling books—the grand temples, the complex inventions, techniques and leaps in medicine that had been discovered and implemented long before they ever reached European shores.

"That word does not fit."

Enrique's mouth was downturned. His eyes wide and jaw set. A pattern of sorrow mixed with something else.

"I know."

Now Zofia knew what else his expression said. He understood.

A sound in the alley made them both jump.

"A Sphinx," he hissed under his breath. "Don't move."

Zofia stayed still as the lamplight twisted into a familiar reptilian shape. Tasked with tracking down stolen House-marked items, the Sphinx operated for and answered to the Order. As the Sphinx stalked past their hiding spot, Enrique and Zofia sank farther into the shadows. Behind him limped a thief, his arm bent at a wrong angle, his wrist broken and bleeding into the Sphinx's jaws.

Zofia averted her eyes. The moment a Sphinx targeted someone, the Forgery in their crocodile masks took over. They moved inhumanly fast, and their jaws snapped through skin and bone on whatever they caught first.

The man was lucky the Sphinx had only gone for his wrist.

When the Sphinx and the thief had passed, a clanging sound at the Exhibition on Colonial Superstitions caught her attention. The security guard had finished his shift, and the door to the exhibition swung open. Once the night security guard finished locking up, he pressed his palm to a pane of glass. It glowed a brief shade of blue, then faded. The man looked around him. In the distance, beggars huddled into corners for the night. Skinny cats dissolved into shadows.

Enrique adjusted his outfit of a threadbare shirt and coat. "Remember what Séverin said. The theft has to look like an accident."

"No explosives," she said, bored.

"*No* explosives."

Zofia did not mention that she brought her fire tape, incinerator, and matches. Just in case.

Enrique pulled a mask over his head. The guard started walking toward the street. Lantern light glinted off the edge of his top hat. Enrique ambled toward him, swinging an empty bottle of wine he'd found near the trash heap.

"You there!" Enrique hollered. "Have you got any coin on you?"

The guard recoiled. Zofia moved farther into the lean-to, which meant losing sight of Enrique. But she still heard him. The scuffle. The guard shouting. Coins hitting the ground. Enrique's drunken apology reverberating off the buildings.

Now it was her turn.

Zofia crept through the trash. Like Enrique, she was dressed as a beggar. Albeit, a slightly better kept one. Acting like someone else was easy, a relief, even. She had a script. She followed the script. The end.

"Sir!" she called.

The guard walked faster.

"Sir, you dropped this!"

She ran forward to catch up to him right before he left. As she ran, she was careful to keep her gel-covered hands from touching anything more than she had to. The man turned, glancing down at her open palm full of silver coins.

"*Merci*," he said, uneasily taking the coins.

Zofia held still. She pulled her cheeks into a grin that looked like hopefulness. She bent her knees to appear shorter. More childlike. If this didn't go as she planned, there was one other way. Her necklace was hidden under a high collar, and she felt its dangerous pendants like chips of ice against her skin.

"For your trouble," he said gruffly, dropping one silver on the ground.

Zofia grabbed his open hand, leveraging it so that she trapped it in a flat grip with both hands.

"Thank you, sir," she said in falsetto. "Oh, thank you so much."

The man quickly yanked away his hand. Then he ran off into the night. Zofia watched after him, then she looked at her hands. The gel was Streak of Sia, a Forge material first developed in ancient Egypt that retained the shape of prints. Specifically, handprints. Normally the gel was bright blue and frigid to the touch, but Zofia had altered the formula, turning the gel colorless and warm as human skin. It was said the Fallen House could do more with the Streak of Sia. That they could Forge the gel not just to remember handprints, but to *leave* prints on a person that would allow them to be tracked. But such technology, if it had ever existed, had died with the Fallen House.

At the entrance of the Forging exhibition, Enrique stepped out of the shadows. His beggar costume had been shucked off for a plain, dark suit and top hat.

"Got it?"

She held up her hand. Enrique kept an eye out as she pressed her hand to the windowpane. It glowed a dull blue. *Match*. On the heavy doors, the iron locks unbraided, falling into a noisy pile.

The inside of the Forging exhibition was far larger than the outside suggested. The gallery stretched into a long row of darkness, lit up by occasional points of light in front of glass display cases. Though the outside looked like steel and glass, the interior allowed no natural light. Instead, large murals covered the windows. All along the back wall stretched panels of brocade fabric. They were so silky and bright, they looked almost wet.

Enrique pulled a Forged spherical detection device—one of her own inventions—from his pocket. He tossed it in the air. As it slowly spiraled downward, light burst from the sphere, illuminating the room's contours.

The place seemed empty enough to Zofia, though she didn't like how it looked. Too closed off, despite the space.

"There's no one here," she said. "And there aren't any recording devices. Come on—"

Just as she stepped forward, Enrique grabbed her from behind and quickly pulled her against his chest.

"Get *off*—"

"Easy, phoenix, easy," Enrique said, low in her ear. "Look at the floor."

The sphere had rolled to a stop near one of the many podiums. A spiraled grid of red light radiated out from the object, netting across the entire floor.

"They hid the recording devices in the floor?"

"Rather clever of them," said Enrique, releasing her. "We'll have to go slower than I thought."

Zofia glanced at the front door, the pile of iron chains just on the other side. Enrique had slipped extra cash to the madame of a brothel the next night guard frequented, so the man wouldn't arrive for at least another twenty minutes. That should have given them plenty of time.

But they'd planned their time assuming the recording devices would be on the wall. Not the floor.

"As long as we don't touch any of the red light, it'll be fine," said Enrique.

He took the lead. He stepped carefully and completely within the bounded space of red light. Zofia followed, matching him step for step. Within five minutes, her calves started cramping. Every space became narrower. She could hardly fit the whole of her foot into each one. Zofia rose on her tiptoes, hands out to the sides for balance. Enrique did the same.

"Nearly there," whispered Enrique. "We just crossed the seventh podium, and I marked it at the ninth."

Zofia didn't look up from her feet. The darkness cinched tight around her. She knew it wasn't a locked room. She knew it, and yet, she thought she could feel the air touching her. Soft as a feather dragged across her skin. Bile reared up in her throat. *It's open. It's open.* She looked up. She had to see the sky. Had to know it wasn't a wall. That the podiums weren't students. That the electric whirr wasn't laughter.

Enrique stopped a foot away from her. "We're here! I can see the artifact—"

Her shoe slipped.

The red line across from her snapped in half.

Beams of light shot down from the ceiling. Outside the exhibition hall, sirens screamed into the night.

Enrique turned to face her. "*What did you do?*"

Zofia looked up wildly, but her gaze went not to Enrique or the black column where the artifact sat, but to the man leaning against the wall behind them. In the dark, he had melded in with the shadows, but the light revealed him. His eyes narrowed, lips pulled in a sneer as he raised his hand. Light glanced off a raised blade.

"Watch out!" screamed Zofia.

The man thrust the blade. Enrique pivoted out of the way. Instinct took over. When it came to socializing, Zofia had difficulty knowing the right moves. But fighting was different. It was all patterns, anticipation of the movement of muscle. *That* she could do. Zofia reached for her necklace. At her touch, the Forged pendants shifted.

Enrique jumped to her side.

"Get the artifact," said Zofia.

He looked between her face and the pendant, brows quirked for barely an instant. The man with the knife made a grab for her. She thrust up her elbow, catching him in the nose. Before he could yelp, she caught him sideways with a right hook. The man growled, backhanding her. Zofia's face stung as she reeled back. Then, she clicked her heels together. Steel spurs spun out from her shoes. The man lunged once more, and she kicked out, swiping his kneecaps so he fell, writhing, onto the floor.

The second he was down, Zofia raced to Enrique. He was busy wresting the square-shaped artifact off the wooden block. Behind her came a loud groaning sound. The man had pushed himself off the ground. As he lumberd toward them, a gold chain spilled from the collar of his shirt.

"Foolish girl," he rasped.

He reached for something in his cloak. Zofia ripped off another pendant, flinging it at his face. Chemically speaking, it was nothing more than a metal oxidizer and metallic fuel, but Zofia had Forged it to do more than just flash with light once. She had bent her will to the object, encouraging it to draw from the very air itself. Now it sparked and burned, hissing against the man's face. His hands sprung apart as he batted uselessly at the pendant.

"Got it!" yelled Enrique.

Three policemen appeared at the front of the entrance.

"*Arrêtez!*" shouted the first police officer.

All three of them looked up. The man's mouth twisted into a grin. He reached for the hat on his head, then flung it toward the police officer. Zofia caught a strange sheen to its brim.

The second Zofia realized what it was, she waved her arms to get the police officer's attention. "*Move!* It's a blade!"

Too late. The brim swept across one of the police officer's throats. Blood bloomed down the man's shirt.

"No!" she screamed. "No!"

The man grabbed her wrist. She tried to twist out of his grip, but he was too strong. Instead, she grabbed the gold chain around his neck. The man spluttered as the chain broke off in her hand, the force of it throwing her to the ground.

"You don't know what you're stopping," the man wheezed. "This is the start of something new. A *true* revolution."

He stalked toward her. The dark shape of him choked off the light. Zofia staggered, crawling backward as she reached for the Forged tape concealed on the underside of her collar. She peeled it off, throwing it between her and the man. As she threw it, she willed it: *Ignite*.

Flames spurted up from the ground and heat shimmered in the air. Just through the flames, she saw the man's face. Livid and red in the glow.

Enrique helped her stand, his voice sounding faraway as he rallied her: "Move, move!" The exit was within reach. One step, then another, then running. The glass doors flung back. Footsteps slapped the pavement. The scent of fire stung her nose. Her mouth tasted like iron and salt from accidentally biting her tongue, and her ears rang out with the man's last word: "Revolution."

10

LAILA

Laila couldn't find enough breath to pull into her lungs.

Hypnos had sent her head spinning.

Tristan and Séverin will be dead within the hour.

"What do you want me to do?"

Hypnos clapped his hands. "I *adore* when people ask me that."

Laila narrowed her eyes. "Why don't you—" she started.

But Hypnos ignored her, crossing the room to Laila's large, gilt mirror propped up on her vanity.

"Allow me to show you the scene I just left behind on the floor of the Palais."

Hypnos pressed his hand to the mirror, and the image rippled. The reflection changed from Laila's dressing room to an eye-level perspective of the audience facing the stage. In the mirror's reflection, men lit up their cigars. Waitresses weaved through the audience wearing wings made of newsleaf, each sheet covered in the words of the French constitution: *Liberté, Equalité, Fraternité*. Laila eyed Hypnos suspiciously. Only the courtesans and dancers of the Palais knew the mirror's abilities.

He met her gaze and shrugged.

"Please, *ma chère*, this room is not the first dancer's room I've been invited to."

A flicker of movement in the mirror stole Laila's response. A Sphinx.

"We anticipated one Sphinx in the crowd," said Laila uneasily. "That's nothing new—"

Hypnos pointed at the mirror. From the eastern hall, a second Sphinx. It paced back and forth. At the table nearest it sat the House Kore courier. At first, Laila's heart lightened. Maybe Séverin and Tristan had gotten there earlier than she expected. Maybe Tristan had just put the decoy on the House Kore courier.

"That must be Séverin—" she started.

Just then, right on schedule, a third Sphinx stepped through the doors of the western hall. Beside it walked a Sûreté officer in plain uniform. *Séverin and Tristan.*

Tristan spotted the House Kore courier on the other side of the room.

"Don't!" Laila yelled.

She knew even as she yelled that it was useless. The mirror relayed only images. Not sound. No one could hear her.

If he walked forward, she wouldn't be able to see him anymore. The mirror only allowed a look at a strict width of the audience. Tristan looked as if he was about to take a step forward when something yanked him backward. Abruptly, a group of men stood from their table, cutting Tristan and Séverin from view. When the men cleared, Laila caught a glimpse of Tristan and Séverin hiding behind a wide, marble column. Any moment now, the two genuine Sphinxes would recognize the imposter. A violent image flashed before her eyes. Séverin and Tristan facedown in a pool of blood.

Laila whirled to face Hypnos. "Get a message to them! Besides, you're a patriarch of the Order. Can't you call off the Sphinx?"

"The moment I step outside my home, my every action is recorded and submitted to the Order at the end of every month," said Hypnos, tapping his lapel where a mnemo bug in the shape of a moth was pinned. No wonder he'd come here. All dressing rooms were Forged to nullify any recording devices.

Outside her door, someone began to beat drums, her cue to enter the stage. Laila eyed Hypnos's fancy clothes, from the watch and the mnemo bug to the crescent-moon cuff links of his sleeves.

"Are all your accessories House-marked?"

Hypnos's gaze turned haughty. He stroked his matching crescent-moon brooch. "Of course. Far too pretty to be on commoners."

Laila had an idea. She unclasped her dress, candlelight catching on her Night and Stars costume.

Hypnos's eyebrows skated up his forehead. "Oh, heavens," he said. "I don't blame you in the least. But I can't have the death of my hired associates on the conscience of my irresistibility."

"Your virtue is safe with me." Laila winked. "How would you like to cause some drama?" she asked, shrugging off the rest of her gown. Her Forged peacock headdress tickled her skin.

Hypnos's teeth flashed in the candlelight. "I live for it, lovely."

L'ÉNIGME DID NOT take the stage as planned.

She did not take the stage at all.

Laila descended the main staircase instead of the stairwell that led directly to the stage. She told no one—not the stage manager, musicians, or even her fellow dancers. Which was just as well. When the grand courtesan had trained her, she had told her the only rules to follow were instincts and color palettes. Tonight, Laila followed both.

At the top of the staircase, she waited. In one hand, she carried a half-empty bottle of champagne. Her other hand brimmed with strings of pearls, a set of emerald earrings, and two crescent-moon cuff links. The two Sphinxes had not moved from their posts. Tristan and Séverin were nowhere to be seen.

"Hypnos!" she hollered.

The crowd turned. The French horn and piano music cut off sharply. Hypnos sat at a table, his arm around a beautiful man. When he looked up at her, he flashed a wicked smile.

Laila walked down a few steps, swaying her hips generously so the light caught on her spangled corset. She hadn't faked a lover's spat in six months. She owed it to the crowd.

Gingerly, Hypnos slid his arm off the other man.

"You lied to me," she said loudly.

Hypnos stood, putting up his hands. "My darling, I can explain—"

Laila threw the champagne bottle in a wide arc. Some people dove out of the way. Others raced to catch it before it fell, but they were too late. The champagne bottle smashed to the floor, glittering shards spinning out across the dance floor. The Sphinx nearest the stage lifted its head. Its nostrils flared.

"She meant nothing to me!" cried Hypnos, dropping to his knees.

"*She?*" repeated Laila. "I was talking about a *he.*"

"Oh." Hypnos winced. "Him too?"

"I am through with this!" announced Laila. "*All* of this!"

From her vantage point on the stairway, Laila broke the streams of pearls. They rained down on the audience. As the crowd dove for the pearls, the second Sphinx lifted its head.

"L'Énigme is not performing today!" yelled Laila, and then she turned on her heel, disappearing up the stairs.

The stage manager huffed, but she didn't care. Her contract allowed—and, frankly, encouraged—one outburst and cancelled performance a year.

She was just doing her job.

The moment Laila was in her room, she touched the mirror and watched the scene unfurling on the Palais floor. Séverin and Tristan weren't there. But neither was the House Kore courier. On the floor, the two real Sphinxes crouched on their knees, pawing through the stray pearls and jewels, their hands wet with champagne. Tossed in with all that rubbish had been Hypnos's House-marked cuff links and the crescent-moon brooch. Laila was fairly certain one of the cuff links had fallen between the floor panels, which meant they'd be searching for ages.

Laila changed out of her costume, and then selected a violet *crêpe de Chine* dress from her wardrobe. Polished amethyst pendants Forged to drink in the moonlight adorned the sharp V of the waistline and the tips of her billowing sleeves. Laila paused to swipe more rouge on her lips before taking a specially commissioned staircase behind her wardrobe that led to the servants' exit and the cellar that served as a holding cell. At the cellar, she pressed her ear to the door.

Behind the wood, the voices were indistinct. After a moment, she heard a chair scrape back. Then, a door slamming shut.

If all had gone to plan, Tristan had finished interrogating the House Kore courier while Séverin discovered the Horus Eye location. Laila was still straining to hear more sounds when the door swung open. She lost her footing, and her head thudded against someone's hard chest. She looked up, a scream caught in her throat. *Sphinx*. Its jaws were cracked wide. Reptilian eyes like a gold coin slit down the middle. It caught her with one hand, and then with its other, pulled back the mask to reveal a disheveled Séverin. He grinned.

"Had you there for a moment, didn't I?"

"*God*," said Laila, clutching her heart.

"A mere mortal, at your service," he said, bowing.

The Sphinx mask had mussed his hair, and Laila's hands twitched with the memory of her fingers combing through it, the surprising texture of it like roughened silk. She shoved aside the memory. She knew all the carefully cobbled pieces of him. He was deception steeped in elegance, from his sharp smile to his unsettling eyes. Séverin's eyes were the precise color of sleep—sable velvet with a violet sheen, promising either nightmare or dream.

Séverin held open the door, and Laila brushed past him. The basement holding space was narrow and lined with bookshelves and rusting cutlery. Tristan was in the middle of peeling off his Sûreté uniform in exchange for a swallowtail coat and top hat. He waved a shy hello at her.

Laila blew him a kiss. "So? Did you get the catalogue coin?"

Séverin grinned. "Yes."

"Where's the courier?"

"With a stiff drink, I imagine."

"Did you keep the coin or—"

"Returned it," said Séverin. "No point holding on to it once we had the coordinates."

"Good," she said. She'd begun to feel rather guilty for the courier and the thought of landing him into even more trouble with his employers didn't sit well with her. "What happened back there with the Sphinx schedules?"

Séverin rubbed his hand through his hair. "I couldn't tell you. Zofia Forged the schedule perfectly. Tristan delivered it on time. A clerical error, perhaps. But you saved us. Feigning a lovers' spat with Hypnos?" He shuddered.

"On the contrary, it was quite fun," said Laila. Séverin seemed to go rigid, and Laila felt the slightest thrill. "He was the one who came to warn me, anyway."

"He did?" asked Tristan and Séverin at the same time.

"I did."

The three turned to the doorway. Hypnos leaned against the entrance. He held up his mangled mnemo bug, a sign that for the time being, at least, he was not recording anything.

Hypnos grinned at Tristan. "Ah! I used you as bait!" He walked forward, with his hand outstretched. "How do you do?"

Tristan crossed his arms. "I should set one of my spiders on you. They're very venomous, you know."

Hypnos looked around the room. "Are they present?"

Tristan faltered. "Well, no, not exactly, this is when Goliath eats, you see, and—"

Séverin cut him off. "Why are you here?"

"We're in business together, are we not?" asked Hypnos. His gaze swept over the room as he tilted his head to one side. "Where's that handsome historian?"

"On business," said Séverin tersely. "Which is the only topic I am willing to discuss with you."

"Ah, yes. *Business*. So. Were you successful in finding the catalogue coin?"

Séverin eyed him for a moment. Then, he nodded.

"We have the exact coordinates for the Horus Eye in House Kore's collection. Now, we just need the invitation."

"My domain, naturally."

"And I'll need a guest list and the name of the private security organization the matriarch of House Kore hires for her event."

"Done!" said Hypnos, clapping his hands. "Is this what teamwork is like? How . . . hierarchical." Hypnos winked at Laila. "Hello, lover."

"Ex-lover," she said, a touch fondly.

Hypnos reminded her of Enrique. If Enrique's wits had been fed on champagne and bitter smoke for the better part of a decade. Séverin's face darkened. A small muscle in his jaw twitched, as if he were chewing down an imaginary clove to calm his temper. He stalked forward, placing himself between Laila and Hypnos.

"You and I should talk privately," he said to Hypnos.

"I'll come for tea tomorrow."

"There's no need for you to come to the hotel."

Hypnos's shoulders dropped, his voice pitched like a child's. "But I want to!" He grinned and spoke normally again. "And I *always* do what I want. I shall see you tomorrow."

Hypnos blew Tristan two kisses, which Tristan pretended to squash under his heel. Then, Hypnos pushed past Séverin and bent over Laila's hand.

"I shall keep your identity secret, L'Énigme. And before I forget, I must tell you I adored your costume. So shiny. I'm rather tempted to see if it will fit me."

Hypnos glided out the door. Once he was gone, Tristan's shoulders dropped, and he released his breath.

"I really don't want him at the hotel."

For a moment, a cold, hollow look flickered on his face. Laila knew how protective Tristan was of Séverin, but she'd never seen him look like that. A moment later, his expression melted into a warm smile.

He beamed. "Oh, I liked your costume too, Laila. You looked beautiful."

Laila bowed, then glanced at Séverin. He'd taken unusual care with how he dressed. The color of his silk pocket square matched the silvery shade of his scar. On the second button of his shirt, he'd pinned an elaborate ouroboros brooch, one that she knew dug painfully into his skin because he'd told her. His shoes were scuffed hand-me-downs from his father, the long-dead patriarch of House Vanth. Laila's chest tightened. Today, Séverin had dressed in subtle pain. Laila recognized it because she did the same thing to herself every night when she took off her clothes, splaying her fingers against the long scar down her back as she tried to read her own body. Sometimes the pain was a reminder of where she was . . . who she was . . . and what she wanted to be.

Séverin's eyes flashed knowingly to hers, and Laila forced herself to smile wryly.

"Tristan and Hypnos admired my outfit," she said, resting her hand on her hip. "No compliment from you?"

"I didn't have a chance to look," he said. His smile didn't meet his eyes. "Too busy avoiding certain death. It's terribly distracting, you know."

He could say what he wanted, but she hadn't forgotten how he'd watched her yesterday. How still he stood. How his eyes darkened, leaving only a halo of violet. Men had looked at her a thousand ways and times, and none of them had made her feel as she did yesterday. The almost-painful exquisiteness of being unveiled by a glance. It made her feel aware of everything about her—skin stretched over bone, silk clinging to her limbs, her breath heating the air. The kind of awareness that makes one feel alive.

It terrified her.

It was the same reason why after that one night, she knew it had to end there. There was no point entertaining that awareness when, in less than a year, she wouldn't even exist. But she still remembered.

She remembered that she'd reached for him first, and he was the first to break it off.

Laila had to leave.

"The driver is waiting for me," she said.

On her way out, she gazed over her shoulder at Séverin.

"Be sure to appear very sad at L'Eden. After all, if you really were my lover, you should be utterly devastated both by my public dismissal of you and by my marvelous costume."

She did not wait to see his expression.

II

ENRIQUE

Enrique collapsed in his favorite blue armchair in the stargazing room. A thunderstorm rattled the windows, and the curtains covered in embroidered constellations shook like rags of night sky.

"Someone was waiting for us."

"Revolution man," said Zofia softly.

He looked up. Zofia was curled warily in the armchair across from him. As usual, she chewed on a matchstick.

"What did you say?"

"Revolution man," she said, still not looking at him. "That's what he talked about. About the start of a new age. Also, the sensor should have picked him up, but it didn't."

That had bothered Enrique too. It was almost as if the man had watched them from somewhere, materializing only after they had secured the area for signs of any recording devices or other people. But there was no way he could have gotten in. The entrance had been locked. The windows were all covered with murals. The exit had been closed and barred until the police officers had broken it open.

All that was in that room were the Forging displays and the massive mirror wall.

Zofia opened her palms, and a golden chain spilled out. A pendant no larger than a franc dangled from it. She brought the chain to her face, turning over the pendant.

"Where did you get that?"

"He wore it on his neck."

Enrique frowned. Behind Zofia, the hands of the grandfather clock tilted slowly to midnight. All around them, the stargazing room bore signs of their planning. Papers and blueprints covered every surface. Different sketches of the Horus Eye hung from the ceiling. Until now, this had felt like any other acquisition: planning, casing, squabbling over cake.

Until the man had raised a knife to him.

It struck him then. The cold knowledge that perhaps someone didn't want them to find the Horus Eye and would do anything to make sure they didn't find it. Enrique pulled the artifact from the breast pocket of his jacket. According to his research, it had been placed above the entrance of a Coptic church in North Africa. Enrique turned over the artifact in his hand. It was made of brass, its edges jagged. When he ran his thumb along the top, he could feel the depressions of grooves, but it was too caked with verdigris to see properly. The back of the square showed chisel marks from where it had been hewn off the base of a statue depicting the Virgin Mary. According to the locals, the square at the base of the statue emanated a strange glow when someone stepped into the church carrying evil in their hearts. He'd never heard of a stone Forged to do such a thing except verit. If this square held a piece—or pieces, though that seemed impossible—of verit, then perhaps it had detected a weapon on a man who had entered the church. Perhaps the man truly was bad, and when they'd noticed the glowing stone, they'd accosted him, found the weapon, and made their own connections. There was always an observation at the root of a superstition.

"It's a honeybee," said Zofia suddenly.

"What?"

She held up the chain pendant. "It's in the shape of a honeybee."

"A strange fashion choice," said Enrique, distracted. "Or a symbol, perhaps? Maybe he sympathized with Napoleon? I'm fairly certain honeybees were thought to be a symbol of his rule."

"Did Napoleon like mathematicians?"

"What does that have to do with anything?"

"Honeybees make perfect hexagonal prisms. My father called them nature's mathematicians."

"Maybe?" said Enrique. "But seeing as how Napoleon died in 1821, I don't think I'll have the opportunity to ask him."

Zofia blinked at him, and a pang of guilt struck Enrique. She couldn't always process jokes the way the others did, and sometimes his attempts at wit came off severe rather than sophisticated. But Zofia didn't notice. Shrugging, she placed the honeybee chain on the coffee table between them.

Enrique turned the artifact over in his hands. "Where did he come from, though? Was he waiting the whole time, or was there a door there?"

"No doors except the entrance and exit we noted."

"I just don't understand what he wanted. Why wait for us? Who was he?"

Zofia glanced at the honeybee necklace and made a noncommittal *hrmm* sound and then stuck out her hand. "Hand me that."

"Have you never heard the saying 'you attract more flies with honey than vinegar'?"

"Why would I want to attract flies?"

"Never mind."

Enrique handed it to her. "Be careful," he said.

"It's nothing but brass with some corrosion," she said disdainfully.

"Can you take off the corrosion?"

"Easily," she said. She rattled the square. "I thought you said this could be solid verit inside? This looks like the superstitious charms sold in my village. What proof did you have? What was your research?"

"Superstition. Stories," said Enrique, before adding just to annoy her: "A gut instinct."

Zofia made a face. "Superstitions are useless. And a gut cannot have an instinct."

She took a solution from her makeshift worktable and cleaned off the square. When she was finished, she slid it across the table. Now, he could make out a gridlike pattern and the shape of letters, but little else. In the stargazing room, the fires had been banked. No lanterns were allowed so as not to disrupt the view of the stars, and only a couple of candle tapers stood on the table.

"I can barely see," said Enrique. "Do you have flint to light the match?"

"No."

Enrique sighed, looking around the room. "Well, then I—"

He stopped when he heard the unmistakable sound of fire ripping from a match. Zofia held a tiny fire out in her hand. In her other hand, she took a second match and struck it against the bottom of one of her canine teeth. Firelight lit up her face. Her platinum hair looked like the haze of lightning on the underside of a cloud. That glow looked natural on her. As if this was the way she was meant to be seen.

"You just struck a match with your teeth," he said.

She looked at him quizzically. "I'll have to do it again if you don't light the candles before these burn out."

He quickly lit the candles. Then he took one and held it over the metal disc that had slipped out of the compass, examining it. On closer inspection, he saw writing on its surface. All the letters on the square were concentrated in the middle, but there were enough squares for twenty-five letters to be written vertically and horizontally.

S	A	T	O	R
A	R	E	P	O
T	E	N	E	T
O	P	E	R	A
R	O	T	A	S

His heart began to race. It always did whenever he felt on the verge of discovering something.

"Looks like Latin," said Enrique, tilting the disc. "*Sator* could mean 'founder,' usually of a divine nature? *Arepo* is perhaps a proper name, though it doesn't seem Roman. Maybe Egyptian. *Tenet* means to hold or preserve . . . then there's *opera*, like work, and then *rotas*, plural for 'wheels.'"

"Latin?" asked Zofia. "I thought this artifact was from a Coptic church in North Africa."

"It is," said Enrique. "North Africa was one of the first places Christianity spread, believed to be as early as the first century . . . and Rome had frequent interaction with North Africa. I believe their first colony is now known as Tunisia."

Zofia took one of the other candles and held it close to the disc.

"If the verit is inside, can I just break it?"

Enrique snatched the brass square off the table and clutched it. *"No."*

"Why not?"

"I am *tired* of people breaking things before I get a chance to see them," he said. "And besides, look at this switch on the side." He pointed to a small toggle sunken into the width of the square. "Some ancient artifacts have failsafes to protect the object within, so if you smash it, you might destroy whatever is inside it."

Zofia slouched, nesting her chin in her palm. "Perhaps one day I'll discover how to chisel verit stone itself."

Enrique whistled. "You'd be the most dangerous woman in France."

As a rule, it was impossible to break verit stone. Every piece that existed at the entrance of palaces, banks, and other wealthy institutions were raw slabs that had naturally come apart during the lengthy mining and purification process. All of which made procuring a gravel-sized piece of verit unheard of, even on the extensive black market that usually suited their purposes.

"The words are the same," said Zofia.

"What do you mean?"

"They're just the same. Can't you see it?"

Enrique stared at the letters, and then realized what she meant. There was an *S* in the upper left and bottom right corner. An *A* adjacent to both. From there, the pattern made sense.

"It's a palindrome."

"It's a metal square with letters."

"Yes, but the letters spell the same thing backward and forward," said Enrique. "Palindromes used to be inscribed on amulets to protect the wearer from harm. Not just amulets, though, come to think of it. There was one in ancient Greek found outside the Hagia Sophia church in Constantinople. *Nipson anomēmata mē monan op-ʃin.* 'Wash the sins, not only the face.' It was thought the wordplay would confuse demons."

"Wordplay confuses me too."

"I shall withhold comment," said Enrique. He studied the letters once more. "There's something familiar about this arrangement . . . I feel as though I've seen it before."

Enrique walked over to the library within the stargazing room. He was looking for a specific tome, something he had come across during his linguistic studies in ancient Latin—

"Found you," he said, pulling out a small volume: EXCURSIONS TO THE LOST CITY OF POMPEII. He quickly scanned the pages before he found what he was looking for.

"I knew it! This arrangement is called the Sator Square," he said. "It was found in the ruins of Pompeii in the 1740s, commissioned by the king of Naples. Apparently, the Order of Babel helped fund the excavation alongside Spanish engineer Roque Joaquín de Alcubierre in hopes that it would reveal previously unknown Forge instruments."

"Did it?"

"Doesn't look like it," said Enrique.

"What about the palindrome's meaning?"

"Still under scrutiny," he said. "Nothing else has appeared like it in the ancient realm, so it's either a riddle or a cryptogram or a very bored inscription by someone who was about to be killed by a gigantic volcano. Personally, I think it's a key . . . Figure out the code and the brass square will unlock. Maybe there's some math involved here . . . Zofia? Any ideas?"

Zofia chewed on the end of a matchstick. "There's no math to it. Just letters."

Enrique paused. An idea flying to his head.

"But numbers and letters have plenty in common . . ." he said slowly. "Mathematics and the Torah led to gematria, a Kabbalistic method of interpreting Hebrew scripture by assigning numerical value to the words."

Zofia sat upright. "My grandfather used to give us riddles like that. How do you know about that?"

"It's been around for some time," said Enrique, feeling his academic tone creeping into his voice. He had a bizarre urge to sit in a leather chair and acquire a fluffy cat. And a pipe. "Mathematics has long been considered the language of the divine. Besides, the system of alphanumeric codes doesn't just belong to the Hebrew language. Arabs did it with *abjad* numerals."

"Our *zeyde* taught my sister and I how to write coded letters to each other," said Zofia softly. She twirled a strand of platinum hair around her finger. "Every number matched its alphanumeric position on the alphabet. It was . . . fun."

At this, the barest smile touched her face. Not once had he ever heard her talk about her family. But no sooner had she mentioned them than she set her jaw. Before he could say anything, Zofia grabbed a quill and scraps of paper.

"If I take all these letters from your Sator Square, and look at their position in the alphabet and add them up, here's what we get."

$$SATOR \Rightarrow S + A + T + O + R = 19 + 1 + 20 + 15 + 18 = 73$$

$$AREPO \Rightarrow A + R + E + P + O = 1 + 18 + 5 + 16 + 15 = 55$$

$$TENET \Rightarrow T + E + N + E + T = 20 + 5 + 14 + 5 + 20 = 64$$

$$OPERA \Rightarrow O + P + E + R + A = 15 + 16 + 5 + 18 + 1 = 55$$

$$ROTAS \Rightarrow R + O + T + A + S = 18 + 15 + 20 + 1 + 19 = 73$$

"That hardly looks helpful."

Zofia frowned. "Separate the numbers. The first line is seventy-three. Seven plus three is ten. Move to the next line. Five and five is ten. Each of them becomes ten when treated as a separate integer. Or, perhaps it is not ten. Perhaps it is just one and zero. See?"

"It's like the I Ching," said Enrique, impressed. "The movement of zero to one is the power of divinity. *Ex nihilo* and all that. That would fit if there's a piece of verit inside this square because the stone was believed to examine the soul, the way a deity might. But that doesn't give us a hint to how to open the box itself. Plus, do the letters look like they're . . . *sliding*?"

Zofia held up the metal square, tilting it back and forth. She pressed the letter *S* and moved her finger. It dragged a couple spaces to the right.

For the next hour, Enrique and Zofia copied out the letters on at least twenty different sheets of paper before cutting them up, and trying to arrange them as they went. Every now and then, his gaze darted to her face. As she worked, Zofia's brows were pressed down, her mouth slanted in a grimace. In the past year or so that she'd worked for Séverin, Enrique had never spent much time with Zofia. She was always too quiet or too cutting. She rarely laughed and scowled more than she smiled. Watching her now, Enrique was beginning to think she wasn't really *scowling* . . . maybe this was just the face she made when thinking . . . as if everything was an exercise in computation. And here, with the numbers and the riddle before them, it was like watching her come alive.

"Language of the divine, language of the divine," muttered Enrique over and over to himself. "But how does it *want* to be arranged? I see *A* and *O* which could theoretically be said to represent the *alpha* and *omega* power of God. Those are, coincidentally, the first and last letters of the Greek alphabet, said to suggest that God is first and last."

"Then take out the two *A*s and two *O*s," said Zofia. "Wouldn't it make sense if it stood apart?"

Enrique did as she suggested. Maybe it was the light in the room or the fact that his eyes were strangely unfocused in exhaustion, but he thought of home as he muttered a quick prayer. He thought of kneeling with his mother, father, Lola, and brothers in the church pews, heads bowed as the priest recited the Lord's Prayer in Latin: *Pater Noster, qui es in caelis, sanctificetur nomen tuum* . . .

"Pater Noster," breathed Enrique, his eyes flying open. "That's it. 'Our Father' in Latin."

His eyes skipped over the arrangement of letters, hands moving furiously as he moved the bits of paper into a cross:

"Zofia," he said. "I think I know how to use it."

He took the metal disc from her, then dragged the letters into the PATER NOSTER formation, with the *A*s and *O*s placed outside of the cross. The square split down the middle, and a ghostly light shimmered before them. Zofia reeled back as the top half of the brass square slid away, revealing four gravel-sized pieces of verit stone that could ransom a kingdom.

12

SÉVERIN

Séverin was ten years old when he was brought to his third father, Envy. Envy took them in after Wrath accidentally drank tea steeped with wolfsbane. It was not a peaceful death. Séverin knew, for he had watched.

Envy had a wife named Clotilde, and two children whose names Séverin no longer remembered. On the first day with Envy, Séverin fell in love. He loved the charming whitewashed house and the charming children who were the same age as Tristan and him. When the men in suits and hats had dropped them before the house, Clotilde had told them, charmingly, of course, "Call me Mama." When she said that, his throat burned. He wanted to say that word so badly his teeth hurt.

Clotilde allowed them almost one perfect week. Milky tea and biscuits in the morning. Warm hugs in the afternoon. Pheasant shimmering in golden fat for dinner. Cocoa just before bed. Two feather-down beds down the hall from the other two children.

And then, before the week ended, Séverin had heard Clotilde and Envy fighting behind closed doors. Séverin had been on his way to her tearoom. In his hand were flowers that he and Tristan had spent all morning picking.

THE GILDED WOLVES ❧ 139

"I thought they were heirs!" Clotilde yelled. "You said this was our chance to earn back a place!"

"Not anymore," said Envy, his voice heavy. "One has an immense fortune, though he won't see a penny of it until he comes of age."

"Well, what are we supposed to do? Feed and clothe them on that measly allowance from the Order? This week's meal cost a king's ransom! We can't go on this way!"

Finally, Envy sighed. "No. No, we cannot."

That was the end of milky tea and biscuits, of warm hugs in the afternoon, of shining pheasant, of cocoa in bed. That was the end of "Mama," for now she preferred to be known as Madame Canot. Séverin and Tristan were relocated to the guesthouse. The other two children no longer sought them out. The only blessing was that Tristan and Séverin were given a tutor from the university. And as it was all he was given, Séverin abandoned himself to it.

After Madame Canot moved them to the guesthouse, Tristan cried for weeks. Séverin did not. He did not cry when Christmas dinner was only for Envy and his wife and children. He did not cry when Envy's daughters received a silk-eared puppy for a present, while Tristan and Séverin received a scolding for keeping their narrow, chilly rooms unkempt. He did not cry at all.

But he watched.

He watched them fiercely.

SÉVERIN STARED AT the bone clock.

He'd moved it from its original place on his bookshelf to his desk to help him concentrate. Behind him, late afternoon sun poured through the tall, bay windows of L'Eden.

It had been two weeks since they'd uncovered a few precious pieces of verit stone and the Horus Eye location from the catalogue coin. In three days, they would leave for House Kore's Spring Festival celebration at Château de la Lune, House Kore's country estate.

On those sprawling grounds hid the Horus Eye, the rare artifact that could see the Babel Fragment.

The acquisition that would change everything.

And yet one fact kept pressing at the back of his skull . . . Enrique and Zofia had reported that a man had been waiting for them in the dark of the exhibit. That fact haunted all of them. Tristan, especially. Not that this particularly worried Séverin. Tristan was always the most terrified out of them, always concerned they were on the brink of death, always looking for a way out of it. Only this time, Séverin hadn't indulged him.

Last night, they'd been laying traps in the garden, trying to catch whatever creature had been killing off all the birds.

"You're sure it's not Goliath?" Séverin had asked.

"Goliath would never do that!" said Tristan, blushing. "But forget the bird killer. What about the man that almost killed Enrique and Zofia? Séverin, this acquisition isn't *safe*."

"When was it ever going to be safe?"

"But no one was after us before. They could hurt us. *Really* hurt us."

Tristan scowled. "I bet it's Hypnos. I bet he's leading us into a trap. How else would someone know we're after the Horus Eye?"

"He swore an oath of no harm. He can't break it."

"But what about someone working with him?"

"Our intelligence cleared all of his guards."

"But obviously there's someone—"

"—likely from House Kore," said Séverin. "They've had teams dedicated to finding their matriarch's missing Babel Ring, and they might have mistaken Zofia and Enrique for the thieves."

"You're too excited to see what's right in front of you! This is different! And you're not listening to me!" shouted Tristan. "Honestly, it's all about your ego. What's the point of this—"

"*Enough.*"

Tristan had flinched. Only when Séverin looked down did he realize he'd slammed his hand against the desk. But he couldn't help it.

"What's the *point*?" Séverin had repeated. "The point is getting back what was taken, but you don't get that, do you? You were always used to Wrath, but I wasn't. I used to have a family, Tristan. A fucking future. What do I have now?"

Tristan opened his mouth, but Séverin spoke first. "I have you, of course," he'd said.

Tristan eyed him warily. Tense. "But?"

Séverin turned his palm skyward, eyeing his silver scar. "But I used to have more."

Tristan had stormed out. When Séverin had gone to talk to him, he'd found the Tezcat door locked. No matter how many times he knocked and twisted the gilded ivy leaf . . . he couldn't get through.

Apparently, Tristan wasn't the only one angry with him. Laila was acting unusually distant, and no matter how many times he ran through their interactions, he wasn't sure what he'd done.

A knock at his door jolted him from his thoughts. He straightened in his chair. "Come in."

At first, all Séverin's mind registered was raven hair. Something caught in his chest. A hundred memories just like this. Laila entering his study unannounced every single week, sugar sparkling in her hair. In her hand, a new dessert she simply couldn't *wait* for someone to try.

"Um, hello?"

Enrique stood inside his office, carrying a piece of paper and looking very bewildered.

Séverin shook himself. He needed more sleep. He glanced at Enrique, noting the dark circles beneath his eyes, his usually impeccable black hair twisted into horns. Sleeplessness frayed at all of them.

"What've you got there?"

"Well, considering the way you were looking at me, I feel like I should be holding the secret to world domination. Sadly, I am not." Then Enrique grinned widely. "Out of curiosity . . . *who* did you think I was?"

Séverin rolled his eyes. "No one."

"Didn't look like no one to me."

"Enrique. What've you got for me?"

Enrique collapsed into the chair across from him and slid a piece of paper scrawled in sloppy notes across his desk. "You asked for a report on honeybee imagery, but there's nothing particularly ground-breaking here for me to tell you. Same as I told you before. They appear across a cultural spectrum of mythology, most often as por-tents of prophecy given the ancients' understanding of their honey, or as psychopomps, creatures capable of spiriting the dead from one world to the next. In terms of how it relates to France, all I could find is that Napoleon Bonaparte used them as part of his emblem, perhaps trying to make himself seem more aligned with the ancient Franco kings, the Merovingians."

Séverin reached for his tin of cloves. "That's all?"

"That's all," said Enrique. "And it's not like we can go back and take a look at the area of the Exposition where we were attacked either. It's crawling with police officers. And while I'm not saying we don't have someone on our tail, I am saying the man's necklace and pendant was just a honeybee ornament. Maybe he had some-one in his family who once worked for Bonaparte."

"Maybe."

Enrique eyed him. "Is there something you're not telling me?"

Séverin waved his hand. "No, no. Thank you for this. Just keep digging up what you can find."

Enrique nodded, then pushed back his chair. As he stood, his gaze fell to an object on Séverin's desk. The bone clock that had allegedly belonged to the Fallen House.

"Is that new?" asked Enrique.

"Old."

"The markings on it are . . . distinct. Though why someone would choose to twist perfectly good gold into the shape of human bones is rather macabre. And is that a pattern of a six-pointed star? It almost looks as if—"

"It is."

Enrique's eyes widened. "It's a relic of the Fallen House? Why do you have it?"

"It serves as a reminder."

Enrique shifted on his feet. "You don't . . . I mean . . . You're not planning to—"

"The last thing I want is to emulate the Fallen House," said Séverin. "I'm only looking for the Horus Eye. I have no intention of trying to unite every Babel Fragment and build my way to the heavens or whatever it was the Fallen House intended to do with them."

"I wonder why they did it," said Enrique quietly, fixated on the bone clock.

"I believe they thought it was their sacred duty. Though, how they went about doing so led to some nasty murders, or so I'm told. Who knows. Who cares. The Fallen House fell. This bone clock is a reminder of that."

"You have such cheerful taste, Séverin."

"I try."

Enrique stared at the clock longingly. He always got that look whenever there was an object he desperately wanted to analyze. Séverin sighed.

"*After* this acquisition, you may inspect it—"

"Mine! Huzzah! I win!" Enrique gave a little wriggle of joy, straightened his jacket, and then collected himself. "Meet you upstairs?"

"Yes. Get everyone ready. I want to run through the layout of Château de la Lune. Hypnos will be here too, with the invitations and new identities."

Spots of color touched the top of Enrique's cheeks.

"He's been coming around a lot, hasn't he?" Then, as if to explain it himself, he added, "I mean, I guess he *has* to."

The patriarch of House Nyx had been over quite a lot, though always undercover. The Order wouldn't take kindly to them socializing even though the second he came of age, they'd deemed Séverin forever beneath their notice. It made Séverin suspicious. As much as he wished that everyone found Hypnos's company repulsive . . . they didn't. Well, most didn't. Tristan refused to speak to him. Someone had even played a prank on him by hiding his shoes, though no one confessed to it. Hypnos hadn't been mad at all. Instead, he'd clapped excitedly. *Ah! A prank! Is this what friends do?*

It was not.

Though Hypnos refused to be swayed.

"I think L'Eden's cuisine is the most deciding factor."

Enrique laughed. "Probably."

Séverin chewed on a clove. When Enrique left, he opened a concealed drawer in his study and took out the file he'd had stolen from the coroner's office.

Enrique had guessed right. There was something he hadn't told them: The House Kore courier was dead.

He had been found in a brothel with his throat cut, and all his personal effects removed, save for the catalogue coin. It had either been left on his person by accident or intention. Séverin remembered when he and Tristan had interrogated the man. How when he removed his catalogue coin, it was not on his body as they had imagined, but inside his mouth, hiding under his tongue like a golden drachma placed as payment to the ferrier of the dead. But when the coroner had looked in the man's mouth, he found something else hiding behind his teeth:

A golden honeybee.

EVERYONE WAS ALREADY waiting in the stargazing room.

Tristan paced back and forth, spinning a daisy with golden petals in one hand. It was, Séverin remembered, a prototype for the hotel's summer installation: the Midas Touch. Zofia sat with her legs crossed beneath her, a matchstick dangling from her lip, her black smock striped with ash. Enrique hunched over a book that he handled with kid gloves. Laila reclined on her chaise. Her hair was elegantly coiffed, and she wore a dove-gray gown with pearl beading at the neck. In her hand, she lazily twirled what looked like a piece of black string. Séverin looked at it closely. Not a string at all . . . a shoelace. Not that he'd paid remarkable attention to Hypnos's choice of footwear, but he was fairly certain those belonged to him. Laila met Séverin's gaze and flashed a conspiratorial grin. She was reading Hypnos's objects. Séverin smiled back.

"Where's Hypnos?" he asked, looking around the room.

"Who knows." Tristan scowled. "Do we have to wait for him?"

"Given that he has our identifications and invitations—yes. It's the last piece left to plan."

At his name, the door swung open. In walked Hypnos wearing a dark green suit and shoes studded with emeralds.

"I come bearing gifts!" he announced.

Enrique didn't look up from his book. "*Timeo Danaos et dona ferentes.*"

The five of them fixed him with blank stares.

"What?" asked Zofia.

"It's from the *Aeneid*," said Enrique. "'Beware of Greeks bearing gifts.'"

"I'm not Greek."

"Same principle."

But when Enrique said it, a smile twitched at his lips.

"Are those our invitations?" asked Laila, looking at the handful of golden cards in his hand.

Hypnos fanned them out on the coffee table. "One for each of you. Except Tristan, who has to be there anyway to landscape the gardens. For your invitations, I've arranged that you will arrive Friday in time for the midnight feast. You will depart Saturday at midnight, as Sunday is reserved strictly for Order members."

"Perfect," said Séverin. "In and out."

"First invitation goes to our aging Oriental flower expert all the way from China, Monsieur Chang," said Hypnos.

He held out the gold card to Enrique.

Enrique didn't take it, but rather stared at the card like it was a disease. "Are you serious?"

"I'm Hypnos."

"Well, *I'm* not Chinese. I'm Filipino and Spanish." Enrique took the card. "That's terribly offensive."

Hypnos shrugged. "Terribly convenient too; the matriarch of House Kore is obsessed with all things Chinese. Next, a card for the nautch dancer who is joining the titillating entertainment troupe."

Séverin shook his head. Laila might perform on the Palais stage as L'Énigme, but he knew that for her, dance—the classical way in which she had been trained in India—was considered sacred. Laila took the invitation imperiously, disgust rippling across her features.

"However, the dancers are not technically arriving until the day after the festival starts, so you'll first have to pose as a House Nyx servant."

Laila nodded tightly. "Makes sense—"

"No! It doesn't! Why does she have to pretend to be an Order servant?" demanded Tristan, rising to his feet. "She's not part of the Order! None of us are!"

"Tristan, my love," said Laila with dangerous calm. "If you get in the way of a woman's battle, you'll get in the way of her sword."

Tristan sat back down, his face flushed.

"Oh, so *sweet*!" said Hypnos. "You don't want her tainted by association with me, I assume. Fair enough. However, it would be unwise for you to smuggle all the tools you might require in one travel excursion. Far better, I believe, to separate the burden. What's the saying? Don't put all the baskets on your head?"

Enrique rolled his eyes. "It's 'don't put all your eggs in one basket.'"

"I hate eggs. I like my version better," said Hypnos. He pulled out the next golden card. "The next invitation goes to our government official, Claude Faucher. And, don't worry, every guest is required to wear a mask, and as far as I know, I am the only member of the Order who cares to know what you look like."

Séverin took his invitation, pushing down twinges of relief, guilt, and, though he hated it, outrage. All this time and all that he'd done, and the Order had never once looked his way. His guilt was sharper, though. His mother's Algerian bloodline showed only subtly in his features, but otherwise he could hide in plain sight as a Frenchman. Others could not.

"And finally, an invitation for the Russian Baroness Sophia Ossokina."

Zofia looked around the room even though Hypnos held the card out to her. "Me?"

"*Oui.*"

"I'm to be a *Russian* baroness?"

Zofia might be wandering in a cloud when it came to politics, but under Tzar Alezander, Russia had no love for Jews, and *she* had no love for Russia.

"You'll be grand," said Hypnos, tossing the invitation into her lap.

With nothing left in his hands, Hypnos glanced down at them, unsure of what to do next. He clasped them behind his back. It looked painfully childish. In the light, his emerald-studded shoes looked less grand and more gaudy. Everything about him had been so carefully put together. But it didn't matter how well one's clothes fit if the skin didn't.

Not one of them looked at Hypnos. Or thanked him. Séverin understood that. He saw how each invitation flew in the face of each person's self-image. But he also understood how Hypnos had seen the scenario, how he had worked to ensure that each person could access the Château de la Lune without incident.

"When you are who they expect you to be, they never look too closely. If you're furious, let it be fuel," Séverin said, looking each of them in the eye. "Just don't forget that enough power and influence makes anyone impossible to look away from. And then they can't help but see you."

He didn't meet Hypnos's gaze, but he saw the lines of his shoulders relax.

"Now, as for the Château," he said, bringing up the blueprints by mnemo hologram. The others leaned forward eagerly.

Hypnos's jaw dropped. "How'd you get *those*?"

"I have my sources," said Laila, smiling.

"Part of her useful legion of lovesick men," said Séverin quickly. He didn't want to linger on the pining men in Laila's arsenal. "Now, the mansion itself is nothing we haven't seen in the past. Two salons, grand banquet hall, kitchen, dining room, chapel, crypt, and boot room. The matriarch of House Kore commissioned particular Forged staircases that lead to the servants' quarters, which will be challenging."

The Château itself was situated on nearly fifty hectares of land, and surrounded by a collection of smaller buildings. Squares of purple marked the gardens: the winter and spring orchard. A star marked the observatory. A leaf marked the greenhouse—a sprawling building—and a handful of blue circles marked the estate fountains. A red *X* marked the library. Their target for where the Horus Eye was held.

"These are the core features of the estate," said Séverin. "Tristan, the only one of us who has actually been to House Kore's country estate, noted that aspects such as the tent arrangements and entertainment pavilions change by the season. These"—he pointed at the alternating black and red dashes haloing the buildings—"mark the positions of the hired guards. A total of one hundred men and women with rifles. Every eight hours, the House is paying for the guards to be switched out. Twenty incoming. Twenty outgoing. Presumably so that no one stays long enough to commit any unsavory acts."

Enrique whistled. "One hundred guards? I don't mind leaving parties with holes in my memory. My body, however, is a little different. I'm not trying to end up in the catacombs."

"You're assuming the rifles will be loaded," said Séverin.

"They won't be?"

"Only half, according to our man in the police force. Guess what two places they're guarding the most?"

"Library and greenhouse," guessed Zofia.

"Correct."

Those were, after all, the two features that House Kore celebrated most. The entrance to its otherworldly gardens and its extensive collections.

"But we already knew that," said Enrique.

"Also correct," said Séverin. "But the half of the police force assigned to the library are carrying blanks in their rifles."

Enrique lifted an eyebrow. "And the half at the greenhouse?"

"Fully loaded."

"According to the catalogue coin, the Horus Eye is in the library, though," said Laila. "Why guard the greenhouse?"

"A mystery that only access to the greenhouse can solve. Tristan?"

Tristan had been oddly silent until now. When he looked at Séverin, his eyes were rimmed red. He smiled, but it didn't reach his eyes.

"I can handle that," he said. "With the help of my good friend, the ancient and honorable botanist, Mr. Ching."

Enrique groaned. "Ugh. It's *Chang*. Wait, why am I even correcting this?"

"What about the rifles?" asked Hypnos.

Zofia waved her hand. "My designs are superior."

"Also, how are we getting *out*?" asked Enrique.

"I can help with that," said Hypnos. "I can invoke Order rule to ensure the matriarch must place something in her most well-protected vaults. She won't be able to tell what it is, and it can be anything you need. Getaway clothes, et cetera."

"Fine. But what about weapons?" asked Enrique. "We can't just stroll in armed to the teeth."

"True," said Zofia, frowning.

"I don't know how you'll get around that," sighed Hypnos. "First, the matriarch of House Kore has to throw the party to keep up appearances, but she isn't taking any chances on security after the theft of her Ring. Second, the entrances will all have verit stone, so weapons will be useless. Third, the Sphinxes will be present."

At this, Laila grinned.

She winked. "Trust in cake."

Séverin nodded, knowing exactly what Laila had been working on to bypass House Kore's security.

But Hypnos looked horrified. "Have a care for my figure, *ma chère.*"

It was a silly throwaway comment that had nothing to do with Laila's plans. And maybe because of that, it stole a laugh out of Séverin. Behind Hypnos, Tristan looked stricken.

Séverin's flash of humor crumpled.

He'd promised Tristan the Order would not touch them.

Now look at them . . . Hypnos reaching for a cookie from the plate of treats Laila had made. Hypnos grinning with his two asymmetrical dimples, a smile that Séverin remembered since their childhood. Hypnos sitting among them . . . making them laugh even as Séverin wore that oath tattoo like a dagger pressed to the heart.

Hypnos took a bite of cookie and nodded approvingly at Laila. "Good plan! Now we can all—"

Cold washed over Séverin. "There is no 'we.'"

The four members of his team exchanged glances of confusion.

He would have to be clearer. "Hypnos," he said. "You're employing our services for shared gain. You're not one of us."

Slowly, Hypnos put down the rest of the cookie. His gaze shuttered. When he stood, he didn't look at them, choosing instead to brush invisible crumbs from his fine suit.

"Seeing as we're in a business arrangement, I am privy to information about your progress and will continue to inquire about it," he said tightly. "I will see you in three days' time at the Château de la Lune. Oh, and Séverin—you have never been on the inside of an Order festivity, have you?"

Hypnos knew he hadn't. If anything, it was a well-placed jab that *he* was on the inside while Séverin would always be the orphan circling for a way in. There was no point affirming Hypnos with a spoken answer.

"I should warn you now. It will be as if your eyes are seeing for the first time," said Hypnos, smiling slowly. "And, if you fail at the tasks at hand or get caught, the last time too."

PART III

Letter from Matriarch Delphine Desrosiers of House Kore
to her sister, Countess Odette, upon her
initiation to the Order of Babel

Dear sister,

I so look forward to meeting my new nephew when you come to visit! You asked how I feel having been entrusted with our family's lineage, and I confess I feel a mixture of emotions. I feel awe, on one hand, for the sacred responsibility entrusted to me. And yet, wariness . . . Do you remember the House that fell? Its name has been wiped from the records, so it is known only as the Fallen House. Father said it fell near the time when I was born, but he showed me a letter he received from its executed patriarch. He told me it is a reminder that we do not fully understand the depths of that which we protect. It haunts me, sister, for the executed patriarch wrote:

"I cannot help but wonder if for all that we protect the West's Babel Fragment from the public, we are also protecting the public *from* it . . ."

13

ZOFIA

Zofia liked computing numbers aloud. Math calmed her. Distracted her.

"Two hundred twenty-two squared is forty-nine thousand two hundred eighty-four," she muttered, climbing the marble steps.

In her hand, the golden invitation looked like a flame peeled off a fire. She traced the elaborate letters: *Baroness Sophia Ossokina.*

"Seven hundred ninety-one squared is . . ." Zofia frowned. "Six hundred twenty-five thousand, six hundred eighty-one."

Not as fast as she used to be. That numeral had taken her almost fifteen seconds to compute. By now, she should have felt calmer.

She didn't.

In an hour, they would board the train for the Château de la Lune. By midnight, they would be seated at the opening feast. This wouldn't be like acquisitions in the past when impersonating someone meant memorizing a handful of lines. This meant hiding herself in plain sight. It would have been easier if she was still a sum unto herself. But Séverin and the others made her part of an equation. If she failed, she wouldn't fail alone. It was Séverin and Enrique and Laila, and all the weight of their hopes. It was Hela, who was acting governess to their pampered cousins, waiting for freedom. It was the dream she clung to, that small image she replayed over and over . . . the peace of walking down a street and feeling as though she were no different from anyone else.

Such fragile things swaying in the balance.

Zofia's hands were damp as she crossed the final hallway to Laila's room. She had only visited Laila there once. She hadn't liked it. It smelled too strong. And it was so colorful. Not like the kitchens with their uniform shades of cream.

Before she could knock, Laila opened the door, her smile wide as always.

"Ready?" she asked brightly.

A wave of perfume hit her nose. Zofia scrunched her face, stepping back sharply, her shoulders rounding like a cornered animal.

Laila left the door open, disappearing into her room. She did not invite Zofia inside, nor did she wait for an answer. From where Zofia stood, she could only see a sliver of the room. A hint of green silk on the walls. One window draped in linen curtains so the room was not too bright. Near the threshold was a little jade table. And on it . . . a perfectly pale and round cookie.

Zofia took a step forward and swiped the cookie off the plate. She wanted to step back immediately, but then she caught a glance at the vanity table. Laila was habitually messy. Once, Zofia had tried to rearrange the kitchen, but stopped when Laila threatened not to make any more desserts. The last time she had been here, it was a disaster: pots of cosmetics on the floor; jewelry hanging from light fixtures; the bed not only unmade, but also asymmetrically positioned because Laila "liked to wake with the sunshine on her face." It gave Zofia chills.

Now it looked different.

She poked her head through the door. All the cosmetics on the vanity were evenly spaced apart, exactly as Zofia would have done. But there was an exception. One glaringly tall tube in the middle of an otherwise perfectly descending scale. Zofia's fingers twitched to rearrange it.

Zofia glanced to her left. Laila was fiddling with a long, black dress. Just ahead was another pale cookie balancing on a low trunk near Laila's vanity. Warily, Zofia stepped inside. She padded over to the second cookie and promptly ate it. She felt . . . less terrible. But that might have just been the cookie.

"Nearly finished selecting your outfits," said Laila. Now she was sitting cross-legged on the floor, fluffing up the train of the black dress. "You'll need four outfit changes between Friday's midnight feast and Saturday's midnight ball. And of course, you'll have time to tailor them with whatever incendiary devices you deem fit. I think all of that should fit in your traveling wardrobe."

Zofia's traveling wardrobe stood at the back of the room. It was less a travel wardrobe and more of a travel workspace. When completely closed and locked, it resembled tiers of embossed leather suitcases. When opened, it became something else. All the "suitcases" were attached and Forged to hold compartments containing a chemistry set, lock picks, moldings, vials of diatomaceous earth, iron filings, various acids . . . and dresses. A single piece of precious verit stone lay at the bottom, rendering it undetectable to House Kore's sensors.

"You're going to be fine," said Laila softly. "You have the bearing of a baroness. Now you have to believe it."

Laila took the dress off the hanger, bringing it toward Zofia. Zofia recoiled. She thought of the women she had studied in the lobby. They looked terribly uncomfortable. All cinched waists and pinched shoes. Laughing at unfunny things.

"Try it on!" said Laila. "My couturier at the House of Worth made it especially for you. There's a changing screen right—"

Zofia shrugged off her apron, kicked off her shoes, and started shucking off her clothes.

Laila laughed, shaking her head. "Or that."

Zofia knew that weighted sigh.

Her mother used to make that sound all the time whenever she thought Zofia lacked modesty. "Lacking." Another word that did not fit. It was not as if she had some secret stash of modesty and had used it all up. She had learned what was considered modest. Taking off one's clothes in public? Bad. In private? Fine. This was a closed room which meant private. Who cared? Besides, she never liked the feel of too much clothing. And she didn't understand why she had to be self-conscious of her body anyway. It was just a body.

All the same, Zofia missed the sound of her mother's sigh. After their parents died in the house fire, Hela had done her best not to fill their days with grief, but it seeped into the cracks of their life anyway.

"Tell me when you can't breathe," grunted Laila, pulling the stays.

"That. Makes. No. Sense."

"Fashion, my love, just like the universe, owes you neither explanation nor rationale."

Zofia tried to make a sound of protest, but ended up gasping.

"Tight enough!" announced Laila. "Arms up!"

Zofia obeyed. Black silk shimmered around her. She glanced down, noting the perfectly round beads of jet that frothed at the hem like black waves. They were Forged too, and the waves rippled and pulsed down the fabric. Zofia's mind latched onto the pattern.

"Not discovered until 1746 by d'Alembert."

Laila paused in her ministrations. "You lost me."

"Waves!" said Zofia, pointing at the pattern of black beading.

"Classical physics has lots of waves. They're a beautiful hyperbolic partial differential equation. There's sound waves, light waves, water waves—"

The rest of the room fell away while Zofia talked about waves. Her father, a physics professor in Glowno, had taught her all about recognizing the beauty of mathematics. How one could hear it—even the effect of waves—in something as complex as a piece of music. As she spoke, she hardly felt Laila pulling on the corset stays, sliding her feet into shoes, or tugging at her hair.

"—and, lastly, longitudinal and transverse waves," she finished, looking up.

But it was not Laila's face she saw, but her own, staring back at her in the mirror's reflection. She did not look like herself. There was black smudged on her eyes. Red on her mouth and cheeks. An aigrette fastener, with a white plume and gray pearls, pinned to coiled-up hair. She looked like the women in the grand lobby. Zofia reached up to touch the elegant bun on top of her head.

"You look beautiful, Baroness Sophia Ossokina."

Zofia leaned forward, scrutinizing her reflection. She might look like the women in the lobby, but she was nothing like them. If anything, Laila was. Laila, who was as elegant as a wave.

"It should be you," said Zofia.

Laila's eyes widened in the mirror. Her shoulders fell slightly. A pattern of sorrow.

"I can't," she said softly. "You remember what Séverin said. If you dress to the world's expectations, it doesn't look too closely when you steal from it. Though I do wish I didn't have to go as a nautch dancer." Her mouth twisted on that word. "Nautch dancers used to be sacred in temples. Where I'm from, dancing is an expression of the divine."

"Like at the Palais des Rêves?"

Laila snorted. "No. *Not* like at the Palais. It's not even me on that stage. Even if it were, no one deserves a performance of my faith."

Zofia pulled at the tips of her gloves. The right words kept hitting her tongue wrong. Laila looked at her, concern etched on her features. Then she reached out, cupping her chin.

"Oh, Zofia," she said. "Don't be sad. Everyone hides."

ZOFIA WAS THE first to board the train.

Séverin had arranged for himself, Enrique, and Zofia to occupy an entire block of suites. The others took separate transit. Tristan had left for House Kore's country estate yesterday to handle their landscaping, and Laila had gone with Hypnos, lugging with her a marvelous and gigantic cake that House Nyx would transport. They were all due to arrive at the Château de la Lune at the same time.

Once in her train suite, Zofia yanked down the window's velvet drapes. Just looking at the crowded train platform teeming with people and engine steam made her stomach hurt. Her nose stung from the char of burnt street snacks, and she was getting bored of those Forged posters floated along the platform. Each one advertised different parts of the Exposition Universelle, which would open to the public in four days.

Zofia plucked at loose threads on her dress. Across her lap was the walking stick she'd Forged for Enrique. It was hollow, polished ebony, the top of it fashioned like an eagle with outstretched wings. Zofia sighed, wishing she could have brought her chalkboard. There was nothing to do except wait for Séverin or Enrique. Weary, she counted the cut crystals dangling from the chandelier: 112. Next, she counted the golden buttons sewn into the quilted satin seats: 17. Zofia was about to sit on the floor and start counting the carpet tassels when her compartment slid open.

An old man with a hunched back stood there. He was bald, with splotches of brown on his scalp. He paused at the threshold of the compartment and bowed low.

"What do you think? Took nearly three hours to conceal my unearthly beauty."

Zofia blinked. *"Enrique?"*

"At your service—" He started, looking at her. He paused, and Zofia fought the urge to nestle farther into her compartment.

Be like Laila, said a voice in her brain.

Zofia sat up straight, held his gaze, then did what she'd seen Laila do many times when she looked at Séverin—lift one corner of her mouth ever so slightly, but tilt her head down at the same time . . . wait, now she couldn't see anything, oh, and Laila would sometimes lift up one shoulder—

"What on *earth* are you doing?"

"I am imitating patterns of flirtation."

"Wait. You're flirting. With . . . *me?*"

Zofia frowned. Why would he think that? She just said she was imitating the general strategy of others.

"Maybe I have the methodology wrong. I also saw women do this. Better?"

She relaxed her body. Then pretended there was something on her upper lip and licked it off with a slow swipe of her tongue.

Enrique blinked rapidly then shook his head.

Shaking one's head meant no.

Zofia shrugged and waved her hand. "I'll practice later."

"You . . . don't need much," said Enrique, his voice pitched lower than usual. He wasn't looking at her. She must have been terrible.

Enrique took the seat across from her. Because of the hump on his back, he had to lean forward. The sun hit his face, exposing the faintest seam along his cheek that belonged to a Forged mask.

162 ᴂ ROSHANI CHOKSHI

"In the dark, it won't look like a mask at all," said Enrique, gently touching his face. "I checked. And I won't have to go out into the light either. Apparently, my identity as an aging botanist means I'm also nocturnal."

"So are skunks."

"Splendid."

At that moment, the train lurched forward. The walking stick on Zofia's lap began to roll. She grabbed it quickly and thrust it at him.

"Yours."

Enrique reached for it. "Is it a prop for my disguise?"

"It's a bomb."

Enrique nearly dropped it.

"Don't," said Zofia.

"A *bomb*?" he demanded. *"Maybe lead with that?"*

"It's a light bomb."

"That sounds oxymoronic."

"A light bomb in the sense that it releases a lot of light."

"Oh."

Zofia pointed at the middle of the walking stick. "It's hollow. The filler has a pyrotechnic metal-oxidant mix of magnesium and an oxidizer of ammonium perchlorate."

"What the hell does any of that mean?"

"If you hit it against something, it will explode."

"None of that bodes well."

"And it will produce a flash that will cause your enemy to lose their sight for a full minute. Only use it in emergencies."

"I figured, once you said 'bomb.'"

Zofia pointed at the hump on his back that he had strapped on. She had made the prosthetic last week after Séverin had designed a verit-repelling vessel.

"Give me the hump."

Enrique started laughing.

Zofia tilted her head. "Is rapid disintegration because of an industrial acid funny?"

He stopped laughing. Every line of his body went rigid. He leaned forward, arching slightly as if trying to distance his skin from the hump. "Is . . . is that what's inside this?"

Zofia nodded.

"This is the kind of thing someone would like to know before they attach it to their body."

The compartment slid open again. Séverin stepped inside, dressed in the attire of a government official. On his lapel, the golden Marianne emblem shone. A symbol of the Third Republic of France.

"Thank you for letting me know I was strapping *acid* to my back when you gave me the hump."

Séverin started laughing.

Zofia crossed her arms. She hated when she didn't get the joke. She wished Laila were here.

"What's so funny about disintegration?"

"Nothing," said Séverin. He wiped at his eye. "I needed that. Give it to her. She'll show you."

Scowling, Enrique took off his jacket, unstrapped the hump, then handed it to Zofia. Zofia took out one of her hairpins and gently pried it open.

"I need one of those—" started Enrique.

"It's hidden in the heel of your shoe," said Zofia. "Just click them together and it will pop out."

Enrique let out a whistle. "First, the walking stick. Then the acid. Now this. Not to mention what you do with numbers. I like how you think, Zofia."

Zofia paused, the pin still in her hand. No one had ever said that to her before. In fact, the way she thought was usually the thing that got her into trouble in the first place.

She frowned. "You do?"

Enrique smiled. A real smile. She knew it was real because he always smiled like that when Laila snuck him a second helping of cake.

"I do."

I do.

Zofia returned to the hairpin and lock, but something fluttered low in her stomach. The hump opened with a small *pop*, revealing a glass tube on a velvet bed.

"Piranha solution," said Séverin. "It's what you're going to use when you're escorted to the greenhouse as Monsieur Ching—"

"It's *Chang*!"

"*Chang*, my apologies. Point is, you're going to get us started. Tell me what you're doing."

"This isn't my first—"

"Enrique."

"Hmpf." Enrique crossed his arms. "We arrive at Château de la Lune before midnight. You, Zofia, and Hypnos go off and feast and do what rich people do, even though I'm an honored botanist who has traveled over many, *many* oceans and—"

"Enrique."

"—and then we meet in your rooms and do a final rundown. Between the hours of three A.M. and four A.M., me and Tristan meet in the greenhouse. Then we break open the acid container, raise an alarm, and make sure the greenhouse is sectioned off."

Zofia yawned. She already knew this.

"Correct."

"Tristan will get us both gas masks so we can keep breathing after we use Zofia's chemical death trap, and we show up there again by the eighth hour."

"Yes."

"I don't know why you're so fixated on the greenhouse, though. What do you think is there?"

"At the very least, it's a safe zone for keeping the Horus Eye. But I think it's more than that. Why else would all the guards' guns be loaded there and not elsewhere? It's a little too interesting," said Séverin. "But I won't make any guesses until after the midnight feast. Hypnos is bringing something precious, or so he said. Under Order law, he can demand that any object he deems important be immediately removed and taken to the House's most protected vaults."

"The library," said Zofia.

"Exactly. The House Kore matriarch will have no choice but to put away whatever it is. While Hypnos does that, I'm going to be tailing him and the House Kore matriarch." Séverin removed his tin of cloves from his jacket pocket and popped one into his mouth. "Zofia. Tell him how the piranha solution works."

"It's hydrogen chloride and sulfuric acid, so the chemical process is fairly simple—"

"Not that way, Zofia."

She pointed at the glass vial. "I've Forged the glass with levitating titanium. All you have to do is break it, then throw it into the air of the greenhouse. It will fall slowly and spray acid from top to bottom. But once you break it, don't let it touch your skin. Unless you want to disintegrate."

She started laughing.

Séverin and Enrique stared at her.

"See?" she said. "It's like your joke earlier! Disintegrating!"

"Oh, Zofia," sighed Séverin.

He glanced at his watch, his mouth flattening. "I need to take care of some things. I'll see you when we exit. Separate carriages for all of us."

As they approached the Château de la Lune, the silvery mist reminded Zofia of the light that split the metal Sator Square. She remembered how it felt to watch the letters of the Sator Square slide back and forth, how the numbers had aligned perfectly into a repetition of zeroes and ones. Enrique had called mathematics the language of the divine. When she thought about the power of the Horus Eye, her skin crawled. What it could *do* did not seem within human grasp, but that was the thing about numbers. They weren't like people, who could say one thing and do another. They weren't like riddles of social mannerisms or conversations.

Numbers never lied.

14

SÉVERIN

When Séverin turned eleven, Envy and Clotilde gave them up, and Tristan and Séverin moved into the home of their fourth father: Gluttony.

Gluttony was Séverin's favorite father. Gluttony made funny faces and told funnier stories. Gluttony discarded garments after one day of wearing them. He threw cake with mild imperfections onto the streets. Jewels in storefronts disappeared almost as fast as he smiled. Gluttony had nothing to his name but a dusty, aristocratic title and some fallow land in the countryside. But this did not bother him.

"Aristocracy is just a fancy word for thievery, my dear wallets. I am simply embodying what I was innately born with, you see?"

He did not call Séverin and Tristan by name because he preferred to call children as he saw them. But names or no, he fed them regularly, found them tutors and even a Forging affinity specialist for Tristan. Tristan loved Gluttony, for he read him poetry at night and promised that he could reshape the world as he saw fit. Séverin loved Gluttony because he stoked a hunger within him.

The tutors may have fed him languages and history, but Gluttony taught him diction and how to recognize the accent of wealth. He taught him how to level a man with a turn of phrase, how to order dishes and send them back. He taught him about terroir in wine and the godliness of a dish that satisfied all the senses.

"It's not just the fat, acidity, and salt, my dear wallet. It's about devouring it with your eyes, licking flavors with your sight. And you must never underestimate the importance of presentation."

He taught him how to eat and how to hunger for things out of reach and how to steal without ever looking like you lack for something. He taught him all his tricks and all he knew until the day he took his nightly fifty-year-old aged tawny port with a dash of rat poison. At his funeral, Séverin stole a bottle of champagne from Gluttony's favorite restaurant and left it on his grave.

Of all his fathers, he thought of Gluttony the most.

"Half of winning, my dear wallet, is simply looking victorious."

SÉVERIN, ENRIQUE, AND zofia stood before the train doors. Outside the windows lay true night. Not the hesitant midnight of Paris, where gas lamps and trapped steam smudged the stars and threw the city into eternal dusk. Séverin could smell the countryside. Sweet grass and loam, the spring season too young to melt winter out of the air.

Beside Séverin, Enrique touched his false mustache.

"Am I pretty?" asked Enrique, plucking at his fake beard and patting his hands over his jowls, wrinkles, and age spots. "Be honest."

"'Pretty' is a stretch. Let's call you 'striking.' Or 'impossible to look away from.'"

"Oooh. Like the sun?"

"I was thinking more along the lines of a train wreck."

Enrique let out a wounded *hmpf.*

After two years and countless acquisitions, Séverin knew how his team wore their fear. Enrique wore an armor of ready jokes. Zofia wore hers with mechanical calm, her eyes roving down the train compartment one last time, probably looking for something to count. In the silence, he thought he could see all their wants stretched out and warping the air.

Three days.

Three days and they would find and secure the Horus Eye. With it, Hypnos could protect the Babel Fragment's location—maybe even find House Kore's missing Ring—and his inheritance would be restored. Around him, lantern light flashed against the train's stained-glass panes, turning it a shade of molten gold. Séverin's scar twitched. He blinked, and the image of the golden honeybee found in the dead courier's mouth itched at the back of his thoughts.

A loud knock echoed through the compartment door. His cue to leave. Séverin touched his hat, not looking at them as he spoke.

"After midnight," he said.

The two of them split, heading for different doors and different carriages. Their wants cast out in front of them, large as shadows.

HE KNEW HE WAS NEARING House Kore when the road changed.

His father had brought him here when he was seven years old . . . back then, Tante Delphine—as he had known the House Kore matriarch—had taken him horseback riding. "He's like a son to me!" she'd said. "Of course I shall teach him how to ride." She'd held him close, his spine to her chest, her laugh in his ear. "Next summer, we'll practice jumping. How does that sound?"

But there was no next summer. There was nothing after the day she administered the inheritance test and dropped his hands as if he were rotten fruit.

"Tante?" he'd tried, only for her to shudder.

"You may not call me that. Not anymore."

Séverin quickly shoved down the memory. It belonged to another life.

Ahead, the road split into five lanes that looked like rivers. One lane was polished hematite that looked like a ripple of silver. One lane glowed red and looked like twisted candlelight. The other, a pale blue, looked like a sky scraped of clouds. Beside it, a lane of glass appeared dimpled as if invisible rain kept denting its surface. And last, a lane of smoke. Beyond the five lanes disguised as rivers, fog and mist stretched or pinched into fantastical shapes—three-headed dogs yawning and baring translucent teeth, gigantic hands scraping misty nails down the mountain, women wearing ragged tunics, folding in half as they wept and wept and wept. Beyond that . . . well. Séverin could hear the music. The laughter.

"Lethe, Styx, Phlegethon, Cocytus, and Acheron," he recited softly.

The five rivers in the home of Hades.

House Kore had turned its country estate into an opulent underworld. How fitting, he thought, for this place was his hell.

The carriage door opened on the River Styx. Before him stood an elaborate entrance: a glowing, jade skull of what might have been a monster dragged out of myth, with a row of teeth concealing verit stone. The barest prickle of ice ghosted over Séverin's skin. When they'd tested the verit that Enrique and Zofia discovered, it had worked like a charm.

It will work . . . It has to work.

To the left of the verit entrance stood a group of three guards. Jutting over their shoulders, the points of their bayonets caught the flat, green light of the stone.

"Monsieur Faucher, welcome to House Kore's country estate,"

said the first guard. "If you do not mind, may we check you before you enter through the jaws?"

"Into the belly of the beast, as it were."

The first guard let out a nervous laugh. The lightstick in his hand flashed. "May I?"

"Of course."

Séverin forced himself not to flinch as the penlight neared his skin. Every time he saw a penlight, he thought of Wrath, who had used the penlights to double-check there was no sign left of the Forged mind affinity he used on them. He always knew when the Order was planning their monthly check-in because for twelve precious hours, Wrath would not place the Phobus Helmet on him. It was just enough time for traces of mind manipulation to disappear . . . just enough time that no one from the Order ever believed him.

The familiar light flashed over his pupils. Memory conjured the nightmares of the Phobus Helmet behind his eyes, but just as quickly, the light flashed off, and the guard waved him toward the verit jaws.

Behind him, he heard the scrape of carriages. The others had arrived right on time. Including—judging from the low laugh— Hypnos. Which meant Laila was here, pushing that gigantic icebox of cakes and Forged tools, all hidden by a verit stone concealed in the metal.

As Séverin walked through the verit entrance, he held his breath . . . but the small nub of verit in his shoe had done the job. With the entrance behind him, he headed to a dock choked in fog and mist where Zofia and Enrique were already waiting.

"Welcome to the country estate of House Kore," announced a calm, disembodied voice from the air. "Please be advised that all boats may only transport three guests at a time."

A long boat carved of onyx rose out of the water.

Once in the boat, the false Styx flowed beneath them, leading them toward a cave. The cave walls were hewn onyx, gleaming wet and lustrous. Stalactites dripped down from the ceiling. Within minutes, the small boat glided to a stop in front of another elegantly appointed dock, this one shrouded in mist save for the gigantic pair of ebony doors Forged with the snarling, barking faces of the three-headed guard dog of the underworld. Each head barked:

"In—"

"—vi—"

"—tations."

The three heads kept their mouths wide. One by one, Séverin, Zofia, and Enrique placed their invitations onto the black tongues. The dogs' jaws slammed shut, the heads melting into the wood and stone. A moment passed before the doors swung open. Light and sound and music poured out of the doors, blinding Séverin. The three of them stood, and the boat rocked beneath them. Once more, the dog heads appeared, this time a slip of velvet dangled from their teeth.

"Take—"

"—your—"

"—masks."

They did.

Zofia entered first. Then Enrique. Séverin went last. He couldn't undo this step once he took it. Past the greeting vestibule, a floor of polished black marble drank up the light cast down from chandeliers of etched bone and stained glass. It looked like nothing he remembered as a child, and for that he was glad.

Beneath the light, a delicate pattern spiraled across the floor, like that of a nautilus. A network of crystal vines and quartz veins formed the walls, as if they were sumptuously below the ground. Masked guests clad in black and gray and bloodred moved down the halls. An after-echo of a chimed gong lingered in the air. They had arrived moments after the dinner gong had rung. Only the matriarch and a group of her servants were left. She walked toward them, dressed in an oxblood gown and a choker of black diamond thorns. On her face, a gold mask.

He stared at her a second too long, convinced she'd recognize him. She didn't. The last time he'd seen her, he'd seen the blue glow on the Babel Ring—the color that declared he was the rightful heir—ripped from his sight. The last time she'd spoken to him was the last time he had a family.

"Welcome to our Spring Festival," she said in her smoky voice, her smile tight.

She extended one velvet-gloved hand. Séverin noted the glove of her right hand was heavily padded. Her bones had not yet healed after the theft of her Ring. Enrique bent over her proffered hand and Zofia executed a perfect curtsy. The matriarch whispered something to her manservants, who immediately led them to different parts of the mansion.

Last, the matriarch turned to him. Séverin had prepared himself for this, but practice paled to the reality of her. Eleven years ago, that gloved hand had thrown him in the dark and stripped him of his title. And now he had to kiss it. To thank it. Slowly, he held her fingers. His hands shook. The matriarch smiled. She must have thought him overwhelmed, stewing in his insignificance before this opulence. Before *her*. His eyes narrowed. Séverin squeezed the joints of her broken fingers.

"So honored to be here." He pressed his other hand atop hers, watching her breath hitch, her smile turn brittle. "Truly."

To her credit, the matriarch did not snatch back her hand, but let it fall limply to one side. He smiled.

A tiny hurt was better than none.

*   *   *

SÉVERIN MISSED L'EDEN the moment he sat in House Kore's dining room. It was nothing like the bright green of his hotel. Here, the ceiling had been Forged to resemble the inside of a jeweled cave. Hunks of bloodred rubies and cabochons of emerald and jasper cast stained light onto the onyx table below. Candles like flowers seemed to bloom from evenly spaced piles of snow. On the floor, Séverin recognized Tristan's design—vines that sprouted beside guests, blooming to reveal dainty wineglasses, much to their awe and delight.

As anticipated, his insignificance earned him a seat near the exit, far from the matriarch. Many of the people around him had been, or were soon to be, guests of L'Eden. They might have recognized him had they looked close enough. But they didn't.

Near the head of the table, Hypnos slung back his drinks with happy abandon while the smile on the matriarch's face turned tense every time he spoke. Near the middle, Zofia had perfected the picture of aristocracy: bored and beautiful. She kept moving her fingers to a strange rhythm, eyes roving around the dining room. *Counting again.* When she met Séverin's gaze, he raised his glass to her. She did the same, holding it aloft long enough that people saw.

The meals progressed quickly: pan-fried foie gras, leek sprouts in a rich marrow broth, creamy quail eggs served in an edible nest of spun rye bread, and a tender filet of beef. Finally, the pièce de résistance: a single serving of ortolans. The songbirds were a rare delicacy, trapped and drowned in armagnac, a regional cognac, then roasted and eaten whole. The sauce dribbled thickly onto the plate, streaking ruby bloodlike smears onto the pristine white porcelain. At the head of the table, the matriarch led the meal. She took the crimson napkin and placed it over her head. The guests followed suit. As Séverin reached for his, the man beside him laughed softly.

"Do you know what the napkins are for, young man?"

"I confess, I do not. But I am far too enthralled with fashion to deny a trend."

Again, the man laughed. Séverin took a moment to study him. Like everyone else, he wore a black velvet mask across his eyes. There were wrinkles around his mouth, and his hair was streaked gray. What skin Séverin could see was pale and thin, waxen with illness. The man's mustard-colored suit wasn't obviously Forged, so he likely wasn't aristocratic. Something gleamed on the man's lapel, but he turned before Séverin could get a closer look.

"The point of the napkins," said the man, placing the napkin over his head, "is to hide your shame from God for eating such a beautiful creature."

"Is it our shame that we're hiding or our delusions that we can hide at all?"

Séverin caught the edges of the man's grin from beneath his napkin.

"I like you, Monsieur."

Séverin didn't look too closely at the brown flesh on the plate. He knew objectively that it was a delicacy. Gluttony always said he wished for a dish of ortolan to be his last meal. But Séverin had never approved them for L'Eden's menu. It felt wrong.

Cautiously, Séverin bit into the bird. The thin bones snapped between his teeth. His mouth filled with the taste of the bird's flesh, tender and rich with the flavor of figs, hazelnuts, and his own blood as tiny bits of bone cut the inside of his mouth.

He licked his lips, hating that it was delicious.

Brandy followed dessert, and guests were encouraged to move to a separate lounge. As Séverin rose, he saw Hypnos whisper something to the matriarch of House Kore. Her mouth pursed into a thin line, but she nodded and whispered something to her manservant. Hypnos summoned his factotum from the edge of the room. The man carried a black box.

This was it.

Hypnos had invoked Order rule, and now the matriarch would have to safeguard the object by entering the vault. While the guests streamed out of the dining room, Séverin lingered by the door, pretending he had just seen someone he knew. The matriarch walked out the door, Hypnos on her heels. The left corner of Hypnos's mouth turned up as he passed him. A signal to join. Séverin waited, giving them a head start. Then, as he was about to follow, the man in the mustard suit blocked him.

He wheezed as he spoke, sweat shining on his forehead. "A pleasure talking with you, Monsieur . . ."

"Faucher," said Séverin, pushing down his annoyance. "I did not catch your name?"

The man smiled. "Roux-Joubert."

Outside the dining room, the large staircase blocked off the light. The hall broke off into three separate vestibules. Séverin had memorized the layout earlier, including the entrance to the library where the Forged treasures were kept. He kept to the shadows. From the blueprints, he knew where House Kore kept their mnemo bugs and moved against their patterns of surveillance. At the entrance of a hall full of twisting mirrors, Séverin paused. He reached into the sleeves of his jacket, slicing the silk seams that hid a Forged bell designed by Zofia. He rang it twice, and his steps turned silent.

Between the hall of mirrors and the library was a rotunda full of astrological tools, and a wide skylight. The matriarch, Hypnos, and manservants all had their backs to him. Séverin touched the tip of his shoe to one side of the wall, then quietly ducked into one of the recessed niches on the opposite side. A slender, nearly invisible Forged glass thread stretched across the hall, connected to Séverin's shoe. Outside the niche, he heard the others talking:

"—a moment for me to place the box within my vaults."

"Of course," said Hypnos. "I appreciate it, truly. Though, is it not tradition for us to hold our Rings together as proof of agreement? You know me, I am ironclad to tradition. Right down to my blood."

Séverin smirked at Hypnos's self-jab.

"I don't believe that's necessary," she said, her voice slightly higher pitched. "We are old friends, are we not? Old dynasties and all that is left of the Houses of France . . . Surely, as I am doing you a favor at great cost to myself, we might excuse the formality?"

Hypnos's comment was a test. The matriarch must not have disclosed to the Order that the Ring had been stolen. Her words were proof that she too thought the theft had been an inside job.

"Of course," said Hypnos brightly.

"May I speak frankly with you?" asked the matriarch.

Séverin could sense the hesitation in his voice. But Hypnos answered, "Of course. What are old friends for?"

The matriarch took a deep breath. "I know you are aware my Ring has been stolen."

Hypnos feigned a gasp, but the matriarch must have cut him off.

"Don't humiliate me," she snapped. "Every member of my House that I trust has been searching for it . . . I am not asking for you to set your own guards to finding it, but I ask that you keep your wits about you. I know we've had our differences, but this . . . this damage that might be wrought would affect far more than just us."

"I know," said Hypnos solemnly.

"Very well," said the matriarch. "Now if you'll excuse me."

Séverin listened for the sound of something clicking open. The massive doors of the library unlocking. Moments turned into minutes. Hypnos started tapping his foot. After exactly nine minutes and forty-five seconds, the door to the library opened once more.

"Shall we?" asked Hypnos.

The matriarch said nothing. Perhaps she had taken his arm. Séverin heard their footsteps quickly approaching.

He opened his watch, taking out some mirror powder. He smeared it onto his fingers, dragged them down the wall behind him, and touched his clothes. Instantly, his clothing shimmered, turning the same brocade pattern as the wall. The disguise would last for little over a minute—all he needed. Séverin propped up his foot, ready. But the matriarch stopped just outside the thread, as if to catch her breath.

This was not part of the plan.

"It's beautiful, is it not?" asked the matriarch.

"Yes, yes, it is—"

Irritation flickered in Hypnos's voice. Séverin's fingers twitched. He glanced at his watch. He hadn't been able to get another order of mirror powder in time, and that was all that was left. His clothing shimmered. Less than thirty seconds, and it would vanish. They would see him.

Ten seconds left.

The servants walked past.

Four seconds.

Hypnos escorted the matriarch. Séverin willed himself to breathe, not to let his hands get damp and soak up what remained of the mirror powder.

Three seconds.

The matriarch was about to cross the glass thread. Séverin lifted his shoe. Right on time, she tripped. Hypnos caught her before she fell, but her dress had billowed, lifting high enough to reveal her shoes. Séverin looked intently for the one sign that would have proved his theory, and found it: mud.

"Are you quite all right?" asked Hypnos.

Hypnos crushed the glass thread, spinning the matriarch so her back faced Séverin just as the last traces of powder vanished from his fingertips.

WHEN SÉVERIN ENTERED his room at two thirty in the morning, he found his bed occupied.

"Flattered as I am, get out."

Enrique clutched a pillow.

"No. It's deliriously comfortable."

"You know I hate when my pillows get warm."

"Like this?" Enrique started rubbing his face on the pillows and hugging them.

"Ugh. Just take them."

On Enrique's other side, Tristan lay on his back, staring up at the ceiling. He didn't say anything when Séverin entered. Even when Enrique smacked his face with a pillow, he merely groaned and turned on his side. Blue-black circles hollowed his eyes. He looked exhausted, and he kept flexing his hands, sinking his nails into his palms. He got like this sometimes . . . lost in his own head. And then either Séverin or Laila would have to bandage his hands to keep him from breaking his own skin. Laila moved to Tristan's side, carefully flattening his palms. When it came to Tristan, all of them acted a little differently. Laila coddled, Enrique teased, Zofia instructed. Séverin protected.

Ever since their fight in his office, he hadn't been able to apologize. Everything left unsaid gathered and crackled in the air between them.

Footsteps echoed outside the door. Laila held a finger to her lips, glowering at the room.

The door opened. In glided Zofia. The first thing she did was kick off her heels. With the bed and chair taken, Zofia plopped on the floor.

"How come we had to hide out in the laundry to get in here, and she just strolled into your bedroom?" asked Enrique.

Zofia started rubbing her feet. "We're having an affair."

"It's clearly very torrid," said Séverin.

Zofia grunted.

To Enrique's bewildered expression, he added, "We raised a glass of wine to each other across a dinner table and threw in a lingering look. Voilà. Easiest way to go somewhere unnoticed is to tell everyone where you're going. Now. What do you have for me?"

The door creaked open. All five of them leapt up, hands immediately reaching for knives or fire tape—

Hypnos.

He grinned in the doorway and waved.

"*Why* are you here?" asked Séverin.

"It's my plan too. I helped downstairs . . ."

"You're drawing unwanted attention—"

"On the contrary, I'm affirming your penchant for eccentric proclivities. A rumor I judiciously spread at dinner. And as you just said, the easiest way to go somewhere unnoticed is to tell everyone where you're going. If I left now, and someone saw, it might draw, what was it you said? Oh." Hypnos beamed. "Unwanted attention."

Séverin scowled.

"Fine. Just sit and don't talk or touch anything. Or anyone."

Hypnos sat on the floor beside Zofia.

Laila spoke first. "I confirmed that the only guards with loaded weapons are the ones surrounding the terrariums and hothouse garden wall. I also confirmed they're being regularly transferred. Every eight hours, twenty guards are switched out."

"And the outdoor grounds facing the library?" asked Séverin.

"All blanks in their shotguns."

Enrique and Zofia looked shocked.

"How did you figure that out without firing their rifles?"

"I rummaged through their artillery and wardrobe room. It's right next to the maids' quarters," said Laila.

"But why does the matriarch have her best men guarding her *flowers*?" demanded Enrique. "Does that mean she doesn't care about the objects at all? Maybe the Horus Eye was moved somewhere else—"

"No," said Séverin. "It's here. On these grounds."

"Then why wouldn't she be hiding it in the library where she said it was?"

"It is in a library," said Séverin, thinking of the mud. "She has another one."

"In the greenhouse?" asked Enrique flatly.

"No," said Séverin, grinning. "Beneath it."

"How do you figure that?"

"I saw the mud on her shoes. Besides, you've seen the blueprints. The dimensions of the library are too small for the size of the rumored collection. She has to be accessing the real library underground. That must be why the guns are guarding the gardens. Which is where our next stage comes into play. Enrique and Tristan, are you all set to release the piranha solution?"

They nodded.

"Good. The solution will take about eight hours to work. Laila. What happened with the icebox?"

But Laila didn't have a chance to answer.

"It's all set to be debuted as a surprise to the matriarch for tomorrow evening!" said Hypnos. "I've even arranged for it to be wheeled into the office where the matriarch keeps the physical key to the vault. She can't access it using her Ring anymore, so it's not Forged. Laila's nautch dancer costume has already been hidden under the cushion of the chaise lounge. Once she has the key, she can exit the office dressed as a nautch dancer who presumably got lost. Then, Séverin, the ever helpful gentleman, assists in finding her way while she slips him the key. He gives the key to Zofia, who makes a copy. At dinner, Zofia gives the key to me, and I return it to the study. Me and Séverin go through the House access, while the others go through the greenhouse and we meet in the library vault!"

"Hypnos?"

"Yes?"

"Are you Laila?"

Hypnos hung his head. ". . . No."

"Laila?"

Laila pointed at Hypnos. "What he said."

"Are we clear?" asked Séverin. "Laila gets the key. Zofia makes the copy. Me and Hypnos take the library route, meet you in the underground vault. We get the Horus Eye, and we're out no later than an hour after midnight when our transport comes."

Hypnos, Enrique, Zofia, and Laila nodded as one. Tristan, who had silently been curled up on the bed, was the last to nod.

Enrique left first, escaping down the laundry chute armed with Forged bells that muffled his sounds. Next went Hypnos and Zofia, their heads bent close. Which left Tristan and Laila.

"Stay a moment, Laila?" asked Séverin.

She frowned, but nodded.

Tristan shuffled to him. Séverin shoved his hands in his pockets and looked down at him.

"Listen—" started Tristan.

At the same time Séverin said, "I forgive you."

Tristan paused. "I'm not asking for forgiveness." He swallowed hard, then lifted his gaze. His gray eyes looked bleak. Sleepless. "I don't trust Hypnos. I don't trust the Order."

Séverin groaned. "Not this again."

"I'm serious this time. I just . . . I have a feeling and I need you to listen to me—"

"*Tristan.*" Séverin gripped his shoulders. "You're my family, and I will always protect you. But I won't hear this."

"But—"

"Another word and I will find a way to get you off this acquisition and send you straight back to L'Eden. Is that what you want?"

Tristan's face burned red. Without another word, he stalked out of the room. Séverin stared at the closed door.

"You shouldn't dismiss him like that," said Laila.

He closed his eyes, exhaustion dragging through his bones. "He didn't give me much of a choice."

"There's always a choice, *Majnun.*"

Madman. That name meant only for him. On her lips, it sounded like a talisman. Something that could protect him. Chew up the dark.

He caught her scent as she came closer. Sugar and rosewater. Had she packed that vial of perfume with her? Swiped it down her throat and across her wrists as the train pulled to a stop? Those mysteries were for some other man to uncover. Not him. And then he remembered that he hadn't been alone in a bedroom with her since that night . . .

"*Majnun?*" she asked, tilting her head.

"I've never asked why you call me that," he said, fumbling for something to say.

"That's a secret you haven't earned."

She smiled. Her mouth was red. Not by rouge, but by blood-rush. On her full lower lip, he could see the faint indents of teethmarks. They held him in thrall.

"What will it take?" he asked. His voice was roughened by lack of sleep, and it came out gruffer than he meant it to.

"What will you offer?" teased Laila.

Her hair had come undone from its chignon. He liked her hair best like this: a little feral. A little soft. Wholly her. Wisps of black silk curled around her long neck. She tucked a strand behind her ear, and Séverin wished a strong wind would blow through the room if only so that she'd do it again.

"What do you want, Laila?" he asked. "A feather from a legendary bird? Magic apple?"

"Please," said Laila. "I hate repeats in my wardrobe."

Séverin paused. Wardrobe. The word brought him back to himself. That's what he wanted to talk to her about. The wardrobe was how she'd accessed the guard uniforms.

"Laila, in the guards' wardrobes, I think you could only read the uniforms for the incoming guards. Not the outgoing. I need you to double-check," he said. "We can't have any surprises."

For a second, it looked as if she wanted to say something else. But in the end, she only nodded. "Of course. I'll go right now."

After Laila left, Séverin didn't move from his spot on the wall. He thought of the matriarch's gloved hands, the way he could have crumpled her broken fingers if he wanted to. Even if Enrique hadn't ruined his pillows, Séverin couldn't bring himself to climb into House Kore's bed. What if he'd slept in it once as a child and simply couldn't remember? He fell asleep where he sat, slumped with his head against the wall. And as he did, he dreamt of the snap of ortolan bones and teethmarks on Laila's bloodred mouth.

15

ENRIQUE

Enrique held his walking stick just slightly off the ground, careful not to drop the light bomb on anything. The greenhouse was on the other side of the lawns. Revelers swirled around him. Women in velvet bodices with wolf masks. Men in tailored suits with wings affixed to their shoulders. Around him, waiters and waitresses wearing fox and rabbit masks weaved through the crowd, carrying platters of a steaming drink that granted kaleidoscopic visions. As they walked, some of the waiters changed height, abruptly shooting up into the air on the Forged stilts concealed in their heels and pouring bottles of champagne in slender streams into the laughing, open mouths of guests. Platters of food drifted through the crowd without anyone to carry them. On their surfaces, Enrique spied hollowed pomegranates and pale cakes, oysters on the half shell served on dripping panes of ice.

Unlike the Order of Babel auction, hardly anyone here had darker skin or a lilting accent. And yet, he recognized the decoration. Lovely and monstrous things plucked from tales that grew on the other side of the world. There were Forged dragons out of myths from the Orient, Sirenas with heavy-lidded eyes, *bhuts* with backwards feet. And though they were not all his tales, he saw himself in them: pushed to the corners of the dark. He was just like them. As solid as smoke and just as powerless.

He didn't even look like himself. Or like any man from China that he'd met in the past. He was hiding in a caricature, and it let him pass without comment. Maybe it was an ugly thing to hide behind, but that was why he was here . . . so that he wouldn't have to hide any longer.

The greenhouse loomed ahead. In the dimness, he could make out the strange symbols carved around it. Examples of sacred geometry. Even the footpath beneath him was covered in distinct symbols, tessellated stars inside circles, fractals of stars hidden in the trees. The very eaves of House Kore's mansions spoke of ancient symbology with their repeated nautilus coils.

Enrique was nearly at the greenhouse when he felt someone grab his shoulder. He yelped, almost jumping in the air. He spun around to see Laila hiding behind a tree.

"Glad I caught you," she breathed. Laila slipped something in his hand. "I found these in the guards' uniforms, but only for the ones guarding the greenhouse."

When Enrique opened his hand, all he saw was a candied violet.

"I don't have much of a sweet tooth at the moment, but—"

"Turning down food?" Laila went wide-eyed. "You *must* be nervous. This isn't candy. It's an antidote."

"For what?"

"For the venom," she said, frowning. "Didn't Tristan tell you?"

Faintly, he heard the snap of something underfoot. Laila turned her head sharply and groaned. "I have to go. I think I'm being followed."

Enrique scowled. Laila dealt with this all the time at the Palais, but he thought she'd at least be free of it here for a change.

"Idiot drunks. You have a blade?"

"Multiple."

Laila touched his cheek once, then melted into the night.

The air around the greenhouse sweltered. No revelers came this far, which made sense. Fifty guards with shining bayonets was not exactly what he would call inviting. The greenhouse itself was a massive, imposing structure. Frosted glass, with clear roofs. That earthen, wet smell seeped into the air around it. Along the walls, he saw a familiar pattern. The same one that had been on the gilded mirror of the Palais Garnier: a six-pointed star, or hexagram, inter- twined with crescent moons and pointed thorns and a great snake biting its own tail. Symbols of all four original Houses. There was something about that star that jolted him, though. The star was the sign of the Fallen House, the House that had dared not to protect the Babel Fragment, but *use* it, all because they thought God wanted them to. The hairs on the back of Enrique's neck prickled.

A guard stopped him outside the greenhouse. "And you are?"

Enrique considered a retort, then looked at the bayonet and thought better of it. Bullet or no, that was still a sharp and pointy end.

"Greetings," he said, roughening his voice. He held out his access card. "I am here to assist Monsieur Tristan Maréchal."

"At this hour?"

"Does beauty follow the hours of the day?" asked Enrique, lifting his voice. "Do the heavens simply say 'no, thank you' because it's a bit after midnight? I think *not*! My occupation knows no time. I don't even know what time it is. Or where I am. Who am I? Who are *you*—"

The guard raised his hands. "Yes, yes, very well, I will accept the card. But know that I am under orders only to answer to Monsieur

Maréchal. Not *you*. And the matriarch has requested that no one spend longer than ten minutes in the greenhouse, save for Monsieur Maréchal."

Only ten minutes? Séverin hadn't seemed to know that. The guard held open the door. Enrique walked inside. Tristan was waiting for him, elbow-deep in some hideous bloom.

"Corpse flower!" said Tristan excitedly.

He looked happy enough, but there was that strange blue tinge around his eyes that spoke of sleeplessness. Nightmares, even.

"Not my favorite term of endearment, I must admit."

"No, *this* is a corpse flower."

"Is that why it smells like death?"

"Taxonomy is rarely creative with its names," said Tristan, standing.

The lights of the greenhouse were far brighter than those in Séverin's room. For the first time, Enrique noticed how sallow Tristan's skin looked. Usually, his round cheeks were bright with color, always propped up in a grin. But though he was cheerful enough when he saw Enrique, he had the look of someone depleted.

"Are you well?" Enrique asked. He carefully laid down the walking stick. He wouldn't need it here.

Tristan swallowed. "Well enough. Or, at least, I will be soon."

Soon. When they had found the Horus Eye. When Séverin was named heir of House Vanth, and the world itself might be within reach.

Enrique squeezed his shoulder. "Just one day more."

Tristan nodded.

"What is this place?" asked Enrique, taking off his jacket.

"A poison garden—I made it myself. No spiders allowed, though. Stupid House Kore rules. Goliath would hate it."

Enrique paused, halfway through unstrapping the prosthetic hump. He glanced at his jacket on the floor, where the candied violet lay in his breast pocket. An antidote for poison. It hadn't surprised him that Laila had known, but why hadn't Tristan? He would have planned for it.

Around him, the greenhouse looked far too peaceful to be poisonous, but he recognized venom all around him. Wolfsbane and oleander hung from the glass and steel ceiling. Widow's ivy and black laurel grew in abundance. Larkspur the color of a late-evening sky flourished in the corners, and deadly Pied Piper flutes so pale they looked like orphaned clouds spiraled toward the sky as if they were trying to find the way back home. Enrique positioned his feet more narrowly in the path. Poisonous flowers and piranha solution was a terrible idea to mix together.

"It's beautiful, isn't it?"

Enrique shuddered. "So beautiful I'm driven by envy to destroy it immediately."

Tristan smacked his arm.

Using the key hidden in the heel of his shoe, Enrique unclasped the metal hump. He tossed Tristan a pair of small pliers that Zofia had packed, and a pair of needles. They set to work unlocking the base, peeling back the metal shelling and protective layers until the box holding the piranha solution broke free. Enrique and Tristan took out their foldable gas masks at the same time. Tristan poured some water in the lenses, and Enrique checked for any cracks. None. A single crack, and he'd lose an eye and get poisoned. Or worse.

Enrique held a small hammer in his hand, fingers trembling. If they did this wrong, he'd probably burn off his hands. Then again, he might not even notice because his vision would be the first thing to disappear. Tristan glanced at the door.

One chip.

Two.

The casing broke.

Enrique tossed it high in the air. He and Tristan had about four minutes before they were in any trouble.

"Let's go—" he started, but right then he heard Tristan start gasping.

Tristan grabbed his fingers, nearly crushing them in his grip. His face went from pale to tinged with blue.

A knock sounded at the door.

"What's going on in there?" demanded one of the guards.

"Nothing!" shouted Enrique.

"We are only allowed to accept orders from Monsieur Maréchal. Sir, is everything all right?"

Tristan tugged at his goggles. Then brushed something off his jacket. Petals. Frantically, he pointed at the poisonous Pied Piper flutes. Enrique had once read that the moment one touched the petals, they released oils that could seep into one's skin. Tristan must have accidentally brushed against the flower.

"Monsieur?" demanded the guard. "Do we need to come in? We will take your silence in the affirmative if so."

Tristan's face turned blue.

"He cannot speak because he got too close to a poisonous plant!" shouted Enrique, thinking fast. "If he speaks, he will inhale a toxic fume and . . . and die!"

Outside, the guards began to shuffle back and forth, arguing with one another. Enrique reached out, shaking Tristan.

"Just croak out a word!"

Tristan's eyes turned watery, limpid. Drooping. And then he slumped over.

"No no no no no," muttered Enrique, throwing the tools into the metal hump and fixing it sloppily to his shoulders.

"We're coming in!" shouted the guard.

The doors cracked open a sliver. For a moment, Enrique wondered whether he should just smash the rest of the piranha casing, but he couldn't do that without risking severe burns. Several guards peered through, rifles at the ready.

One of the guards in the back whispered, "Wasn't his hump on the other side?"

But the second one shoved him to the ground. "Monsieur Maréchal! He's been injured."

The other guards were clamoring to get inside. Shouts crowded the air.

"What's that?" asked the first guard, staring at the piranha solution falling slowly from the ceiling.

A heavy mist began to descend on the plants. Plumes of sulfur unraveled into the air.

"I told you that if you let him speak, he would inhale too much toxic fumes. Now look at him. You should leave before you risk serious injury."

"Wait a minute, that solution is eating into the ground—"

"Is it? That's curious. I can't remember it doing that."

The first guard narrowed his eyes. "What happened to your accent?"

"Accent?" repeated Enrique, trying to slip back into his disguise.

The first guard stepped forward. "Your mustache is coming off."

"Toxic fumes. You know. Mustaches are always the first to go."

The first guard cocked his rifle.

"No! Don't do that. Totally unnecessary. There's just something wrong, perhaps, with your eyes."

Enrique lunged for his walking stick. He couldn't have the deaths—or disintegration—of these guards on his conscience.

"There's nothing wrong with our sight, old man."

"Are you sure?" asked Enrique.

He lifted the walking stick high above his head, then slammed it down, flinging his arm across his eyes. A white light burst from the wood, followed by an ear-shattering sound. Afterward he saw two guards lying facedown and unconscious. Enrique stepped over them gingerly, leaned down and whispered, "How are your eyes now?"

But the loud shouts outside the door snapped his victory in half. The piranha solution spread quickly over the terrarium floor, stopping just short of the guards. A blue sheen crept over Tristan's skin. Enrique patted down his jacket, his fingers shaking until he found what he was looking for: the candied violet.

Enrique shoved the candy into Tristan's mouth, pinching his nose and forcing him to swallow. He had two unconscious guards, a thoroughly ruined mustache, and outside, the door shook from the sounds of the security team. Hope was a thin thread inside him, but Enrique reached for it anyway. It was all he had left.

16

LAILA

Laila fumbled in the dark, her breaths shallow and quick.

If you panic, you'll lose even more.

The taste of metal filled her mouth. She winced. The sharp lock pick had scraped the inside of her cheek. She spat it into her hand, then started feeling around for the hinges.

In a way, this was her fault. Three weeks ago, she'd ruined a cake. Séverin, perhaps trying to console her, or more likely get her out of his study, had said, "It's just cake. It's not like there's anything valuable inside it."

"Oh really?" she had demanded.

She'd baked his favorite snake seal into a fruit tart, and left it on his desk with a note: *You're wrong.*

So who was she to blame when Séverin had slid the note she'd written across her kitchen counter, told her about his plan, and grinningly said, "Prove it."

And here she was.

Trapped in a cake.

Sneaking herself into the base had been easy once the whole thing had been assembled. The final task—locking it shut—required Zofia.

Her fingers fumbled until they finally found the clasp. Sweat slicked her palms. The metal needles were wet with spit and kept sliding from her hands. All she could hear was her heartbeat. And then the pick notched into something. She stilled. Listening. Listening for the slight gasp of metal, the muffled snick of things aligning . . .

Pop.

The hinges came undone, clanging to the bottom of the base. Laila grinned.

And then she pushed. But the compartment wouldn't budge. She pushed harder, but there was something blocking her. Wedging the small metal piece between the edges, Laila pried. A gap opened, just enough for her to glimpse what was blocking her exit.

The servant who had wheeled her in must have placed the base of the cake against the bookshelf.

She was trapped.

Outside, the clock chimed eight in the evening. The sound of the nautch dancers' anklet bells chimed through the halls. Her heart lurched as she heard the familiar straining of a sitar in the distance, the musicians tuning their instruments for the dancers. Any second now, and Séverin would be standing outside, waiting to help the lost dancer while she slipped him the key.

But there was no way she could get out in time.

Laila threw her weight against the metal board, but nothing gave way. Another bell chimed. Shoes shuffling outside the door. If Séverin had been waiting for her to slip him the key, he'd left by now.

Folded onto her side in the dark, Laila reached down to remove her slippers. The right slid off. Then the left. She shoved one slipper into the other, twisting them through the gap in the cake base. Her arms shook as she pushed all her weight into those interlocked shoes braced against the bookcase.

At first, nothing happened. The cart didn't budge. And then an inch gave way. More light slid through the base. Laila pushed again, scraping open her elbow.

The wheels of the cart squeaked, rolling backward and giving *just* enough room for Laila to slide out one leg, then the next, before she finally uncrumpled onto the carpet. She let out a breath.

Laila checked the hollow base once more for any strands of her hair or scraps of cloth before making quick work of the locks. On the other side of the door, the sounds of the party reached her. She cast her gaze to the chaise cushion in the corner of the room where Hypnos had hidden her costume.

Laila pushed any tendrils of fear out of her thoughts. She would figure out how to get House Kore's vault key to Séverin later. First, she needed the key itself.

The matriarch's office looked like a sprawling, elaborate honeycomb. Hundreds of interlocking golden hexagons formed the walls, filled with books or plants or etchings of her late husband. The ceiling was a ribbon of gold shot through with crimson, a portrait of still flames. Far from the windows stood a nephrite desk, like Séverin's. The bookcase behind it stretched from floor to ceiling, filled with as many strange objects as actual books: hollow skulls full of dried flowers, animal prints trapped in slick amber, jars upon jars of preserved things. If she wanted to, Laila could trail her fingers across the desk's surface, reading for the image of a key that might have touched it. But instinct stopped her.

On the floor, Laila found a small paper clip and tossed it onto the jade surface. The desk glowed red in warning. Her mouth tightened.

Like Séverin's, the desk was Forged.

She turned to the honeycomb walls, and threw another metal clip. The bookcase did not change color. Not Forged. But that didn't help her get the key from the desk. If it was Forged to remember her touch—or hold her hand hostage—she needed something to counteract it . . .

Like a Forged creature, Séverin's desk had a somno that turned off the warning mechanism. It was just a matter of finding out how to trigger it.

Sometimes people hid a plaster mold of their hands—Séverin hid one behind his bookcase—or there might be a piece of wax with a thumbprint concealed by a window. Chances were, the matriarch had something like that too. All she had to do was find it.

Hauling out the leather armchair, Laila balanced on the seat, letting her fingers trail down the wall of the bookcase. Energy flowed out of her veins. A headache crimped the edges of her vision.

As Laila searched the bookcase, her mind picked up images of contracts, receipts, love letters, and then she caught it: a thumbprint encased in amber. It was hidden in the pages of a book of love poems. She searched for the spine on the shelves, opened the book, and found it. A large amber coin. Laila muttered a quick prayer, then tossed it onto the desk. The red glow faded.

Grinning, Laila jumped down from the armchair. The noises outside the office grew louder. More urgent. There was no use trailing her fingers down the desk, trying to figure out where it kept the key. Forged things never answered to her readings. Laila reached for drawers and cabinets, rifling through papers as fast as she could.

Hundreds of keys filled the drawer inside the left cabinet. Laila plunged her hand through the metals, casting out her senses. The keys weren't Forged, so the images flowed through her. Empty bedrooms. Halls of senate. Order of Babel auctions. And then . . . a dark vault, a ceiling full of painted stars, statue busts, and hundreds upon hundreds of rows filled with strange objects. Her eyes flew open.

The key to the subterranean library beneath the greenhouse.

Laila pulled the key and ran to the chaise lounge near the door. She lifted the cushion and found the nautch costume beneath wrapped in cloth. Quickly, Laila undid the wrappings, but she hadn't anticipated what she would feel the moment she saw the outfits of her youth. The way her soul staggered, folding in on itself at the memories. The raw silk blouse the color of parrot plumage and edged in red. The heavy *gunghroo* bells and *jimmikki* earrings that looked so like her mother's. Laila raised the costume to her nose, inhaling deeply. It even smelled of India. That mix of camphor, dye, and sandalwood incense. Looking at the outfit, a cold fury spread through her. She heard her mother's voice curling through her thoughts: *You want to feel real, my daughter? Then dance. Dance and you will know your truth.* Laila had thrown her soul into dance, giving her body to the rhythmic invocations, the sharp movements that stamped out whole stories with nothing but her limbs. It could be sensuous. But it was always sacred. It was, her mother used to say, *proof* that she had a soul. That she was real.

But to people in the audience . . . it was entertainment designed to be something else.

What had Hypnos called it?

Titillating.

Laila changed her outfit, undoing her braided crown of hair so that it fell thickly down her back. She shoved her House Nyx maid costume into the cushions, hid the amber thumbprint coin back in the book of love poems, and secured the key in her blouse.

The third bell struck.

At the far end of the room, no light appeared at the crack of the door. If Séverin had been waiting for her, he wasn't anymore. The nautch dancers had probably lined up at the stage. She would only draw attention to herself if she ran out now. Laila pulled the silk scarf over her head and slipped outside into the empty hall. By now, the rest of the guests were already seated inside the vast amphitheater. All she had to do was get to the theater.

The guard yawned when he saw her.

"You're late," he said, bored. "The rest of your party is already assembling."

"I was asked to perform a solo piece," she said, crossing her arms.

The man groaned, flipping through the pages of the schedule. "If you can go on now, then—"

"Lead the way."

She scanned the crowd . . . somewhere, Séverin was there.

The guard directed her to the musicians to choose a song. Laila recognized their instruments, and an ache dug into her ribs. The double-sided drum, the flute and veena and bright cymbals.

"Which piece shall we play?" asked the veena musician.

She peered through the curtain at the crowd. Men in suits. Women in dresses. Glasses in their hand. No sense of the story she would have tried to tell with her body. No language with which to decipher the devotion of her dance.

She would not perform her faith to them.

"Jatiswaram," she said. "But increase the tempo."

One of the musicians raised an eyebrow. "It's already fast."

She narrowed her eyes. "You think I don't know that?"

Jatiswaram was the most technical piece, the distillation of music and movement. A piece where she could still perform and set her heart aside.

A few minutes later, an announcer cleared his throat. The stage fell dark. "Presenting a nautch dancer—"

Laila tuned out the presenter. She was not a nautch dancer. She was a *bharatnatyam* performer.

As she walked, two parts of herself merged together. She had done this walk, worn these clothes. The man who had brought her to France as a performer had thrown away the original costume sewn by her mother. Laila was supposed to wear a customized *salwar kameez*, not this ridiculous thing that left her midriff and chest on display. Her hair was supposed to be strung with flowers, with a preserved jasmine from her mother's first performance. Not unbound, and brushing her waist. She looked at her hands, her chest pinching. Her hands felt naked without henna.

A low murmur of approval chased through the crowd when she walked on the stage. When she performed at the Palais, her favorite moment was stepping onto the stage before the lights rose: the adrenaline fizzing in her veins, the darkness of the theater that made her feel as if she'd only just burst into existence. But here, she felt like something held beneath glass. Trapped. Between her breasts, the key to the library felt like a chip of ice. She scanned the crowd. Before each seat was a basket of rose petals to be thrown upon the performer at the conclusion of their entertainment.

The music keyed up.

Even before the light fell on her, she *felt* Séverin before she saw him. A space of cold in a warm room. The lights cast his eyes into shadow. All she could see were his long legs stretched in front of him, his chin on his palm like a bored emperor. She knew that pose. Memory stole her breath. She thought back to that evening . . . on her birthday . . . when she'd felt buzzed with a daring she almost never indulged. She'd cornered him in his study, more intoxicated by the way he'd looked at her than she had been from any champagne. Séverin hadn't gotten her a birthday present, and so she demanded a kiss that turned into something more . . .

Laila could feel the moment he became aware of her on the stage. The sudden stiffness of his body.

He'd never seen her dance before . . . and instantly something changed within her. It was how she felt before she always performed, as if her blood now *glittered*.

She needed him to look closely. If he didn't, he wouldn't get the key on time. But she *wanted* him to look closely too.

Perhaps it was just her fate to be haunted by a night never acknowledged. But that didn't mean she had to suffer alone. Maybe it was cruel of her, but her mother's voice rang in her ears anyway: *Don't capture their hearts. Steal their imagination. It's far more useful.*

And so she did. She sank into the beginning pose, hip jutted, chin tilted to expose the long line of her throat. The music started. She tapped her heels against the floor. The movements so precise it was as if she'd sewn her shadow to the beat.

Tha thai tum tha.

Séverin might have looked like liquid elegance as he lounged in the crowd, but she knew him. Every muscle was strung taut. Rigid. Beneath that posture was something prowling and hungry. She couldn't see his eyes, but she could feel them tracking her. His mouth had gone from a controlled smile to a slack line.

Laila felt a burst of satisfaction.

I won't be haunted alone.

She dragged her hand across her chest. Séverin shifted in his seat. Laila hooked her pinky into the gap of the key. She stamped her foot, glancing at the floor as she concealed the key in a row of bangles. As she sank lower, she smiled to herself.

There was another power in her. A power that sat low and thick in her blood and consciousness. A way to move through a world that tried to keep her to the sidelines.

Steal their imagination.

She hovered on her heels, knees bent in nritta while the pleated emerald of her skirt fanned out. The music grew faster. The rhythm turned urgent.

She flicked her gaze toward the concealed glass key in her hand. Séverin's head moved. Just barely. But she knew he understood. He reached into the basket. Around him, the others did the same.

The music turned faster, building into a climax. Finally, Laila looked directly at him and nearly fumbled. Séverin looked undone. His gaze lit up her skin. She forced herself into the movement, flicking up her fingers . . . a signal.

Séverin tossed the blossoms into the air. The other guests, seeing him do so, followed his movements. A shower of petals rained down, catching in her lashes like snow, brushing silkily against her lips. Laila extended her arm in a flourishing final arc of movement, tossing the key.

It sailed through the air.

Séverin caught it between his palms. A clap. Laila could picture his eyes perfectly, even though she couldn't see them. His dusk-colored gaze darkening, fixed on her. Laila knew she should look at the other audience members, but she couldn't look anywhere but at him, and she didn't want him looking at anyone but her.

As the room burst into applause, the man sitting behind Séverin caught her gaze. He wore a mustard-colored suit, his body entirely too still. Laila shuddered as she walked off the stage. He'd hunched over Séverin like a wraith . . . or a beast on the verge of attack.

17

ZOFIA

Zofia checked the clock. Séverin was late. Already, there was less than an hour before she had to get ready for the ball, and if she didn't have a cast molding of the key, there was no point. It was too bad the matriarch didn't use a handprint to open her vaults . . . she could have used her refined Streak of Sia formula. Then again, she didn't have any of the critical ingredients. They were all back in her laboratory at L'Eden.

Zofia forced herself to sit in one of the corners of the room. It wouldn't help to pace. Half of any acquisition was just the long, *long* stretches of waiting. But all that waiting only brought them closer to their goal.

One more day.

One more day, and then all of this would be behind them.

By midnight, they would be in the vault. With the location of the Horus Eye secured, it was just a matter of taking the object off a shelf. It was a small thing, but with large consequences. Once the

Eye was acquired, everything could change . . . she could pay off her debts and her sister could finally start medical school. When Séverin became a patriarch, he'd have the strings of the world in his hand, and he might even be able to reverse her expulsion from university.

When her parents were still alive, they said that fear grew in places unlit by knowledge. Perhaps if she had more knowledge, then she would not know fear. She could become a scientist or a professor . . . someone who spent her life rooting out the dark unknown with the light of knowledge. She could be like her parents. Like her sister. She could walk down a street or through a crowd. She wouldn't know that tight, breath-pulling sensation of drowning, all because someone had asked about her day and she didn't know how to answer.

Knowledge would make her brave.

And more than anything, Zofia wanted to be brave.

But she was learning how to fit. Or, at least, imitate it. On the other side of the room, her wardrobe faced her. A sable gown hung off the frame. Her outfit for the evening's ball. It'd taken hours to figure out how to make herself ready without Laila, but she'd finally managed.

Just then, Séverin walked inside and quickly shut the door behind him.

Zofia stood. "You're late."

Séverin did not look like himself. He looked out of breath. Wild-eyed. Frustrated. Laila was supposed to give him the key. Had something gone wrong? Panic struck Zofia.

"Is Laila harmed?"

At her name, spots of color appeared on Séverin's face.

"Your face is red."

Séverin cleared his throat. "I was walking fast. And no, Laila looks fine. I mean, she is fine. Never mind. I'm fine. Everything is—"

"Fine?"

"Yes," said Séverin. He handed her the key. "She had to use a different method of delivery to get the key to me."

That was an easy explanation. Though it did not explain why Séverin looked so strange. Zofia took the key and went straight to the fireplace where a chunk of zinc had been melted. From her wardrobe, she pulled out a cast molding from the bottom cabinet of her drawer, prepping the molding.

Séverin leaned against the wall, dragging his hand down his face. "The piranha solution worked."

Zofia was not surprised the solution worked. She had made it, after all. And she was nothing if not exact.

Séverin continued, "As far as I can tell, the greenhouse has been marked off limits. Officially, the story is spreading that one of the guards broke the windows, and the mixture of Forged smoke with the venomous plants led to the fumes."

By now, Tristan and Enrique should be hiding in the expansive gardens. By the ninth hour, their invitations would expire and they would exit the premises in full view of the House Kore security team, who would officially take them off the guest list. Then, Séverin's hired transport would drop them off at one of the unsecured entrances on House Kore's property, and they would meet at the greenhouse.

Zofia pressed the key into the wax.

"As you planned."

"Mm." Séverin reached for the door handle, then paused. He looked as if he wanted to ask her something, then thought better of it. "Top of the hour. Then it all starts."

ZOFIA CHANGED INTO her evening gown. In her velvet wristlet lay a box of matches and two keys: one real and one copy marked by a slight dent. A mask made of frost-colored swan feathers concealed the top half of her face, disappearing into her hair. A gauzy net of fragile, silver thread spangled her dress. All she had to do was tear the cloth, and she had a purifying air filter for herself and Laila to walk through the greenhouse fumes unharmed.

Downstairs, the hall had transformed. Mirrors lined the walls, turning the room into endless space. Down the halls stalked a translucent gryphon, its beaked head brushing the ceiling. Ladies and gentlemen tittered and laughed when one of the illusion-creature's heads snapped at them. In a corner of the room, a glorious cake that could only have been made by Laila glistened, showing eight planets that tilted and swayed gently.

Zofia concentrated on the floor. A glint of a silver spiral caught her eye. She paused, mentally tracing the line . . . she recognized that pattern of spirals. She hadn't noticed it until now, though. The black marble of the floor had concealed it until the chandelier light snagged on the floor's silver veins. The pattern was almost nautilus-like. Precise. Mathematical. It reminded her of the golden spiral, a logarithmic spiral based on the golden ratio. Two quantities were said to be in the golden ratio if their ratio was equal to the ratio of their sum to the larger of the two quantities. Her father had explained it to her in terms of a golden rectangle . . .

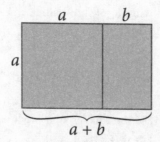

$$\frac{a+b}{a} = \frac{a}{b} \equiv \varphi.$$

The numerical representation was called *phi*, approximately 1.618. Her father had showed her how one could find evidence of the golden ratio all throughout nature: in the spiral of a nautilus shell or the round hearts of sunflowers and pine cones . . . but she had never seen it in someone's home. Zofia blinked, scanning the room as if she'd never seen it until now. Everywhere she looked she saw examples of the golden ratio. In the entrances. The shape of windows. The equation was all over. Numbers were never accidental. There was intention here. But to what purpose, Zofia could not fathom. She moved closer to one of the arches, but a man in a mustard-colored suit blocked her.

"I envy the man who would be the recipient of such an intense gaze. I simply had to know what it might feel like, and so I came to introduce myself."

Zofia quickly ran through what she'd observed other women do. When a man they had not been introduced to spoke to them, they offered their hand. So Zofia did. The man took her hand, lifting it to his lips.

"I don't know you."

He laughed. He wore a mask of small, dragonfly wings. Zofia had never seen a man so pale in her life. A sickly sheen covered his skin.

"Roux-Joubert," he said, releasing her hand. "May I have the first dance?"

She'd hardly noticed the couples swirling around her. Once she'd fixated on the equation of the floor, nothing else seemed to matter.

"I—"

"Please," said the man, though his voice did not sound coaxing. "I insist."

Zofia wanted to say no. But she did not know how fine ladies did such a thing. They would laugh or simper, say something behind a fan. Until now, most of the guests had let her be, knowing she only kept company with Monsieur Faucher, the high-ranking government official. Séverin had been her shelter. If she said no, they would notice she was acting strangely. Zofia felt a flash of panic, as if someone had just locked her into a room. Would the rest of the crowd notice? Would they circle them? Demand to know what was so wrong with her that she couldn't stomach a single dance?

"So many people are watching, Baroness," said the man. A slight sneer curled his pale mouth. "You would not want to embarrass me, would you?"

Zofia quickly shook her head no, and Roux-Joubert pulled her into the dance. The man's hands were somehow freezing and damp with sweat. She tried to pull back, but the man, for all that he looked weak and ill, held tight.

"Where is it that you're from in Russia, Baroness?"

"Poltava."

"Stunning place, I am sure."

Roux-Joubert spun her, and she took the moment to look around the room, hunting for any sign of Hypnos. He should have found her by now. The music picked up, a frantic cadence building in her ears, joining with the erratic pulse of her blood. The floor beneath Zofia felt like cut ice. She couldn't dance well even when she wasn't stressed, and her movements felt less like gliding and more like struggling for purchase. He spun her again, his hand tight on hers, until a warm voice cut through the orchestra's straining—

"Baroness."

Hypnos.

He stood behind Roux-Joubert, one brown hand on the man's mustard-colored suit.

"May I?"

Roux-Joubert's mouth pressed into a tight line.

"Of course," he said, kissing Zofia's hand once more. She shuddered against the icy touch. "I do hope to see you again . . . Baroness."

Hypnos swept her up in the dance. His body was warm and his brown hands dry and hot beneath hers.

"You look like a marvel, *ma chère*," he said.

Other couples moved around them in dizzying spirals. Hypnos maneuvered them to the center of the room, far from the watchful gaze of the matriarch. Zofia moved closer, angling her reticule so he could slip out the original key. She felt his fingers against her wrist, then, just as quickly, they were gone. Hypnos smiled, then whispered in her ear, "I do mean it. You are stunning. Though I did not quite like the look of your friend."

"He's not my friend."

"Am *I* your friend?"

Zofia was not sure what to say to that. Hypnos had threatened to imprison them . . . which did not seem like a thing a friend should do. But he was other things too. Funny. He treated her no differently than anyone else. Zofia looked at his face. She knew that pattern of features: widened eyes, arched eyebrow, forced grin. Hopefulness. Vulnerability, even.

"What would friendship entail?"

"Well, on Wednesdays, we sacrifice a cat to Satan."

Zofia nearly tripped.

"I'm teasing, Zofia."

Her cheeks turned hot. "I don't particularly like jokes."

Hypnos gave her a spin. "Well, in the future, I'll be more aware of that. Friends?"

The dance drew to an end. Near the entrance of the staircases, the clocks chimed the eleventh hour. Zofia weighed his words before dipping her chin. "Friends."

At the conclusion of the dance, bits of the crowd broke off. Many of the invitations to House Kore expired an hour after midnight, and some who wished to leave early began to make their way to the entrance. Zofia stood in the greeting line, scanning the crowd as she waited to say her goodbyes. Somewhere in the crowd, Séverin was plotting the route to the library. Hypnos was sneaking the key back into the office. Tristan, Enrique, and Laila would be waiting for her in the greenhouse. But her mind kept returning to the man who had asked her to dance. Roux-Joubert. His touch reminded her of something . . . but what?

"Did you enjoy your time with us, Baroness?"

The matriarch stood in front of her, a slightly concerned expression on her face. Zofia startled, fumbling for the right words. She had practiced this exchange, but the floors and the man had thrown her off.

"Yes," she said stiltedly. "And . . . and I like your floor."

The matriarch blinked. "What?"

Oh no. Zofia felt that familiar tightness again . . . that sensation of reaching for a step on a staircase that wasn't there. She'd said the wrong thing. She wanted to take it back, but then she remembered Laila's advice. To perform. To own whatever illusion one cast of themselves. So she straightened her back. As elegantly as she could, she gestured to the floor.

"The logarithmic spiral based on the golden ratio," she said. "One of nature's favorite equations."

"Ah!" The matriarch clapped her hands. "You have a fine eye, Baroness. My late husband imbued everything in our home with meaning. Though it is a shame I could not keep the grounds beyond the greenhouse open . . . that is truly a sight."

Zofia felt the barest stab of guilt. It was her fault, after all, that the greenhouse couldn't be accessed.

"A shame," Zofia agreed.

"More so for my landscape artist and his colleague, though," whispered the matriarch. "Pity what happened to them."

The ebony doors opened. Damp fog rolled in through the entrance, sitting low on the hematite river. Zofia knew she was supposed to move, but she couldn't. One of the matriarch's servants leaned in to whisper something in her ear. Zofia felt all the air stolen from her lungs.

She gulped down a breath, the stays of her corset straining. "What?"

The next person in the greeting line tapped their foot. The din of the music played louder. A servant appeared at her elbow.

"What did you say about the landscape artist and his colleague?"

Applause thundered through the hall, drowning out her words. Fire-breathing acrobats had just appeared, leaping down from the ceiling like bolts of lightning. Sulfur stung the air.

"I do hope to see you at the Winter Conclave in Russia!" called the matriarch over the din.

The person behind Zofia kicked at her ankles, and she tripped forward just as the servant took her—rather forcefully—by the elbow. A gift favor was placed in her hand. The matriarch turned to the next person in line.

It happened so fast.

The doors opening, then closing. The boat rising up to meet her and gliding over the silent, Forged water. There was no one else in the boat with her.

Pity what happened to them.

She felt as though someone had grabbed her thoughts in a fist and squeezed. What happened to Enrique and Tristan?

From the dock, Zofia walked past the verit stone structure and handed in her invitation. The guards bid her a good evening. She waited for a moment before Séverin's marked transport drove up to where she stood.

"Straight for two kilometers, stop at the second row of sycamores," she said to the driver.

Whatever had happened to Enrique and Tristan, she would find out soon enough.

Night blurred outside the carriage window as the driver took strange twists and turns about the property, driving them through secure roads with no other transports in sight. Zofia thought about the matriarch's last words and about the others until the carriage slowed to a stop.

"Clear on all sides," said the driver. "Go now."

Zofia stepped out of the carriage. According to the stolen House Kore blueprints, there was an old Tezcat door situated between two unmarked trees that would grant her access directly to the estate gardens.

As with any Tezcat door, Zofia assumed she'd be looking for an object that looked like a mirror. But when she walked to the trees, there was nothing there. Just two sycamores side by side, and all around, the ever-hungry dark. Zofia turned around. The road stretched out on either side. Beyond it loomed a shadowed meadow. She was entirely alone with no path in sight. Maybe it was too dark, she thought. Zofia reached for a particular pendant on her necklace. Phosphorous was one of the only materials that could reveal a Tezcat. She snapped the phosphorous pendant between her fingers, and it emitted a pale, blue light. Zofia looked up, blinded by the sudden radiance.

A shadowy figure was standing inches from her.

A scream caught in her throat. She stumbled backward, reaching for the pendants at her necklace, when she noticed the shadowy figure before her did the same. Zofia went still. Slowly, her eyes adjusted. The light in her hand was not alone. It was twinned by the light in front of her, held in the hands of the shadowy figure.

Zofia was looking at her reflection.

She was looking at herself.

Fascinating, thought Zofia. The technology of how to make a Tezcat door that did not look like a mirror had been lost when the Fallen House had, well, *fallen*. But now she was looking at proof of what they had been capable of making . . . not just pieces which could camouflage doors, but actual portals that pinched together the distance between one place and another.

Zofia reached forward, her fingertips trembling. At her touch, the Tezcat door yielded, bending and absorbing her hand. On the other side, she could feel the same air, the brush of ivy on her skin. Zofia dropped the phosphorous pendant on the ground, crushing it beneath her heel.

On the other side, Zofia found herself in the gardens. Without any guests, the gardens looked eerie. The music of the instruments sounded haunted and lopsided. Broken glasses littered the ground. Gold peeled off the tree bark. Just beyond the trees, Zofia could make out the abandoned greenhouse. A noxious smell rose over the place, and her heart shuddered. Zofia double-checked for any guards, but Séverin's predictions held true: They'd been stationed to the garden perimeters in the event of inhaling any toxic fumes.

And then, a hand on her shoulder.

Zofia jumped.

"Shh, it's just me."

Laila.

Zofia turned to face her and then frowned. "What happened to your costume?"

She was wearing half a blouse and a skirt that sat too low on her hips. It looked far more comfortable than what the other women were wearing.

Laila laughed. "This *is* my costume."

"Oh."

But then, the corners of Laila's lips turned downward. "I heard something when I was hiding. I think Enrique and Tristan might've gotten hurt."

Laila's lower lip trembled. She started walking toward the greenhouse, and Zofia followed.

"Everyone in the servants' hall was talking about what happened at the gardens. There were two men covered in bandages. And . . . and one of them was wearing Enrique's costume."

Zofia's breath knotted inside her. But there was nothing she could do or say. Either they were inside the greenhouse and safe.

Or not.

She tore the outer sheath of her dress, then ripped it in half. One for Laila, one for her. They wrapped it like a veil around their heads as they got closer to the greenhouse. Even with the veil, the fumes still stung her eyes.

The doors were open. Laila looked at her, hope written all over her face.

But Zofia was not certain. An open door didn't mean Enrique and Tristan had done that to welcome them. The matriarch might have ordered the doors opened to allow the greenhouse fumes to dissipate.

Zofia clenched her hands. *Focus*. She started counting what she saw around her. Two doors. Fourteen bars of iron. One moon. Seven linden trees. Four gargoyles hanging off the greenhouse roof, their cheeks pulled in menacing smiles. Six statues beneath six darkening oaks, stone eyes unblinking.

Three steps until the door.

Then two.

Laila went in first, knife out. Inside, the windows were silhouetted with light.

Everything here was burnt down to the ground. They shuffled slowly over the floor of the greenhouse, watching for some slip or dent, some indication of a *door* when someone coughed in the shadows. Laila darted forward, throwing someone from the shadows onto the floor of the greenhouse. It was a police officer with a scarf tied around his head. Laila snarled, raising her knife.

"You . . ." she said. "You must have been one of the men that hurt them. I'm not sorry for what I'll do next."

The police officer waved his arms, his speech panicked and muffled. Zofia felt the thrum of vengeance, the ache of it raw in her heart. They'd hurt Tristan and Enrique. Her . . . her *friends*.

Then the guard tore open a small gap on his towel. "*—waitdontkillme!*"

The man braced his elbows on his knees, his face red. He looked up at them, a faint grin on his face.

Enrique.

"Though I'm delighted you'd avenge me, there's really no need."

18

ENRIQUE

Enrique whistled, and Tristan stepped out of the shadows. Tristan looked at Zofia, who was dressed up in silk and velvet, then Laila, who was dressed in . . . less. Tristan blushed furiously, and Enrique threw the towel at his face.

"You're such an infant."

Tristan scowled, but the expression faded, replaced once more with that pinched look of terror. He'd looked like that ever since the violet candy had released him from the grips of poison. Not that Enrique blamed him. Any brush with death would have left him shaking. Tristan was never at ease outside of L'Eden, and this acquisition in particular had him spooked. While they'd been waiting to return to the greenhouse, Tristan had fidgeted nonstop, nearly destroying an entire rose bush because he kept tearing out the petals.

"I thought you were *dead*!" said Laila, running to them and crushing them in a hug.

Zofia did not move, but she tugged at the edges of her dress.

Enrique saw her glance at him, then back down at the ground, her eyes shining. She didn't have to run to them. He knew.

"That violet candy saved us," said Enrique. "Tristan got poisoned somehow. I think the mask was faulty and let in some of the fumes."

Zofia looked up. "It wasn't."

"I know they're your inventions, but there could always be a mistake," he said. "I hate to be the one to inform you of this, Zofia, but you *are* human."

"Then why do you call me 'phoenix?'"

Enrique couldn't argue with that.

Beside him, Tristan's shoulders slumped.

"So what happened?" asked Laila.

"I think the guards must've gotten a whiff of the fumes, and so they bolted to raise the alarm," said Enrique. "Two guards ended up unconscious and blistered, so we switched out our clothes and have been hiding until an hour ago."

Laila touched his face. "I'm glad you're both safe. Now let's get to the vault. It's nearly midnight. Did you find the door?"

"Yes," said Enrique. "Except we couldn't come in until the fumes had gone down enough that we could walk inside with only the towels. I wasn't going to take a chance with the masks after Tristan got hurt."

Tristan swept aside the plant detritus, revealing a flat, metal door.

"Everyone ready?" asked Enrique. "Minus Tristan, of course."

Tristan was usually fine with playing lookout when it came to acquisitions, but as he opened the flat door, his hands trembled.

"Be careful," said Tristan.

"Just think about what we'll do when we finish," said Laila lightly. "Hot cocoa?"

"Oooh . . . and cake," added Enrique.

Even Zofia smiled.

"Can Goliath join too?" asked Tristan.

The three of them groaned.

As the door opened, a lightless staircase spiraled out below, yawning into the darkness.

"Honestly," muttered Enrique as he hoisted himself down. "Why can't Goliath be on a leash? He's nearly the size of a cat."

"I can hear you," scolded Tristan.

"*Good*. Start thinking about tarantula leashes."

The staircase twisted off to the side and seemed to stretch out for nearly a kilometer. After a while Enrique looked up to see how far they'd gone and whether they could still see Tristan. It was too dark. And it didn't help that the staircase was wet. As he walked, his shoes slipped out from underneath him.

Laila shivered. "It's *freezing* here!"

Enrique agreed through chattering teeth.

They were approaching the bottom of the staircase. Enrique had expected the staircase to lead down to the grand library, but this place looked more like a gigantic atrium. Wet cave walls glistened in a rough, oval shape. Roots dangled above them. When he breathed, a slick, mineral scent coated his throat. At the center of the atrium, a round pedestal protruded like a boulder. Three metal sticks poked out of it. They reminded him of levers, though he couldn't imagine why they would be there. He couldn't even tell if that's what they were. There was no light, save for the small flare Zofia held out, which barely cast more than a puddle of light around them.

"Where's the library?" asked Laila.

Zofia waved the flare. It spread across the cave walls, then disappeared.

"A tunnel," breathed Enrique. "Maybe it's down there?"

He was still looking down the tunnel when he took his foot off the staircase and touched the ground. Hardly a second had passed before he felt it . . . a tremor in the earth. Enrique took a step back, until both feet were firmly planted on the last step.

"Do you feel that?" he asked, his voice suddenly high.

"Do you *see* that?" retorted Zofia.

She pointed up ahead. In the tunnel, a torch flared. The light of its fire caught on the outlines of an amber door.

"That must be the entrance to the library," breathed Laila. A huge grin broke out on her face, and she leapt down the last two steps.

"Wait, Laila—"

There was something strange about the floor. As if it had *read* their presence. But he couldn't stop Laila in time. She landed with both feet on the ground. That same tremor returned, shaking the stairs this time. Enrique tripped, his arms flailing as he landed on the hard earth. Zofia fell beside him, her flare rolling across the ground.

Light—far too grand to belong to Zofia's pendant flare—streamed across the floor.

Slowly, Enrique lifted his gaze. The tunnel was gradually brightening. Where there had been one torch, now there were hundreds. And they weren't alone. That tremor belonged to something . . . a great stone ball rolling through the tunnel. With each rotation, it caught fire from the torches, blazing hot and illuminating the stone atrium. Enrique scanned the rest of the atrium. A grooved, spiral path wrapped around the room, winding to the center.

Enrique pushed himself off the ground. "On second thought, I'm completely fine with the dark and cold."

Laila grabbed his and Zofia's wrists, tugging them to the other side of the atrium.

"If we just move out of its trajectory, then it can crash into the wall, and we run to the tunnel and get to the door," she said. "It's not as if the floor is going to—"

The floor snapped.

Enrique's shoe snagged on a crack in the ground that had not been there a moment ago. The crack spidered across the stone floor, as if it were nothing more than a pane of ice. Enrique fell hard. He scuttled backward, only for his hand to slip.

Inches from his fingers was a plummeting drop. An icy river flowed beneath the ground, rushing dark and roaring. The floor plan must have been Forged to fit together like a puzzle piece, framed above a river so that any trespassers would either die by fire or by water. The only good thing that could be said about the fireball moving closer was that at least he could see what was around him.

"We're moving!" called Zofia.

She was sprawled on a narrow slab of rock not too far from him. Laila stood on the other side, lightly balancing on a piece of the floor no bigger than a dining plate. Far in the tunnel, the fireball gained speed, following a corkscrew pattern that would soon catch up to them.

Enrique glanced at the river. His position had changed. He watched as the room slowly turned. All of the shattered pieces, including the ones they perched on, drifted in a slow rotation around the pedestal in the center of the room.

"All defensive Forged things legally have a somno!" he shouted over the din of the river and the fireball. "We just have to find it! That center pedestal must be the key. Laila, you're getting to the pedestal first. Be ready to tell us what it says!"

Laila nodded. She leapt again, gracefully springing from one slab of rock to another, closing the distance to the pedestal.

Enrique cast about the room. This was not like the auction's holding room. There was no onyx bear with its teeth caught around someone's wrist. No stone body to skim his hands over and find the divots and markings of a release. He was too far away from the cave walls to see if they had any writing. And the rock slabs, as far as he could tell, were nothing but rock.

"Chin up!" called Zofia.

"This really isn't the time for tired motivational phrases!"

"*Enrique.* There's writing up there."

Enrique looked up. On their way down the steps, he hadn't noticed anything above them but roots dangling from the ceiling. With the light from the fireball, he could see more of it, and there was a pattern hacked into the roots . . . a precise arrangement of letters. The rock he stood on spun faster, and Enrique had to pivot on his heels, trying to suss out the words—

E? Mut? Surg?

He squinted.

He looked back at Zofia, thinking she might be able to help, but she was sitting cross-legged on the rock, as comfortable as if she were inside L'Eden's stargazing room. Her gaze was unfocused as she looked around her, her fingers slowly tracing a spiral in the air. Ahead, Laila was getting close to the pedestal.

Enrique's rock moved faster, spinning around the room as it drew ever closer to the pedestal. He craned his neck up, catching the letters as fast as he could, until he saw them fully.

EADEM MUTATA RESURGO

"What does it say?" called Zofia.

The language was Latin. And the phrase somewhat familiar, though he could not tell where he had heard it . . .

"It means . . . *although changed, I arise the same.*"

"Zofia! Enrique!" shouted Laila. She waved her hands, pointing at the pedestal. "There's thirteen levers with numbers on them! They seem attached to some kind of . . . dial? I think? I . . . I can't see it anymore, but you're going to be coming up on it soon!"

Levers.

That was a somewhat heartening fact because it meant it could be controlled.

"If the levers have dials, what if that means there's a numerical pattern here?" asked Zofia.

"Like a key," said Enrique, nodding.

If they put the right numbers into the levers, the fireball should stop and the atrium would right itself.

"Although changed, I arise the same," he whispered to himself before risking a glance at the ball of fire. It had doubled in size and now resembled a flaming carriage that would hit them within minutes.

Zofia dragged her finger through the dirt as she sketched something.

"Think, think," muttered Enrique, stamping his feet.

He'd noticed the layout of House Kore's gardens . . . the pieces of sacred geometry hanging from the trees, even the great spiral on the marble floor of its entrance room. But it didn't help him with the pattern. Arising out of the same thing? But remaining the same? Did it mean something that *built* upon itself—

"A spiral," said Zofia.

"What?"

"We're moving in a spiral."

He blinked. "Obviously, Zofia—"

"But we're moving in a *specific* spiral," she continued. "It matches the pattern of House Kore's floor. And the spiral fits with the riddle! *Although changed, I arise the same*. It's a logarithmic spiral. That means the angle between the tangent and the radius vector is going to be the same throughout *all* points of the spiral—"

His head was spinning, and not just because his square of floor seemed to be moving faster.

"But it would have to be something repeating," said Zofia, talking fast now. "Something that has ancient roots too. A sequence of some kind—"

Enrique followed the spiral. Even the tremor in the ground seemed to move to a particular *rhythm*. Rhythm that might have been found in nature, or poetry. They were closing in on the levers now. He could see the jutting pedesetal.

Up ahead, Laila was crouched on a slab of stone, her body angled toward the pedestal with the thirteen levers.

"Don't jump!" called Zofia.

Just then, the rocks lurched.

Laila teetered. Her rock tipped, canting sharply to one side. She rolled down the slab, just narrowly catching onto the edges. Her feet dangled over the icy river. A livid tremor ran through the atrium, as more light splashed onto the cave walls. The fireball picked up speed, and with it . . . momentum. From where Enrique stood, the fireball verged on leaving the tunnel behind and pummeling straight through the atrium.

"I'm fine!" called Laila, heaving herself onto the slab.

But her rock had been dragged into the churn of the spiral . . . and if they couldn't stop the fireball in time, it would roll into the atrium, and Laila would be caught directly in its path.

"The riddles are a pattern; the pattern is a key," murmured Enrique aloud. Every breath he sucked into his lungs felt stolen. The room grew hotter, and sweat ran down his back. "Thirteen levers. A riddle. A key. Moving floor."

Slowly, an image shifted together in his head. There was only one historical sequence he could think of that fit the pattern.

"The Fibonacci sequence," he said, his head pounding.

Enrique only remembered the sequence because he had tried to impress a lovely Italian girl in his linguistics class. Her fiancé had not been amused, but he hadn't forgotten the numbers . . .

"Zero, one, one, two, three, five, eight, thirteen, twenty-one—" said Zofia rapidly. "Each number is formed by adding the two previous numbers. It fits the logarithm riddle."

The pedestal swam into view, thirteen ancient levers and just enough space for two people to stand.

"It's getting closer!" shouted Laila.

Enrique's head shot up. The fireball moved closer and closer, and directly in its path: Laila.

She had hoisted herself just far enough onto the piece of rock so she wouldn't fall, but she was stuck.

"We've got the code!" said Enrique. "Hold on!"

When the pedestal with the levers came closer, Enrique nodded at Zofia.

"On my count, we leap," he said. "One, two, *three*—"

He jumped. For a moment, everything was weightless. The ground fell away, and a mouth of darkness opened beneath him. He strained, reaching forward, his breath gathered in a tight knot until his fingers hit the rocky ledge. Zofia stumbled beside him. Wrenching himself upright, he grabbed her by the arm. Zofia clung to him as the ground pulled back from their feet, plunging into the icy river below.

"Is this a bad time to mention I only know the Fibonacci sequence up until the number twenty-one?"

"I've got the pattern," said Zofia. "I don't need anything else. Start on the far left."

On each of the thirteen levers was a row for three numbers. He felt around the top of the lever for the small toggles, letting him push the numbers into view. For the first:

0 0 0

Then on the second:

0 0 1
0 0 1
0 0 2

On and on—three, five, eight, thirteen—until he hit the eighth lever, spinning the toggles atop it until the numbers read: 021.

In the distance, Laila screamed. The ball of fire behind her roared livid as the dawn. She turned her face from the heat.

"Wait!" called Zofia.

Tears streamed down her face as her pale hands darted down the levers.

"Thirty-four, fifty-five, eighty-nine, one hundred forty-four," she said. "Two hundred thirty-three!"

Immediately, the ground lurched to a stop. Zofia stumbled, nearly falling over the edge until Enrique caught her. The ball of fire halted. Slowly, it moved backward, heat leeching from the room. Laila had scrambled to another rock once it got close enough. Around them, the floor stitched back together. Grinding sounds of rock and steel whined until the floor was, once more, *whole*.

Zofia's heartbeat thumped wildly against his chest. He could feel her skin, feverish and damp, through his linen tunic. The moment stillness returned to the atrium, she sprang from him, running to check on Laila. Enrique slid onto the floor, rubbing his temples.

When he looked up, both girls were staring down at him.

Laila grinned widely. *"My hero."*

She kissed him on the cheek, and Enrique beamed. He wasn't quite like the heroes he'd dreamed of becoming. He hadn't saved a country from oppression or rescued anyone on his white horse . . . but he still felt rather impressive. He turned to Zofia, about to congratulate her, when she crossed her arms over her chest.

"I'm not going to kiss you like Laila did."

Black ash streaked Zofia's arms and the tops of her cheekbones. It made her eyes look like blue fire, her hair a wisp of candlelight. The farthest thing from his mind was her mouth on his, but when she said it, he couldn't help but look at her lips. They were red as candy. Abruptly, Enrique pinched the bridge of his nose. He must have hit his head because the strangest thoughts kept darting through it.

"I was only going to say that we make a good team, phoenix."

A corner of her mouth quirked up. "I know."

And that was true. Her math, his history. They were, he thought, a bit like an equation where the sum was greater than its parts.

Ahead of them, the tunnel had been plunged into semidarkness. Still, he caught the glint of an amber door, the true entrance to House Kore's library. It was a bit of a walk, but adrenaline raced through him, staving off any twinge of sore muscles and aching bones.

"What was the code for the pedestal?" asked Laila.

Zofia cleared her throat. "Zero, one, one, two—"

"It was the Fibonacci sequence," cut in Enrique.

If Zofia got started on numbers, they'd be here all day.

"Praise Fibonacci," said Laila, pressing her palms together.

"Well, Fibonacci can have some credit, but not all. He was brilliant, of course. But did you know—"

Zofia groaned. Enrique ignored her.

"—the Fibonacci sequence itself appears as early as the sixth century in Sanskrit treatises by the Hindu scholar Pingala. Isn't that fascinating?"

Laila made a face. "So who do we thank?"

"*Me*, naturally."

The tunnel drew to a close, and the three of them stood before the amber entrance to the library. By now, the adrenaline coursing through his veins had faded. Exhaustion crept into the edges of him.

Enrique braced himself for what lay on the other side of the door. The Horus Eye. As Zofia reached for the doorknob, Enrique wondered if it was possible for time itself to pause and expand, as if it were a vast pupil dilating to let in the light. Because he felt as if he could sense each second passing against his skin. As if every dream of his hung low and ripe as fruit for the plucking. If Marcelo Ponce and the rest of the Ilustrados group could see him now, then maybe they'd see him as more than a clever *mestizo* boy, but a hero in the making. Like Dr. Rizal. Like someone who illuminated the dark.

The door swung open.

Warm air gusted over them, and his skin shivered. Once in the dark, and now on the threshold of light, his eyes adjusted.

Across the room, a second door swung open, and two shadows stretched across the floor.

19

SÉVERIN

S *éverin's fifth father was a man he called Pride.*

Pride had married into the Order of Babel. His late wife had been the second-born daughter of a patriarch. Though born wealthy, an investment in far-off salt mines had left them penniless, forcing them to sell their possessions. Bitterness grew like a crust over Pride's home. Pride showed them the collection catalogues of the Order, whispering which items had once belonged to him and his wife. He showed Séverin and Tristan how to take back what belonged to you. How to make a harness that let one slip down roofs and into windows, how to pay off the right guards, how to step with a light foot.

He never used the word "steal."

"Take what the world owes you by any means necessary," Pride had said. "The world has a shit memory. It will never pay its debts unless you force its hand."

SÉVERIN THOUGHT OF Pride now as he met Hypnos at the entrance to the subterranean library. Hypnos slipped the copied key into the amber door. The door swung open, revealing a long trail of steps that descended into the dark. Séverin took a moment to bow his head, the closest he would come to prayer. He whispered the words Pride spoke every time he went to repossess an object: "I've come to collect my dues."

Before him, the whole of the subterranean library sprawled. The room was the size of an amphitheater, and though the floor and ceiling was packed earth, a luminous underwater shine danced across the top. A small moat surrounded the library. It looked to be a built-in coolant system to regulate the temperature of the treasure room. Forged lanterns and thuribles floated down the neat aisles that sprang out of the ground. Objects loomed into sight: caryatids and drinking horns, broken crowns and canopic jars, mirrors that floated in midair, and an azure jug that poured a continuous stream of wine.

"Oh no, shiny things," moaned Hypnos, clapping his hands to his heart. "My weakness."

Though the library could bring kings to their knees, it wasn't the sight Séverin craved. He walked down the aisle, toward the back end of the wall where an amber door identical to the one they had walked through now swung open. Three figures stepped into the room. Enrique, with a stunned expression on his face. Zofia, bewildered and clutching her necklace. And then Laila . . . streaked with what looked like ash. Laila in that same dancing costume he hadn't been able to shake from his thoughts ever since she'd thrown him the key.

Hypnos waved hello, and then he leaned down to whisper in Séverin's ear, "You're staring."

Séverin looked abruptly away. He reached into his jacket for the silver tin of cloves and popped one into his mouth.

"Any trouble?" he asked.

"Yes," said Zofia, matter-of-fact. "There was a fireball and the ground broke, and we thought Tristan and Enrique were dead."

"*What?*"

"Tristan is fine," soothed Laila. "He's upstairs now, standing guard."

"Did you say fur ball?" asked Hypnos. "Like a puppy? How endearing."

"She said *fireball*."

"Oh. That is decidedly less endearing."

Séverin clapped his hands together, and everyone fell silent.

"The convoy for the next guard shift comes in an hour. We've got five empty seats on that convoy to get us out of here, so let's get moving. We know the Horus Eye is in the west quadrant and eighth hall, but there could always be unexpected surprises. Zofia?"

Zofia tore the second layer of her dress. At her touch, it broke into five strips that fell to the ground. She wrapped one strip around her hands, and it molded instantly to their shape, turning into a pair of translucent gloves.

"Forged rubber," she said, raising her palms. "That way no object can detect a human touch."

Laila shuddered. "Yes, let's not get stuck to anything just by touching it."

"And let's not leave prints either," added Enrique.

"Or blood," said Séverin, glaring at Hypnos. He wasn't going to get trapped into that letter scheme again. "Enrique?"

Enrique pointed at the shelves. "Collections are tricky things. Sometimes there're even decoys of objects. The Horus Eye should be about palm-sized, with a glass or crystal piece in the pupil to see through, although age might have clouded it so it looks stained."

Hypnos looked around at the group, as if he were just seeing them for the first time.

"You know, in this lighting, you lot are rather fearsome."

"*All lighting*," corrected Enrique.

The moment everyone had slipped on their gloves, Séverin led the way to the eighth hall.

"Once we have the Horus Eye, we'll walk out—"

"That's *it*?" asked Enrique, his voice rising. "But it's House-marked—"

"Shhhh, beautiful," said Hypnos. He held out his hand, where his Ring—a bright crescent moon—gleamed. "This Ring is welded to my skin. If it's taken off and not delivered to a blood heir within a fort-night, the House mark fades. And I know for certain the matriarch had no time to pass it on to her abominable nephew."

"So . . ." Enrique looked around the room. "*Technically* . . . we could take anything right now?"

"Focus," warned Séverin.

Around them, the library stretched for nearly a kilometer under-ground. As the world's largest purveyor of ancient Egyptian arti-facts, House Kore's shelves overflowed with Forged treasures plundered from pharaohs' tombs and scrolls encased in glass and sand that had been lifted from the foundations of crumbling temples. But though the owners and artisans of the objects had long since passed, the power within them still crackled. Glass beetles with lightning storms flashing across their carapace scuttled into the shelves. Once or twice, a telescope's eye turned toward him, and Séverin saw not the dirt floor and treasures mirrored behind him, but a skull hovering over his head, a ripped rose on either side of him. Shaken, he kept walking.

As they neared the eighth aisle, a cold wind gusted into the hall. Zofia reached for her necklace. Laila stood back, fingers skimming down the wooden beams of the shelves. She turned to Séverin, her chin dipping ever so slightly in a silent signal: *Safe to enter*.

Séverin entered first. Then stopped. He heard the others rounding the corner, the shuffle of their feet abruptly stopping. Enrique stood at his shoulder and groaned.

"You've got to be kidding me."

The entire eighth aisle . . . were Horus Eyes. All of them were bronze and the size of one's hand. All of them had a perfect glass pupil and were completely identical. Only the objects stuffed between their spaces on the shelves distinguished them. Odds and ends not worthy enough to be catalogued. Silver ankhs dangled from slender hooks, and broken canopic jars were shoved alongside bits of pottery strewn about the shelves.

Zofia stepped forward. "Not all of the Horus Eyes are Forged."

"How do you know?" asked Enrique.

Zofia touched her palm, not looking at anyone directly. "They're just not."

"She's right," said Laila, taking her hand off the Horus Eye closest to her.

Hypnos eyed her shrewdly, and Laila gestured at the shelves. "It's nearly impossible that so many would actually be here. In existence."

"Fair," said Enrique. "In which case, we're looking for a special Horus Eye amongst the decoys. Presumably, looking through the correct Horus Eye will reveal a Babel Fragment, so it won't show the floor beneath you. It will show something else."

Hypnos groaned. "But there's got to be *hundreds* of Eyes!"

"All the more reason to get started." Séverin moved to the first shelf. "Shall we?"

There were fifty sections, ten for each of them. Séverin began reaching for the Horus Eyes. Every time he could see his shoes through the glass, he put an Eye back and reached for another. One after another after another, and each time he saw the ground reflected at him. Three sections. All of them decoys.

Séverin slid yet another decoy into its section when a slip of silver cloth fell. When he reached for it, his fingers skimmed across the surface, as if it were a pane of ice. He'd never seen anything like it. And frankly it was just so *lustrous*, like a mirror poured onto the ground. He pinched the edges of it, lifting it off the floor and stowing it away.

Across from him, Laila paused in running her hands along the Horus Eyes. Her gaze swept from his face to his jacket pocket and lingered there. He couldn't seem to hide anything from her.

Séverin cleared his throat. "Enrique? Zofia? Anything?"

Enrique shook his head. Zofia didn't answer. Séverin turned, about to move back to the shelf when he saw Laila struggling to pull a Horus Eye from its shelf. There was a large, black tome wedged next to it. The base of its spine seemed stuck to the wooden board.

"I can't get to it!" said Laila. "The Horus Eye is stuck behind this book."

Séverin couldn't have explained why the hairs on the back of his neck suddenly raised. He didn't like how that book was stuck to the shelf. It felt too intentional. Besides, there was something unnerving about the ink-stained pages and how the charred leather-bound cover looked far too smooth to be made of animal skin. Even the library felt entirely too still and silent in that moment. Before he could warn her, Laila pried the book off the shelf. The moment she wrenched it from its spot, it split down the middle. Indigo plumes spilling out from the opened pages.

"Get back!" yelled Séverin.

Laila dropped the book and darkness erupted from the pages. Amidst the dark, a snatch of white slipped from the page to the floor. It was a slender white feather.

Before, he thought the cavernous library had been still and silent. He was wrong. *This* was silence. All the sounds he had taken for granted—rustling fabric, whirring insect wings, running water—disappeared. Shadows seeped in from all sides of the library, rushing to give the book's smoke new shape. A snout formed. Teeth glinted. Paws covered in blood-slick fur outstretched. Séverin could see Laila, her mouth shaped into a scream. He darted between the thing's legs toward her just as a low snarl reverberated through the library. Slowly, the five of them looked up.

The shadow creature towered above them, the top of its head stretching far above the high shelves. The front of its body belonged to a lion, the hindquarters belonged to a hippo, and its head swung back and forth, crocodile jaws snapping. The creature slammed its paw against the floor.

"Duck!" hollered Séverin.

The five of them ran to the end of their respective sections.

"Ammit," said Enrique, loudly.

"What?"

"That's what *that* is," he said. "The devourer of souls from Egyptian mythology."

"But we're not in Egypt!" wailed Hypnos. "What's it doing here?"

"I'm guessing they brought it over to protect a powerful Horus Eye," said Enrique.

"Which means you must have found the true one," said Séverin.

The ground thundered. The snuffling sound of an animal searching for something filled the air.

"If we went back and got the Eye, maybe it will disappear," said Zofia.

Hypnos choked back a laugh. "That's *your* experiment, *ma chère*. Enjoy. I am *not* going out there."

"Not all of us have to," said Séverin.

He looked over his shoulder.

Ammit breathed heavily, its head lowered, eyes half-lidded and unfocused. Near its foot was the white feather that had fallen onto the ground. Ammit paced back and forth across that small section. The fur on its body bristled as it hunched protectively near the shelves.

"It's definitely guarding something," said Séverin.

Now all they had to do was lure it away from that thing.

"You four go around the other side of the shelf and get to the section with the Horus Eye. When you're close enough, signal me. I'll jump out. Ammit will come after me. Then all you have to do is close the book and grab the Eye. Got it?"

All of them began to creep to the other side of the shelf except one: Laila.

"You're far too fond of martyrdom, *Majnun*," she said. "I'm not leaving you."

Yet, he thought.

"It's your grave, Laila."

"As long as it's my choice."

The two of them peered through the cracks in the shelves. Zofia, Hypnos, and Enrique crept ahead . . .

Ammit didn't move. Its whole body was rigidly trained in Séverin and Laila's direction. Zofia leaned forward, her fingers inches away from the book. Hypnos and Enrique crouched on either side of her.

Then, Enrique met Séverin's eyes, nodding once.

Zofia reached for the book. Ammit's neck twitched, as if it were about to turn. Séverin jumped from his hiding place.

"Hungry?"

The creature roared.

Steam blew from its nostrils. It pawed the ground, then charged. The floor trembled. Objects rattled off the shelves. A ripe, putrid scent wafted from the creature, choking off the mineral scent of the air. Séverin braced himself, digging his heels into the floor. In the distance, he saw Zofia reach for both sides of the book, slamming it shut. Beside her, Enrique plucked the Horus Eye from the shelf.

"Good-bye!" he shouted, waving.

But Ammit kept charging.

Séverin saw Zofia frowning, looking up, then looking back at the book. She opened it and closed it again, but nothing happened. He pushed away the panic. Sometimes Forging defense mechanisms took time. Just another moment and it would work. It *had* to work. Ammit ran closer. Séverin could smell its rank breath, like flesh left to curdle in the sun's heat. He gagged. Ammit raised its paw, opening its mouth. Blood-flecked teeth shone in the light. At the back of its mouth was a blazing, sunken furnace in the precise shape of a feather that reminded him of a lock awaiting a key. Séverin paused. For a single moment, he took his gaze off Ammit, searching the floor for the white feather, which must be the key to triggering the creature's somno. All he had to do was force the white feather into its mouth.

But he had looked away from the creature a second too long.

Its shadow engulfed him. Before he could throw up his hands, Laila dove from the shelves, shoving him out of the way just in time.

He grunted, stumbling backward. Laila pulled his arm, dragging him behind another shelf in the same instant that Ammit charged into the wall. It snorted, shaking its head.

"Feather," said Séverin. "Get the feather."

Laila darted off to grab it. Seconds later, Ammit had freed itself from the wall. It reared back on its legs, turning to face the hall. Séverin crawled forward. Enrique and Zofia were holding spears they must've grabbed from a nearby shelf. Hypnos clutched the Horus Eye to his chest. Laila was closest to the creature. In her hands gleamed the white feather. Ammit eyed Laila like prey, tilting its head to one side. As if considering.

The rest of the world seemed to fall away in that moment.

Not her.

"No . . . No no no," Séverin rasped, forcing himself to stand. He waved his hands. "Over here!"

But Ammit was not distracted.

Laila's gaze darted to Séverin's, then back at the creature. She squeezed her eyes shut. There was no way she could get the feather to him. She held out her hand and the creature charged at her. Distantly, Séverin heard the others shout. He didn't think he made a single sound even as every ounce of his body screamed. Ammit charged at Laila, pinning her down with a paw. Pain twisted across her face, but she fought back, thrusting the feather forward where it disappeared into Ammit's mouth. Ammit's head swung, blocking Laila's face from view. A loud howl rumbled through the shelves, and then Laila's hand fell slack on the floor.

Séverin's mind numbed at the edges, zeroing in on her fallen hand. It was silly how well he knew her hands. He knew her hands were always cold even when it was blazing hot outside. He knew there was a small burn on the tip of her index finger. He remembered because he'd been in the kitchens with her when she yelped after touching a scalding pan. Séverin wanted to call a doctor, a retinue of nurses, declare a war on pans if he could . . . but Laila refused.

"It's a tiny burn, *Majnun*," she'd said, laughing off his panic.

"I know," he'd said.

But I cannot stand to see you hurt.

Ammit tossed back its head. The world turned weightless. Cracks showed through the creature's body, the eerie blue of twilight. Then, in a burst of light, the creature vanished. But Laila didn't stir on the floor.

He rushed to her, gathering her body close. She felt too light in his arms. The others approached warily, but he didn't turn.

"Laila?" he called, shaking her.

Open your eyes.

Her head lolled to one side, and something in him snapped. He brought his lips to her ear and whispered, "Laila, it's your *majnun*." *Your madman*, he thought, though he did not say it. "And you will drive me well and truly mad if you do not wake up this instant—"

She stirred, groaning. Then she opened her dark, fathomless eyes.

"Thank *God*," breathed Enrique, crossing himself.

Zofia looked stricken and pale. Even Hypnos, who Séverin thought had only seen them as a means to an end, had tears in his eyes. Enrique helped Laila to stand, and Séverin stood too. He brushed himself off and straightened his suit. He didn't trust himself to look in Laila's direction.

"Thank every pantheon of deities for Laila and Zofia because you two"—Séverin pointed at Enrique and Hypnos—"are useless."

Hypnos's hand fluttered to his throat. "I was frightened. You know what fear does to one's complexion?"

"Enlighten me."

Hypnos blinked. "Well, I don't know *precisely*, but it's nothing good, I can tell you that much."

"We got the Eye?" tried Enrique.

He turned, as if he was going to give the artifact to Hypnos when Séverin held out a hand.

"Don't give that to him," he said.

"Why ever not?" demanded Hypnos.

"You'll perform the inheritance test, *then* you may have your Eye—"

Hypnos crossed his arms. "My conditions were—"

"Acquire the eye and in return I will have my inheritance restored," recited Séverin. "You never once specified that in acquiring the Eye, it had to be passed over to your possession immediately."

Hypnos opened his mouth and closed it. Finally, he grinned. He wasn't angry at all. In fact, he seemed relieved.

"Touché."

Hypnos wandered off in search of the black box he'd placed in House Kore's care. Minutes later, he returned with a heavy black box.

"For you, my lovelies."

He took off the top. Inside gleamed five pairs of guard uniforms and hats. They pulled on the clothes quickly. Then, hats adjusted, they made their way to the exit separately.

"I shall be at L'Eden day after next to honor my promise," said Hypnos. His gaze rested on each of them, something hungry and searching in his gaze. "I look forward to being in the presence of another patriarch."

THE STAIRCASE TO the greenhouse was a short distance away, and yet even that made Séverin impatient. He wanted to be on that step already. He wanted to be in L'Eden, wandering through his grand lobby, holding out his scarred palm for the two Rings test and watching the matriarch of House Kore's face as she declared him blood heir of House Vanth. When he blinked, he saw the future poured out before him, rich and golden as mythic honey, each taste an edible prophecy—Tristan smiling, his pockets full of flowers; Enrique buried under the weight of books; Zofia and her spontaneous combustions; Laila, her heart's quest satisfied, lounging across from him with a smile fashioned just for him. Pain lanced through Séverin and he winced at the sharpness of it. Unripe, untested joy. The kind that doesn't know any better than to explode furiously behind the ribs. He didn't know what to do with it. He wanted to hold it at arm's length before it could devour any more of him, but then he felt Enrique tugging at his sleeve.

"Zofia has a spear."

Séverin looked behind him. "Zofia, I said not to take anything but the Horus Eye." He pointed at the spear. "You can't keep it."

Zofia glared at him. "You stole a silver cloth and it's in your jacket pocket."

Séverin considered this. "You can keep the spear."

"Not fair!" said Enrique. "*I* didn't take anything!"

"You're getting a completely different reward."

"Ah, yes," said Enrique dreamily. "Destiny. Deliverance. *Dessert.*"

"No more debt," added Zofia.

"What will you do, Laila?" asked Enrique.

"Oh, you know. I'll go wherever my search takes me," said Laila, with a secret smile.

The others thought she was looking for the means to return home, her arms loaded with treasure. But Séverin knew what she sought. He knew that Paris was merely a stop along the way, and the thought folded his joy in half even as it steeled his resolve. If he let her, she could lay waste to his heart. *What a foolish thought.* She was Laila. The famous L'Énigme. Who was to say she'd even have him again?

"What about Tristan?" mused Enrique. "What's he going to do?"

Zofia lifted her spear. "Build an army of spiders."

Everyone laughed, even Séverin, but his cheer had an edge to it now. At the top of the staircase, he pushed open the door.

"Tristan?" called Laila.

"We got attacked by a hippo!" shouted Enrique.

Séverin didn't move. He swept his gaze across the greenhouse. Something was wrong. Heavy fumes and veils shadowed the ground, moving slowly across the acid-scorched dirt. A black sheen caught Séverin's eye. Mist rolled out of the way. A faint ringing built up in his ears. The sound of fear howling in the mind.

"Tristan," he said softly.

Now the mist disappeared entirely, revealing a small garden chair dragged in the middle of the room. Atop it, his head lolled to one side, sat Tristan. And on his head, a contraption that haunted Séverin's every nightmare. A pale metal diadem, blue light snapping back and forth. A Phobus Helmet. The words of Wrath flared through his head.

Your imagination hurts you far worse than anything I could ever do.

Under enough pressure, the mind might even . . . crack.

Séverin tried to run to him, but Forged knives materialized in the air, a blade grazing his throat. A second later, the Horus Eye was torn from his hand.

"Thank you, dear boy," said a weak voice.

Séverin slowly turned his head to the side. Roux-Joubert stood before him, thin and quivering. He dabbed his mouth with a handkerchief flecked with blood. A honeybee pin gleamed unmistakably on his lapel.

"Though really, I should be thanking your friend here," he said. He tapped the side of his own temple. "His love and his fear and his own cracked mind made it easy to convince him that betraying you was saving you. Though he did have some help from the lovely baroness. It was her very hands that led me to you."

Zofia slowly lifted her hands, horror clear on her face. Roux-Joubert must have slipped something on her . . . but how?

Roux-Joubert bowed. "Thank you, Mademoiselle, for being such a willing participant. I do love an idiot girl."

From behind the garden chair, the Forged knives drifted toward Tristan's neck.

"*Stop!*" shouted Séverin.

"You don't wish to put him out of his misery?" asked Roux-Joubert mildly. "I must admit I was not always as, well, *kind* as I might have been. But if you wish him alive, then let us make a deal,

Monsieur Montagnet-Alarie. According to Tristan, you are in contact with Hypnos, the patriarch of House Nyx."

Séverin said nothing.

"I take your silence as agreement," he said, with a terrible smile. "In three days' time, you will meet me and my associate inside the Exhibition on Colonial Superstitions at midnight. At that time, you will bring me the Babel Ring of House Nyx. I already have House Kore's, but now I desire the matched set . . . Do we have an agreement?"

Tristan shook violently in the chair. His eyes were shut tight. One of the knives started to rotate, its point brushing the topmost button of his shirt—

"*Yes*," said Séverin, breathless. "Yes, I agree."

The knife halted.

Beside him, Laila trembled with rage. "You'll never find the Babel Fragment—"

"*Find* it?" Roux-Joubert laughed. "Oh, my dear. I already know where it is." He paused to cough into his blood-flecked handkerchief. "Three days, Monsieur Montagnet-Alarie. Three days to give me the Ring. Or I will burn down your world and everything that you love with it."

Roux-Joubert checked his watch.

"You made a very detailed schedule, Monsieur. Best to be on that guard convoy now. I wouldn't want you to miss your ride home," he said, waving the stolen Horus Eye in his hand. "Not when you have so much to do."

"I—"

"—will find me?" guessed Roux-Joubert, laughing softly. "No, you won't. We have been hiding for ages, and none have found us yet. When the time comes, we'll make ourselves known. After all, this is the start of a revolution."

PART IV

From the archival records of the Order of Babel
The Origins of Empire
Mistress Marie Ludwig Victor, House Frigg of the Order's Prussian
faction 1828, reign of Frederick Wilhelm IV

In olden times, there was some debate as to whether the Babel Fragments were separate and distinct artifacts, or whether they were once part of something greater . . . something that was then hewn apart and flung across the soils of different kingdoms.

It is my belief that if they fell from the heavens separately, they were never meant to be joined.

God always has His reasons.

20

LAILA

Laila stood in the Seven Sins Garden.

Tristan's workshop deep within Envy looked as it always had. There was his old trowel, the wood gone dark and sculpted by the pressure of his fingers. An unfinished terrarium holding a single golden flower. The ruler Zofia had made him because he didn't like uneven spaces between his plants. The packet of seeds from the Philippines, a gift from Enrique that Tristan was planning to plant in summer. A plate from the kitchens where a thin film of mold grew over a cookie. He must have stolen it when she wasn't looking, gotten distracted, and forgotten all about it.

The tips of Laila's fingers buzzed numb. Cold touched their edges blue. It was too much, her body protested. But Laila couldn't stop. Roux-Joubert's words about Tristan haunted her.

His love and his fear and his own cracked mind made it easy to convince him that betraying you was saving you . . .

Cracked mind. It was true that some were more susceptible to the effects of mind affinity Forging than others, but Tristan . . .

Tristan hated Hypnos.

Tristan washed blood from his palms every time he dug his nails into his skin.

Tristan ached.

Guilt grabbed her by the throat.

All of yesterday had passed in a blur. The convoy. The switch. The guards in Tristan and Enrique's disguise placed onto an infirmary bus, their clothes exchanged, and none the wiser. Then came the carriage ride home. Empty-handed and raw.

In the carriage, Séverin looked each of them in the eye as he spoke:

"This acquisition is not done. We're going to get the Horus Eye back, and we're going to do it before those three days are up. And when we do, we'll rescue Tristan from this mess," he said. "Our number one priority is finding out who Roux-Joubert is and where he's hiding. We can't save Tristan if we don't know who has him."

Laila had come here to look for clues of Roux-Joubert's location or identity. But she had ended up trying to answer the question of Tristan. She read everything in his workshop, but found nothing. Nothing but what she had known the whole time. His laughter. His shyness. His curiosity. His *love*. For all of them. Séverin, especially.

Behind her, Laila heard the soft crunch of branches. She turned around sharply. Séverin had changed out of the guard uniform and into a dark suit. His hair was mussed, dark waves falling across his forehead. With the dawn rising around them, he looked like a stubborn vestige of night, and her breath caught.

"Well?"

He leaned against the threshold. But he did not enter.

"Nothing," she said.

Laila looked at him closely. His jaw was clenched tight. The sweep of his shoulders brittle. She could not see his eyes, but she imagined they burned in that moment.

Laila crossed over to where he stood. He didn't move. Didn't change his position at all. She didn't even realize what she was doing until she'd done it. She touched him . . . folding his hands between hers. She held tight even when a tremor ran through his fingers. As if his soul had flinched.

"I found nothing *at all*. Do you understand me?"

Look at me, she willed. *Look at me.*

He did.

Séverin's violet eyes burned cold. In his gaze, she saw her guilt mirrored. What had they missed that let Roux-Joubert capture— and *hurt*—Tristan? What had they done wrong? They let each other stand like this, mutually clasped. Maybe it was just because it was still dark out, and the memory of this moment would dissolve with the sunlight. Or maybe it was because in that vast silence of uncertainty, they could feel each other's pulse against their fingertips, and that cadence meant they could be many things, but not alone.

A second passed. Then two. There was relief in this second, in holding and being held, but then he let go. He always let go first.

Laila shoved her hands into the pockets of her guard disguise, her face burning.

Séverin nodded in the direction of L'Eden. "Hypnos is on his way."

"Are you . . . are you going to tell him Roux-Joubert wants his Ring in exchange for Tristan?"

Séverin's gaze went flat. "Are you asking whether I'm going to sell him out?"

Yes.

"No, of course not!" she said hurriedly. "You aren't, right?"

He raised his eyebrow. "Do I look like a wolf to you, Laila?"

"That depends on the lighting."

The corner of his mouth lifted. A ghost of a grin.

"I'm not planning to walk into a trap," he said. "I am, however, planning to set one."

IN THE STARGAZING room, Hypnos sat utterly frozen in his chair.

He looked at each of them in turn. His hands were flat against the tops of his thighs. Pity twisted through her. Though Hypnos was the tallest out of all of them, he looked like a child. His shoulders caved. He had worn that same bemused expression ever since they told him what happened to the Horus Eye. But that hadn't shocked him nearly as much as Séverin admitting that Roux-Joubert had proposed an exchange. Hypnos's Babel Ring, for Tristan.

Hypnos laced his hands tight. "So. Am I to understand that you brought me here to inform me you're going to turn over my Babel Ring to Roux-Joubert because you prefer to stab me in the front versus the back?"

Zofia tilted her to head to one side. "Does that make a difference?"

Laila winced. Hypnos looked horrified and then . . . hurt.

"Why are you telling me this?" he demanded.

Séverin leaned forward in his chair. "I'm telling you this to gauge whether or not you would be interested in being bait."

Hypnos regarded them, his expression curiously blank. "You . . . you aren't going to give me to him?"

"And end up with two Rings gone? No."

Hypnos rose to his feet slowly. "But the easier option is to protect yourselves."

"I'm confused. Do you *want* me to?"

"Of course not, *mon cher*! I just want to make sure I understand what's going on here."

Laila frowned. Why did Hypnos seem so delighted? She knew he wasn't happy about Tristan being captured. His whole face had crumpled with sorrow when he heard the news. She'd even read his jacket to be absolutely certain, but the objects didn't lie. Hypnos had nothing to do with Tristan's imprisonment.

"What's going on here is that I need you to play bait," said Séverin, enunciating his words carefully.

Pure, unfettered relief spread across Hypnos's face.

"What's going on here"—said Hypnos, his voice rising as a bizarre grin spread across his face, —"is that you *care* for me. We're all *friends*. We're friends going to save another friend! This is . . . this is *amazing*."

Laila wanted to hug him.

"I never said that," said Séverin, alarmed.

"Actions have a better voice than words."

Enrique, who had been assembling the last bits of a projection, looked up and shook his head.

"It's *actions speak louder than words*."

"Whatever. I like my version better. Now. Let's discuss this friend bait business."

"*Bait* business," Séverin corrected under his breath. He reached for his tins of cloves. "Before we plan anything, we need to know who it is we're dealing with. And you need to start telling the truth."

Hypnos blinked. ". . . Truth?"

Séverin's tin of cloves shut with a decided snap.

"Roux-Joubert not only admitted to stealing the matriarch of House Kore's Ring, but also said that he already *knows* where the West's Babel Fragment is hidden, so then what's the point of the Horus Eye? What else might it do if not to see a Babel Fragment?"

"How do we know he's not lying?" asked Enrique.

Laila knew he wasn't. Roux-Joubert had thrown his handkerchief into the dirt when he left. Lies always left a slimy film to her readings, as she measured up what the object had seen and what the person had said whilst holding it. But there was none of that to the handkerchief.

"Instinct," said Séverin glibly, but his eyes cut to hers for confirmation. "Besides, I know Hypnos is lying. Even in the library when the Horus Eye came up, his gaze shifted. So, tell us the truth, *friend*."

Hypnos sighed. "Fine. I wasn't particularly forthcoming, but that's not my fault . . . It was a secret my father told me not long before he died. He never told me what, exactly, the Horus Eye did, but he said that should House Kore's Ring ever be taken, I must find the Horus Eye and keep it safe. He said the Eye had an effect on the Fragment."

"As in . . . it reveals a Fragment's location?"

"I'm not sure."

"He never said what *kind* of effect?"

Hypnos swallowed hard. "He never had the chance."

"Then why did you want the compass in the auction?" asked Enrique.

"My father had been after it," said Hypnos tightly. "He said he didn't want even rumors of the Eye's ability getting in the wrong hands."

"Did House Kore know what the Horus Eye could do?"

"Not quite," Hypnos admitted. "My father told me House Kore was under the impression that looking through the Horus Eye would reveal all somnos in weaponry, and that's why they were destroyed during Napoleon's campaign."

"What about the Order? Do they know?" asked Enrique.

"No," said Hypnos, a touch smugly. "The secret was only with the French faction and as far as I understood, only House Nyx."

"What does Roux-Joubert want with the Horus Eye then, if he knows where the West's Fragment lies?" asked Laila. "Not to mention that he has House Kore's Babel Ring and now wants yours too."

Hypnos worried his lower lip between his teeth and then looked up at them. He held up his hand, and his Babel Ring, a simple crescent moon with a pale blue sheen, briefly flared with light.

"My Ring does not just guard the location of the Babel Fragment . . . it is said to have another capacity, though I confess I'm not sure how it works . . ."

"What?"

"It, well, it supposedly *awakens* the West's Babel Fragment itself."

"Awakens?" repeated Laila slowly. "What, so a Babel Fragment is something slumbering beneath the ground? I thought it was a rock."

"That's what most people think, but the truth is no one knows what it looks like." Hypnos shrugged. "It's also why every hundred years, the knowledge of the Fragment's location changes, moving to another group of Houses within the West. The Order uses a special mind-affinity tool where those who know the knowledge forget it instantly after one hundred years. They even use it upon themselves. It's not supposed to be beheld."

All of them fell silent, and then Enrique spoke. "But you don't know if awakening the West's Fragment requires, say, both Babel Rings or just one?'

Hypnos shook his head. "The Order has never specified. Sometimes the stories say it's three Rings. Sometimes it takes just one. Who can say? The Babel Fragments haven't been disturbed in thousands of years. No one would dare."

"What happened the last time someone succeeded in disturbing a country's Fragment?" asked Laila.

"Ever heard of Atlantis?"

"No," said Zofia.

"Exactly."

"It's a mythical city," said Enrique.

"Well, *now* it is."

"But we still don't understand what Roux-Joubert wants with the West's Fragment," said Séverin. "The last group that tried to disturb the Fragment was the Fallen House, and they sought to join all the Fragments together. Maybe Roux-Joubert wants to emulate them, but we don't even know why the Fallen House tried what they did in the first place. Do you?"

"I do," sighed Hypnos, looking around the room. "But first, where's the wine? I can't discuss the end of civilization without wine."

"You can have it after," said Séverin.

Hypnos grumbled. "The Fallen House believed that Forging was a subset of alchemy. You know, transforming matter and turning things to gold and such. But that was only one part of mastering their secrets. The most important aspect was theurgy."

"Which is?" asked Zofia.

Enrique pressed the heels of his hands into his eyes. "*Theurgy* means 'the working of the gods.'"

Zofia frowned. "So, the Fallen House wanted to understand how gods work?"

"No," said Séverin. A terrible smile bent his mouth. "They wanted to become gods."

Laila shuddered. Silence fell over them, broken only by the metallic chime of Séverin opening his tin of cloves.

"We're not going to find Tristan without figuring out who Roux-Joubert is," he said. "We know he's not with either House Nyx or House Kore. When he was at the dinner, the matriarch didn't acknowledge him, and he didn't sit with the other House members. So, we presume that he's functioning outside the Order, or that someone in the Order is acting through him. We also know he has access to the Exposition Universelle because that's where he first laid a trap for Enrique and Zofia, and it's where he's demanded that we do an exchange."

"In three days," said Enrique. "Perfectly timed for the opening of the Exposition Universelle."

"So?" asked Zofia.

"So, it means he's waiting for a built-in audience," said Séverin. "There's something he's planning on that date. You heard him. All his talk of 'revolution'? What better stage to launch one than the world fair?"

Hypnos deflated. "That tells us nothing."

"We also know that Roux-Joubert wears a honeybee pin," said Enrique.

"So? Today I'm wearing underwear. It's hardly monumental."

Zofia frowned. "Why did you specify *today*—"

Enrique jumped in, "The man who accosted us at the Forging exhibition also wore a honeybee pendant on a chain."

The chain in question currently dangled from Laila's hands. Zofia had brought it to her earlier while they were waiting for Hypnos to arrive. The chain itself was not Forged, exactly. Something about it called to Laila's senses. But images that should have been sharp in her mind now felt blurred, as if swiped with oil. Someone had tampered with the item. The only thing she knew for certain was that wherever Roux-Joubert was . . . it was underground. She could feel it. The lightless cold of it. Damp on the walls. Nails with crescents of dirt. And a symbol scrawled in light . . . pointed. Like a star.

"Roux-Joubert also has a strong Forging affinity," added Zofia begrudgingly. "He managed to tamper with a Streak of Sia formulation. Usually, the formula copies handprints, but theoretically, there are ways for the Sia formulation to act like a homing mechanism. He must have figured out the way, and that's what led him directly to us."

"Who said it was *his* affinity, though?" asked Laila. "He could have someone working for him."

Enrique shuddered. "Don't forget the gentleman with the blade-brimmed hat who accosted us in the exhibit. It could be him. What else do we know?"

"He's underground," said Laila.

The four of them turned to face her. Hypnos rested his chin on his hand, eyeing her suspiciously. "And how do *we* know that?" he asked.

"I don't owe you all my sources," said Séverin protectively. "Does Roux-Joubert remind you of anyone?"

Hypnos shook his head. "I'm sorry, *mon cher*, but I haven't heard that name at all. I can always return to Erebus and check, of course. My house holds many secrets."

Enrique cleared his throat. "There's something, though, about the honeybees . . . I'm starting to think it's not a coincidence that both he and the man from the exhibition wore one."

"Not again," groaned Hypnos. "It's nothing but a symbol—"

Laila hissed in her breath. She could practically see Enrique brandishing a sword.

"Nothing but a symbol?" repeated Enrique quietly. "People die for symbols. People have *hope* because of symbols. They're not just lines. They're histories, cultures, traditions, given shape."

Hypnos blushed and plucked at his vest.

Enrique turned to Séverin. "Can you get the lights?"

Séverin snapped his fingers and drapes swooshed down to cover the bay windows. He snapped again, and a large black screen crept over the domed glass of the stargazing room.

Hypnos snorted. "And you call *me* dramatic."

Ignoring him, Enrique straightened the cuffs of his sleeves. "I've been doing research on honeybee symbology for some time now," he said. "But I only recently connected what Roux-Joubert said to the man who accosted us in the exhibition hall. Both spoke of revolution. Both wore that honeybee chain. Now, historically, honeybees have some mythological resonance, and I think I found a clue . . ."

"Normally you'd be gloating by now," pointed out Laila.

Enrique sighed. "Let's just hope I'm wrong about this clue."

He placed a small projection sphere on the coffee table. When he touched it, two images appeared side by side. They appeared to be mnemo scans of pages in textbooks or from museum displays.

The first image showed a square, golden plaque. On it was a winged woman. From the waist up, she was human, but waist-down, she was a bee. The next image showed a faded painting of a Hindu goddess, bees radiating from the halo of her heavy crown.

"Bee deities are not uncommon throughout mythology," said Enrique. "The image you see here is a representation of the Thriae, a triplicate bee goddess—a recurring motif of trinity goddesses— who had the gift of prophecy. The other is a representation of Bhramari, a Hindu goddess of bees. Am I pronouncing that correctly, Laila?"

"It's Bruh-mah-ree," she corrected gently.

Enrique made a note and continued, "Where the honeybee motif gets interesting and potentially connects us to France is that honeybees were emblematic of Napoleon's rule, though the reasons for why he chose his reign to be represented by a honeybee are contentious."

The image on the wall changed to show a bee embroidered on a rich, velvet robe.

"Some say that when he moved into the Royal Palace at Tuileries, he didn't want to allocate any resources to redecorating, but also didn't want the French Royal emblem of the embroidered fleur-de-lis everywhere, so he turned it upside down. When he did that, it looked like a honeybee, and there you have it."

Séverin sat up straighter. "Do you think Roux-Joubert has some connection to Napoleon?"

"It's possible," he said. "Napoleon *did* lead multiple campaigns throughout North Africa and the Middle East to explore the area. He had a corps of at least two hundred experts, including multiple linguists, historians, engineers, and delegates from the Order of Babel who provided a range of Forging services. Their discoveries"— he paused to press the mnemo bug and change the image—"were fascinating."

The next image showed a slab of dark rock, covered in what looked like rows of text.

"In 1799, that corps of explorers discovered the Rosetta Stone, and sparked a worldwide interest in ancient Egyptian artifacts, with many of the Forged instruments or objects going straight to House Kore. Bees were sacred in ancient Egypt as well because they were said to grow from the tears of the sun god, Ra. But I think the other reason they held such interest to the Order of Babel was because of their honeycombs."

"Honeycombs?" asked Laila. Honeycombs were delicious, but hardly the kind of ancient item she imagined would capture the interest of the Order.

"I didn't think of it until I remembered something Zofia had said."

"Me?"

Spots of color appeared on Zofia's cheeks.

"You were the one who mentioned the perfect hexagonal prisms of honeycombs."

"What's so great about a hexagon?" asked Hypnos.

"Geometrically speaking, hexagonal prisms are the most efficient shape because they require the least total length of wall," said Zofia, her voice rising slightly. "Honeybees are the mathematicians of nature."

"*This*," said Enrique, changing the display yet again, "is a hexagon."

"*I*," said Hypnos, clearly bored, "am a human."

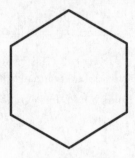

Séverin's jaw fell open. "I see it."

"See what?" demanded Zofia and Hypnos at the same time.

Séverin stood. "Extend the lines and you get—"

Enrique smile was grim. "Exactly."

"You get *what*?" demanded Laila, but then the image on the wall changed, and she saw what formed when the lines of a hexagon were extended:

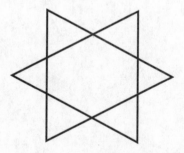

Laila felt a cold thud in her heart. She recognized that symbol in the blurred images of the necklace chain. In her hands, the pendant felt a touch colder than the rest of the necklace.

"It's a hexagram," said Enrique. "We know it as an ancient symbol that's taken on all kinds of meanings throughout various cultures, but it also—"

"—is the crest of a House in the Order," said Séverin, staring at the six-pointed star. He absentmindedly rubbed his thumb along the long scar on his palm. "A House that was supposed to be dead."

Hypnos gripped the armrest. "You don't think—"

Séverin cut him off with a nod. His eyes looked hollow.

"The Fallen House has risen."

21

ZOFIA

Zofia could not concentrate. Every time she blinked, she heard Roux-Joubert's words echoed back to her: "I do love an idiot girl."

Idiot.

It was just a word. It had no weight, no atomic number, no chemical structure with which it could bind to and thus make it real. But it hurt. Zofia squeezed her eyes shut, gripping the black table in her laboratory so hard her knuckles turned white. She felt the word like a slap to the face. In Glowno, she had once asked a theoretical question about physics. Her teacher told her, "You'd have better luck setting your desk on fire and seeing if the answer appears in the smoke."

And so Zofia did.

She was ten years old.

When she came to the École des Beaux-Arts, it was much the same. She was too curious, too Jewish, too strange. To the point where no one had pushed back at the idea of locking her in the school laboratory.

But not once had anyone been hurt by how she thought. Or rather, how she didn't think.

But Tristan? Slumped over in a chair, knives floating at his throat . . . *she* had done that to him. Tears stung Zofia's eyes. She could work her way through mathematical riddles as if it were walking down a street. But a conversation was a labyrinth. And in her effort to navigate it, she had led Roux-Joubert right to their hiding spot in the greenhouse.

Something was wrong with her.

"Zofia?"

She looked up, blinking rapidly. Séverin was standing in the doorway. A silver cloth dangled from his hand.

"May I come in?"

She nodded. This was it. He was going to tell her to leave. That she wasn't welcome here anymore after what she did. But he didn't do any of that. Instead, he slid the silver cloth across the black table. Zofia recognized it as the piece that he'd stolen from the library of House Kore. She touched it gently. It felt like cold silk, and it had the strangest *heft* to it, as if it were pushing back against her hand.

"We have two more days before we have to meet Roux-Joubert in the Forging exhibition with Hypnos's Ring."

"You're giving him the Ring?" she asked.

"I'm showing it to him."

Zofia frowned. "What's the difference—"

"Let me worry about that," said Séverin. "I've got the others working on figuring out where the Fallen House headquarters are. But I can promise you that we won't let them take the Ring. And we won't let them take Tristan."

Zofia's shoulders fell. Everyone else was working on something. Except her.

"But I saved an important job for you," he said softly.

Zofia stilled. "You did?"

"You're the only phoenix I've got," he said with a small smile. "Roux-Joubert couldn't see that. Which is rather advantageous, wouldn't you agree? He may not know now. But he will soon."

Zofia's hand curled into a fist. She felt as if fire had shot through her belly. *He will.* This must be what vengeance felt like. It made her . . . hungry.

"What do you need me to do?"

Séverin pointed to the silver cloth. "Can you figure out how this works? I think it could be useful."

"Yes," said Zofia breathlessly. "I can."

The moment she reached for the silver cloth, the rest of the world disappeared. Someone could have set her laboratory on fire, and she wouldn't have noticed. The moment she gave herself to her work, she gave *all* of herself. A new cadence seemed to buzz through her blood: She was no idiot; she would bring Tristan home; she would make this right.

It was nearly nighttime when Zofia looked up from her work to hear another knock at her door. Laila walked in carrying a platter of food, a steaming mug of tea, and a single round cookie.

"You haven't eaten all day."

Zofia's stomach grumbled loudly at the sight of food. She patted it absentmindedly. She hadn't noticed.

Laila placed the platter onto her worktable. "Eat."

Zofia felt itchy just looking at the worktable now. The corner of the platter hung off the edge. It wasn't even. And now it looked messy.

"I will take away the platter and put it somewhere else when I see you take five bites. And don't scowl at me."

Zofia dutifully shoved five bites of food in her mouth.

Laila pointed with her chin to the teacup. "Drink."

Zofia drank the tea.

Only then did Laila remove the platter, place it off to the side of a different counter, and position it *just so*, with none of the corners hanging off the edges and arranged perpendicular to the wall.

"Any progress?"

Zofia eyed the silver cloth on the table. She was beginning to think that for what Séverin had asked of her, she might not be able to do this entirely inside L'Eden.

"It works like a Tezcat door," said Zofia. "The actual filaments of it are made of obsidian."

Laila tilted her head to one side. "Is that why it looks like a mirror?"

Zofia nodded. "But it does more than that." Zofia rummaged through her toolbox and pulled out a sharp knife.

"Um, Zofia—"

Zofia plunged the knife into the cloth. The cloth didn't tear. Instead, it *bent*, as if absorbing the impact of the blade.

Laila swore under her breath. "What in the *world*?"

"It repels matter," said Zofia. "No solid matter can penetrate it."

Laila dragged her fingers across the surface of it.

"What does Séverin want with it?"

Zofia chewed her lip. She wasn't sure that she could answer yet because it depended on something back in the dark halls of the Forging exhibition. A place she was not looking forward to exploring once more.

"Have the others found the headquarters of the Fallen House?"

Laila sighed. "No. They think the answer is in an old bone clock. Apparently, it once held the locations of the Fallen House meetings or something. Don't get me started. Personally, I think we should use the meeting location and just track who goes in and who leaves."

Zofia thought back to the man who had been lying in wait for her and Enrique. The detection sphere hadn't revelead his presence, and at the time both exits had been accounted for, which meant he had entered some other way. She hadn't noticed anything that might have concealed their assailant, but studying the silver cloth made her think perhaps she had missed something.

"That won't work."

"Why not?"

"They're using a different route."

"That's impossible," said Laila. "There's only the entrance and exit, and both join at the same road."

Zofia reached for her box of matches and her necklace with the phosphorous pendants, shoving them into the pockets of her black smock. If the theory churning in her mind was right, then she couldn't waste any more time. After all, Tristan was counting on her.

Zofia was already headed to the door when Laila blocked her.

"Where are you off to?"

"I have to go to the Exposition Universelle. I have to find a way into the Exhibition on Colonial Superstitions. I can climb over walls or stun guards or whatever I have to do—" she said, even as panic started pushing itself through her bloodstream.

"Zofia," soothed Laila. "Let me help. We can get in and get out, and hopefully no one will be jumping over fences."

Zofia looked up, confused. "We?"

Laila winked. *"Oui."*

"How?"

"You have your talents," said Laila. "I have mine." And then she scrutinized Zofia's outfit. "But you are not wearing that."

"Why not?"

"Because, my dear, we are without armor. And beauty is its own armor. Trust me."

ZOFIA WAS EXTREMELY itchy.

"I hate this," she declared, plucking at one of the outfits Laila had shoved her into.

It was a nice enough color. Pale pink. With frills around the bodice and a neckline that felt at once scratchy and ticklish.

"Garments are an art," said Laila, walking briskly.

"I'll never get out of it."

"As it so happens, some would consider disrobing an art too."

Zofia grumbled, but kept up her pace. It was nearly nighttime. Lights spilled out across the Seine River. Up ahead loomed the Eiffel Tower, the entrance to the Exposition. Zofia had watched the Tower being built, growing from scaffolding to spire. It was a bold, staggering lattice of rivets and steel bolts. No one would call it beautiful, but that hardly mattered to Zofia. Beauty did not move her. But the Eiffel Tower did. It was immensely awkward. If the streets looked sewn together with a neat hand, la Tour Eiffel was the ungainly needle pinning it all into place. It lanced through the grand boulevards, elegant cupolas, and buildings draped in sculpted gods. It would never blend in, but always demand witnessing. Zofia suspected that if la Tour Eiffel could talk, they would understand each other perfectly.

Past the Eiffel Tower stretched out the Esplanade des Invalides. Even in the dark, Zofia felt her breath catch. It was as if she were no longer in Paris. Gone were the familiar boulevards and docile cafés with their wicker chairs. Now, sprawling tents covered the streets. On the sidewalk were low tables crowded with water pipes. Men in robes and women with their heads covered walked briskly down the cobbled lanes.

Laila pointed out the water fountain, the bell-shaped minaret, and the mosque paneled with bright blue tiles. Around it were salons and restaurants. The tang of unfamiliar food coated the air so thickly that Zofia was tempted to stick out her tongue.

"We're on Cairo Street," said Laila, keeping her voice low.

Although Paris was full of tourists, the Exposition had not yet officially opened, and the streets were empty, save for the very wealthy who had procured tickets early. Small units of guards carefully patrolled the spaces, making sure no one had snuck in before it was open to the public. On the other side of the street, Zofia spied a handful of guards walking toward them.

"Act calm," said Laila under her breath. "You look like anyone else. As if you belong here, so there's no reason for them to feel alarmed. And under *no circumstances* should you take off running."

A guard strolled up to them. Zofia thought he would direct his questions to Laila, but he didn't. He acted as if she wasn't there at all.

"I'm afraid you and your maid can't be here, Mademoiselle," he said to Zofia. "We have been having some troubles with security—there was a disturbance here a week ago. We will have to ask you to remove yourself to a different sector of the Exposition Universelle."

Beside Zofia, Laila stiffened.

"She isn't my maid," said Zofia automatically.

Laila winced. And Zofia realized that was not what she was supposed to say. "I mean—"

Another guard started walking toward them. His eyebrows were slanted down.

"Mademoiselle, what's your name?" asked the first guard.

"I . . . I . . ."

Zofia tugged nervously at the silken sheath cover on her dress. Hidden in her sleeve was a box of matches. There were sharp spurs concealed in the heels of her shoes. But she didn't want to use them.

Laila jumped in. "My mistress does not simply hand over her name like some common token!"

The first guard looked taken aback. "I meant no offense—"

"You should apologize anyway!" scolded Laila.

"It's just that she seems to match a description for a person involved with the recent disturbance. A girl, of about her height. With white-blond hair. It's not a very common coloring."

"She is a rare and exquisite flower," said Laila, tugging on Zofia's arm. "Let us go, Madame. We were lost, is all—"

"If she could but stay a moment longer, my colleague will be able to confirm that she is not the woman we seek. I am dreadfully sorry, but protocol is quite strict before opening day."

Zofia recognized the second guard approaching them. He was the one who had cradled his friend who died at the hands of the man with the blade-brimmed hat. The man stopped short when he saw her. His hand went to the Forged device at his hip.

Zofia grabbed Laila's arm.

"Run!" she cried, sprinting down the road.

Laila took off after her. Zofia's heart pounded in her ears. She could hear the guards shouting. Behind her, tents crashed and tables were overturned as Laila threw them to the ground, blocking their path.

"This way!" said Laila, pulling Zofia through one of the twisting streets.

Shouts erupted behind them. Zofia flew past a spice table, overturning cinnamon and pepper in heaps onto the ground. A slew of foreign curses chased her shadow, but there wasn't time to apologize. Zofia followed Laila through the twisting streets of the colonial pavilions until they arrived at a corner that plunged into the dark.

On the other side of the alley, the streets changed once more.

From Cairo to an Annamite village, where the wooden thatched peaks of pointed huts unfurled in front of them. A colorful rickshaw streaming ribbons sped past in the direction of a large theater outfitted with palm fronds. Down the street, Zofia could see the darkened archway of the Exhibition on Colonial Superstitions.

And just behind her, she could hear the pounding footsteps of the guards.

Laila started waving her hands wildly. "I can't get the rickshaw driver's attention!" she called.

The footsteps were gaining on them. Zofia had an idea. From her sleeves, she pulled out the matches, struck one against her teeth, and set it to the outer sheath of her dress before jumping in the middle of the road. She tore off the first, burning layer, which now flared into a long column of fire.

The rickshaw driver braked hard.

"I got his attention," announced Zofia, stomping the fire out with her foot. The rest of her dress, made of Forged flame-retardant silk, gleamed, completely unsullied.

Laila's mouth fell open, but then it pulled into a wide grin. She waved a bag full of coins.

"For your services. And your silence."

The driver, a boy no older than thirteen, beamed a gap-toothed smile. The two of them hopped into the rickshaw just as the guards appeared.

"Get down!" said Laila.

Zofia slid farther down in her seat. The rickshaw itself was little more than a covered tricycle. But at least it could get them to the exhibition.

Laila whispered directions to the driver. Once they sped away down the road, she flopped backward in her seat, breathing hard.

"See?" said. "What did I tell you earlier?"

Zofia gripped the edge of her seat. "That some people consider disrobing an art?"

"No, not that!" said Laila, as the driver blushed. "I said that beauty was its own armor."

Zofia considered this. "I still don't like dresses."

Laila merely smiled.

INSIDE THE FORGING exhibition, the lights had been kept dim. The only pinpoints of luminescence were beneath each of the podiums. Zofia kept herself near the wall.

"What are we looking for, Zofia? Another entrance? A hidden door?"

Zofia shook her head. "Us."

She reached for the phosphorous pendant from her necklace, remembering how it had revealed the Tezcat door at House Kore. That mirror had been a gift from the Fallen House. And if the Fallen House was behind the theft of the House Kore Ring, then what if she and Enrique had missed something the last time they were here? What if the whole time they had been walking through the exhibition, thinking they were unseen, someone had been watching them from behind a concealed mirror?

With Forging, detecting the presence of a Tezcat required a burning phosphorous formula. Zofia snapped her phosphorous pendant. She held it out where it looked like a piece of chipped-off blue flame.

"Don't walk in front of the flame," instructed Zofia.

Laila nodded. The two of them made their way slowly through the exhibit. Zofia let the light of the phosphorous pendant climb up the brocade walls. On the left, nothing moved. Zofia held out the pendant as she made her way to the place in the wall where the man with the honeybee pendant had been waiting as if he had slid out of the wallpaper itself. The light climbed over the brocade slowly, glittering over the golden embroidery, and then—

Laila sucked in her breath.

The wall changed. At first, it showed nothing but cloth, but then the surface of it rippled, turning liquid and silver. A Tezcat door, exposed. In its reflection, Zofia caught Laila's eye.

"They're coming through here."

22

ENRIQUE

Enrique was hanging upside down from his armchair.

He groaned aloud. "It makes *no* sense."

Hypnos, seated on the black-cherry chair beneath him, raised his nearly emptied wineglass. His third such glass, if memory served Enrique.

"Try wine."

"I doubt that will help."

"True, but at least you won't remember." Hypnos drained his glass, then set it aside. "How come you have an armchair? I want one."

"Because I live here."

"Hmpf."

Sometimes Enrique found his thoughts worked better when he was dangling upside down. It helped that he could see the floor beneath him, all the documents they'd found on the Fallen House fanned out across the carpet. And in the middle of it all, encased in a thin quartz terrarium: the bone clock.

It was a feast for both a symbolist and a historian. It was not an ordinary clock, though it had a face and numerals and hands that pointed to various hours of the day. Twisting symbols stretched around the clockwork. Carved maidens who drew veils over their faces. Grinning beasts that disappeared beneath silver foil foliage. Sepulchers that opened and closed in the space of a blink, forcing one to wonder whether there was something that had crept out of their hollow spaces. At first, Enrique had thought the Forged symbols were intentional. But after hours of observation, he had become disillusioned. Symbols meant something, but they could also exist to confuse the eye. Something that he was not willing to share just yet with Hypnos.

All his life, symbols had been a source of comfort. They felt like stories that reached out beyond the confines of time. And yet, everything about this clock felt like a taunt. To make it worse, every time he looked at it, he was forced to reckon with the hours sliding past. Every hour that went by with Tristan's life hanging in the balance.

A loud huffing sigh broke through his thoughts.

"How am I supposed to think under these conditions?" demanded Hypnos. "What happened to the wine?"

"You could always try water for a change," said Séverin from the doorway.

"Water is boring."

To an outsider, Séverin looked no different than he normally did. Dressed in an elegant suit. Irritable, but restrained. As if this minor glitch were nothing to worry about. But the closer he got, the more little details popped out. The slope of his shoulders. The creases under his eyes. Ink stains on his fingers. The threads on the cuffs of his sleeves unraveling.

Séverin was coming undone.

Séverin took two steps inside the stargazing room before stopping.

"Can't find a seat?" asked Hypnos.

Enrique righted himself. Of course, Hypnos had spoken in jest. There were a number of empty seats, but to Enrique they felt like unsteady ghosts. There was the black cushion on the ground where Tristan should be sitting, hiding Goliath in his pocket. The green, velvet chaise lounge from where Laila would be brandishing her teacup like a queen's scepter. The high stool with its ragged pillow where Zofia would be leaning forward, a matchbox twirling in her hand. And then Séverin's seat, the black-cherry armchair where Hypnos currently sat.

In the end, Séverin chose to stand.

Enrique looked behind him to the door. "Where are the girls?"

Séverin fished around in his pocket and held up a note. "Laila and Zofia went to investigate something at the Forging exhibition."

That made Enrique sit up straight. "*What*? That place is crawling with security guards. And if there's someone from the Fallen House there, then—"

Hypnos started laughing. "Oh, *mon cher*. Did you want them to ask for permission?"

"Of course not." Enrique blushed.

"Ah," said Hypnos, his gaze narrowing. "Then perhaps you're nursing a bit of a wound for not being invited along with them. Which girl, I wonder, has laid claim to some corner of your imagination . . ."

"Can we just get back to work?"

"Laila, I wonder? The living temple goddess?"

Enrique rolled his eyes. Séverin, on the other hand, went entirely still.

"Or is it the little ice queen?"

"Neither," he said sharply.

But even as he said the words, he couldn't help remembering that one of the last times he'd been in this room was with Zofia. Together, they had cracked the code on the Sator Square. Together, they had found something. He'd just thought they made a good team. Yet even as he remembered it, he saw Zofia in the train compartment. The light catching on her candle-bright hair. Her pale fingers tracing the neckline of her velvet dress as she practiced, of all things, *flirting*.

Enrique shook himself. His head was a snarl of too many impressions. Tristan's closed eyes, the dead stare of the figures on the bone clock, the peppery scent of Hypnos's skin, and light catching on Zofia's hair.

"When will they be back?"

"In an hour," said Séverin. "Where are we on the clock?"

"Nowhere," grumbled Hypnos.

"Have you tried taking off the glass covering?"

"What would that do?" demanded Enrique. "It's far too delicate as it is. Maybe that's why it's called a bone clock in the first place. Fragile bones and all that. I lifted the covering once and examined it with kidskin gloves, and the silver immediately started flaking."

"Fine, fine," said Séverin, although he didn't sound very convinced. He turned to Hypnos. "What about any headway on the Fallen House?"

"There's nothing here that we haven't already discussed. The Fallen House believed it was their sacred duty to rebuild the Tower of Babel. They sought to do that by"—Hypnos paused, squinting as he held a piece of parchment to his face—"'harnessing the power of the dead.' I have no idea what that means. It sounds both sinister and terribly unfashionable."

"Well, they were always cryptic," said Enrique, gesturing at the famed bone clock.

At the height of their power, the Fallen House had never once revealed where they held their meetings. Only their infamous bone clocks, their Forged objects of communication, could reveal the meetings' location. Supposedly, the clock also contained a failsafe method allowing a non-House member to locate them in case of emergency, but Enrique was starting to think that was nothing more than rumor.

"How do we know Roux-Joubert is even at the Fallen House's original meeting place?" asked Enrique.

Séverin turned over the honeybee chain in his hand. "He'd consider it a point of pride. As if he were intentionally continuing a legacy."

Hypnos snorted. "Him and *who else*? You told me that man kept saying 'we,' but the Order has tightly controlled anything even resembling recruitment to the Fallen House. They had the leader executed, and the rest of them were given the choice of death or a strong mind affinity alteration that would wipe out any recollection of the Fallen House."

"But so many of those members must have been with the Fallen House for most of their adult lives, wouldn't mind affinity make them—"

"—a shell of their former selves?" finished Hypnos. "Yes. Which is why a shocking number of them chose death. Fanatics."

"Some must have escaped both death and punishment, though," mused Séverin. "Perhaps they were driven deep underground."

"My guess is that it's a clever, deranged man and his hench person with that blade hat you mentioned. The Fallen House loved to travel in packs, like they were wolves or some such. Trust me, if he had more than one person on his side, he would've brought them all for that little showdown in the greenhouse," said Hypnos. At this, even Séverin nodded in agreement. "Also: Who wears a blade hat? What if it slips and then you end up slashing your face? Detestable."

Enrique shuddered, crossing himself. "At this rate, we're not going to find Roux-Joubert or his henchman. Nothing on this clock is helpful. Not even the notation."

He pointed at the one word scrawled just beneath the sixth hour marking: *nocte*.

Midnight.

"It's just the name of the clockmaker," said Séverin.

"I wouldn't be too sure . . . It might be a directive, a rule of some kind meant to inform us how to look at the clock."

"Can I just see the clock without the protective covering?" asked Séverin.

"Only if you promise you won't smash it."

"I promise I won't smash it."

Enrique narrowed his gaze and then nodded in the direction of the bone clock. Gingerly, Séverin lifted the glass covering. He considered the bone clock beneath, the silver foil clinging to the exquisite statues.

And then he shoved it over, where it toppled to one side.

Hypnos squealed. Enrique leapt out of his chair.

"What did you do?" he demanded.

"I did what I wanted. It's my clock."

"But you *promised*!" wailed Enrique.

"True, but my fingers were crossed."

Hypnos faked a gasp. "Oh no! His fingers were crossed!"

Enrique shot Hypnos a scathing glare. "Séverin, you could have damaged a symbol, some critical piece of information, and now we'll never find Tristan—"

"I gave you nearly four hours," said Séverin. "You're brilliant. If there was anything to find, you would have sniffed it out by now. That you didn't is proof enough to me that, in the clock's current state, there is nothing worth finding."

"I . . ." Enrique hesitated.

Truthfully, he was both flattered and insulted. But looking at the place where the bone clock had toppled over, mounting horror replaced all that. Silver dust now spangled the air, a consequence of the delicate foil that had covered the symbols on the clock. Evening light glanced off it, creating sharp and slender shadows on the face of the machinery.

"Now you've done it," said Hypnos. "He's lost the ability to speak!"

"Oh, shut up, Hypnos—" started Séverin.

Enrique tuned out both of them. He crept forward slowly, his heart hammering. There was a new pattern on the body of the bone clock, like ink sluicing between grooved wood. Words hewn out of light and silver and shadow. Where the silver had peeled away, a flat paleness revealed itself. Off-white. Like . . . like . . .

Hypnos scuttled backward on his hands. "Dear God, is that clock *actually* made of bone?"

At the same time, Séverin squinted. "There's writing on that clock."

It hadn't been clear until now. The hand that had cleverly disguised the words on the clock was cramped and narrow, the words barely legible Latin that Enrique quickly translated:

I have been with you all your life
Though I appear only in strife
My quantity will let you see
All this world was meant to be

Enrique moved closer to the clock, his fingers hovering over the words that now appeared.

When Enrique looked up at him, there was a renewed light in Séverin's eyes. Something that hadn't been there until now. The three of them sat once more on the ground. Hypnos with his knees pulled to his chest. Séverin, legs crossed, arms crossed. And then Enrique, who was now happily sprawled out, a pen and notebook beside either hand as he began to transcribe the riddle's words. This was the first breakthrough they'd had in hours, and he could feel the strength of it like an unaccounted for burst of sunshine in the veins.

"My quantity," mused Séverin aloud. "That suggests the answer is twofold. Both the answer to the riddle and how it relates to the clock. Perhaps the quantity has something to do with the numbers on the clock face?"

"Yes, but the clock only goes to twelve," said Hypnos. "What's in your body that there's only twelve of that shows up in times of strife?"

And thus began the most excruciating hour of Enrique's life. At first, there was talk of teeth which Séverin instantly dismissed. "*Who only has twelve teeth?*"

Together, they combed through different riddled answers but nothing fit. The minutes stretched by. Not one of them had disturbed the bone clock where it lay. Hypnos had gotten up and started to wander in circles, moaning for wine. While Séverin had turned inward once more, his fingers worrying the tassels on Tristan's cushion.

"Stupid clock that may or not be made of bone."

Séverin lifted his head. "What did you say?"

"I said the clock may or may not be made of bone."

"Bone."

Hypnos muttered, "I could use a quick one."

Enrique ignored him. "Could that fit? As an answer?"

"'I have been with you all your life,'" read Hypnos aloud. "True. Or that'd be deadly terrifying. Though some people, I honestly believe, are born without spines. And next we have, 'though I appear only in strife.' What? I don't think that fits."

Enrique fell quiet. The strife bit had thrown him off too, at first. Bones didn't *appear* in strife, floating before someone like ghosts. But they certainly showed. He had seen it in the Philippines, when he accompanied his father on rides through the provinces of Capiz and Cavite to check on the rice production of the paddies they owned. On the road, leaned up against whitewashed churches and houses that looked like a strong breeze might make them fold over in defeat, crouched the beggars. Young and old, it didn't matter. Their eyes were all the same: flat and vacant. The faces of those whose hope had hardened and shrunk from too much of life. There, he saw the children with their too-sharp ribs ridging their shirts. Knobbed elbows stained with dirt. Eyes unsettlingly wide in faces sculpted by starvation.

"I think 'bone' fits," he said quietly.

Hypnos cast him a strange look. Enrique had no desire to be the focus of that attention, so he said, "The last two lines fit as well. We know that the Fallen House had some macabre interests. It's possible that meant using bone. In which case, that line, 'all this world was meant to be,' might fit with their own interests and not all humans' everywhere. Which leaves the second-to-last line—'my quantity will let you see'—as the final hint. Maybe it means the number of bones found in a human body. How many are there, anyway?"

"Two hundred and six," said Séverin instantly.

Enrique frowned. "Do I want to know why you had that answer immediately?"

Séverin's smile gleamed wolflike. "I doubt it."

"But how do we get 206 to show up on a clock?"

Séverin let out a soft laugh. As if he were remembering something. "Six minutes past two. Two-oh-six. Two hundred and six."

The three of them stared at the clock. Some crackling energy that had not been there before now wafted out of it. Enrique had the bizarre notion the clock could now sense that they knew how to drag out its secrets.

Slowly, Enrique pushed the hour and minute hand. Hypnos and

Séverin had moved closer without him noticing. He saw the scene, suddenly, in his mind's eye, as if from afar: three boys kneeling around a clock made of bone, the light behind them rendering them sharp shadows brought to life, and he felt that thread of hunger sewing them all together in the moment, so that when it came right down to it, perhaps their souls would have been indistinguishable.

Enrique waited.

He waited for the Forging power to unravel into the air, to push back. But he felt nothing.

"It's not working," said Hypnos. "Did we get it wrong?"

Enrique's heart seized. He hoped not, but then—

"We didn't follow directions," said Séverin, pointing to the little script on the clock's crescent: *nocte. Midnight.*

"But midnight is hours away!"

Séverin's gaze shuddered. He rubbed the scar on his palm, then reached for his tin of cloves. He chewed one thoughtfully, ignoring the tension building up with everyone else.

"At least by then, the girls will be back."

Séverin left not long after that to attend to L'Eden business, which left Enrique and Hypnos alone in the stargazing room. Enrique wasn't sure what he should do. In the end, both of them returned to what they had been doing before—poring over the shredded documents of the Fallen House. Searching for clues in the detritus. The shadow of evening stretched over them. Food had been called up and eaten without either of them lifting a head from their research. Always, the bone clock stared back. Waiting. Smug. When Enrique looked at the room, he saw the strange pall over it. The cushions upturned. Tristan's pillow shoved under a chair so no one could sit in it.

"Why are you helping us?" Enrique realized the words were out of his mouth before he could even think them.

Hypnos looked up, his face unguarded. "Is it so strange to think I might have reasons of my own for wanting the Babel Ring found?" he asked.

"That's not an answer. You could be doing this work from home. I've heard the House Nyx library is the envy of scholars. You don't have to be here."

Hypnos was quiet for a moment, and then he folded his hands on his lap. "If I had someone on my side . . . someone of equal standing to me, then maybe life in the Order would be . . . easier."

Enrique processed this. "You *want* Séverin to become a patriarch?"

Hypnos nodded. "When we were little, I thought we'd grow up and be kings or something. A whole kingdom to divide between us." He glared at Enrique. "Do *not* tell him I said that."

Enrique mimed a zip over his mouth, and Hypnos relaxed once more. He looked so young, so unlined, and yet his ice-colored eyes looked ancient.

"The truth is I need someone on my side," said Hypnos. He wrapped his arms around his knees. "Someone who might understand what it means to live in two worlds as I do. I have tried and I have failed. I cannot be both the descendant of Haitian slaves and the son of a French aristocrat, even if that is what I hold in my heart. I had to choose, and perhaps the Order forced my hand in this. But what no one tells you is that even when you decide which world you will live in, the world may not always see you as you would wish. Sometimes it demands that you be so outrageous as to transcend your very skin. You can change your name. Your eye color. Make yourself a myth and live within it, so that you belong to no one but yourself."

Enrique's mouth felt dry. He knew exactly how that felt. The feeling like his own skin betrayed him. That his own dreams didn't match his face and would therefore never come to pass. "I understand."

Hypnos snorted. He dropped his head back against the couch, and the light caught on the long line of his throat. Hypnos looked like a seraph who spent his whole life in ripe sunshine. He had always been beautiful, but now the light gilded his beauty into something unearthly. Enrique used to feel a twinge of shame when it came to his feelings . . . He used to pray that when it came to attraction, his body would just choose between men and women, and not both. It was his second-oldest brother, bound for priesthood, who told him that God made no mistakes in crafting their hearts. Enrique still hadn't quite parsed out his own relationship to faith, but what his brother said had made him stop hating himself. It made him stop turning from what lay inside him and embrace it. But it wasn't until he arrived in Spain for university that he started doing more than just looking at beautiful boys. He was reminded of it now, staring at Hypnos . . . and he was far too distracted to realize the other boy had noticed.

Hypnos swiped his thumb across his lips. "Do I have something on my mouth?"

"No, not at all," said Enrique, turning quickly.

Hypnos muttered something that almost sounded like: *That's a pity*.

TIME MARCHED STEADILY toward midnight.

By then, Laila and Zofia had returned. They shared their findings with one another—the bone clock and the hidden Tezcat—and settled down to wait in the stargazing room. The chairs had lost some of their ghostly attributes, and everyone took a seat, leaving only Tristan's cushion untouched.

In those final stretches to midnight, Enrique thought he could feel everything . . . From the heat vibrating off Hypnos's hand, which was just an *inch* too close, and the glow of Zofia's candlelight hair as she bent her head to inspect her newest invention, to the sugar crystals from the cookie Laila had snuck him and the cold of Séverin's fury as he stared at the clock. Enrique, who had always dreamed about what magic might feel like, thought he had found it then: myths and palimpsests, starlight sugaring the air, and the way hope feels painful when shared equally among friends.

At the stroke of midnight, they slid the clock into position: six minutes past two.

Light burst across the room.

Laila jerked backward, but Zofia leaned toward the light. Curiosity flickered across her face.

"It works like a mnemo bug," she observed.

The vision contained in the clock splayed across the room, blotting out the glimpse of the stars overhead.

A hall full of bones. Grinning skulls crowded together. Compacted earth where a great spiraled pattern like the logarithm floor of House Kore spread out across an abandoned auditorium. And Enrique thought he might even be able to sniff out the smell of that place regardless that he could only see the image of it. Great crosses made of femurs, and an eerie lake where stalactites dripped their mineral tears. Here, finally, was the secret hiding place of the Fallen House. The place connected to the Forged exhibition. The place where, somewhere, Tristan lay trapped in the dark.

Enrique didn't know who spoke first, but the truth of the words brushed against his skin, raising the hairs along the back of his neck.

"The Fallen House is waiting for us in the catacombs."

23

SÉVERIN

Séverin's sixth father was a man he called Greed. Greed was a pretty thief with a petty trust fund, and often resorted to stealing. Greed liked to keep Séverin as a lookout while he ran his "errands." On one such occasion, Greed broke into the home of a rich widow. He cleared out the curio cabinet, which was full of precious porcelain pieces and elaborate glasswork, but then he saw that atop the cabinet was a clock made of jade. Séverin had been standing outside, watching the street. When he heard the steady clip of horse hooves, he whistled, but Greed shushed him. He reached for the clock, only for the ladder beneath him to crash. The heavy clock fell on his head and killed him instantly.

Greed taught him to beware of reaching too high.

SÉVERIN PLACED A clove on his tongue, chewing slowly as he mulled over his information.

They knew where the Fallen House hid.

They knew what the Fallen House wanted: the Babel Fragment rejoined.

Everything else was just a matter of timing.

As the light from the bone clock dissolved, Hypnos sighed. "Technically, all House heads are supposed to report any Fallen House activity to the Order."

"Technically?" repeated Séverin. "Technically, we don't know if someone from the Order is acting through Roux-Joubert."

"Which is why I said 'technically,'" added Hypnos. "I *have* to report to the Order, but they never specified *when* I had to do that. I could supposedly do it after we find Roux-Joubert, when we're sure that no one from House Kore was involved in stealing the Ring."

"Sneaky."

"I'm following someone's example."

"Do you really think someone from the Order would be behind this?" asked Enrique. "Wouldn't they be betraying the whole point of the Order?"

"Never underestimate the human capacity for betrayal," said Laila quietly.

Like the rest of them, she had avoided her usual seat on the velvet chaise lounge. Instead, she leaned against the bookcase, the train of her green silk dress tucked over her legs. Laila rubbed the back of her neck, her fingers disappearing behind her collar to trace her scar. She thought of it like a seam, as if it made her more ragdoll than human, but to Séverin it was just a scar. Scars sculpted people into who they were. They were scuffs left by sorrow's fists, and to him, at least, proof of being thoroughly human. And then, unbidden, came the memory of touching that scar, how it felt cold as glass and just as smooth. He remembered how she tensed when he touched her there, and how he'd kissed the length of it, desperate to show her he knew what it meant and it didn't matter. Not to him.

Suddenly Laila looked up and their eyes met. The slightest color touched her cheeks, and he wondered if she was remembering too. She looked away from him abruptly.

"What's the plan?" she asked.

Séverin forced his gaze to the others. "We infiltrate the Fallen House's meeting location in the catacombs. We take back both the House Kore Ring and the Horus Eye."

"I doubt he'd leave the Ring lying around on the ground," said Laila. "Wouldn't he be wearing it?"

Hypnos wiggled his fingers. "He can't. He might have managed to tear it off, but it's still welded to us."

Séverin nodded, then added, "Looking through the Horus Eye will give us the Fragment's location, which, assuming there's no sign of House Kore's involvement in the theft, we'd then relay directly to the House Kore matriarch. That way, the Order can dispatch people to protect the site of the Fragment and immobilize Roux-Joubert and his accomplice."

"How are we entering the catacombs?" asked Laila.

"Through the normal route on rue d'Enfers."

"But they can just escape through the hidden Tezcat in the exhibit," pointed out Hypnos.

From where she sat, Zofia drew out the silver cloth and dangled it before them.

"No, they can't."

"Is *that* supposed to impress me?" asked Hypnos, horrified.

"This cloth is impenetrable," said Zofia.

"It's true," said Laila. "She stabbed the poor thing."

"Fascinating as that is, it's still no bigger than a handkerchief," pointed out Hypnos.

"I know," said Zofia. "I can reproduce it."

"A *hundred* handkerchiefs? I'm quaking."

"You should," said Zofia mildly.

"Zofia, if you can manipulate the size of the silver cloth, I wonder if you can play with one other thing."

Séverin took out a mnemo bug from his pocket. It was small and lightweight and cold to the touch. And yet in its Forged body, it could hold the image of a mind's eye and project it into the air.

"*A mnemo bug?*" groaned Enrique. "What's that going to do? Record the moments before our inevitable death? Because I don't actually want a souvenir of that."

"Just trust me."

"Maybe I could stay behind," said Hypnos. "I could be a point of contact on the street or—"

"What happened to being excited about teamwork?" asked Séverin.

"That was before I realized how little regard you hold for mortality."

"If you follow the plan, your mortality will stay intact."

Hypnos looked highly suspicious. "What is this plan of yours, *mon cher?*"

Before Séverin could answer, Zofia struck a match against her tooth. "Crocodile teeth."

The four of them turned to her. Séverin laughed. Zofia had guessed exactly what they were going to do.

"Great minds think alike."

Zofia frowned. "No, they don't. Otherwise every idea would be uniform."

BY NOW, SÉVERIN'S mouth burned, but he still reached for another clove. He wasn't sure where he had first heard that the aromatic herb helped preserve memory. A hotel guest, perhaps, leaving a present for him on the eve of his or her departure. Now, he couldn't stop the habit. Memories unsettled him. He hated the thought that he might have missed something, and he didn't want time warping how he remembered things because he didn't trust himself to remember without bias. And he needed to. Because only then, only with absolute impartiality, could he detect where he had gone wrong. As he made his way to the grand lobby of L'Eden, he combed through— for the thousandth time—his last moments with Tristan. Tristan had been trying to warn him of something, and Séverin had turned him away. Was it then? Did Tristan step outside and get trapped by the Fallen House? Did he try to knock himself unconscious when they showed him the Phobus Helmet, the way he used to when they stayed in the home of Wrath? Roux-Joubert's words found their way back to him with perfect clarity and for a moment, Séverin wished the cloves he chewed didn't work half as well: "His love and his fear and his own cracked mind made it easy to convince him that betraying you was saving you . . ."

Guilt curdled in his stomach. He should have listened.

Séverin stood at the base of the grand staircase that opened into the lobby, surveying L'Eden. Except Tristan wasn't here, and Séverin was alone. Then, from behind him, came a thin and reedy sound.

"Mama?"

Séverin's spine stiffened.

He turned and saw a young boy clutching a ragged teddy bear. Children rarely stayed at L'Eden with their parents. He had expressly forbidden any "family-friendly" allure and had succeeded up until now. For a moment, Séverin was riveted by the sight of the child. Where he went, he rarely saw young children. And he forgot that he had ever been so small, barely hip-height and utterly lost.

"Mama?" called the little voice again.

What had happened to the boy's parents? Had they actually presumed to abandon him . . . *here*?

Fat tears slid down the child's face, and Séverin fought down the urge to yell at him.

Why mourn those who didn't want you? he wanted to scream. *You'll be fine without them.*

But then a woman rushed past him, gathering the boy in her arms and laughing. "Darling, did you not hear me say I was only going to check with the concierge for a moment?"

The boy shook his head, sobbing, and his mother held him close. Right then, his jealousy was a living thing, settling into his heart, pulsing through his veins. Of course, the boy hadn't been abandoned. Of course, he had only been temporarily misplaced.

"What is wrong with me?" he murmured, turning away from the sight of the boy and his mother.

Across the sea of guests, his factotum caught his eye and waved. Séverin waited at the end of the staircase, occasionally nodding his head in acknowledgment to various guests until his factotum appeared. In one hand, he carried a small box that he held at arm's length. Distaste rippled across his features.

"Sir, we can easily find someone else to perform this . . . task."

Séverin took the box. Inside, a handful of brown crickets chirped and jumped. "I would prefer to see to it myself."

"Very well, sir."

Out the corner of his eye, he saw a sleek cheetah bound across the lobby. "And please inform the Marchessa de Castiglione that if Imhotep eats someone's poodle again, the hotel is not responsible."

His factotum sighed. "Yes, sir. Anything else?"

Séverin closed his hands into a fist. "The guests with the child . . .

tell them their room is under construction. Find them comparable lodgings elsewhere. The Savoy perhaps."

His factotum eyed him suspiciously. "Very well, sir."

AT THE ENTRANCE to Tristan's workshop, Séverin pinched the gilded ivy leaf of the Tezcat door only to stop short.

He wasn't alone.

Silhouetted by candlelight and bent over a glass terrarium was Laila. She was singing a lullaby, though not particularly well, and dropping crickets into Goliath's cage. Now he wished he'd let someone else come. He hated seeing her like this . . . going through routines, settling herself into a life she couldn't wait to leave behind.

He took a step toward the table. Around her gleamed the miniature worlds that Tristan crafted. Minuscule spires lording over a painted sky. Gardens where porcelain petals gathered dust. Amidst it, Laila looked like an icon. Her hair was pulled over one shoulder, and he imagined he could smell the sugar and rosewater sprayed at the hollow of her throat.

Not wanting to alarm Laila, Séverin set down the box of crickets. But he ended up placing the box near the table's edge where it nearly slid and toppled to the ground. Séverin rushed to grab it, only to stab his thumb on a concealed thorn.

"Majnun?" said Laila, whirling to face him. "What are you doing here?"

Séverin winced and gestured at the box of crickets. "Same as you, it seems. Although you managed to do so without injury."

"Here, let me," she said, walking toward him. "I know he keeps bandages around here somewhere." Laila rummaged through one of the drawers until she found a length of gauze and a pair of scissors.

"For a moment I thought you might be the elusive bird killer on the grounds."

Séverin shook his head. It was a pesky problem, but chances were, it was just a cat.

"I'm sorry to disappoint," he said. He brought his pulsing finger to his lips, intent on sucking the skin as he would any cut, but Laila batted away his hand.

"You could get an infection!" she scolded. "Now hold still."

She reached for his hand. Séverin did as she commanded. He held still as if his life hung in the balance. Right then, it seemed as if there was too much of her. In the air. Against his skin. When she bent her head to tie the gauze, her hair trailed over his fingertips. Séverin couldn't help it. He flinched. Laila looked up. Her uncanny eyes, so dark and glossy they reminded him of a swan's stare, bored into his. One corner of her mouth tipped up.

"What's wrong? Do you think I'll read you?"

His pulse scattered. She had told him before that she could only read objects. Not people. *Never* people. "You can't do that."

Laila raised one slender eyebrow. "Can't I?"

"That's not funny, Laila."

Laila waited a beat, then two. Finally, she rolled her eyes. "Don't worry, *Majnun*. You're quite safe from me."

She was wrong about that.

FOR THE NEXT eighteen hours, none of them slept. Enrique spent so much time scouring books in the library that Laila had arranged for his bedding to be sent there. Hypnos was scarcely seen without a drink in his hand—*the better to help me think!*—and spent all his time corresponding with his own spies, accomplices, and guards. Zofia, meanwhile, lived up to her nickname, for she spent half the day submerged behind veils of smoke. And Laila . . . Laila kept them alive. Her hands were always working . . . pouring tea, offering food, rubbing tired scalps, grazing the edges of objects, while her smile stayed as still and knowing as ever.

One day, then two, and now midnight was nearly upon them.

Far away from the glitter and glamour, midnight soaked the gritty streets. Beggars slept huddled in corners, and skinny cats slipped around stone corners. Séverin and Laila walked lightly, their shoulders hunched against any curious glares. Séverin had never had any interest in seeing the catacombs. He knew that it was an underground ossuary holding the remains of *millions*. Cradled in its earth were the bodies of duchesses and aristocrats, plague victims, and those whose heads had been snapped off by a guillotine's teeth. Countless, unnamed individuals who were now nothing more than ghastly halls and arches made from grinning skulls and cracked jaws.

Laila shivered as they got close. Slowly, she plucked off her gloves, then reached down to touch the metal fence surrounding the entrance. She closed her eyes, then gave a tight nod. *Roux-Joubert was here.* Calm washed over him then. He thought of the stories he'd heard growing up about the underworld. The tale of Orpheus, who looked behind him and lost everything. He wouldn't be that. He would descend and ascend, and lose nothing but a handful of time. He swallowed hard against the doubt lodged at the back of his throat and took the stairs. Above his head, a sign carved in stone declared

Arrête! C'est ici l'empire de la mort.
Stop! This is the empire of death.

PART V

From the archival records of the Order of Babel
The Origins of Empire
Mistress Hedvig Petrovna, House Dažbog of the Order's Russian faction
1771, reign of Empress Yekaterine Alekseyevna

We must be vigilant in the boundaries of our work.

We protect and preserve.

We do not pretend at being gods.

Our Babel Rings carry the power to reveal the Fragments, but some have forgotten that this power does not confer godhood. We might have been better served to call them wax wings. A reminder for those who wish to reach for that which they should not. There are Icaruses, Sampatis, Kua Fus, and Bladuds. Those who reached and failed. Their fall, the better to remind us. Their smashed bones upon the ground, a necromancer's reading of the fate to befall those who forget.

24

❧ ❦ ❧

ZOFIA

Two hours before midnight

Zofia glared at her bed. On it were three different outfits. One was dark, one was light, one was covered in multicolored embroidery. She was aware, distantly, that there was more she was supposed to notice, but she couldn't fathom it and so she didn't try. Instead, she reached for the letter pinned to one of the sleeves. It was a list written out in Laila's neat hand.

Step 1: Zofia, brush your hair. I tried to help before I left, but couldn't find you. Or did I see you on the western hallway near the wisterias?

Zofia felt a stab of guilt. Laila had seen her. But Zofia had seen the brush and disappeared down another hall.

Step 2: I laid out three dresses for you. The dark one will be the least distracting because there are no asymmetrical frills. The light one will be the most comfortable. The embroidered one is for if you feel nervous because then you can count the stitches while you're waiting.

Zofia brushed her hair and reached for the embroidered dress.

Step 3: *On your vanity is a pot of rouge and a pot of kohl. Use them only if you wish. Cosmetics do not mean that you need them. They can be anything you desire them to be. Enhancement, armor, et cetera.*

Zofia stared at the last step. She could not explain why it calmed her, but it did. On her vanity, she found the cosmetic pots Laila had mentioned. Zofia did not keep many things on her dresser beyond the wash basin and a clean towel. At home, she never spent much time on her face or hair. It inevitably ended up frustrating her, and she would simply turn to Hela for help. But Hela wasn't here. Not yet, anyway. And if tonight went wrong, perhaps she never would be.

Once she was dressed, Zofia double-checked the pockets and skirts. All her clothing had some Forged aspect to them, and the embroidered dress was no exception. Her pelisse was made of Forged sulfur silk that could burst into flames—perfumed so as not to offend the nose—and she had altered her shoes along with Enrique's and Hypnos's to include blades in the heel.

In her drawstring reticule lay a mnemo bug and the silver cloth. Zofia fumbled, her hands damp as she tightened the reticule's drawstrings. Just as she was about to leave her room, she caught a faint glow on her bedside table. She paused. It was a moonflower, Forged by Tristan to soak in starlight and serve as a night-light for those times when she got hungry and wanted to sneak down to the kitchens. Tristan was always working on botanical inventions the way Zofia already tinkered with new engineering developments. She smiled, thinking of the last invention he'd been working on: Night

Bites. Projectile ink that could temporarily blind a person, much to Laila's despair.

Zofia touched the moonflower softly. These past few days she had taken to sleeping in her laboratory and had not left the moonflower on her windowsill. A scrap of light clung to its petals, casting a luminous pool on the wood of her night table. Carefully, she picked it up, then lay it atop the items in her reticule. Tristan was never without a flower, either in his pocket or between his fingers. He would need one for the ride home.

Zofia walked toward the lobby. On the wall, the Forged torchlight seemed too bright. She rubbed her skin, scalded. Normally, she never entered through a hall where people could see her. But Séverin's instructions before he left had been strict.

Be seen.

The thought made her nauseous. Zofia looked down from the top of the staircase. For a split second, the staircase did not appear at a slanted diagonal, but rather a steep fall, her body leaning off a precipice that fell straight to the floor. She swayed—

"All right, phoenix?"

Enrique was at her side, his arm around her waist. He removed it at once.

"I apologize. I thought you were going to fall."

Zofia gripped the bannister. "I was."

Zofia glanced at Enrique. Like her, he had dressed with care. She recognized the subtle armor of his clothes. Her invention where buttons could turn to marbles and make someone slip. The silk square in his pocket could become an iron shield. But then her gaze went . . . *up.* To his face. She had looked at his face at least once a day for approximately 730 days, and in that time it had not altered. It was still an objectively handsome face. She had noticed the lingering stares that followed him whenever he walked into a room. But her awareness of his features felt . . . different. More heightened.

"Um . . . Zofia?"

Zofia blinked, then realized she had raised her hand to touch his face. She pulled her hand back, looking at it thoughtfully.

"Your face is different."

Enrique patted his cheeks softly. "Bad different? Good different? Am I still handsome, at least?"

Warmth zipped through the base of her spine. How odd. It was uncomfortable. But not painful. "Yes," she said, and then took to the stairs.

The two of them wandered through the crowd. In one corner of the lobby were Turkish princes sitting around a game of chess. A woman whose hair looked like a sheet of ink drifted past them, her bright red sleeves touching the floor. The concierge desk was a circle of chaos. Room keys zipped through the crowd, knocking against the wrists of guests like dogs eager for a treat.

"How long do we have to stay here?" asked Zofia.

"Just until the clock strikes ten."

Zofia glanced up at the large grandfather clock near the entrance of L'Eden. Ten minutes to go.

"Where's Hypnos?"

"Ask and you shall receive, *ma chère*."

Hypnos appeared at their side dressed in a bright purple, velvet coat. He waved his fingers. His Babel Ring twinkled there.

"You're flaunting it!" Enrique scolded.

"Relax, it's fake."

Zofia eyed him. Where had Hypnos hidden his, then? A patriarch or matriarch could never be without their Ring because it was welded to them.

Enrique made a huffing sound.

"Fine. What about the rest of you? What are you wearing?" he demanded. "Séverin said go for *subtlety*."

"Someone might recognize me. And if they do, then dressing with subtlety would only attract more attention—it's that unusual. Besides, I'm wearing all my accoutrements of good luck." Hypnos lifted the inside of his lapel, revealing massive brooches made of cut jewels. "A good deal of my inheritance if I'm being honest—"

"You look like an insect!"

Hypnos fluttered his hand to his chest. "How rude! Zofia, am I an insect?"

Zofia shook her head.

"Thank you—"

"You don't have the characteristics necessary to be an insect," she said. "You would need two pairs of wings, a body segmented into three parts, and six legs to be an insect."

She had learned that from Tristan.

Enrique burst into laughter.

When the clock struck ten, the three of them piled into a carriage. The drive to the Exposition Universelle was short, and when they stepped out, the crowd had formed a thick press along the Champs-de-Mars. Lightbulbs flashed up and down the Eiffel Tower, and fireworks spangled the night sky. Zofia pushed through the crowd, feeling that edge of panic rising in her lungs. People hemmed her in on all sides. She couldn't even see the road, and they had hardly taken five steps—

"Make *way*!" shouted Hypnos, prodding at people with his walking stick.

Enrique looked horrified. He shaded his face with his hand. And then, Hypnos sighed.

"Be that way." He unscrewed the top of his walking stick. "Cover your mouth and nose, my dears."

Zofia did not see anything, but she felt a fine mist against her skin. One by one, people's noses wrinkled, and they took a step away from Hypnos, clearing a path down to the exhibition. When they had gotten through to the other side, Hypnos stoppered the stick and smiled.

"I hired a Forging artist with mind affinity to make a people repellent. Sadly, it doesn't last longer than a minute, but it makes for a delightfully useful walking stick."

Enrique looked envious. "Well, *my* walking stick emits a bright light."

Zofia felt a flare of pride. She had designed that stick.

Hypnos lifted his chin. "*Mine* can . . ."

Zofia ignored them. She had no interest in listening to two boys compare their sticks.

Past the streets teeming with vendors hawking souvenirs and cafés boasting exotic offerings loomed the glass and metal archway of the Galerie des Machines, a testament to the inventions that would usher them into the new century. And right beside it, the Exhibition on Colonial Superstitions. Earlier, Hypnos had planted House Nyx guards at the exhibit, and when the guards saw them, they stepped aside and granted them entry. The place was empty at this time of night, with most of the tourists having abandoned the exhibits to see the fireworks shooting off the sides of the Eiffel Tower.

As before, neat rows of illuminated podiums striped the floor. On each of the podiums were written descriptions of the Forged object on display and the country of its origin. Zofia reached for the mnemo bug in her reticule.

The wall concealing the hidden Tezcat door towered above Zofia. At barely four feet eleven inches she was not unaccustomed to feeling small, but it was what stood on the other side of the Tezcat that shrank her. She had beheld the secrets hidden in the bone clock. The ossified auditorium covered in what looked like a gigantic logarithmic spiral. Bones pressed into the walls.

On most acquisitions, she was off to the side or hiding in their final meeting location and running interference as needed. Never at the forefront. Never the one controlling the aspects. Zofia swallowed hard against that lump of misgiving. Things changed. Tristan needed her. She would not fail him.

The silver cloth that had taken hours to Forge slid from her hands to the floor. Zofia gathered herself, looking at her sleeves and counting the neat, embroidered stitches until a pleasant hum ensnared her thoughts. At the two ends of the wall crouched Hypnos and Enrique.

Zofia pretended to look at one of the objects on the podium. And then, under her breath, she muttered a single word: "Go."

Hypnos and Enrique reached for the opposite ends of the silver cloth, now adhered to the length of the entire stone wall. The cloth itself was invulnerable to matter, but it could still be torn from a wall, and so she'd lined the fabric with Forged adhesive. Even if someone were to come in after they left, they wouldn't be able to take it down from this side of the wall.

As one, they clicked their heels together. The Forged stilts concealed in their shoes unclasped, shooting them straight into the air. The silver cloth stretched out from the ground, like a waterfall pouring upward until it covered the entire wall.

That done, Zofia reached for the mnemo bug. She rubbed the small button on the right wing. Every time her skin brushed against it, she felt a buzzing trill zip through her veins. Though the mechanics of the bug required an affinity for matter, its internal mechanism used affinity of the mind. The object was linked to how her brain processed an image, and with that image, it could then project the "mind's eye" into hologram form.

"What shall I do, pretty?" asked Hypnos. "Sing? Dance?"

"Why do I have to be in the view of the mnemo bug?" asked Enrique. "Can't I just be off to the side?"

"What would Séverin do?"

"Probably glower attractively and stare into space."

"And chew a clove," said Zofia.

Enrique grinned. "Definitely that."

"Now?" asked Hypnos.

"Not yet," said Zofia. They had to get the timing perfectly right, otherwise Séverin and Laila might be exposed.

Around them, the clock struck eleven.

Zofia adjusted the lens, then said, "Start posing."

25

LAILA

One hour before midnight

Laila's foot slipped on the slick floor of the catacombs. Her pulse turned jagged in her ears. Slowly, she felt her way through the dark. Up ahead, she could just make out Séverin. A tall, imposing shape that cut through the thick shadows of the bone-warped halls.

Laila did not dare to touch the bones lining the walls around her. She had never tested her ability against a skull. In India, the dead were cremated. Legend went that those who weren't properly buried became *bhuts*, or ghosts. Though she knew she couldn't read anything living, she didn't want to take her chances with the dead.

Above her, coin-shaped carvings in the ceilings cast green light onto the floor. Laila shuddered, thinking of the warning at the entrance to the catacombs.

Arrête! C'est ici l'empire de la mort.
Stop! This is the empire of death.

She could barely stand to look at this place. Even the air offended her. It had the unstirred and cold texture of a sepulchre, and she could feel it frosting her throat with every inhale. As she turned a corner, she saw a child-sized skull and nearly vomited. Everything reeked of a *cost* to be paid, and Laila did not know what had been the cost of her existence. Is that what the *jaadugar* had used when he crafted her body?

"Here," whispered Séverin.

Laila crept up beside him. The closer she got, the more she felt as though a hand had pressed down on her thoughts. When they had seen the Fallen House's location revealed in the bone clock, it had imparted more than just an image, it had given knowledge. Laila shook her head. She didn't like how it felt, like something parasitic sitting on her thoughts, tugging the very reins of her mind.

Now, beside Séverin, she thought there had to be a mistake. There was nothing but another shelf of bones, this one hammered into an archway with a row of grinning skulls teetering at its apex. A faint slit of light shone through the hollows of skull eyes. Laila held her breath as Séverin placed his hand to the wall of bone. His hand disappeared, sinking to his wrist.

"Another Tezcat," he said. A ferocious grin split his face. "And it's not even protected."

The Fallen House had relied on the secrecy of their location and not much else. Not once when she and Séverin had walked down the halls and held out their Forging devices had they picked up even a hint of additional security.

"Ready?"

Laila nodded. Séverin's main task was to find Tristan. As for her, all she had to do was read the room. Literally. Somewhere on the other side lay not only the Babel Ring of House Kore, but also the Horus Eye stolen from the subterranean library. After that, Hypnos could relay the information to the Order, and Roux-Joubert and his accomplice would be stopped.

"I'll go first," said Séverin.

For a moment, Laila wanted to stop him. This place unnerved her. But maybe it was superstition. In the end, she watched him sink into that wall of bone, her heartbeat ringing loudly in her ears.

Laila waited a beat. Her hand brushed against the small satchel at her hip. She drew it aside, removing the small knife strapped to her thigh. She inhaled deep, her body recoiling at the sensation of damp air, and then walked straight through the wall.

On the other side lay the auditorium, identical to the one the bone clock had shown them. Dirt terraces carved into the wall, sloping downward into a wide stage. The stage itself reminded her of a snail's shell. A strange whorl grooved deep into the earth. When they had first glimpsed it in the bone clock's projection, Zofia had mused that it was another logarithmic spiral and then launched into an explanation that Laila completely tuned out. Séverin, though, thought it was something else. A mechanized pathway, not unlike a waterwheel activated by the churning of a liquid, or the fireball that traveled in a corkscrew pattern back in House Kore. But they had no clues about what it was supposed to lead to. Behind the stage, tattered scarlet curtains hung from the ceiling, utterly still. Faded, golden embroidery covered the scarlet drapes. The symbols of the four Houses of France. An ouroboros—a snake biting its own tail—edged the curtain. House Vanth. A crescent moon shaped like a pale and ghastly grin hovered in the center. House Nyx. Thorns and tightly furled buds crosshatched the space between the snake and the moon. House Kore. And within the snake, six points touching the scaled body, a giant hexagram. The Fallen House. Behind those curtains, guessed Laila, must be the entrance to the Exhibit on Colonial Superstitions. Laila tried not to think about Hypnos, Enrique, and

Zofia. How close they were and how unreachable. She murmured a prayer as she scanned the rest of the view.

To the left of the stage was a shut door. Laila could just make out the sound of someone playing a violin and another person talking in low murmurs. The hairs on the back of her neck prickled, but she didn't panic. This was as they had planned. Naturally, Roux-Joubert and his associate would be there. In an hour, they'd step through the Tezcat, presumably to take Hypnos's Babel Ring before returning to the catacombs. A flicker of movement to the right of the stage caught Laila's attention. She reached for the dagger at her hip. At the same time, Séverin grabbed her hand, his grip like steel.

Tristan.

He was slumped over in a chair. The Phobus Helmet still wrapped around his forehead. Even from a distance, Laila could make out a flash of blue flickering across the glass like sparks of lightning. Her gaze flew across his body. To his white-knuckled clench on the armrests. The brittle way he held his legs, straight out and locked. Laila squeezed her eyes shut, forcing back the tears that prickled.

"Why haven't they taken off that cursed thing?" he asked hoarsely. "Why are they still hurting him?"

She didn't have an answer to that . . .

"We'll take it off. It'll be over soon."

Séverin paled, but he managed a curt nod. Laila forced herself to look beyond Tristan's face and to the area surrounding him. There was a large workshop table, strewn with mechanical bits—the ends of tools, a wooden awl, a jar of buttons. And then, sitting on a scrap of velvet . . . the Horus Eye. Something else gleamed just beyond it. It was too far to tell, but that blue sheen raised her spirits. It might be the Babel Ring.

Séverin held out his hand. Laila dug through the satchel. Next to a small pouch of Tristan's Night Bites lay a tiny snuffbox. She opened it, revealing a new and precious supply of mirror powder. Séverin took a pinch, dusting his hands and touching the dirt floor. His image rippled, melding in with the terrace. As he moved, it looked as if there was an invisible bump on the terrain, traveling quickly down the slope. Laila did the same, then raced down the steps. Even with the Forged muffling bells, she went on tiptoe. A dancer's instinct to move with precision. The ground beneath them was slick, covered in grime and gravel. All it would take was one fall and then the landslide of pebbles would give away their location.

At the base of the terrace, Laila and Séverin crept around the edges, working their way to the shadowed alcoves where Tristan sat. Séverin ran to him, grabbing his wrist. He waited a moment, then loosed his breath.

"His pulse is racing."

At least he had a pulse.

Séverin crouched on the floor, reaching for the straps that bound each of Tristan's legs to the chair. His hands trembled. This close, the helmet around Tristan's head gleamed a sinister blue. Tails of light whipped through the top, as if tentacles rippled over his skull. His eyes roved beneath closed lids.

"What did they do to you?" Séverin murmured under his breath. He spared a glance at Laila. "Grab the Eye and start looking for the Ring."

But Laila felt rooted to the spot. Something felt *off*. It nagged at her, itching at the back of her skull.

"Séverin, wait."

"I'm getting him out of here," he said fiercely. One knot done, Séverin turned to the straps and bindings on the other leg. All the while Tristan didn't move, didn't twitch. As if he couldn't feel a thing. "That's final."

Laila turned to the worktable. There was the Horus Eye. Beside it, the Ring.

All of it there, ripe treasure for the taking. But she couldn't swipe it off the table. Something stayed her hand. Instead, she touched the wood that faced Tristan. The images it had witnessed sank through her thoughts, pulling her away from the surrounding scene. *The stage. The curtains pulled back as a man with a blade-brimmed hat stepped through. Roux-Joubert coughing, blood escaping from his handkerchief and flecking the wooden table. Tristan screaming. A cloth shoved past his lips.*

Laila pulled back her hand, her heart racing wildly. Out the corner of her eye, she could sense Séverin. His hands working on the knot. Distantly, she heard him.

"Laila, grab the Eye and Ring. What are you waiting for—"

She saw herself touching the Horus Eye. It felt as if she were outside her own body. She felt herself straining her perception, trying to read it as she would with any un-Forged object. But the Eye was Forged, and whatever secrets it held drew away from her touch. Next, she reached for the Ring.

Images slammed into her.

The tools on the table. The cast molding of zinc. Blue lights on a thread. Tristan screaming as the Ring was made.

"Now hush, boy, be quiet or I will meld that Phobus Helmet to you. Is that what you want? Don't you see your place in the grand revolution? Don't you understand what must be done to awaken the future?"

Laila yanked back her hand.

She shouldn't have been able to read it.

It was fake.

"Séverin!" she called, not caring that her voice had risen, that someone might hear her. She reached for his hand just as he touched the helmet. But she wasn't fast enough. Séverin reached out with both hands. The moment he lifted it off Tristan's head, the blue lights cut off abruptly. Beneath it, Tristan's head lolled to one side. They had not changed him out of the clothes from the greenhouse. He was covered in his own filth. Séverin turned to Laila, a victorious smile blooming on his face. Laila blinked. It happened so fast. One moment, the blue lights disappeared. The next, they *flared* to life. Lightning curled, coiling around Séverin's arms. He fell backward, his head thrown back, body trembling—

"No!" cried Laila.

She kicked the helmet away from his hands, reaching for Séverin. His eyes rolled back.

"Majnun."

He didn't move. In the distance, Laila heard a door opening. Voices growing more insistent. The whining screech of metal on metal as the curtains were scraped back. Laila's mind splintered. She had to leave. Or she could hide Séverin here, cover him in enough mirror powder that no one would find him until everyone else joined her. She had the Horus Eye at least.

Laila rocked back on her heels, then winced sharply. Something had jabbed into the back of her neck. She reached up with one hand— and felt flesh. The cold, clammy skin of someone's wrist. And beneath that wrist, a blade.

Laila went still. She snatched her hand away, her back rigid as a board. In a moment, she would have to turn. Slowly, she moved her head. As she did, she slipped one hand into her satchel. It was still open, now fallen across her lap. Her fingers closed around a Night Bite.

"Please," said a shaking voice behind her. The voice of the person who held a knife to her. "Please."

Something snapped inside her. She knew every contour of that voice. How it dipped low in a laugh. Rose high in excitement. She looked behind her: Tristan.

Tears streamed down his face. But even as he wept, he did not lose his grip on the knife that he held to her throat.

"Please," he begged, and he did not sound like himself but like a boy haunted and hunted. "Please, you don't understand."

26

SÉVERIN

Fifteen minutes before midnight

Séverin opened his eyes.

He was kneeling. He knew that much. His knees ached. The muscles of his neck throbbed. When he looked down, he noticed his hands were bound together. As if in prayer. His mouth tasted sour. A hint of clove burned on his tongue.

"Do you know where you are, Monsieur Montagnet-Alarie?"

Séverin glanced up. Roux-Joubert stared down at him. Séverin shifted from one knee to the next, feeling the heavy weight at the bottom hem of his left pant leg. Before he'd stepped foot into the catacombs, he'd placed a time-weighted bag full of diatomaceous earth and sulfur in the lining. A trail, he'd hoped, but now he wasn't sure the others would find it in time.

Séverin bit his lip, hoping the pain would jog his memories. He remembered entering the catacombs. He remembered seeing the strange grooves carved along the floor of the stage. He pushed himself, new images rising to the surface of his thoughts. *Laila.* Laila screaming at him, reaching for him just as he was reaching for the helmet that had been stuck tight to Tristan's head.

"He's fine, my boy," said Roux-Joubert, as if he could read his thoughts.

Séverin bit back a growl.

Roux-Joubert had laid a trap for them. And he had placed irresistible bait for Séverin: Tristan.

Séverin looked up. The scarlet curtains, once pulled close, had been flung back. The Tezcat door sprawled before him, towering like a great beast of polished obsidian. Through the Tezcat, he could see the Forging exhibition. Objects hovering above black podiums. The stingy light of sulfur lamps draping the scene in shadows. But that was not all that he could see. Standing just on the other side of the Tezcat, feet planted firmly in the Forging exhibition, their hands shoved into pockets and smug grins on their faces were Enrique and Hypnos. Séverin looked away from them, his heart beating fast in his rib cage. His gaze swept the stage. Only two people stood there. Roux-Joubert, dressed in a black suit, his honeybee pin prominent and polished on his lapel. Behind him, a stout man with a strange bowler hat, the brim of it gleaming as if . . . as if it were a blade.

Séverin tried to twist his neck to look behind him, but he couldn't. Laila and Tristan were gone.

"Where are they?" he croaked.

"They're waiting to bear witness," said Roux-Joubert.

He took a step toward Séverin, then stopped. He reached for a handkerchief in his pocket, coughing violently. Even now, his head still swimming with the remnants of nightmares, Séverin could see the other man was not well. The handkerchief was blood-splattered.

Séverin opened his mouth to speak when the man in the blade-brim hat held out an object from behind his back: the helmet.

Blue sparks traveled up the glass exterior, and Séverin shuddered. That thing was the last object he had touched before collapsing. He remembered how it had invaded his thoughts. Images darting through his mind, grabbing his soul in a tight fist—his mother screaming at him: *Run! Run, my love! Run!* Tristan crouched in a rose-bush. The cuts of thorns crosshatching his skin. Golden-skinned pheasant on a dish. Laila's hand falling limp to the floor. Ortolan bones cutting the inside of his mouth.

Nightmares. All of them.

"The Phobus Helmet needs no introduction to you," said Roux-Joubert. "Though you do seem surprised to see it. It was banned about ten years ago by the Order of Babel. Quite a pity, considering it produces excellent results. No one motivates you better than yourself. And who knows you better than, well, *you*?"

Séverin remembered Tristan's face when he pulled back the helmet. The bruises beneath his eyes. As if he hadn't slept in days.

"It's astounding what one might reveal in their worst nightmares," said Roux-Joubert.

The man in the blade-brim hat pulled up a chair for him, and he sat, crossing his ankles and smoothing the front of his jacket as if they were sitting down for tea.

"Including an acquisition of a Fallen House bone clock."

Séverin's gaze hardened.

"Oh, don't worry, my boy. It's still particularly impressive that you were able to figure it out. Frankly, I wasn't sure you would, but I left the trap there just in case."

Séverin fought against the ropes binding his wrist, but they didn't budge.

Roux-Joubert got up from his chair. In the sulfurous lighting of the catacombs, his face was drawn. Almost yellow from illness.

"Shhh . . . Shhh . . . Don't do that. You shouldn't hurt yourself. Let someone else do that. Otherwise, where's the fun?"

He touched Séverin's face, trailing a nail down the side of his cheek. But then Roux-Joubert winced. He grabbed his sleeve, as if there was a wound there that needed tending. Slowly, he drew up the fabric, revealing a long gash covered in a bandage that was stained yellow.

"This is the price of godhood," rasped Roux-Joubert. "A price that we tried to pay once before."

Séverin looked behind Roux-Joubert. Enrique and Hypnos stood there, clearly inside the exhibition and talking to each other, throwing something up in the air as if they had all the time in the world. Séverin wetted his lips. His voice sounded hoarse, but he needed to talk. Needed, more importantly, to keep Roux-Joubert talking.

"Godhood?"

"Of course," said Roux-Joubert. A manic gleam shone in his eyes. "Have you never wondered about why only some humans can Forge? It is an essence alongside the blood. One capable of being harnessed by the power of the Babel Fragment itself. God made us in His image. Are we not gods, then?"

Once more, Roux-Joubert lifted his sleeve. He tore off the yellow-stained bandage, revealing pale skin crosshatched with scars.

"It was hard," he admitted. "To hurt oneself. To flay oneself. But—"

He took a glowing knife from his breast pocket and dragged it across his arm. He winced, but when his blood ran, it was not red, but gold. Gold as ichor. As the blood of a god.

"—it is worth it. The Fallen House made a discovery of our blood years ago. With the right tools, we could harness the essential essence within us that allowed those of us with the affinity to Forge. But that is just the beginning. It gives one power over more than just matter and mind—it gives one power over the spirits of other men. I'll show you."

Séverin jerked back, but the ropes bound him into place. Roux-Joubert took a step forward. He pressed the knife point against Séverin's cheek, dragging it downward. Séverin tensed. His breath turned jagged, his pulse leaping wildly. When he had finished making the cut, Roux-Joubert pressed the broken skin of his arm to Séverin's face. Séverin cried out, but Roux-Joubert only pressed harder.

Roux Joubert's voice was low, damp against Séverin's neck. "I could make you an angel, Monsieur Montagnet-Alarie."

A searing pain rent itself across Séverin's back. He screamed. Something shoved through his shoulder blades. He exhaled a shaky breath then looked behind him. The slender point of wings shoved through his suit, sharp as finials. Wet, pearl-pale feathers rose steadily into the air as they dried.

"Or I could make you a devil."

Séverin doubled over. A new pain gripped him, shooting through his temples. His vision blacked out, then restored just as horns shot out from his forehead, curving around the backs of his ears.

"I could change you."

The very cells of Séverin's being quivered until, in an abrupt rush, it fell away. The horns pulled back into his skull. Wings furled tight against his spine.

Roux-Joubert gasped—Séverin could not tell whether from triumph or pain. He looked up to see the other man squatting, rocking on his heels. He was grinning and smiling so hard Séverin thought his teeth would crack. Roux-Joubert licked his lips, but no blood fell. Gold flaked off onto his chin, spattering the front of his jacket.

"But we cannot remake the world on just the power given by one Fragment, you see? If we were to *join* them, then perhaps such imaginings as I might have performed would be permanent. I could *remake* you. Remake the entire human race in the images of *new* gods. Imagine it. No more of this hideous mixing of blood. A purity. Assured and filtered through the holy relics passed down to us from the first ages."

Séverin fought through a wash of pain. His tongue felt leaden. "You know, I was told once that an ancient civilization in the Americas made gods by sacrificing humans." He smiled. "If you'd like me to drive a stake through your heart, you need only ask."

Roux-Joubert laughed. "It's far too late for that. It is time for revolution. Soon, the Babel Fragments will be joined together . . . but first, they must be awakened. Only then can we fulfill the promise and potential that the Lord set out for us."

Even through the haze of pain, Séverin's mind latched onto something: *first, they must be awakened . . .*

"And what promise would that be?" he asked.

"Why, to make the world anew, of course."

The man in the blade-brim hat hoisted the Phobus Helmet. Séverin recoiled. He would do anything—*anything*—not to wear that cursed thing again.

"And it's nearly time," said Roux-Joubert.

He looked over his shoulder, grinning widely at the image of Enrique and Hypnos.

"Your friends have been most helpful. Which makes me think that perhaps I owe you something . . . a thank-you, of a sort. All this time, you wished to know where the West's Babel Fragment lay, did you not? Perhaps you wanted to alert the Order? Warn them, even?"

Séverin said nothing. His gaze flicked to the image of Hypnos and Enrique. Still laughing.

Don't look . . .

"You'll soon find out," said Roux-Joubert, smiling. "You know, I rather like you. I think you could fit very well among our rank, Monsieur Montagnet-Alarie. Should the doctor decide to let you live of course."

Blearily, Séverin ran the word through his mind. *Doctor*. What *doctor?* Roux-Joubert coughed again, this time more harshly. He dabbed at his mouth, spittle glossing his chin.

A sound echoed from the stage. Séverin forced his head to raise. Laila stood there. Behind her, holding a knife to her throat . . . Tristan. Séverin couldn't look away from him. Tristan's eyes were the same piercing gray they had always been. But Tristan's eyes held no betrayal, only grief . . . and when he saw Séverin, his eyes widened. His mouth opened as if to speak, but something held him back. Séverin's gaze flew to Laila. Laila, who was . . . *mouthing* something to him. Beside her, Tristan's eyes glistened.

Séverin couldn't read her lips. His head still felt fuzzy from the Phobus Helmet. But he watched her hands. How they squeezed Tristan's wrist. As if she weren't fighting back . . . but reassuring him.

Before him, Roux-Joubert tore off the honeybee pendant from his lapel. He twisted it sharply, and the ground ruptured beneath them.

"Now it begins."

Séverin tried to take advantage of the chaos. He lurched forward, but an object whizzed through the air, sharp and whistling. The blade-brimmed hat of Roux-Joubert's accomplice caught the edge of his jacket, pinning him to the ground.

"That would be a poorly thought out move on your part, Monsieur Montagnet-Alarie."

Séverin could only watch as the ground beneath him changed. The deep, spiraled grooves set into the earth glowed a faint blue.

Bones peeled off the walls. They began to merge, cobbling themselves together into terrible shapes. The dead were bent into thrones and crosses, grotesque skeletons wearing crowns, and cruelly formed beasts. He felt a cataclysm rising inside him, of true Forged power, not the ornamentation and posturing of the Order, but the very thing that had sewn itself into humanity.

"Are you familiar with the word 'apotheosis,' Monsieur?" asked Roux-Joubert. Ichor dribbled from his lip.

Séverin didn't respond.

"It's . . . a moment of *ascension*. From mortal to immortal. Man to God. And you shall witness it, but you shall not be alone. The doctor will see what I have done, and I will be glorious beyond reckoning," he wheezed.

Roux-Joubert raised his hands. All along the walls, the bones shivered. They peeled off the walls—skulls, femurs, necklaces of teeth—careening down from the terraces, knitting themselves together. The bones clasped together, the sound like thunder.

With the scarlet curtains fully drawn back, the image on the Tezcat mirror shivered. Across, Enrique and Hypnos had not registered the danger. They smiled and carried on, not even raising their heads.

"Séverin," called Laila softly.

Her dark eyes were wide and glossy. There was a plea to her voice. One that Séverin didn't know how to answer. Because maybe Roux-Joubert was right. Maybe there was no hope. They had intended to deliver the Horus Eye to the Order. To show them where the Babel Fragment lay hidden. They thought the Babel Fragment would be far away, hidden somewhere far from the Fallen House.

At that moment, the ground pitched forward. Séverin went sprawling as the dirt rose to meet and sting his face. His skin smarted from the slash that Roux-Joubert had left near his temple. He lay there, straining against his ropes, his cheek flattened onto the slick

THE GILDED WOLVES   319

gravel of the catacombs. He inhaled a shuddering breath. In the end, their assumptions had been wrong.

The Babel Fragment was *here* . . . hidden deep beneath the catacombs.

Roux-Joubert dropped the Ring of House Kore to the ground. The Ring sank through the dirt, and lightning crackled through the ground. Then, from his jacket, Roux-Joubert removed another Ring . . . this one darkened by time. A cruel six-pointed star. The missing Ring of the Fallen House. It joined the Ring of House Kore, and the skeletons drifted into the air.

"It's waking," said Roux-Joubert.

Séverin lifted his gaze. The skeletons flung themselves at the Tezcat door. He knew what they were doing. They were trying to break down the barrier. And once they did, they would be there for all the world to see . . . for just on the other side lay crowds of tourists; the entire Exposition Universelle would witness the rebirth of the Fallen House.

Roux-Joubert wheezed, then forced a smile onto his face. "Let's greet your friends, shall we?"

27

ENRIQUE

Midnight

Enrique watched as a skeleton hurled itself at his face.

He turned to Zofia, who, along with Hypnos, crouched beside him in the starless dark of the catacombs terraces. He barely recognized his own voice as he combed his thoughts for a joke. "I was *so* confident about my outfit, but you know, looking at it . . . it lacks a sort of internal rhapsody, you know what I mean?"

Zofia fixed him with those feral blue eyes. "No."

Beside them, Hypnos let out a strangled cry, clutching his ringed hand to his chest. The whites of his eyes gleamed.

"They're waking it up . . ."

The Babel Fragment.

All this time, Enrique had thought of it the way everyone else had . . . as a rock, perhaps, something manageable enough to be carried. But now he could *feel* the power of the Fragment coursing through the catacombs. It wasn't a rock. Maybe it wasn't even an object, but some other force restrained beneath the ground.

Enrique watched, his eyes widening, as blue light spangled across the stage. More bones peeled off the walls, assembling into ragged skeletons. A harsh scent cut the air: minerals and rain, singed hair and metal. A tremor ran through the earth, the terraces quivered and dirt crumbled down the walls, falling in the space between his shirt and neck. Enrique recoiled, but he didn't look away from the scene. Tristan, teary-eyed, stood with a knife pressed to Laila. But Séverin . . . Séverin had been caught. He didn't know how. They had only just arrived in time to hear Roux-Joubert gloat. *To make the world anew*. To reset the human race. A hard lump formed in his throat. Enrique thought of the people he'd met over the years. The dark and the fair, the ones whose languages sounded spiced. The ones kept in makeshift villages, commanded to entertain. The ones who watched and jeered or tamped down their horror. The ones who reached for hands they could never hold openly in the street. All of them. Stitches in a tapestry that had no horizon. The Fallen House couldn't erase them. It seemed impossible . . . but all Enrique had to do was look at Séverin's folded-over form to remember. Great gashes in the back of his jacket. A dirtied feather clung to his shoe. Remnants of wings he had sprouted with nothing more than Roux-Joubert's blood against his torn skin.

Hypnos raised his hand slowly, staring at his false Ring.

"I thought . . . I thought if anything my ring might be the missing piece to keep the Fragment from waking, but I was wrong—"

Beneath them, Roux-Joubert let out a roar. He raised his hand, backhanding Séverin. Laila looked as if she wanted to scream, but instead, clamped her lips tighter.

"What did you do to the Tezcat?" demanded Roux-Joubert. "The doctor cannot enter!"

Thanks to Zofia's adhesive and the silver cloth, the Tezcat door hadn't broken. That was one small blessing. And if the Tezcat door couldn't open, then whoever was on the other side couldn't come in . . . All this time they thought it was just Roux-Joubert and the man with the blade-brim hat.

They were wrong.

The skeletons hurled themselves against the obsidian glass. A fine seam appeared, chunks of it breaking and falling onto the ground. The image of Enrique and Hypnos began to malfunction. They smiled, turned their heads, smiled again. It was nothing more than a mnemo recording splayed across the silver cloth. And yet, with every tear, a new scene took form, showing the Forging exhibition in real time. When they'd left, the exhibition had been empty. But now, they saw the dark shape of a gathered crowd, silhouetted by the dim light of the room.

Waiting.

Waiting to enter.

Séverin screamed as the Phobus Helmet was slammed onto his head. Hypnos leaned forward, nearly giving away their location. Zofia grabbed his wrist.

"Séverin said not to go down there. No matter what."

"That was before he got caught! He needs help!" said Hypnos. "If the Babel Fragment is awake, then we have to put it back to sleep . . . it cannot stay like that! The entirety of civilization is at stake, don't you understand? Can't you feel it?"

"Think for a moment," said Enrique, his heart racing. "Roux-Joubert wanted the Horus Eye for something. You said that it would have an effect on the Fragment, remember?"

"But I don't know what effect that is—"

"You keep saying the Fragment is *awakening*," said Zofia. "It is an object. It cannot be awake. Unless you are suggesting that it's akin to a Forged creature. In which case, it has to have a somno to deactivate it."

Hypnos squeezed his eyes shut.

"The Horus Eye," he said slowly. "What if the Horus Eye puts the Fragment to sleep?"

Enrique swallowed hard, turning his face from the scene of nightmares below them.

"It would explain why he wouldn't want us to have it," said Enrique. "He wouldn't want anyone to stop them."

"What about my Ring, then?" asked Hypnos. "If he already has two Rings, then why would he have wanted mine?"

Enrique's mouth twisted into a grimace. He thought of the way Roux-Joubert kept hurting Tristan . . . he thought of Séverin writhing there . . . the ugly words that left Roux-Joubert's lips to remake the world.

"Power and greed always have appetites," he said. "Taking your Ring would be a step toward that."

Hypnos's jaw clenched. "Then we must give him what he wants. Or, at least, an illusion of it."

Enrique nodded tightly. He looked through the hiding place to the Horus Eye lying on the wooden table, all but forgotten. Perhaps Roux-Joubert thought he'd won and that there was no need to protect it, for it wasn't as though anyone else knew what it could do.

Zofia's eyes snapped to the floor. She reached for something in the dirt, a trail of pale powder that she pinched and rubbed between her fingers.

"Curious . . ."

Hypnos cradled the fake Ring to his chest. "We were supposed to take the Horus Eye to the Order. We can't do that now. And we can't leave them."

Enrique stared at the Ring, and then at the brooches and jewels set against the rich velvet of Hypnos's jacket. *A great deal of my inheritance*, Hypnos had said. Which meant that it was House-marked.

"If we can't go to the Order, then we can bring the Order to us," said Enrique slowly, a plan forming in his head. "Hypnos, give us those. I want to send a signal."

Hypnos's eyes widened, a smile touching his lips. "The Sphinxes."

Enrique nodded. The Sphinx would be able to track anything House-marked, even if it led them down to the catacombs. Plus, their eyes could record images . . . and the Order would have no choice but to believe the Fallen House had once more risen. Hypnos tore off the brooches. A blue light, once marked onto the back of them, flared red. He rolled them one by one onto the ground.

Enrique glanced at the auditorium below. The ground rippled, dirt cascading in waves.

"It's nearly *here*," said Roux-Joubert. He grabbed Séverin by the lapels. "Tell me how to open the Tezcat. What did you *do*?"

Distantly, Enrique heard Séverin's wheezing response, "You know, for someone who wishes to play god, you're not very omniscient."

Enrique looked away, but he still heard it: a resounding *crack* as Roux-Joubert brought his fist to Séverin's head.

"Hurry, hurry—" murmured Enrique, rocking on his heels. He wished he had his rosary. He needed something to do with his hands. He couldn't just watch.

A ripping sound blared beside his ear, the hiss of a struck match. Below, Roux-Joubert paused. Enrique looked to his side. Zofia had struck a match and was now holding it against the ground.

"Zofia, what in the—"

"He told me he'd leave an emergency path," said Zofia, pointing at the pale powder on the ground. "This substance is highly flammable."

Enrique felt the grin spreading on his face even before he realized he was smiling. Fire in this place would buy them time. But it was dangerous . . . they had to work quickly.

"Then by all means, phoenix. Light it up."

Zofia lowered the match to the powder.

On the stage, blue veins of light emerged on the floor. The shape of them: nautilus-like and vast, stretched across the very walls. Enrique couldn't see what the others were doing, but he could feel the power of the Babel Fragment. It felt like something that could level kings and twist immortality. He opened his mouth, wanting to receive it like a sacrament.

Hypnos lunged forward, snatching Zofia and Enrique by the backs, of their collars.

"Move!" he shouted.

He pulled them back, just as a strong burst of wind swept through the corridors. Enrique shivered as something nameless coiled through him. He felt it at the corner of his soul. A knowing there, like a creator's thumbprint. It was too late to stop Roux-Joubert from stirring the Fragment from its rest.

Because it was wide awake.

28

LAILA

One minute after midnight

Laila fell to the floor as the force of the Babel Fragment hit her. Her vision fuzzed. Blue streaks wrinkled the dirt stage, like ice cracking across a lake. Light lashed through the floor, a dark expanse opening in the middle of the stage, terrible and lightless, a chasm where stars went to be unmade.

Laila touched the floor, spreading her fingers in the hard dirt, feeling it bite into her nail beds. She had never been able to read anything Forged. Always, it was as abrupt and stark as a light turned off in a room. But this time . . . this time she could do more than just read the Forged power licking through the room.

She could understand it.

The vastness of it seized her from her own body. She was everywhere, *everything*, in that moment. She was at the top of a mountain, snow caught in her hair. She was on the floor of a palace, the sweet-smelling resin stinging her nose. She was clutched in the hand of a priest, placed in the mouth of a god, *forged*—in the old sense of the word, existence hammered into being—in a furnace of time. Points of connection mushroomed across the plane of her mind. Her consciousness scattered. She was infinite—

Laila gasped.

She pulled back her hand from the dirt. Points of blue blinked and dimmed on her skin. What did it mean that it called to her this way . . . if this was a place where stars could be unmade . . . what about her? Would she unravel here?

Who was she? *What* was she? Her mother called her beloved. Her father labeled her blasphemous. Paris named her L'Énigme.

"Laila?" breathed Tristan.

Laila.

She was Laila. The girl who made herself. This moment—shining and distant—crashed around her. Her senses rushed back to her and with them, fear. She knew it was not desperate imagination that let her see the flash of matchlight far above in the terraces. *Zofia. Enrique.* They were here. Séverin was still swaying, kneeling. Blood dripping down his mouth from the cut along his cheek. She could feel Tristan's hands on her shoulders, cold and quivering. She touched his wrist lightly, letting her hair fall over her face so as to conceal the gesture from Roux-Joubert.

The earth was not all that she had read.

When she'd kneeled on the ground beside an unconscious Séverin, Tristan had held a blade to her. And then he forced the hilt into her hand. *Please. Make it stop.* The wooden hilt had dug into her palms, splinters cutting into her skin, images lancing through her mind. In her visions, she saw Tristan forced under waves of nightmares that warped his doubts and made them seem real. They'd tortured him.

And then they'd tortured him with the knowledge of what he had let happen. Laila had handed him back the knife, closing her fingers around his in the stolen seconds before Roux-Joubert had arrived with his associate.

I know what they did. It's not your fault.

Tristan had wept against her. He didn't even ask how she knew, he simply trusted, and the weight of it left her aching. She would not let anyone make Tristan cry. Never again.

"Laila?" whispered Tristan.

She shook her head, careful not to speak. The Night Bite was cold on her tongue. She only had one chance to use it, and she needed to time the moment just right. Laila glanced up, focusing on Séverin. Even now, even bruised, he looked like a king. His gaze stern. Unflinching. But not on her.

Roux-Joubert screamed louder. "Get that Tezcat open!"

The man with the blade-brim hat shrank. The obsidian chips of the Tezcat had fallen off, crashing and splintering on the ever-rolling floor. But the Tezcat did not budge. On the other side, the crowd of cloaked people remained unmoving.

The rest of the Fallen House.

Laila shuddered to look at them . . . so pale . . . so still.

"Sir, there's no way . . . there is something blocking it," said Roux-Joubert's associate, removing his hat and placing it on his chest. "I . . . Perhaps you might use your blood? As you did before? The strength of your ichor will surely be enough."

Roux-Joubert swallowed, his eyes wild. He touched his arm gingerly. "I do not like to keep the doctor waiting. But I have nothing left to give."

Tristan squeezed Laila's arm. She could sense his panic, the quick inhale he drew into his lungs.

"But you . . ." said Roux-Joubert, turning to Séverin. "What essence lies in the veins of the blood heir of House Vanth? I was told not to spill your blood . . . proof, perhaps, that the doctor sees some worth in you, but I find myself tempted."

Laila nudged Tristan. He hesitated, and then he drew her hair in a tight fist, yanking her head forward. Laila winced. But it was part of the plan.

"Please," she murmured. "A moment."

Roux-Joubert's eyes widened. He smiled, and the waxen skin around his lips cracked from the effort.

"Rather devoted whore you have, boy," he said, sneering at Séverin. "It seems she wishes to say goodbye. Why not. I always planned to be benevolent."

Séverin went still. His gaze burned into hers. Laila let herself be led by Tristan. Then, lightly, she touched Tristan's wrist. She needed Séverin to know that she had seen what truly happened. That he had to trust her.

Séverin blinked slowly. In the gloaming of the catacombs, his lashes cast spiked shadows onto his face. When he raised his gaze to her, blue glinted in those violet depths.

Tristan shoved her forward.

Laila didn't wait. She grabbed Séverin's face, fingers threading in his hair as she lowered her lips to his, memories and promises tangling together.

We can't do this again.

I know.

His eyes flew open, pupils blown wide. His mouth opened beneath hers and she could taste him. Blood and cloves. Her hand pressed into the cut of his cheek, and he winced into her mouth.

Kisses were not supposed to be like this. Kisses were to be witnessed by stars, not held in the presence of stale death. But as the bones rose around them, Laila saw fractals of white. They looked like pale constellations, and she thought that, perhaps, for a kiss like this, even hell would put forth stars.

29

SÉVERIN

Séverin should never have closed his eyes. He didn't even regis-
ter it happening because the whole moment seemed to occur outside the scope of his reality. Of course, she would kiss him as the
world unhinged around them. Why not. Logic danced at the edges of
his senses when Laila brought her lips to his.

Séverin seized her lips, felt her yield, tasted her.

She tasted impossible.

Like candied moonlight.

And then something hard rolled onto his tongue. Night Bite. He
remembered, in a rush, how she had tucked it into her satchel right
before they had left. Logic righted itself. Whatever horizon tipped
deliriously in his mind now settled, restored.

Of course, it wasn't a real kiss.

They had sworn off those.

Roux-Joubert yanked her back. "My moment of mercy is done."

Séverin's eyes narrowed. "Then come and kill me."

Roux-Joubert's smile gleamed manic. "If you insist."

He slid out a knife. Séverin waited, tensing.

Come closer.

Roux-Joubert held out the knife.

And then, far above in the hidden shelves of the terraces, Séverin heard a *snick* of a match. A crackle lit up the air. Sulfur stamping out the stench of death. A sudden heat warmed his back, illuminating Roux-Joubert's face as flames sprang to life in the catacombs.

Séverin pushed the Night Bite to the front of his teeth. Just as the other man turned, he spat.

Ink splattered everywhere. Black billowed out from his mouth, fanning across Roux-Joubert. Séverin jolted back as the blade grazed his neck. Roux-Joubert stumbled. A cyclone of ink surrounded him. The man in the blade-brim hat rushed toward him. Séverin struggled against the bounds of his rope. He tried to shuffle on his knees, moving out of the way. His knee skidded on the wet gravel, pitching him forward. Light gleamed off the blade and Séverin's breath gathered in a tight knot—

Tristan launched himself at the man. Séverin tumbled, his temple knocking against a sizable boulder. Laila rushed to him, undoing the knots, swaying even as she tried to free him. The very ground beneath them was treacherous. Tristan rushed over to them, his eyes wide.

"Séverin—"

"Later," he said. He reached out, squeezing Tristan's hand, and then he pulled back.

Roux-Joubert howled off to the distance, but Séverin shoved aside the sound.

Laila fumbled with the rope.

"You're welcome," he said when the ropes slid off his wrists.

Laila hoisted him up to his feet. "What?"

"You're welcome," he said, shoving a grin onto his face. He could already feel it. A tense pull in the air. He had to break it now if they were going to put the Babel Fragment back to rest, to get on with the rest of their lives. "For giving you a reason to kiss me."

Her eyes went wide, but she didn't have a chance to speak.

"Thank God for Zofia," breathed Tristan, helping him up.

The ground lurched again . . . the Babel Fragment had broken through the surface of the earth. It was as wide as the stage, but he didn't know how deep. Instinct told him the moment it was fully resurfaced they were out of options.

"The Horus Eye," said Tristan weakly. "The Horus Eye will put the Babel Fragment to rest. That's what he said. We have to put it somewhere in the ground . . . there's a pattern, I—"

The rest of his words descended into stammering.

"I'll get the Eye," said Laila, nodding fast.

The Horus Eye was still on the wooden worktable where they had found Tristan. Laila sprinted over the falling bones. The earth around them continued to rattle as the Babel Fragment pushed itself up and out of the ground. All he had to do was figure out *where* to put the Horus Eye in the ground.

A scream rent through the air. Séverin turned, shoving Tristan behind him . . .

Roux-Joubert had found a new source of power.

The man with the blade-brim hat was dead. Blood spurted from the man's opened throat. Roux-Joubert crooned as he plunged his fingers through the gash. Ink from the Night Bites still splattered across his face, but it faded faster and faster . . . a dim golden glow wound up Roux-Joubert's hands.

"Not enough, not nearly enough," he rasped. "But it will have to do."

Roux-Joubert stumbled forward, pressing his hands to the

Tezcat. The smell of something singed and melting filled the air. There was a moment of utter incandescence . . . light shining through the cracks. On the other side, the man in the mask put forward a single finger . . .

The Tezcat door began to peel and break.

30

ZOFIA

Five minutes after midnight

Zofia peered over the edge. The Tezcat had snapped in half. Smoke rose and curled out, escaping through the ragged door that now left the entire Forging exhibition exposed to the catacombs. This wasn't supposed to happen. It went against the calculus. Follow the rules. Follow the rules and everyone would get out safe. Follow the rules and the Fallen House would be caught.

But that wasn't what had happened. In the scene below, she saw a dead man. Beside him, the blade-brimmed hat, blood pooling around his slashed throat. Roux-Joubert stood there with his hands pressed to the Tezcat, a molten substance dribbling down his arms as he raised them high. The obsidian peeled off like petals. It wasn't supposed to be possible, thought Zofia, staring. But then . . . the Fallen House should never have survived. As the gaping cracks in the Tezcat grew wider, the ground surged even more. Chandeliers of bone rattled above them. Zofia felt something tangled in her hair.

She shook her head, and the teeth of forgotten skulls scattered across her lap.

"They're after the Horus Eye!" said Hypnos excitedly. "Laila is on her way to it right now!"

True enough, Laila was still crossing the ground, making her way to the unprotected Horus Eye where it lay on the wooden worktable.

But it wouldn't be enough.

Now they knew the Horus Eye had to be placed in a particular area in order to activate the somno of the West's Babel Fragment.

The question was *where*.

From where they crouched, Zofia could see a pattern rising through the ground. It was the dead center of a logarithmic spiral, identical to the one that adorned the floor of House Kore. But there was no way Laila would be able to tell.

"We have to show them," said Zofia. "They can't find the center otherwise."

"We can't go down there!" said Hypnos. "Séverin told us not to."

Zofia's hesitation lasted no longer than a blink. Some internal calculus shifted and weighed. Instructions used to be safe. They drew lines in her life, told her to stay within them and safety would follow. But safety hadn't. Safety hadn't followed in the classroom of the École des Beaux-Arts. It hadn't come when Roux-Joubert cornered her in the ballroom of House Kore. And safety hadn't arrived now . . . here, in this nightmare realm of hovering bones, of blood seeping into the dirt, shining knives and peeling stones. Of her friends in trouble. Of a *force* rising through the ground and tainting the air.

Instruction had no place here.

"I don't care what anyone *told* us to do," said Zofia.

Enrique's face split into a wide grin. In one hand, he drew out the walking stick that concealed a light bomb. In the other, he took out a length of rope.

"Let's go."

The two of them got ready, but Hypnos hesitated.

"If I go with you, I'll die."

"It's a high likelihood, but not a certainty," pointed out Zofia.

"Not helping," said Enrique.

The two of them looked at Hypnos. His pale eyes were unfocused. His mouth set, and then he clenched his hands.

"I'm coming with you."

Zofia bounded down the steps of the terraces, her feet slipping on the gravel. She reached into her sleeves, pulling out a thin Forged rod of pure silver. Forging required a will, and hers crackled inside her. *Ignite*. Ropes of lightning zipped and twisted down the metal.

Laila was the first to look up and notice her. In her hands was the precious Horus Eye.

"Zofia!" she cried.

Warmth jolted through Zofia, but she didn't stop. She walked past her, to a flat disc of earth. It was unlit and, as she knelt to brush the surface, *painted*. She looked up to where Séverin and the others stared at her.

"This," she said, holding out the rod for light. "This is where you've got to place the Horus Eye to activate the Fragment's somno."

Too much dirt covered the depression where the Eye should sit. Séverin ran over, Tristan close on his heels. The six of them dug, tossing the dirt. Grit flew into Zofia's eyes, into her mouth. But she didn't stop. She didn't stop when Roux-Joubert started laughing loudly and the Tezcat door, now fully melted, became an entrance point for the rest of the Fallen House.

"*Faster, faster—*" called Séverin.

"Useless. Manicured. Nails," panted Hypnos.

But then a blast of light made them break apart. Zofia was shot backward.

"Zofia!" screamed Enrique.

She pushed herself up, blood pounding in her ears. Zofia grabbed for the lightning rod tucked back into her sleeves, but then she looked up . . .

They were surrounded.

A man wearing a pale helmet, like that of an insect, stared at them, his head cocked to one side. Cloaked figures surrounded them, their hands up, metal honeybees embedded in their palms. The blast forced all of them back. There, buried in the dirt was the Horus Eye. Hypnos tried to dig, but a member of the Fallen House grabbed his wrist.

Roux-Joubert knelt on the floor beside the man in the mask, rocking back and forth.

"Please, Doctor. Please, you promised me, and I have given all that I can . . ." he said, revealing his torn arms.

Zofia shuddered. Roux-Joubert did not bleed like a normal man. A sticky, yellow liquid had crusted into an ochre shade. It splashed down the front of his tunic, staining his pants.

"I have brought you the Babel Ring," Roux-Joubert whispered. "Is it not time for my apotheosis?"

The man Zofia could only assume was the doctor raised one gloved hand.

"You brought us the Babel Ring . . . with additions," he said. His voice was flat. Stripped of affect or accent. "I admire tenacity, young ones. I truly do. But you do not understand that in which you meddle. It is your choice, however. Free will was a gift from Him and a gift I intend to maintain for the new age. Will your blood mark the threshold of this new age? Or will it help forge it into existence?"

Zofia felt Séverin's gaze on her as it swept through the group. However, it was neither she nor Séverin who answered the doctor, but Tristan. Tristan grabbed the blade-brimmed hat that lay not far from him, then flung it out at the crowd. The doctor dodged it, and Tristan let out a growl. And then the doctor clasped his palms together, as if in prayer, and said, "I have my answer then."

The Fallen House drew out their knives.

31

ENRIQUE

Enrique had always imagined what it would feel like to be a hero.
This was not how he imagined it.

He thought that, at *least*, he would have a flaming sword. Instead of a stick. That emitted light. But as he whirled onto the members of the Fallen House surrounding them, at least he could rely on one thing: Heroes always made do.

He swung the light baton against the members nearest him. For now, there were nearly twenty people, but the gash in the Tezcat door remained open, and though it was empty now, there was no way of knowing whether it would stay that way. Chaos broke around him. Séverin wrestled away one of the cloaked members, shoving them backward. He swiped something from his shoe, a thin thread of silver that Laila caught. Together, they circled five of the hooded figures. Tristan spat out a billow of black ink and whooped happily.

"Now, Zofia!" screamed Séverin.

Zofia lunged forward with the lightning rod. The silver light turned her hair and skin incandescent. She thrust out the rod, and a current of electricity coursed down the silver thread, crackling and snapping. Cloaked figures screamed, then slumped over, unconscious.

But not everyone fought. The doctor. Roux-Joubert sat on the floor beside him, blank-eyed and dazed, lips blue and mumbling as he rocked back and forth and held his mangled arm to his chest.

Every chance they got, they dug into the ground, trying to free up the exact space where the Horus Eye might fit . . . but the Fallen House was relentless.

"They should be here soon," said Hypnos, wild-eyed, glancing constantly up at the rafters.

He'd left half of his House-marked possessions up there, a ripe scent the Sphinxes had to follow. But the Order hadn't arrived. No help was coming.

Laila collapsed in the dirt beside him, her face haggard. In her hands was the Horus Eye. Before them, the ground had almost nearly cleared when a handful of Forged knives launched into the air, a blade poised at each of their throats.

"I think this has gone on long enough, don't you?" asked the doctor mildly.

Enrique could not see his eyes, but he could feel the man's gaze on him and Hypnos.

"Your friends will die. And then you will die. But you can avoid this . . . This can be a new world. For all of us. I see your heart, young Patriarch. I see how you struggle . . . how you do not know which world you belong to, how you feel as though the color of your skin will determine the color of your future. It does not have to be that way. Join us." The doctor paused, and Enrique imagined that behind his pale mask, he was smiling. "Save yourself . . . save your *friends*. She won't put down the Horus Eye until she knows that she's lost. All you have to do is give me your Ring."

Enrique watched as Hypnos struggled to stand. He looked behind him, gaze resting on Tristan, Séverin, Laila, Zofia, and finally . . . Enrique. Hypnos's shoulders dropped, his mouth flattening to a taut line. He paled, but then managed a nod. He reached into his jacket, wincing with effort as he drew out his true Ring.

"Ah, I see the young patriarch has seen reason," said the doctor.

Séverin's face shuttered, but he held still. Shock rippled across Zofia's face. How could he? They'd been *friends*, hadn't they? Hadn't they spent hours in the stargazing room? Had he imagined everything?

Enrique dropped his gaze to the dirt floor, the smoothed surface where the perfect mold of a Horus Eye was now partially exposed. The knife pointed at his throat dragged up his skin, as if sensing what he wished to do. Laila met his gaze over the blade, her dark eyes wild.

Hypnos kept his back to them as he stepped forward.

"I shall give it to you," said Hypnos.

Laila screamed, "What are you doing?"

Hypnos neither turned nor answered. He was nothing more than a rigid shadow. Roux-Joubert wept at the doctor's feet.

"It's happening . . . I shall be a god," he whispered.

Slowly, the knives dropped from their throats. Enrique breathed deep, something in his chest finally loosening. When he looked up, he saw a small smile flicker on Laila's face as she looked at Hypnos. Enrique frowned, then his eyes darted to Hypnos. He was still standing, still speaking with the doctor.

"I want assurances that nothing will happen to them."

"Very well," said the doctor. "Now give me your Ring."

Behind his back, Hypnos held out three fingers.

Three.

He curled the ring finger down . . .

"Wait," said the doctor.

Two.

A beat of silence passed.

"This isn't the true Ring," said the doctor, his voice rising. "You would betray your own like this, Patriarch? For these people?"

"I rather like them," said Hypnos.

He looked over his shoulder then, the barest of smiles lifting his mouth.

"But then—" Roux-Joubert said.

Enrique scrambled at the dirt, clearing the space.

"Now, Laila!"

She pitched forward, slamming the Horus Eye into the mold. Bright light flashed all around them. The blue light of the rising Fragment started to fade. Little by little, whatever energy had seeped into the catacombs now folded in on itself, like something slipping into ice only for the ice to re-form and wipe away any proof.

The doctor growled, but the moment the Horus Eye touched the ground, he recoiled. As if he couldn't touch it.

And then, standing at the top of the terraced steps came a low, hair-raising growl: The Sphinx had arrived.

"My Lord," called Roux-Joubert from the floor. "Please."

The doctor drew back his foot.

"You led us into a *trap.*"

"I c-can't live like this much longer."

"Then perhaps you shall not live long at all," said the doctor. He raised one hand, and the uninjured members of the Fallen House fled through the Tezcat, disappearing into the night. Now, the Babel Fragment had fallen back to rest . . . two frail lights emerged from the ground. One was the Ring of the Fallen House. The other, the Ring of House Kore. The doctor tried to grab both, but then hissed out as if in pain. He dropped the Ring of House Kore to the ground, then shoved the other onto his hand before fleeing through the Tezcat.

Now, the room was nearly empty. The four of them were still huddled together. A handful of unconscious members of the Fallen House dotted the floor. Blood seeped from the sprawled-out body of Roux-Joubert's accomplice, his blade-brim hat flung out beside him. Roux-Joubert coughed, covering his mouth with stained hands. All around them, the bones of the catacombs crumpled to the ground, zipping back into the niches they had lived in for centuries . . .

Enrique swayed where he stood, feeling the rush of a thousand people coming around him. The din and shouts of members of the Houses. The mirror seamed up. But beyond the handful of unconscious members, there was nothing left of the Fallen House.

Beside him, he heard Laila let out a cry. Only then did he turn and see Hypnos sprawled out, the cold lights of the catacombs playing across his skin.

32

SÉVERIN

Séverin didn't move until he felt Tristan's hand clapping his shoulder.

"We're alive."

The same could not be said for everyone, though. The Fallen House may have disappeared once more through the Tezcat, but they had left people behind. Soon, they would be uncloaked, their identities known and their location recorded. Séverin looked up to the line of Sphinxes prowling down the terraces . . . their eyes recording all they saw around them. Soon, the whole Order would know who had betrayed them.

Across from him, Hypnos stirred, groaning.

"I'm *dead*," he moaned.

Laila was the first one to rush to him, propping up his head on her lap.

"Well now, this is just proof. An angel stares upon my lifeless form," said Hypnos, flinging his arm over his forehead.

Séverin forced down the smile pushing at his lips. He hadn't imagined how it would feel the moment he thought Hypnos had betrayed them. Like a knife twisting in his gut.

"He's not so bad," said Tristan begrudgingly. "Please don't tell him I said that."

"I won't, so long as you forgive me for not listening to you earlier."

Tristan heaved a sigh. "That depends on one thing."

"And that is?"

"Did someone feed Goliath?"

Séverin laughed, and the force of it—raw, unfettered—scraped his very lungs.

"You only narrowly escaped death, and your first question is about a spider?" demanded Enrique. "What about *us*? We just risked life and limb to save your ungrateful self!"

"Technically, Goliath is a tarantula," said Zofia.

She was beaming in Tristan's direction.

Hypnos propped himself up on his elbows. "What's the difference . . ."

"Now you've done it," sighed Laila.

"Well, mygalomorphs—" started Tristan, only for Séverin to clap his hand over Tristan's mouth.

"He'll tell you later," he said tiredly.

"Later," repeated Hypnos. "Like . . . at tea? Tomorrow?"

Séverin smiled. "Why not."

In the catacombs, more voices joined the din of the Sphinxes pawing through the detritus, searching for the House-marked items.

"We should get out of here," said Séverin. "Leave the cleanup to the Order." He looked at Hypnos. "Which means you."

Hypnos scowled. "And soon, *you*. Don't look so damn smug."

Séverin wanted to snatch that response straight out of the air and hold it tight . . . *Soon* he would be a part of the Order. House Vanth would be dead no longer. And the Order, the same people who had denied him, would be begging for his help.

Enrique held the Ring of House Kore in his hand. He gave it to Hypnos.

"Don't take all the credit."

"I couldn't if I wanted to," said Hypnos. "Those Sphinx probably saw it all."

But he smiled even as he said it.

"Let's go home," said Séverin.

Around them, the world had fallen into a semblance of peace. The skeletons, once animated by the essence force of Roux-Joubert and his dead associate, had returned to their place of rest. Roux-Joubert writhed on the stage, sobbing and howling. He crawled forward, trying to grab Séverin's ankle, but he shook him off.

"You took it from *me*," rasped Roux-Joubert.

Séverin ignored him. The Order would deal with him. The six of them trudged back toward stairs that led out of the catacombs.

Séverin could hardly believe it. They'd fought the Fallen House and survived. The matriarch of House Kore would witness what had transpired, and, with a well-placed word from Hypnos, they would come to L'Eden and administer the test of two Rings. House Vanth would be restored. Why couldn't the five of them do this forever? Plus Hypnos—six of them.

So many things blurred through Séverin's head at that moment. He thought about the pale mask and the mystery of the doctor. He licked his lips and thought he tasted the remnant of Laila's not-kiss. He risked a glance at her and realized she was already looking at him, her dark eyes wide, color flushed on her cheeks and down her neck. Séverin looked away first. There was too much joy to take in. The sound of Enrique and Zofia squabbling over whether or not the key to unlocking the Babel Fragment had been mathematically based or symbology based.

"—impossible to detect without locating the center of the logarithm spiral!"

"Okay, but *after* that. That was me! Why can't we share credit fifty-fifty?"

"If you would like to divide this up statistically, I am entitled to seventy-five percent."

"*Seventy-five?*"

Laila smiled, occasionally smoothing Tristan's hair from his forehead even as he fussed and protested.

"I'm hungry," sighed Enrique. "A bone-in steak would be perfection."

The others gave him strange looks. He looked around the catacombs and shrugged.

"What? I'm hungry. What about you, Tristan? What do you want?"

"This," Tristan said quietly. "Just this."

PART VI

From the archival records of the Order of Babel
The Origins of Empire
Master Emanuele Orsatti, House Orcus of the Order's Italy faction
1878, reign of King Umberto I

I think the greatest power is belief, for what is a god without it?

33

❦

ENRIQUE

Enrique opened a gift box sent from Laila. Nestled inside a swath of inky silk lay a golden wolf mask, one that left the lower half of his face free. The mask had been expertly Forged, and the short, gleaming hairs bristled, as if touched by an invisible wind. Enrique half wondered if the second he put it on, he'd start howling. Tucked behind the mask was a short letter from Laila:

For the Palais's full moon party tonight . . . may it be the start of a new phase for us all.

He grinned despite himself. Tomorrow, Hypnos and the matriarch of House Kore would come to the hotel and reissue the inheritance test to Séverin. Everything was changing. He could almost see it in the air, like the afterburn of the sun pressing against his closed eyes.

All the more reason to celebrate.

Yet, he couldn't leave behind what had happened in the catacombs. A week had passed, and yet every night, he jolted awake, the stench of something burning in his nose . . . the silk sheets beneath his hand feeling like damp, bone-studded dirt. According to Séverin, the Order had already begun their interrogation of the caught Fallen House members, and there was another object the group had been searching for: an ancient book known only as *The Divine Lyrics*.

Enrique rummaged through the papers on his desk, ignoring the latest rejection letter from *La Solidaridad* and the hasty invitation to tea from the Ilustrados . . . something about the name of that title nudged at the dark of his thoughts. But then the clock struck, and he let out a curse. He could search later.

For now, he had a party to get to.

Enrique tied the mask's ribbons around his neck and entered the hall. The carriage would be waiting for them downstairs, and if they got there early enough, he might have time to eat an entire bowl of chocolate-covered strawberries. Just before he got to the staircase, a familiar silhouette made him stop short. "Don't you have your own house?"

"Hello to you too," huffed Hypnos. "As a matter of fact, I have procured a permanent set of suites in L'Eden. I imagine I'll keep seeing more of you anyway."

"You're like a plague."

"What was that? I'm all the rage?" Hypnos cupped a hand to his ear, then grinned.

Enrique rolled his eyes.

"Well, I have to stay here. On official *Order business*. It's my duty as the patriarch of House Nyx."

From the other side of the hall, Zofia emerged, dressed in her usual black leather smock and a tight-fitting cap that let out a single curl of candlelight hair. Wherever Zofia went, she carried that laboratory scent with her, as if she were always faintly burning. It was beginning to grow on him.

"Tell me you're not wearing that to the Palais party," said Hypnos, horrified.

"I'm not going."

"Why not?" asked Hypnos. "We're all celebrating!"

Zofia grimaced. "I have work—"

"Oh posh," said Hypnos. "Join us! Just change out of whatever that is you're wearing, and we can go! Feast upon the offerings of the town! Pour out libations to life itself!"

"What about your attire?"

"What's wrong with my attire?" Hypnos asked, plucking at his outrageous velvet suit. The collar had opened at the throat, and Enrique remembered how his pulse had leapt that first time they had met. How Hypnos's fingers had coasted down his chest.

Enrique shook himself and turned to Zofia. "Come out with us, phoenix. Your work won't go up into flames if you take an evening off."

"Very true," said Hypnos. "Besides, remember how we decided to be friends?"

Zofia glowered. "Please do not suggest that we are now going to sacrifice a cat to Satan. It's not even Wednesday."

"*Friends*," he said, ignoring her comment. "May go on outings. To the theater. Or concerts." He glanced at her smock. "Although one might suggest less ascetic apparel. Should you decide to join, we will be waiting here."

Zofia huffed and turned on her heel without comment. Enrique watched her go, feeling the slightest pang. He understood how she felt. Shaken, still, by what happened in the catacombs. Eager to concentrate on anything but her own thoughts.

"I think everyone could use a distraction from last week," said Hypnos. "You especially."

Enrique looked up, startled at how close the other boy stood. He had only just noticed. Around them, the lights of the hall had dimmed. The only illumination came from the gilded baroque patterns along the wall. Hypnos smelled of neroli and jasmine, the scent more concentrated at the base of his throat—Enrique could see a slick swipe where the other boy must have applied the pomade.

"Perhaps you're in need of convincing?"

"Unless you have a treasure trove of jewels and undiscovered Forged instruments, I am not sure what you have to offer," joked Enrique.

"Well, there's always this."

Hypnos bent down and kissed him.

34

ZOFIA

Zofia looked at the dresses covering her bed. It seemed as though someone had melted a rainbow atop her duvet—rich, nearly edible looking colors covered every inch of it. Laila was to blame.

Yesterday, Laila had left a trail of cookies leading from her laboratory to her bedroom. When she opened the door, she saw a wardrobe filled with gowns of pale lilac and dove gray, rich sable and gold-streaked chestnut.

"Voilà!" Laila had said, delivering a low bow.

"What?"

"Your new wardrobe! I stole your measurements a while ago and had these commissioned. You can even wear them underneath that butcher's smock you call a uniform."

Zofia had taken a couple steps forward, lightly stroking the silk. It was soft and cold beneath her hands. She liked silk far better than she liked other materials, which Laila had laughed at. *Who would have thought the engineer would have the most expensive taste?*

"Until when?" asked Zofia.

"What do you mean?"

She'd always had to return the gowns she wore for acquisitions. Zofia was used to this. Even in Glowno, she and Hela had only one fine gown to share between them.

"They're *yours*," said Laila. "For the keeping. And wearing. Which means you must actually wear them."

Hers. Zofia let out a breath. The gowns were worth far more than her salary, and yet, with so many to choose from, she could even send one to Hela. The thought warmed Zofia's face. What did she say to someone who had done something like this for her? "Thank you" was inadequate. She needed to parse apart the moments that had led her here. She glanced at the floor where a bitten cookie lay on a tray.

"You lured me here with a path of cookies."

"Who said it was a path? It could have just been artfully strewn cookies. You made it a path by following it, and assuming it had any intention."

"I—"

"I know."

And that was all she needed to say.

Now, Zofia ran her hand across the dresses. She reached for a gown that Laila had described as "blue as the heavens." Once she had clasped all the buttons, she evaluated her reflection. Her hair looked like a cloud of snow. Her eyes were blue. That was all she really noticed. Looking at her reflection for more than a minute at a time was excruciatingly boring. Zofia turned away to slip on the ivory gloves. She pinched her cheeks a couple times—the way she had seen Laila do—and then headed for the door, her heartbeat thundering in her chest.

She'd never done this before, and she wasn't sure what to expect. All her life, she'd felt far too analyzed to willingly put herself in people's line of sight. But maybe that could change. She had Laila and Enrique to thank for that. With them, she never felt as if every sentence was a labyrinth to navigate. Séverin was a little more difficult. He often said only half of what he meant to say, according to Laila. Hypnos, on the other hand, said *all* he meant to say, but Enrique had told her she was only to take *half* of it seriously, which made processing his sentences a bit of a chore. With them, she did not feel as if there was a part of her missing. It made her feel brave, to wander into this strange terrain as she did now where she was no different from anyone around her. That perhaps she was enough . . . that her company could be desired and sought out just like anyone else's.

Ahead of her, the lights of the hotel's hallway had dimmed. Down the grand staircase, she could hear the sounds of a violin and a pianoforte. The vaulted windows overhead revealed a clear night sky decorated with an immeasurable number of stars.

When she got to the end of the hall, Zofia stopped short. Enrique and Hypnos had not moved from their spot. Their eyes were locked on each other, heads bent low in conversation and then—just as suddenly—*not* in conversation.

Zofia could not move. Cold spread through her, swirling from the new, embroidered heels Laila had hid next to her work boots and climbing up her body and her new dress and her ivory gloves that had already rumpled and fallen past her elbows. She watched as Hypnos's hand slipped around Enrique's neck and he deepened the kiss. She was reminded of all that she could not detect. All that she could not do. She could storm into a room, but she could not command its attention through charm. She could face herself in the mirror, but she could not spark imaginations with her face.

Zofia stepped back. She should stay in the world she knew.

And not reach for one she did not.

Slowly, she turned on her heel, careful to tiptoe softly so that no one heard or saw her. In her room, she stripped off the blue dress and gloves. Then she put on her rubber gloves and donned her black smock.

She had work to do.

35

SÉVERIN

Séverin hooked his walking stick around the carriage's velvet curtains, scanning the damp streets. The Palais des Rêves stood in the distance, casting curves of amber light that feathered into the night like wings. If Laila were here, she would say the lights looked like a blessing of angel feathers. He grinned. If that were true, it was no blessing. It was a declaration. Only Paris would rip out seraph wings and string them onto its buildings as if to say one thing:

This was no place for angels.

He rapped the top of the hansom with his cane. *"Arrêtez!"*

Beside him, Tristan jerked awake.

"We're here already?" he asked, rubbing the sleep from his eyes.

Tristan hadn't been sleeping well in the past week. Sometimes, Séverin found him curled up in the greenhouse, a pair of pliers in his hand, surrounded by unfinished terrariums . . . including one creation where an array of crimped jasmine petals looked unnervingly like milky bones set into the earth.

"Where are the others?" asked Tristan.

"Probably inside," said Séverin.

Enrique had been giddy to attend the full moon party at the in-famous Palais, and Séverin would've bet money he'd try to get there early just for the desserts.

"Don't forget the mask," said Séverin.

"Oh, right."

Each of them had been given a wolf mask. He'd wear it, but he drew the line at baying at the full moon or whatever festivity the Palais had planned.

Tristan jumped out of the hansom, then paused, patting one of his jacket pockets.

"Forgot I had this," he said, drawing out an envelope. "The fac-totum asked me to give it to you. He said it's urgent."

Séverin took the letter. "Who's it from?"

"Matriarch of House Kore," said Tristan, his mouth twisting.

He hadn't quite warmed to the idea of Séverin regaining his House after the inheritance test was reissued tomorrow. Every day, Tristan had to be assured that nothing would change . . . and every day Séverin reassured him. He wasn't going to ignore him like last time.

Séverin stuffed the letter in his pocket. "She marks *everything* urgent."

It was beginning to get annoying. Invitations to tea? Urgent. Queries about his marital status? Urgent. Thoughts on the weather? Urgent.

TONIGHT, THE PALAIS felt like a devil's dream of heaven, full of golden wolves and gleaming teeth and stars white as milk. Inside, the Palais had been redecorated for the full moon festivities. Wait-resses darted between tables, trailing burning seraph wings. The obsidian floor looked like a void flecked with stars. Patrons in wolf masks sat in velvet chairs, tossing back their liquor and howling with laughter.

Everywhere he looked, he was surrounded by gilded wolves. And for whatever reason, it made him feel perfectly at home. Wolves were everywhere. In politics, on thrones, in beds. They cut their teeth on history and grew fat on war. Not that Séverin was complaining. It was just that, like other wolves, he wanted his share.

Tomorrow, he would have it.

At the center of the room near the stage, Enrique and Hypnos waved them down. Séverin made his way over and sank into the armchair.

"Where's Zofia?"

"She decided not to come for some reason," said Hypnos.

The corner of Enrique's mouth tugged down for an instant, but he quickly hid it in a smile.

"More strawberries for me," he said, reaching for the silver bowl full of sweets. "Also. *You're late*. You're lucky L'Énigme's performance got moved to a later slot."

"What?" snapped Séverin.

He'd timed their arrival precisely so they *would* miss her performance. When Laila danced, he felt like everyone else in the room when they watched her. As if his soul's salvation balanced on the turn of her wrist, the lift of her chin. He couldn't go through that again.

"Why?" he asked.

Enrique shrugged. Even behind his mask, Séverin thought his gaze was a little too knowing. "Ask her yourself."

Too late, he saw her walking toward them. Unlike the others, she wore no wolf mask but a white headdress fixed with several white peacock feathers. A dress the color of moonlight clung to her. Heads turned when she walked. She smiled radiantly, and for good reason.

According to Hypnos, they might have a lead on the ancient book she'd been searching for these past two years. She might finally have a way out of Paris.

Laila didn't greet anyone, but walked straight for him. She braced her hands on either side of his chair and leaned close. "Laugh," she whispered, her breath hot against his skin. "Now."

"Why?" he murmured.

"Because the proprietor of L'Eden has never stepped foot inside the Palais, and now you've caused quite a stir. More than one of the dancers wants to know whether you're spoken for, and while I love them, I don't want them running around the hotel trying to get your attention."

Heat zipped up his spine. She wanted it to seem like he was hers.

"Jealousy looks good on you, Laila," he said, smiling.

Laila scoffed, but her grip on his chair tightened a fraction. "I've got a reputation to protect. So do you. It'll draw too much attention. So laugh."

"Make it worth my while."

Maybe it was the smoke in the air, or the dimming lights and eyeless wolves, but the words—meant only to tease—slipped out wrong. Laila drew back an inch, her eyes dropping to his lips. Everyone else in this room could have vanished on the spot, and he wouldn't have noticed. In her eyes, he saw an answering . . . *something*. A flash of radiance. And for the first time, he wondered whether she thought about that stolen night the way he did. If it haunted her too.

But then the performance cymbal was struck, and she pulled back from him. He let out a delayed laugh, hoping it would be enough.

"*Presenting L'Énigme!*" exclaimed the announcer.

The ceiling spotlights spun toward her, and Laila turned without answering. Séverin cursed under his breath. What the hell was wrong with him? He hunched his shoulders and felt the sharp corner of the envelope in his jacket.

"What was *that* about?" asked Enrique.

"Nothing," said Séverin brusquely.

He didn't have to see Hypnos's or Tristan's eyes to know what kind of looks they were exchanging. His face burned as he pulled out the envelope and ripped open the letter. Better to look harried than humiliated, he thought.

L'Énigme took the stage and the entire theatre burst into applause, rising to their feet and stamping the ground. In the din, he almost couldn't process the letter, but then the words hit him:

ROUX-JOUBERT ESCAPED.
DO NOT LEAVE L'EDEN.

The letter dropped from his hands. Séverin felt like he was moving through water. He couldn't stand up fast enough. Around him, the howls of the audience turned to shouts.

"Fire!" shouted someone beside him.

The curtains had caught in an instant. A wildfire clawed up toward the balconies, moving with unnatural speed.

Tristan clutched his arm. "Dear God—"

Séverin followed his gaze to the hall where Roux-Joubert stormed through the entrance. With every step, he threw sparks of fire onto the ground. More velvet curtains caught fire and smoke thickened the air. Overhead, the chandelier swung dangerously as the crowd stampeded. From the podium, the announcer yelled for the guards, for *order*—

But all Séverin heard was Roux-Joubert.

"It doesn't work that way, dear boy," said Roux-Joubert, smiling. "You cannot go without leaving something behind."

Roux-Joubert's gaze went to Laila. She had managed to clamber down from the stage, and now ran toward the table. She reached out, and Hypnos grabbed her hand. The blade-brimmed hat sailed toward them. Séverin launched out of his chair, throwing his body across hers until they both crashed to the ground—

Her heart beat furiously against his, and he wanted to bask in that cadence forever. All around him, footsteps pounded into the ground, shouts stamping the air. His eyes seamed shut, his whole body tensed for a blow that never came.

"Oh no, oh no—" cried Enrique.

Séverin opened his eyes, pushing himself off Laila and the ground. But she must have seen something before him because she let out a strangled cry. Séverin turned, and he thought the world had split.

He was wrong. Laila had never been the intended hit of the blade-brim hat. A metallic smell stamped into the air. Tristan swayed. He opened his mouth, as if he were going to speak. On the ground, the hat had fallen onto its top, the blade gleaming. A thin line of red stained the collar of Tristan's shirt. The line widened. Blood spilled down the front of his jacket. Tristan crumpled to the floor. His head fell back, knocking against the stone.

Séverin didn't remember rushing to him. He didn't remember gathering Tristan's body and holding it close. Around him, the others had crowded close. He knew they were shouting, running for help, moving so fast as if reality wouldn't be able to catch up to them. But he knew the truth. He knew the moment he touched Tristan's chin, turning it toward him. His gray eyes were still wide, but death had stolen their luster forever.

PART VII

From the archival records of the Order of Babel
The Origins of Empire
Mistress Hedvig Petrovna, House Dažbog
of the Order's Russian faction
1771, reign of Empress Yekaterine Alekseyevna

It is said that when one among us dies, the memory of their blood lies in the Ring.
The Ring always knows who its true master or mistress is.

36

SÉVERIN

Three weeks later . . .

Séverin sat in his office, waiting for his guests. On his desk, afternoon light spilled across the wood, thick and golden as yolk. It startled him sometimes. The audacity of the sun to rise after what had happened.

The door opened, and in stepped the matriarch of House Kore and Hypnos. Hypnos was dressed in black, his pale eyes rimmed red.

"You missed the funeral," he said.

Séverin said nothing. He didn't want to mourn. He wanted to avenge. He wanted to find the Fallen House and open their throats.

The matriarch startled when she looked at him, recognition flitting across her face. He hoped her hand still hurt.

"You . . ." she started, raising her hand. But then she caught sight of her Ring and folded her hands across her lap.

"The French government and the Order of Babel is indebted to you and your friends for your service in restoring my Ring and preventing what might well have been the end of civilization," said the matriarch stiffly.

Hypnos clasped his hands in front of him. "There is no reason to delay this any longer. House Vanth will be restored. You'll be a patriarch."

He pulled his Ring from his finger and set it on the desk. Then he glared at the matriarch until she did the same. From the inside of his breast pocket, Hypnos withdrew a small blade.

"It will only hurt for a moment," said Hypnos gently. "But then you can reclaim what is yours. You can be a patriarch in time for the Winter Conclave in Russia. The whole Order will recognize you then."

The matriarch did not look at Séverin; her lips were clamped in a tight line. Séverin stared at his desk. Here it was, the moment that he had worked for . . . a repeat of the two Rings test. He had imagined this moment a thousand times. His blood—the same blood denied and deemed false—smeared on their Rings, the blue light that would spiral up his arms, sink through his skin. He imagined it would feel like deliverance. Like wings shaking loose from his skin. The impossible made possible—the world turned edible, the sky a cloth he could drag down and wrap around his fists. He had not imagined it would feel like this. Hollow.

"What's a little more bloodshed," he said, pushing the Rings across his desk.

Hypnos stared at him oddly. "I thought you wanted this."

Séverin watched the Rings roll across the wood. He blinked, and no blue light swam behind his eyes. He saw fair hair, nails with crescents of dirt. Downcast gray eyes.

Why can't this be enough? Sometimes I wished you didn't even want to be *a patriarch.*

A memory came to him, unbidden, of the day Hypnos had tricked him into an oath. Séverin remembered looking at Zofia, Tristan, Enrique, and Laila through the glass door. They had been drinking tea and cocoa and eating cookies. He remembered wishing to grab that moment and press it beneath glass. And look at where it had gotten him. He had sworn to protect Tristan, and now Tristan was dead. He had promised to look out for the others . . . and now the Fallen House, who had seen *each* of their faces, was still out there. Waiting. Without them by his side, they'd never find the Fallen House. And with them at his side, they walked with death ever at their shadow. He couldn't let them get hurt. But he couldn't let them get too close either. When he blinked, he remembered Laila's body beneath his, the cadence of her heart. A siren song. Guilt snapped his thoughts. For the song of her heartbeats, he'd never wash Tristan's blood from his hands.

The matriarch's eyes widened.

"Do you?" she asked. "Do you want this?"

"No." He stood abruptly and walked to the door, ushering them out. "Not anymore."

37

LAILA

Three months later . . .

L aila stood in the hallway outside Séverin's office. In her hands, she carried the latest stack of reports. He'd told her there was no need to send them by personally, but she couldn't keep herself away any longer.

Sometimes she wondered if grief could break someone, for all of them bore fractures, new hollows. Enrique hardly left his research library. Zofia lived in the laboratory. Hypnos's charm seemed knife-honed, desperate.

Grief snuck up on her sometimes, and she was not sure how to defend herself from the force of its surprise. Just last month, she had started crying because the cocoa in the kitchens had gone stale. No one ever drank it but Tristan. And then there was the stray Night Bite she had found, gathering dust beneath her bed. She had stopped wearing black crepe two months ago, but that did not stop her from wandering the gardens of L'Eden, as if she might still catch a glimpse of a fair head and the edge of a laugh.

But lately, Laila wasn't sure what to do. Séverin sent her objects to read, but she was beginning to think grief had sapped her abilities.

It all started after the funeral.

Laila had gone to Tristan's workshop. She wasn't sure what she was looking for. Some token, perhaps. Something happy that might keep at bay the last image of his death, blood caking his hair, gray eyes dimming, Séverin's face a mask of broken dreams.

But what she found was not happiness.

It was a secret drawer, one that not even Séverin had known about. Within it lay the pinned bodies of wingless birds. Laila had shuddered at the sight. Here lay the mystery of the birdless grounds of L'Eden. Slowly, she had touched one of the iron stakes pinning them in that rictus of death and an image rose to her mind. Tristan laying traps. Tristan catching them, cooing to them, weeping when he tore out their feathers, cushioning the small worlds that he crafted with such love in the dark of his workshop. She heard how he whispered to the struggling creatures: "See? It's not so bad . . . you don't have to fly."

Against her will, she remembered Roux-Joubert's words in the greenhouse . . .

"His love and his fear and his own cracked mind made it easy to convince him that betraying you was saving you . . ."

She'd burned it. All evidence of it. And now she couldn't even tell if what she had seen was true. When she reached for the memory of it, it was like kneading a fresh bruise. She never told Séverin. She could not bear to let him see this. Already, he walked through the halls of L'Eden as if he had seen enough ghosts for a lifetime. Why give him demons to see too?

Laila faltered at the door, about to turn when it suddenly opened.

Séverin stood wild-eyed before her, shocked at her presence. Her face burned. That moment where she'd leaned over him, that evening where he'd hungrily whispered "make it worth my while," now felt like antiques of a different era.

"Laila," he said, exhaling it like a curse he wished to be rid of. "What are you doing here?"

Laila had been waiting for this. She'd gathered every scrap of courage to speak these words. For the past two years, she thought that having a deadline on her life should make her pull back . . . but Tristan's death changed that. She didn't want to glide through life, unfeeling. She wanted to know everything while she could. She didn't want the ghosts of thresholds not crossed hanging over her. She didn't want one night. She wanted a chance. It was that conviction, more than anything, which made her drop the reports to the floor, step toward Séverin, and kiss him.

38

SÉVERIN

*S*éverin's seventh father was Lust.

    Lust taught him that a broken heart made a fine weapon, for its pieces were exceptionally sharp.

One day, Lust became obsessed with a young man in the village. The young man shared his affection, and both Séverin and Tristan spent many a night laughing at all the strange sounds that echoed through the halls. But then one day, the young man came to the villa and said he had fallen in love with a woman of his family's choice, and he was to marry her within the fortnight.

Lust was furious. Lust did not like to be jilted, and so he found the young woman. He made her laugh, made her love him. And when she told him she carried his child, he forsook her. The girl took her own life, and the young man she would have married went mad.

So, Séverin suspected, did Lust. He spent days sitting on the stone balcony, his feet dangling out, his whole body tipped forward as if he were daring the world to give him wings at the last second.

The day before Séverin and Tristan left for Paris, Lust whispered to him: "Lust is safer than love, but both can ruin you."

* * *

SÉVERIN BROKE OFF the kiss, startling backward.

"What the hell was that?" he spat.

Confusion flickered on Laila's face, but she masked it quickly.

"A reminder," she said uncertainly, her eyes on the floor before she lifted them to him. "To live again . . ."

Live?

"Turning into ghosts is not what the dead deserve."

She came closer. There was so much hope in her face that he felt the ache of it in his bones. Memory bit into Séverin. He remembered how he reached for her instead of Tristan, how he shielded her against one he'd sworn to protect. How could she dare to speak of what the dead deserved?

Ice crept into his heart. A sneer twisted his mouth, and he laughed, walking back to his desk and leaning against it.

"Laila," he said. "What do you want me to say? Would you like me to quote poetry? Tell you there's witchcraft in your lips that resurrected me?"

Laila flinched. "I thought in the catacombs that—"

"Did you really think that kiss meant something?" he asked, smirking. "Did you think one night meant something? I can barely remember it. No offense, of course."

"Stop this, Séverin. We both know it meant something."

"You're delusional," he said coldly.

"Prove it," she said, her voice barely above a whisper.

Séverin's eyes flew open. She was standing right in front of him, her footsteps silenced by the plush rug beneath them. He steadied himself as he reached out to touch her cheek. The slightest tremble ran through her body.

"You're blushing, and I've hardly touched you," he said. He forced another sneer onto his lips even as his foolish heart leapt. "Do you really want me to go through with this proof? It will only humiliate—"

Laila wrapped her arms around his neck, drawing him against her. Séverin's hands gripped her waist, as if she were an anchor. As if he were drowning. And maybe he was. A sigh, once trapped in her throat, turned into a moan when his tongue slipped into her mouth.

"Laila," he murmured. He said her name again, whispering it like a prayer.

He lifted her off the ground, turning sharply and settling her on the desk. Her legs fell to either side of his hips. They were pressed so closely together that the light from his nephrite desk could not squeeze between them. He filled his hands with the black silk of her hair. This was what a kiss that meant nothing supposedly felt like. As if he could not touch her enough, taste her enough, as if this move-ment alone would leave his body riddled as an addict's. Her neck was hot silk against his lips. He felt drunk. And then, he felt her hand skimming to the space where his shirt joined his pants, and he stopped short.

He stepped back. Her legs, once wrapped around his waist, fell, and her heels hit the front of the desk.

"See?" he said hoarsely. "I told you. Nothing."

Fury flashed across her face. "You know it wasn't. And if you really think that, you're a fool, *Majnun*."

He winced at the last word. When he finally looked at her, her sable eyes appeared raw. He didn't even remember reaching for the words that flew out of his mouth, but their venom chilled his teeth. "Go ahead," he said. "Call me whatever you wish. It's impossible to be hurt by someone who's not even real."

He couldn't doubt what he felt afterward. The lightning crack in the air as something in Laila unmistakably broke.

39

SÉVERIN

Two months later . . .
November 1889

Séverin held up a gigantic fur stole that, until very recently, might have been a silver fox. Or may have been a shiny weasel. He could never tell with these things. Glossy chips of garnet shone in the fur so that it looked blood-flecked.

"What the hell is this?"

"It's your birthday present, *cher!*" said Hypnos, clapping his hands together. "Don't you *love* it? Perfect for our upcoming trip too. Russia is frigid, and the last thing you're going to want at the Order's Winter Conclave is to sound snobby through chattering lips. It just won't suit."

Séverin held the fur stole at arm's length.

"Thank you."

Séverin picked up the protocol of the Winter Conclave. They would be staying at a palace, it seems, with separate suites allowed for—Séverin squinted as he made out the world—*mistresses*. He rolled his eyes. Many of the Order factions of the Western world would be in attendance, particularly those factions which guarded a continent's Babel Fragment. If the Fallen House sought to join all the Babel Fragments of the world, then it was no longer just the problem of France.

"What about Laila?" asked Hypnos.

The paper slipped from his hands.

"What *about* Laila?" he asked, not looking up from his desk.

He hadn't seen her since that night in his study. He pushed away the memory.

If everything went to plan, they would find her precious book. She would leave Paris, and he would be free of his guilt.

"Are you no longer working together?"

"We are."

Enrique had become, albeit grudgingly and with much attitude, a conduit between the two of them. Laila might not speak to Séverin anymore, but he still had what she wanted: access to artifacts and the intelligence collected by the Order. And she still had what he wanted: insight into the objects that held precious secrets. Séverin would pack a box full of this or that collector's or curator's personal effects and have it sent to her, and a progress report on finding the Fallen House. Laila would return the box with notes about the person attached, along with anything she'd picked up from the Palais. It was a method that suited both of them.

"Have you asked her to join us at the Winter Conclave?"

Séverin nodded.

"And has she responded?"

He sighed. "No."

That was another problem. He couldn't figure out what she wanted, what would make her join.

"Ah, lover spats," sighed Hypnos.

"Laila is not my lover."

"Your loss, *mon cher*." Hypnos shrugged and looked up at the clock above the office doorway. "Your birthday party is in full swing downstairs. You do know that, don't you?"

"Mm."

"Are you going to make an appearance?"

"This late in the evening, I doubt it will be remembered," he said.

Hypnos rolled his eyes, bowed, and swept out of the office. Séverin forced down a yawn. He wanted to stay in his study, but there was nothing left to do. Happy birthday, indeed. Last year, Tristan had the bright idea of baking a living *entremet* pie and filling it with four and twenty blackbirds as an homage to the nursery rhyme that Séverin had found funny when he was eight. Zofia built the cage-pie with a Forging mechanism to open when Séverin blew out the candles. Enrique found a first edition nursery rhyme book containing "Sing a Song of Sixpence." Laila had made the jam. But once the candles had been blown and the cage sprang open, none of the birds wanted to leave as they vastly preferred Laila's pie. And then Tristan had wanted to keep them. And Enrique was furious because there were bird droppings all over the library books. The pie was inedible after that, but Laila baked him a cupcake and left it on his desk the next day with a small candle.

Séverin almost laughed, but it died halfway past his lips.

There would never be another birthday like that.

Right before Séverin left his office, he grabbed an ouroboros mask from his desk. The brass snake mask formed an intricate figure-eight pattern that hid his eyes, so he could watch the revelries from the top of the bannister. L'Eden was in the grips of a masquerade ball. Acrobats spun down from the rafters, grinning masks plastered eerily onto their faces. Everyone had come out for the event.

Zofia wore a mask with a pointed beak, her cloudlike hair fluffed around her like ruffled feathers. Enrique stood beside her, a grinning monkey mask on his face, complete with a tail. Hypnos had eschewed a mask in favor of a sweeping, phoenix train Forged into the semblance of twisting flames.

At the doors, a line of twelve women wearing peacock feathers poured into the lobby. They were utterly dazzling.

But they were not her.

Behind him, he heard his factotum call out: "Please welcome the stars of the Palais des Rêves, who are performing a *very* special dance in honor of Monsieur Montagnet-Alarie's birthday!"

The crowd cheered. Séverin turned on his heel. His suite was just off to the western alcove, disguised behind a Tezcat door of a long, oval mirror encircled by an ouroboros. The snake was Forged so that it continually slithered, continually chasing after its own tail. It was only by catching it by the throat as if one were to throttle it that the snake would still. It was also how one could access his suites.

Séverin's room was rather spartan, which he preferred. There was a large bed with an ebony headboard. A sheer, golden canopy Forged so that anyone who touched it between the hours of two in the morning and four in the morning—prime murder hours, he was told— would be snarled in the threads.

Séverin rubbed the back of his neck, dropped the snake mask on the floor, kicked off his shoes, and yanked his shirt out of his pants. When he breathed deep, he wondered whether he was beginning to lose his mind. Impossibly, he thought he could smell Laila. Sugar in the air. A faint aroma of rosewater. She was haunting him. He pressed the heels of his hands against his eyes. What was wrong with him? He trudged forward a couple steps, ready to collapse into his bed when he stopped short.

His bed was already occupied.

"Hello, *Majnun*."

Perched on the edge of his bed and wearing a gown that looked cut from the night sky was Laila. She shifted under his stare, and faint stars zoomed across the ends of her dress. Blearily, Séverin wondered whether it was really her. Or whether she was some phantasm scraped together from all his longing. But then the corner of her mouth lifted in a knowing smile, and he was jolted back to this moment.

They hadn't spoken in weeks, and yet the *way* to talk to her—the push-pull of jokes—floated back to him, as easy as breathing. She no longer looked wide-eyed and bruised, the way she had when they had last spoken in the study. If anything, she looked like an icon. Terrible and beautiful. Untouchable.

And here he was. Disheveled and tired and not willing to show it.

"And what brings the celebrity of the Palais des Rêves back to my bed?" he asked.

She laughed, and even though he was clothed he might as well have been standing naked.

"A proposition," she said lightly.

He raised his eyebrow. "One that has to do with my bed?"

"As if you'd know what to do with me in your bed," she said, glancing at her nails.

He most certainly did know—

"My proposition has to do with the Winter Conclave in Russia."

"You'll come with us?"

"On my own terms."

"What do you want?"

Laila tipped forward. The light clung to her skin. "I want special access. I don't want to hide in a cake. Or pose as a maid."

And just like that, he understood.

"You want me to make you my mistress."

"Yes," she said. "Hypnos declined, which left you as the only logical option. With the fête in three weeks' time, I can hardly expend the effort into ingratiating myself with someone else."

He tried not to think about how she had gone to another man first. He tried, and he failed.

She reached for his hand, and he noticed that she wore jewelry now. Heavy, uncut rocks on her index fingers and thin, beaten strands of gold around her wrists. She had never worn jewelry in the hotel. They had always gotten in the way of her baking.

When she touched him, he stiffened.

"What do you say, *Majnun*? It will only be in name, I assure you," she said. Her voice was low, suffused with an almost professional quality of seduction that knocked the wind from his lungs even as every corner of his mind fought to withstand her. "You need me. You know it. If I am not there, then all your plans to find *The Divine Lyrics* disappear."

Now her fingers traced the line of his neck, the underside of his jaw. He couldn't breathe.

"Fine," he bit out.

"Promise?" she whispered. "I need to hear you say it."

He swallowed. "I promise I will declare you my mistress and take you to the winter fête," he said.

"Promise that whatever you discover you will share with me?" she pressed.

She had undone his first button. Her hands were on his chest.

"Fine, yes, I promise," he said hoarsely.

Laila leaned in, her face inches away from his, damson-dark lips parting softly.

"Good," she said.

Something was burning his skin. He hissed, looking down at his wrist to see that her stack of bangles had not been bangles at all, but coils of iron wire, Forged from the same material as an oath tattoo and now seared into his skin by his own promise. The burning lasted for less than a blink before the metal disappeared beneath his skin.

"I have learned not to trust what you say," said Laila. "So I took my own precaution."

"How—"

"I learned from the best," she said, patting his cheek.

He caught her wrist in his hand.

"You should be more careful with the promises you extract," he said, his voice low. "Do you know what contract you have just entered?"

"I know exactly what I'm doing," she said, her eyes narrowing.

"Do you?" he asked. "Because you have just agreed to spend every night in my bed for the next three weeks. I will hold you to that."

"I know that, *Majnun*," she said, softer this time. "Just like I know how that will hold no temptation for you. You might even have to kiss me on occasion, simply to prove that I am to you who you say I am. But that means nothing. Remember?"

She slid down from the bed and made her way to the door.

"Happy birthday, *Majnun*," she said, as the door closed. "Sleep well."

He did not sleep at all that night.

40

HYPNOS

Hypnos walked briskly down the halls of Erebus.

It was freezing outside, and the fires had been banked for the night, which meant that it was bound to be a chilly reception for the matriarch of House Kore. Her fur stole was wound tightly around her body. If she hadn't bothered to take it off, then that meant it would only be a short visit.

"Why did you come here at this hour?" he asked tiredly.

If she was offended with his lack of decorum, she did not show it.

"The Winter Conclave is nearly upon us."

"Hilariously, Madame, I do own a calendar."

She licked her lips, her eyes darting to the door.

"Your friend, Monsieur Montagnet-Alarie . . . are you quite certain he will not ask for us to administer the two Rings test?"

Hypnos frowned. Who could say for certain what occurred in Séverin's head. Perhaps he would ask again. He had refused out of grief, but perhaps with enough time, he would think that his own inheritance might be worth it.

"I can't say for certain."

The matriarch closed her eyes. "Make sure he doesn't ask. At least, not until he's helped the Order find the Fallen House."

"What aren't you telling me?"

She hesitated, and then began haltingly: "We administered the two Rings test on him when the former patriarch of House Vanth was killed in that fire."

"I already knew that, and everyone knows those results were falsified—"

"They weren't."

Hypnos paused. "What are you saying?"

"I'm saying that he's not the blood heir of House Vanth, and he must never know."

AUTHOR'S NOTE

I was eating breakfast and haphazardly listening to *NPR* when I first heard about the human zoo that displayed Filipinos. The Philippine village was one of the largest—and most visited—exhibits during the 1904 World's Fair in St. Louis, Missouri, where visitors were particularly interested in seeing the "primitive" tribe of the Igorots forced to butcher and eat dogs.

That piece shocked me. I couldn't believe I'd just heard the words "human zoo."

It was that piece of history that guided me into the world of *The Gilded Wolves*, specifically the events of the Exposition Universelle of 1889, a world's fair held in Paris, whose major attraction was a human zoo—then called a "Negro Village"—which was visited by twenty-eight million people. As a Filipina and Indian woman, colonialism runs in my veins. I couldn't reconcile the horrors of that era with the glamour of it, which, up until then, was what stood out in my imagination of the 19th century: courtesans and the Moulin Rouge, glittering parties and champagne.

I wanted to understand how an era called La Belle Époque, literally *The Beautiful Era,* could possess that name with that stain. I wanted to explore beauty and horror through the eyes of the people on the sidelines. And, ultimately, I wanted to go on an adventure.

Research itself was an adventure. I learned that Filipino national hero Jose Rizal truly had been in Paris in 1889. I learned far too much about the history of ice manufacturing, which never ended up in the book. I learned that while Belle Époque Paris enjoyed artistic and scientific leaps, it also perpetuated the deep anti-Semitism spreading through Europe, particularly in the Russian empire.

While I took many liberties with time and truth, it never felt right to untangle the beauty from the horror of the 19th century.

When we revise the horror and sanitize the grotesque, we risk erasing the paths that led us here.

History is a myth shaped by the tongues of conquerors. What appears good may eventually sour and curdle in our collective minds. What appears bad may later bloom and brighten. I wanted to write this trilogy not to instruct or to condemn, but to question . . .

Question what is gold and what glitters.

ACKNOWLEDGMENTS

For the longest time, I did not think I could write this book. The scope felt unimaginable. The puzzles were snarls of nonsense. The characters hissed at me when I got too close. But I found my way into this world and I kept my head above water thanks to the following people. To my family at Wednesday Books, I am so grateful for your support. Thank you to Eileen, who made me a romance reader and saw this tale from its origins as a half-baked lump of words and a Pinterest board. To Brittani, Karen, and DJ—thank you for igniting the fuel! To Thao, you're my dream champion of an agent. I wouldn't want to be in the trenches with anyone else. Thank you, also, to my family at Sandra Dijkstra Literary Agency for all that you do and especially to Andrea, who has brought these stories overseas. To Sarah Simpson-Weiss, assistant extraordinaire, how did I ever exist without you? To Noa, I'm so grateful for all your guidance and humor and invaluable feedback.

To my amazing friends . . . thank you to Lyra Selene, my rockstar critique partner who read this story a thousand times. To Ryan:

a thousand heartfelt *meeps*! To Renee and JJ, illuminated and glam oracles. To Eric, who let me borrow his name. Russell and Josh, who have patiently witnessed me in all manner of disheveled deadlineness. Marta, Zan, and Amber, who kept me sane and grounded and laughing. To Katie, who helped me with the maths. To Niv, Victoria, and Bismah: I couldn't have written a tale about friendship without you.

To my incredible family: Mom, Dad, Ba and Dadda, Lalani, my aunts and uncles, and future in-laws. Your support brought me here and keeps me going. A special thanks to my Alpesh Kaka and Alpa Kaki, in whose home I first read the treasure hunt thrillers that inspired this story. Shiv, Renuka, Aarav (I will never forget seeing you for the first time), Sohum, Kiran and Alisa, Shraya—I do not say this often enough, but I love you. A special thanks to my cousin, Pujan, whose brilliant insight into the art world made me rethink how I observe pieces of history. To Pog and Cookie, the beta readers who will tell me first: what fresh hell is this. I am deeply proud to be your sister.

To Panda and Teddy, who can neither read nor write, but seem to grow fluffier to soak up my writing despair. Thanks.

To Aman. I wouldn't want to be on this journey with anyone else. You bring magic to my world.

And last, to my readers, thank you so much. You guys fill my heart.

Read on for a sneak peek
of the next book in
The Gilded Wolves world,
The Silvered Serpents

I

SÉVERIN

Three weeks before Winter Conclave . . .

Séverin Montagnet-Alarie looked out over what had once been
the Seven Sins Garden. Rare, coveted blossoms once coated
the grounds—milk-petaled aureum and chartreuse golden moss,
skeleton hyacinths and night-blooming cereus. And yet, it was
the roses that his brother, Tristan, loved most. They were the first
seeds planted, and he'd fussed over them until their petals ripened
red and their fragrance bloomed to create something that looked
and smelled like melted sin.

Now, in late December, the grounds appeared stripped and bar-
ren. When Séverin breathed deep, cold seared through his lungs.

The grounds were almost scentless.

If he wanted, he could have asked his factotum to hire a gardener with a Forging affinity for plant matter, someone who could

maintain the garden's splendor, but he didn't want a gardener. He wanted Tristan.

But Tristan was dead, and the Seven Sins Garden had died with him.

In its place lay a hundred Forged reflection pools. Their mirror-still surfaces held images of desert landscapes or skies quilted with dawn light when nighttime had already stolen across the grounds. The guests of L'Eden Hotel applauded his artistry, not knowing that it was shame, not artistry, that had guided Séverin. When he looked in those pools, he didn't want to catch sight of his own face staring back at him.

"Monsieur?"

Séverin turned to see one of his guards striding toward him.

"Is he ready?" asked Séverin.

"Yes, Monsieur. We arranged the room precisely as you requested. Your . . . *guest* . . . is inside the office outside the stables, just as you asked."

"And do we have tea to serve our guest?"

"*Oui.*"

"*Très bon.*"

Séverin took a deep breath, his nose wrinkling. The rose canes had been burned and yanked out at the root. The grounds had been salted. And yet, even months later, he still caught the phantom scent of roses.

SÉVERIN HEADED TOWARD a small building near the horse stables. As he walked, he touched Tristan's old penknife, now tucked into his jacket pocket. No matter how many times he washed the blade, he still imagined he could feel the small bird feathers and bone splinters that had once clung to the metal, remnants of Tristan's kills . . . proof of the twisted violence his brother had tried so hard to hide.

Sometimes he wished he'd never known. Maybe then he would have never gone to Laila's room. All he'd wanted was to dissolve her ludicrous oath to act as his mistress during the Winter Conclave.

But he didn't find her. Instead, he had found letters addressed to Tristan, and his brother's gardening satchel—the same one Laila swore had gone missing—untied beside them.

I had thought not reading your objects was for the best, my dearest Tristan. But every day I ask myself if I might've caught the darkness inside you earlier. Perhaps, then, you might not have turned to those poor birds. I see it in the blade. All those kills. All your tears. I may not have understood all of you, but I love you wholeheartedly and pray you might forgive me—

Even before this, Séverin knew he'd failed in his only promise to Tristan: to protect him. Now he saw how deep that failure stretched. All he saw were paths not taken. Every time Tristan wept, and he'd left the room to give him privacy. Every time Tristan had furiously stomped into his greenhouse and stayed there for days. He should've gone. Instead, he let his brother's demons feed on him.

When he read those letters, it wasn't just Tristan's dead stare that swam before his eyes but everyone's gazes—Enrique, Zofia, Hypnos. *Laila.* He saw their eyes milky with death, death that he'd let happen because he hadn't been enough to protect them. Hadn't known how.

Eventually, Laila caught him in her rooms. He'd never quite

remembered all that she'd said to him, except for her last words: "You cannot protect everyone from everything. You're only human, Séverin."

Séverin closed his eyes, his hand on the doorknob of the office.

"Then that must change."

SÉVERIN CONSIDERED HIMSELF something of an artist when it came to interrogation.

It came down to the details, all of which needed to look co-incidental rather than controlled: the chair with uneven legs; the room's cloying scent of too-sweet flowers; the too-salty snacks provided earlier. Even the lighting. Concealed glass shards refracted the sunlight, casting glares on everything from the walls to the ceiling, so that only the wooden table laden with a warm and fragrant tea service earned notice.

"Comfortable?" asked Séverin, taking a seat across from the man.

The man flinched. "Yes."

Séverin smiled, pouring himself tea. The man before him was thin and pale, with a hunted look to his face. He eyed the tea warily until Séverin took a long sip.

"Would you like some?" asked Séverin.

The man hesitated, then nodded.

"Why . . . why am I here? Are you . . ." his voice dropped to a whisper, ". . . are you with the Order of Babel?"

"In a fashion."

Months after they broke into House Kore's home, the Order of Babel had hired Séverin's crew to find the Fallen House's hidden treasure, rumored to be in an estate called the Sleeping Palace, though no one knew where that was. In exchange, Séverin would be allowed to catalogue and analyze these treasures for himself, a privilege unheard of outside the Order. Then again, he *should* have been one of them, but he no longer wanted that mantle. Not after Tristan.

The Order claimed they wanted the treasure to gut whatever power the Fallen House still had left . . . but Séverin knew better. The Fallen House had shown their cards. They were snakes that cast large shadows. Without their treasure, they would be irredeemably weakened, true, but the real reason behind the Order's search was simple. The colonies brimmed with treasure—rubber in the Congo, silver in the Potosi Mines, spices in Asia. The lost wonders inside the Fallen House's hoard were too tantalizing not to pursue, and Séverin knew the members of the Order would fall upon it like wolves. Which meant he had to get to it first. He didn't care for its gold or silver, he wanted something far more precious:

The Divine Lyrics.

A treasure the Order would not even notice had gone missing, for it had always been considered lost. The lore of the Order of Babel held that *The Divine Lyrics* contained the secret for joining the world's Babel Fragments. Once joined, the book could rebuild the Tower of Babel and thus access the power of God. It was an effort that had gotten the Fallen House exiled fifty years ago. And yet, the book had long been missing, or that was what everyone had thought . . .

Until Roux-Joubert's tongue slipped.

After the battle in the catacombs, the captured Fallen House members proved to be useless informants. Each had not only taken their lives, but also burned off their faces and fingertips, thus escaping recognition. Only Roux-Joubert had failed. After he killed Tristan, he bit down instead of swallowing the suicide pill required to take his secrets to the grave. He had died slowly over weeks, and in a fit of madness began to speak.

"The doctor's papa is a bad man," he said, laughing hysterically. "You know all about bad fathers, Monsieur, you sympathize I am sure . . . oh how unkind . . . he will not let the doctor into the Sleeping Palace . . . but the book is there, waiting for him. He will find it. He will give us life after death . . ."

He? The question haunted Séverin, but there was no surviving record of the last Fallen House patriarch, and though the Order seemed disappointed the Sleeping Palace could not be found . . . at least they felt reassurance in the knowledge the Fallen House could not find it either.

Only he and Hypnos, the patriarch of House Nyx, had continued searching, scouring records and receipts, hunting for any inconsistencies which eventually led them to the man who sat in front of Séverin. An old, shriveled man who had managed to hide for a very long time.

"I have paid my dues," said the man. "I was not even part of the Fallen House, merely one of its many solicitors. And I told the Order before that when the House fell, they gave me a draught, and I remember *nothing* of its secrets. Why drag me here? I have no information worth knowing."

Séverin set down his teacup. "I believe you can lead me to the Sleeping Palace."

The man scoffed. "No one has seen it in—"

"Fifty years, I know," said Séverin. "It's well hidden, I understand. But my contacts tell me the Fallen House created a special pair of lenses. Tezcat spectacles, to be precise, which reveal the location of the Sleeping Palace and all its *delicious* treasures." Séverin smiled. "However, they entrusted these spectacles to a unique person, someone who does not know what they guard."

The man gaped at him.

"H-how—" He caught himself, then cleared his throat. "The Tezcat spectacles are mere rumor. I certainly don't possess them. I know nothing, Monsieur. I swear on my *life*."

"Poor choice of words," said Séverin.

He removed Tristan's penknife from his pocket, tracing the initials on it: *T.M.A.* Tristan had lost his surname, and so Séverin had shared his. At the base of the knife was an ouroboros, a snake biting its tail. It was once the symbol of House Vanth, the House he might have been patriarch of—if things had gone according to plan . . . if that dream of inheritance had not killed the person closest to him. Now it was a symbol of all he would change.

He knew that even if they found *The Divine Lyrics*, it would not be enough to protect the others . . . They'd wear targets on their backs for the rest of their lives, and that was unacceptable. And so, Séverin had nurtured a new dream. He dreamt of that night in the catacombs, when Roux-Joubert had smeared golden blood over his mouth; the sensation of his spine elongating, making room for sudden wings. He dreamt of the pressure in his forehead, the horns that bloomed and arced, lacquered tips brushing the tops of his ears.

We could be gods.

That was what *The Divine Lyrics* promised. If he had the book, he could be a god. A god did not know human pain or loss or guilt. A god could *resurrect*. He could share the book's powers with the others, turn them invincible . . . protect them forever. And when they left him—as he knew they'd always planned to—he wouldn't feel a thing.

For he would not be human.

"Are you going to stab me with that?" demanded the man,

pushing back violently from the table. "How old are you, Monsieur? In your twenties? Don't you think think that is too young to have such blood on your hands?"

"I've never known blood to discriminate between ages," said Séverin, tilting the blade. "But I won't stab you. What's the point when I've already poisoned you?"

The man's eyes flew to the tea. Sweat beaded on his brow. "You're lying. If you poisoned the tea, then you'd be poisoned too."

"Most assuredly," said Séverin. "But the poison wasn't the tea. It was your cup's porcelain coating. Now." From his pocket, he withdrew a clear vial and placed it on the table. "The antidote is right here. Is there really nothing you wish to tell me?"

TWO HOURS LATER, Séverin poured sealing wax onto several envelopes—one to be sent out immediately, the others to be sent out in two days. A small part of him hesitated, but he steeled himself. He was doing this for them. For his friends. The more he cared about their feelings, the harder his task became. And so he endeavored to feel nothing at all.